Ramb

and

The Internet Newsletter

John E. Carson

AMI

An Aspirations Media Publication

First Printing Apirl 2006

Copyright © 2006 by John E. Carson
Cover and Interior Illustrations Copyright © 2005 Darryl Taylor
Layout Copyright © 2005 Jennifer Rowell
Design: Jennifer Rowell and John E. Carson

LIBRARY OF CONGRESS CONTROL NUMBER: 2006920970

ISBN: 0-9776043-1-4

MANUFACTURED IN THE UNITED STATES

An Aspirations Media™ Publication
www.aspirationsmediainc.com

Author's Note

"This is a work of fiction. Any references to people or places living or dead are purely coincidental."

So many stories start with this phrase and this one is no exception. This story was inspired by the tall tales I told my own children when they were young. This book was created to pass the legacy on to our grandchildren and I have used many ingredients in cooking it up.

The products mentioned in the story are not endorsements but rather the character's preferences or a device to tell the story with. The trademarks of Reebok, Seven-Up and Kool-Whip are representative only of the necessity mentioned, as are any other products or companies mentioned. Admiral Foods is a work of fiction and the real product Cool Whip is owned by Kraft Foods.

A La Vie Russie is a real place however and they have given their permission to use their name back when I started this project.

Likewise, The Agency and all references to Agents, COM links, etc. are pure fiction created for the same reason as the products above.

The character Rose is also fictional though she does tell the story. And she tells it in her own way as only she can. Being twelve years old some allowances must be made for her technical accuracy and style. The story is not written as I would tell it but as Rose has told it to me. The short chapters and quick pace of the story are representative of the way she writes her newsletter. The words and phrases she uses are part of her character and we both have only one goal in mind-to entertain you.

Many thanks are now in order. First to my wife and co-author, Marlene Rose, without whom none of these stories would be possible and who this book is dedicated to. Second, our children, Christine and Brian who are now grown with families of their own. They always believed in me even when I didn't believe in myself. Also, to all the people, family, friends and co-workers who encouraged me and last but not least, Lee and Chad Corrie who made this book possible.

Now, on with the show!

John Evan Carson

November 30, 2005

Main Prologue

"Oh, Grandpa!" I would say as I rubbed my six-year-old fingers across the polished gold sailing ship on his pocket watch. Even at six I knew when he was stretching the truth.

"Now listen, Rose, there is always some truth to every story. It's up to you to find it and get a hold on it."

So I'd be quiet and listen as he told me one tall tale after another, drifting with his stories as the old rocking chair squeaked back and forth.

We searched for brick seeds on the beaches, walked the pipe farms in Paraguay, hacked our way through the wire forests of Peru and escaped the porcelain mines in Russia. We flew over carpet farms and blasted for Kool-Whip in the Arctic.

I loved his stories!

One day Mother came to me and told me Grandpa would not be coming back. He was off on another adventure to a wonderful place. It would be a long one and some day we would join him there.

I sat in the old rocker and cried. As I drifted off to sleep I thought I could hear his voice.

"Now listen Rose, get a hold on it! It's up to you to carry on! Find your own adventures - and the truth in every story! I'll be watching over you. Some day we'll talk all about it! Now promise me you'll smile! I'm on the greatest adventure yet!"

"I will, Grandpa, I will..."

When Grandpa died he left me with the gift of curiosity and a longing for adventure.

I didn't realize how soon it would begin.

The Porcelain Mines
in Russia
TAXI
New York
Reebok
Ramblin' Rose

Chapter One

Porcelain mines in Russia? Whoever heard of such a thing?

Hi! My name is Rose. Ramblin' Rose. They call me that because I ramble from one thing to another when I talk. I talk about everything! I ask a lot of questions. I want to know about the whole world! And I don't always believe the answers I get. I have to find out for myself!

At twelve years old, I am the youngest editor ever of the school paper at The Brookhaven School For Girls. I also publish it on the Internet for other curious kids (of all ages!). My English teacher, Ms. Canfield says I'm a natural reporter. She also says I have a "great imagination".

She does not always believe the stories I write are true. "However, we must encourage our students' creativity!" She says. So, I keep writing the stories. I happen to know they are true. You can judge for yourself.

We live in a big old house by Minnehaha Creek in Minneapolis. I like being in the Midwest because it puts me in the middle of all the action. Besides, being twelve, I don't have a lot of choice in the matter.

My parents are both "professionals" and the house is very nice. Since my Dad works for the government (and I can't tell you what he does - or his name - secret, you know) we have a lot of security systems and even a chauffeur! He's really my bodyguard, but he gets me around.

My Mom is a corporate whiz kid. She is President (with a capital "P") of an on-line firm specializing in rating and analyzing trends for big corporate entities. She is always on the go. Which leaves me (an only child), Richard, the chauffeur slash bodyguard and my dog Samson the Great (Sam for short), a big black Newfie Mom likes to take to dog shows. Her hobby. "And good protection for a young girl!" She says. I like to fall asleep on him.

There I go ramblin' again! I'm telling you all this so you will be more likely to believe me when you read the stories I have written. One day I may win a Pulitzer Prize! There are other things you should know but I'll tell you as we go along. Now that I have you here, I wouldn't want to bore you.

It all started like this...

It was Thursday. Richard picked me up from school. Mom and Dad were at work and probably would be until evening. We drove up to the house and Richard got out of the limo. After checking the security he opened the door and let me out. I went into the house, while Richard pulled the car around back, and went about his chores.

When I opened the front door, Sam was there to greet me, as always. He liked it when Mother was away so he would not get scolded for playing. He knew better than to jump on me and knock me over, so he sat there with his tail swishing on the marble floor of the entryway. I sat down my books and hugged his neck.

"Get the toy!" I said.

He had the toy ready and woofed as he picked it up. So we played Tug-of-War. Sam always won, pulling me across the slick floor while I tried to hang onto the slippery handle. Today was no different. Except that the toy slipped out of my hands and sent me crashing backwards into the china cabinet.

I landed on my backside as several collector plates toppled off of their easels behind the glass doors, taking other precious pieces with them on the way to the bottom shelf. One of them was Mom's latest find, a rare porcelain plate from Russia. The one she wanted to show off on Saturday at her big party!

Mom had been planning this party for weeks! She had invited several big corporate clients- one of who had a wife who collected rare expensive porcelain!

I think she bought that plate just to impress her! I knew I was dead!

Frantically I cleaned up and replaced what I could. Sam laid on the Oriental rug with his paws over his nose, covering one eye. He knew we were both dead!

I took inventory- two broken plates and one cup- not as bad as I thought. But could they be replaced? And could I replace them before the party? Even Dad might not be able to save me this time!

I had to do something. I wrote down the information from the broken plates I had pieced together and looked for some Super Glue.

Then I called Aunt Susan.

Susan was Mom's older sister. She was in her "thirties" and single. She was fun and since she didn't have any kids of her own she'd kind of adopted me.

I liked Susan. She thought Mom was "too intense!" Mom and Susan had inherited their parent's fortune but both wanted to make their own way in the world.

Susan was a world traveler. She had been her Dad's favorite and followed him in the shipping industry. She was a tomboy the son they never had. Mom was always jealous of her. She had to "outdo" her. Because of their rivalry Grandpa sold the business, leaving Susan as a life-long consultant with pay! As well as the family fortune she split with Mom. Mom wanted nothing to do with the business and went out on her own. She left Connecticut after college and came to Minneapolis.

There I go ramblin' again! Anyway, back to our story...

Susan said she would come over this evening and keep Mom occupied and away from the china cabinet! I went to my computer and started searching. That's when I met Zip!

The computer was personalized just the way I liked it! The Horror theme popped up and I smiled when I heard the old sound clip saying "It's Alive! It's Alive!" My parents had the family filter on and all kinds of security built in and God knows who was watching us! They also expected their little girl to have the Peanuts or Cathy theme. So it was only natural to run the Horror theme!

My plan was to go to my usual search engine and find out about Russian porcelain. From there I could see a list of manufacturers and get in touch with one of them to find a replacement plate. Then, with Susan's help we could arrange an overnight express to put the new plate in before Mom ever knew what had happened! It would have worked great -except for Dad.

Dad was always doing something with our computers. "Security, you know! Top secret!" and "We are not just average citizens!" How many times would I hear him say that in my lifetime? I think he liked to spy on me and see if any boys were talking to me. Protect his little girl you know-oh no! Now I'm talking like him! Sheesh!

This time I noticed the shortcut to the search engine was missing. In its place was something called SAFE SEARCH.

"Safe Search! What the heck is that? I suppose Dad is trying to protect me from the Internet again!" I said out loud, though it gave me a good feeling to know that he cared.

4

I didn't have time to wonder about it so I clicked on it. Then I really got a surprise!

The monitor screen went blank! I was afraid the computer had crashed and was about to say some un-girl like things when I noticed static-like noise in my right ear. I turned my head and about fell out of the padded swivel chair! Materializing next to me was a man! It was like the transporter beams on the old Star Trek TV show. Only this wasn't Captain Kirk! He looked like a ghost! I could almost see through him.

"Who and what are you? How did you get here...?" I asked.

"I am Zip. It's an acronym for Zonal Information Program. I am a search engine."

"Not like any search engine I've ever seen! And I've never seen one outside of my computer! How can you do that?"

"I am a hologram. I have many files on you and know your preferences and all your search history. I am the result of a joint program developed by your government and mine."

"Who is "Your" government?" I was careful now, being the daughter of a secret government agent. "And how did you get into or out of my computer? I don't have access to my Dad's computer or passwords."

The ghostly hologram responded. "My Government is from far away. We are the Del-Tones, and have been operating from Area 51 in cooperation with your government. Your father works with us. But that is a story for another time. Your time on your current project is short. We are aware of your crisis, and are here to help. The party your mother is planning is very important to world affairs, and we are interested in the results. There is much at stake. However, we are limited to Zip as a contact device. We must also have your word on secrecy in order not to jeopardize you or your family as well as our joint program."

"Wow you ramble as much as I do! This is too intense!"

"To repeat," It said, "I am personalized to you, and so will have many of the same attributes..." I stopped him. "Can you really take any form?" I asked, thinking of my neighbor, Steve. He was the fourteen-year-old son of the people at the end of our block and I had a crush on him.

"What form would you like?" Zip asked.

I resisted temptation, and forced my mind back on the original reason for this highly unusual search.

"Are there really porcelain mines in Russia?" I asked.

Chapter Two

"Porcelain mines in Russia?" Zip replied. "Do you want to do a search? I'm a search engine, not an encyclopedia... though I do have access to one, and use it frequently."

"I've always wondered whether there was such a thing. My grandfather used to tell me stories when I was little. They sounded true, but I know they couldn't all be. Things like pipe farms, growing bricks, the wire forests in Peru, and the porcelain mines in Russia, where our sinks and tubs are chiseled out right there in the mine, and then sent to factories where they smooth and polish them. I've always wondered about that one. Today's catastrophe made me think of it. I do need to find out about porcelain though; porcelain plates, to be specific."

"We can do a search on Porcelain," Zip replied. "Do you want it on screen, or 3-D?"

"Wow. A 3-D picture search! Let's do that!"

Zip's ghostly head nodded, and he seemed to disappear. In its place was a barely visible, large, clear cube.

"Too intense!" I said, copying my parents, and Aunt Susan. It was one of their favorite expressions. I had grown up with it, and found myself saying it a lot.

Inside the cube, I could see the white letters of the word "PORCE-LAIN" floating and a list forming under them. It was a list of sites about porcelain, and there were a lot of them! I chose the one that said Russian...

While the site was coming up, I wondered about Grandpa's story. There was always some truth in every story. This was going to be good! Still for some odd reason I felt a little sad. My sadness was lightened by the activity in the search cube. From the center of the almost invisible box came light and sound as the site came up.

"Wow! This is like being at the Omni Theater!" I said, as the site continued to run.

Just as I began to listen to the narration from the cube, I heard a voice calling

"Hel-lo!" It was Aunt Susan!

"Up here!" I hollered back. "Come on up!"

I turned my attention back to the cube as Aunt Susan made her way up the stairs. Aunt Susan was curious about the voices coming from my room, and when she reached the doorway she said, "What is that?"

I couldn't answer right away because I was kind of hypnotized by the cube. My mind was absorbing information and memorizing it. It probably looked like a scene from a science fiction movie. Aunt Susan walked up behind me and put her hand on my shoulder, breaking the spell.

"Hi Aunt Susan, glad you're here!" I wasn't that far gone. I could see Aunt Susan was a little bewildered by the cube, so I brought her up to date while Zip played on.

"And that's the whole story. I've got to replace that plate by Saturday morning!"

"Who is the plate for? I know your Mom was going to use it as a good-will gesture," Susan replied. "I'm not sure of their names. I know they have important ties to Russian capitalists, though. And the lady does collect Russian porcelain..."

"Hmmn. Knowing your parents like I do, I would say it's critical to replace that plate. There is probably more at stake here than just grounding you for life."

That being said, Aunt Susan turned and addressed Zip.

"Zip, I'd like to make an international phone call."

"Certainly," Zip replied, seemingly unconcerned about another user giving him commands.

Dad programmed Maybe Aunt Susan into the computer, and because she was included in our home security system, she could let herself in and come and go as she pleased. Of course, she had a Top Secret security clearance also. Her travels as a consultant for her father's shipping business put her in touch with the State Department a lot. Hmmn! Maybe there was more to Aunt Susan's occupation than we knew about, or should I say I knew about... anyway, I was glad to have her help, though I'm sure I could have handled it alone.

Zip prompted Aunt Susan for the number, and I was surprised when she took an address book out of her purse, and read the number for the Gzhel Porcelain factory in Russia...

The very same name stamped on the bottom of the plate. But Susan hadn't looked at the pieces yet!

Zip brought up a picture from the video cam on the other end and a portly white haired gentleman appeared before us. A hologram!

"Susan! So good to see you! What can I do for you? I did not expect to see you so soon. It was only a month ago that you picked up the plate."

He was speaking in Russian, but Zip was translating. Aunt Susan greeted him back in Russian, which she spoke fluently, of course. For my benefit they continued in English. I was surprised to hear him say Aunt Susan had picked up the plate! Boy, she had a lot of explaining to do.

Chapter Three

I tugged at Aunt Susan's sleeve like a little kid. It was the only way I could get her attention! She was telling Zip to call my school.

"Aunt Susan! Why won't you stop and talk to me?"

"No time. Our plane leaves in an hour. I'm calling your school to arrange for you to take tomorrow off. Then I will leave a message for your parents to tell them you're with me. I'll explain everything on the way. Now go pack quickly, and light - we're going to New York!"

With that she turned back to Zip as he connected with the school. I heard her say something about a "family emergency" as I opened the closet, and started to pack. Who can pack in one minute? But it was only for a day so I just threw in some jeans, a top, and a few of the bare necessities.

New York! I wanted to bring all of my "cool" clothes. But Aunt Susan was motioning me to hurry as she called Richard to pull the car around and be ready for us. She mumbled something to him I couldn't hear, and told Zip to stay in touch.

My questions were building up, and I felt like I would explode as we ran out of the front door. Aunt Susan pushed the remote on her car keys. The trunk flew open, and she reached in for a suitcase that was already packed, slammed the lid, and threw her keys to Richard.

I felt like I was being swept away by a raging river as we jumped into the backseat of the limo, and Aunt Susan opened her purse. She took out her cell phone, and turned it on. It had a small screen, and an Internet connection. "Zip, are you there?"

"I'm here," Zip replied. "The tickets are waiting for you at the gate. You are booked first class as VIPs, the reservations are made, and the antique shop is expecting you."

My head was reeling. Aunt Susan had picked up the original plate for Mom, knew about the party, knew about Zip, apparently was working with Richard, we were on our way to New York to pick up a duplicate plate, and now Aunt Susan was talking to Richard again, giving him instructions. I looked in the mirror, and saw Richard smile and wink.

"Hey, lighten up, Rose. You look like you're being kidnapped," he said.

Well of course I did. My whole world had suddenly changed. People were not who I thought they were. I knew Dad was an agent, but it never occurred to me Mom and Aunt Susan could be too. And I always thought of Richard as just a chauffeur. Now he was an agent too! This was too intense! I started to ask how this all happened, but we were already at the airport.

Richard pulled the limo over, and grabbed our bags. He took us to the gate, where we were met by the stewardess. Aunt Susan flashed her security ID, and we walked onto the plane, leaving the other passengers wondering whom we were. I couldn't wait to get seated, and start firing my questions at Aunt Susan! It was hard for a rambler like me to keep from talking this long!

Before I knew it we were in the air, and I was suddenly very tired. What a day!

Chapter Four

I woke up about an hour later, and looked out the window. We were somewhere over Illinois. It was dark out, and dinner was being served. Aunt Susan looked over at me and said, "Hi, sleepy head!"

I was calmer now, and refrained from asking Aunt Susan any questions. I let her talk while we were eating. I hadn't realized how hungry I was. Aunt Susan handed me the printouts from Zip about the Russian porcelain.

Seeing my questioning look, she explained. "I thought you might like something to read on the way. I know you write a newsletter for your school, and you'll need to print something - but there are things about this adventure you can never tell anyone."

"Aunt Susan, what is really going on?" I asked as the stewardess cleared our plates. The food in first class was a lot better than the snacks the rest of the passengers got. Personally, I liked Oreo cookies...

"I know you have a lot of questions, Rose. It's really not as complicated as it seems. You know your Dad works for the "Agency", well; your Mom and I do too. Don't ask any questions yet. We can't talk freely here. Anyway, your Dad was working for the Agency when he met your Mom. In fact that's where he met her. I introduced them.

"You see, your Grandpa had built a huge shipping business. He was quite successful when World War II started, and had quite a few influential ties around the world. He did a lot for the Allies, procuring needed supplies, and dealing with foreign companies. When the war was over he was asked by the State Department to continue working with the government. Under-cover of course. He was single until he met your grandmother. She was twenty-five, and he was forty-five. They had two girls, your Mom and I. We grew up in the "Cold War" days of the late Sixties and the Seventies. Neither of us were interested in the shipping business, but when our Mom died, we were out of high school and looking for adventure. Of course, Grandpa sent us to college, and when we graduated we had a choice of taking over the business, or going our own ways."

Aunt Susan stopped for a drink of water. She was getting a little emotional, remembering her parents, who were both gone now. Grandpa had died when I was seven- five years ago. Mom had gone into business, and soon became the owner of her own consulting firm. Aunt Susan had taken a life-long post as a consultant for her Dad's business, traveling around the world, arranging deals, and doing PR.

A little more composed now, Aunt Susan continued, "Anyway, The Agency contacted us about working for them. We had grown up around it and spent a lot of time with Dad on his trips and hanging around the office. He loved to show us off, and I think sometimes our presence helped soften up his contacts, and swing things his way. It was all very exciting, and we didn't mind.

"In college, we met your Dad. He was a handsome young man with a cause. He worked for The Agency, and talked about making the world a better place from inside the System. In the late Seventies and early Eighties he was a real change of pace. So many people wanted to tear down the System, or so they said. Most of them did not really know what was going on. Then they started going the other way.

Anyway, he was clean cut, and more like the people we were used to being around. I went out with him, but he was always interested in your mom. Today we are the best of friends, and all work for The Agency. Richard also works for The Agency. He was your Dad's partner on many assignments. When you came along, he became your bodyguard also. The Agency monitors your house and activities because your parents work in "sensitive" areas, and your Dad is known to have made some enemies. We wanted to keep you out of all of this - at least until you were older, for your own safety."

"Whew! I knew about Dad, but this is too much! My whole family is..."

"Shhh! I told you to be careful."

"But what about Zip?"

Aunt Susan explained that Zip was a program developed by the government. My Dad was one of the first to test it. Zip was set up for The Agency to monitor and help the agents as well as provide security. With a cell phone link they were never alone. It also monitored all the security in our house, the phones and computers, listening for any possible threats and even all of my activities on the computer, including my newsletter!

So far I had only published one, and it was an introduction. I was worried about my searches, but Aunt Susan assured me Dad valued my privacy. I was thinking about the neighbor boy, James, and all the chats we had... I was going to be a lot more careful from now on!

"Anyway, young lady, now that you know, you have been deputized."

"Yes, but what about the plate that started all of this?"

"I'll tell you in the taxi when we get to New York. Now I'm going to take a nap."

Reclining her seat, she turned her head and signed off. I decided to read about the Russian porcelain. I wanted to know everything I could. I was not going to be left in the dark again!

From time to time I looked out at the lights below, and read about porcelain. I still wanted to know if there really were porcelain mines in Russia.

Chapter Five

The printout began with a definition of Kaolin, from the Chinese "kaoling" or "high-ridge", named for the hill where it was first discovered. It is pure, soft, white clay which retains its color when fired. It was sent to Europe in the 18th century. Pure kaolin is used to manufacture fine porcelain and china. Impure varieties are used to make pottery, stoneware and bricks; also as filler for pigments and in the manufacture of paper.

It is now mined primarily in South Carolina, North Carolina, Georgia, Pennsylvania, and Alabama. The term "kaolin" is often applied to other porcelain clays, which are not discolored by firing. It's chief constituent is the mineral kaolinite, a hydrous aluminum silicate formed by the decomposition of aluminum silicates, particularly feldspar. What the heck was feldspar? I wondered.

I had to look up from the printout to digest this somewhat technical information. Just because we were involved in a matter of international importance centering on the breakage of a rare porcelain plate, and I remembered the stories my grandfather had told me about the porcelain mines in Russia where he said our sinks and bathtubs were chiseled out of the walls of the mines and sent to factories for finishing, did not mean I was fascinated by porcelain! Still, my curiosity was being satisfied, and I was getting an answer to my question. It was rather interesting - and if I was going to miss school tomorrow, at least I was learning something. And, it would make a great story for my newsletter! The material did come from the Internet.

While Aunt Susan slept, I read on:

The making of porcelain in Russia began with Peter the Great (1687-1725). In his efforts to develop trade for Russia, he engaged artists from around the world to live and work in Russia. When his daughter,

Elizabeth (1741-1762) became empress she continued to search for qualified artisans and eventually a porcelain factory was established in St. Petersburg.

Now the text turned to a history of Gzhel porcelain. Gzhel is the name of a village in Russia famous for its pottery since the 14th century. Using the famous local clays, Gzhel offers a mix of fine and folk art in the familiar blue and snowy white style. So, in a sense, there really are porcelain mines in Russia!

Grandpa, I think you exaggerated just a little bit! I couldn't wait to check out his other stories!

I looked down at the next page, and got another surprise!

It said, "Rose, keep reading, don't look up, and don't look surprised. We are being watched - and I knew I could only tell you what they already know. I had Zip add this to your printout while you were packing. If they find out why we are going to New York it will blow the whole operation. They have been watching you and your family for a long time. They know who we are, what we do, and are always watching for a chance to use you as a "bargaining chip" with your parents. The Agency provides security, but anyone can be listening - even from a distance, and anyone can be an enemy agent.

"The plate you broke was one I had picked up at the porcelain factory in Russia a month ago. Your mother was to present this plate to the Russian couple at the party this weekend. They are Russian capitalists who have moved their operations to the U.S. in order to help the cause of capitalism. They are opposed by hard-line communists who are against democratization, and want to return to communist rule. They will do anything to sabotage it.

"The couple we are referring to own a distribution center in the Midwest dedicated to art - especially porcelain - Russian porcelain. It is etched very fine, but the gold edge of the plate contains the names of companies in the U.S. sympathetic to the communist cause to warn this couple of companies and people to avoid doing business with. There is a back-up plate, and we are on the way to pick it up. A special tool is needed to see the information, and if the second plate is not needed, it will be sold as a regular piece. No one would ever know of its special properties. Now, destroy this as discreetly as you can."

This was definitely too intense! I felt like a secret agent. This whole thing had gotten way too big! I was excited and scared at the same time. I looked around at the other passengers. A businessman talking on a cell phone, a sophisticated middle-aged woman dressed very expensively, a very heavy salesman, and a young couple obviously on their honeymoon. Hmmm! Any one of them could be an enemy agent!

That was just the first class section though! What about the rest of the passengers? I thought if I could get up and walk through the plane, I would be able to check out the others, too. As I stood up, the stewardess came over to see if she could help. There was a concerned look on her face. Was she a spy too?

"Can I help you, miss?" She asked.

"No, I just need to go the bathroom," I replied; hoping my nervousness didn't show. My heart was pounding in my chest, and I turned to the curtains headed for Coach.

"We have restrooms right up front for First Class, why don't you use them?"

"Of course," I replied. "How silly of me." Was it a suggestion, or an order? Now I was really shook. I was going to destroy the evidence. Had she seen me read it? I wanted to wake Aunt Susan, but I was determined to be a good agent, and handle this myself. While I was in the restroom I looked for a way to dispose of the paper. I did not want to leave it behind for someone to find later. I thought about the trash receptacle, but decided against it. I couldn't throw it out the window...

Suddenly, the Captain's voice came on the loudspeaker. "Attention passengers, please return to your seats. We are approaching New York, our destination, the John F. Kennedy Airport."

I scrambled back to my seat, crumpling the page, and stuffing it into my back pocket. I thought it would flatten out when I sat on it. Rats! Now I wouldn't get to check out the other passengers. I still had the evidence, and it didn't flatten out...

At least I wouldn't have to sit on it long! I shook Aunt Susan and looked out the window at the lights of New York. I would just have to check the passengers as they got off the plane. They couldn't fool a master spy like me!

Chapter Six

The bustling of the passengers woke Aunt Susan from her sleep. With the skill of a veteran traveler she sat up and stretched. Regaining her focus, she looked past me out the window. "Coming in to J.F.K., eh?" I could tell she'd been here before.

"Yes. I'm sorry I didn't wake you sooner." Well, I was and I wasn't. I was sorry I didn't dispose of the paper in my back pocket. It was constantly reminding me of its presence. "What's the plan, Aunt Susan?"

"Well, we won't have to wait for our luggage. There will be a cab waiting for us in the ramp. Richard will have called ahead. The cab will take us to our room, and in the morning we'll go shopping. Now, I don't want to hear another word out of you until we get to our room. Understand?"

I wanted to tell Aunt Susan about the page in my back pocket. I started to talk, but thought better of it. Usually I talk any time a thought enters my mind. Hey, I just thought of something... well, that answered my question right there. I guess thoughts can enter your mind, or they can come from the inside... this was deep.

Anyway, I kept quiet while my thoughts rambled on. I knew Aunt Susan was aware of the situation, and it wasn't safe to talk even in the cab. Still, I was going to check the passengers when we got off the plane.

Looking out the window, I watched the lights of New York get closer and closer.

It was an awesome sight. The electric blue of the landing strip lights held my attention as the airport drew near. Soon, I knew I could carry out my plan. I was not going to let Aunt Susan do all of the work.

It was a perfect landing. I wanted to tell the Captain what a great job he had done. We grabbed our bags and headed down the ramp to the gate. We were among the first to disembark, and the stewardess said goodbye in her very professional way. As Aunt Susan and I were about half way to the gate, I turned to look at the passengers behind us. That's when I noticed the stewardess talking into a cell phone as she watched us walk away. Hmmn.

My heart was beating faster now. Was she an agent? Theirs or ours? Was she setting us up? Could she see the ball of paper in my back pocket? I wanted to tell Aunt Susan to turn around and look, but it was too late. We were already in the airport. And besides, Aunt Susan said she did not want to hear another word until we were in our room. It was going to be a looong ride!

I kept turning my head to look at the other people, and Aunt Susan spoke up; "Why are you doing that? Look at the airport, not the people. You look too suspicious. Act like a tourist."

"How soon before we get to the hotel?" I broke protocol. Aunt Susan said to act like a tourist - so I did. Besides, there was no way I could be in New York for the first time, be a spy, be in a situation like this, and be a "rambler" - and Not Talk! Sheesh!

"We'll be there soon. Now you are acting like a tourist. It's okay to talk - just don't "talk". Get it?"

NOW I get it. Duh! Well, I could talk! It would be easy to act like a tourist.

There was nothing special about the Yellow Cab waiting in the ramp. It looked just like all the other ones lined up. But, as we approached the curb the driver got out, and offered to take our bags.

I watched other people getting into cabs, but did not see any familiar faces, so I turned my attention back to the approaching driver.

"May I take your bags?" He repeated, as he reached for Aunt Susan's.

"The flap is open," she said.

"Yes, but the bag is zipped," he replied. And with that, Aunt Susan handed him the bag.

I guessed it was a password, and handed him mine too. The Agency must have sent him. We climbed into the back seat and the driver pulled out into the exit lane. Soon we were rolling down unfamiliar roads. It was eleven o'clock at night, and even though I was tired, the excitement kept me awake. When we were on the open road the driver looked into the mirror and smiled.

"Susan!" He said, "It's been a long time. Welcome back to New York! And this is…"

"Rose," I answered, not wanting Aunt Susan to speak for me. The driver was handsome, and seemed more like a chauffeur than a cab driver. A chauffeur or an agent!

"Well, Rose, my name is Steven. It's a pleasure to meet you!"

I was pleased by his attention, and for the first time since the adventure began I felt like one of the team. An equal. I turned to Aunt Susan, "Where are we going?"

"We're going to the Sheraton. Steven, is the room secure?"

"Yes, and you are both checked in. We'll have you there in a jif."

I thought he was talking about peanut butter, or using a code, but caught on quick. He meant soon.

"Good," Aunt Susan replied. "And you'll pick us back up at 8 a.m.?"

"Yes. Your plane leaves at 5 p.m. tomorrow. I'll stay with you all the way." Steven told her.

During the ride I had missed all the lights. I did notice one thing; there were a lot of cabs in New York!

Aunt Susan was looking at the rearview mirror. She had glanced at it several times. Steven caught her look, and opened the glove compartment. He pushed a button, and a small printer started working. In a few minutes there was a page of information about the car behind us. "Taillight Cam," Steven explained.

Aunt Susan explained how she was routinely followed; sometimes because of an assignment and sometimes just to keep track of her whereabouts. So far they hadn't been able to break Zip's security. If the car behind us was following us, it may or may not be connected with our mission.

The driver of the other car caught on to our attention and turned off. I thought it was over.

Aunt Susan and Steven kept watching, though. I questioned them as Steven drove right past the hotel without a glance at it.

"Sure enough! The old dodge!" Steven said.

Aunt Susan explained that it was a standard trick. A double tail. There were two cars following us. The first one wants you to notice them and then turns off to make you think they are spotted, and pretends to give up. The second one takes over, and follows unnoticed.

And that was just what happened.

It was late and Steven knew he had to shake the tail before we got to the hotel. Now he had driven right past it, and couldn't go back. Or so I thought. But that is exactly what he did! Of course! He would make the tail think the trick had worked!

As we turned into the hotel the second car drove on. I looked at Aunt Susan, and was proud of myself for catching on.

"Now we know it wasn't just surveillance " Aunt Susan said. "But I still don't think they know our objective."

"Don't worry, Susan," Steven said. "I have a plan for shaking them. Tomorrow Rose gets the five-dollar tour of New York." He smiled and winked at us in the mirror.

Chapter Seven

The night air was cold as Steven took our bags from the trunk. I stood alone on the sidewalk, and looked out at the lights. For the first time today I realized how far away from home I was. I missed it. I was glad I brought my favorite jacket, and pulled it tight around me. It's funny how I had never really appreciated it before. Now it was my link to Dad and Mom, Sam and Richard, and my whole familiar world. Amazing how much could fit into a jacket! I zipped it up to keep anything from falling out in this strange place.

Clutching my bag tightly, I stayed behind Aunt Susan as we walked through the plush hotel lobby right to the elevators. I did not want her to notice the tears I was holding back. As she opened the door of our room I made a beeline for the bed by the window and opened my bag.

Aunt Susan sensed my need for privacy, and quietly went about getting ready for bed.

"We'll talk in the morning," she said. "Seven a.m., sharp! ' Night, Rose!"

Soon I was left alone. I reluctantly took off my jacket and Reeboks(. Oh, I wondered, why did I have to break that plate? Being a spy was not as much fun as it had seemed.

I was glad I had brought pajamas, and was re-assured by the familiar feel of them. The room was quiet as Aunt Susan turned off her light, and was soon asleep. I looked out the window for a few minutes and wondered how anyone could feel alone in such a big city. But I did. Terribly alone. We had traveled before, and I had even been to camp for a summer, but this was different.

One day in New York. It was only one day and I'd be back home. Then everything will be fine! But, some things would never be the same again...

As I turned off the small brass lamp on the cherry wood table next to the bed, I thought of Sam. Clutching the extra pillow on the double bed, I did not want to think about tomorrow.

I thought about home, and just before I fell asleep I whispered, "'Night Sam", but he wasn't there to lick my face.

Chapter Eight

I did not want to wake up. I could hear someone moving around as I drifted in and out of sleep. In my dream state I thought I was home, and waited to be licked any moment by Samson the Great! Mother must have come in to wake me. I looked at the clock.

"Seven a.m.! I'm late for school!" I dropped off again, then woke up with a jolt-

jumping out of bed, expecting to see Mother prodding me to get up. Any second now Samson would start licking my face...

Instead, I found myself in a strange room and Aunt Susan was telling me to hurry, and get ready. New York! I thought it was only a dream. But I really was in New York, and somebody named Steven was going to pick us up at 8 a.m. I stumbled into the bathroom - waking up in stages.

The cold water on my face, and the reflection in the mirror were both bringing me back to reality. I looked at my hair. It was hopeless. Even though it was only shoulder length, it would take too long to fix. I decided to shampoo it in the shower, blow-dry it, and throw it in a quick ponytail. I was too young for make up (even in New York) and the blue eyes looking back at me were still a little bloodshot. I must have been more tired than I thought.

The bathroom had double sinks outside of the shower. Aunt Susan was busy getting ready as I brushed my teeth, and checked for zits. The shower had cleared the cobwebs, but the butterflies were still in my stomach.

It was going to be a busy day, but it sure beat school! And I was going to get to see some of New York! I hurried to get dressed. Clean jeans, sweatshirt and Reeboks. After all, I didn't want to look like a kid from Minnesota!

23

At 7:45 we were eating a quick breakfast of rolls and juice as we waited for Steven. At 8a.m. we walked through the lobby doors, as Steven pulled up to the curb in the now-familiar cab.

The short night did not show on him at all. He must have been excited about seeing Aunt Susan.

"Good morning, ladies!" He said, as he opened the car door for us.

Aunt Susan looked sharp in a knee-length gray skirt, white blouse and gray jacket; a business suit, conservative, with black shoes-low heeled, and a gold pin on her lapel. She carried a small handbag, and I envied the confidence in her smile.

Steven was struck! He talked to us through the rear-view mirror as he pulled out of the drive.

"Here is the plan. We know we are going to be tailed, and we don't want them to know where we are going. So, after a brief tour of the sights on Fifth Avenue, we'll stop while you two shop. Then we'll go for lunch, and I'll tell you the rest."

Steven was quiet for a few minutes, concentrating on his driving. Even though it seemed second nature for him. I looked out the window at the fall day. I was excited about everything. The butterflies in my stomach were excited, too. I did not recognize any of the sights of course, but noticed we were on the Van Wyck Expressway.

"Steven, what did you get on the taillight cam printout? Anyone we know?" Aunt Susan asked.

Steven handed the paper over the back seat. I took it from his hand, and saw a picture I recognized... a big, heavy set, actually a fat man in his forties... the salesman on the plane! He was an enemy agent!

Now my stomach was tied in knots! I was glad I did not stuff Aunt Susan's message into the seat on the plane! I read down farther - NAME: Vladimir Petchenko, AKA: John Henry - U.S. COVER: Salesman working in the United States dealing in Russian porcelain, an imitation of Gzhel Porcelain, mostly sold as decorative pieces through home fashion and discount stores. Actually working for old hard-line Soviet movement.

The report went on, but I did not read it. A wave of fear went through me, and Aunt Susan took the paper from me. Puzzled at my expression she quickly scanned the document and said, "Rose, are you okay?"

"Aunt Susan," I said, "I saw him on the plane! He was sitting in first class with us! I think he saw me trying to hide the message Zip printed out!" I was being reminded again that this was not a game.

"Relax, Rose. I saw him too. It's all part of the business. I'm used to being followed, but I did not think they were aware of our current mission. They must have found out about the plate I picked up in Russia. I'm not sure how much they know. They may not know about the second plate. They don't know the first one is broken. They don't know why we are in New York. We could just be a couple of rich girls on a shopping trip. That's how we need to make it look. Just relax, and remember we are not alone."

"Okay, Aunt Susan. But I can't help being a little scared. This is serious, isn't it?" I said as bravely as I could.

"Hey, I thought you were a reporter! You need to look at this objectively. Disconnect a little. This is a part of the world, and has been forever. You're almost a teenager now, and the world needs you. I know you are up to it. Enjoy the ride."

Aunt Susan's words re-assured me a little. She was right. I was in such a hurry to grow up and get out into the world. But I was twelve. At twelve I could go either way, a kid, or a growing-up young woman.

Actually, it was a neat place to be. It was an age I'd never experience again. Some days I enjoyed the flexibility of being able to act like a kid. I could hide and play, or sit in Dad's lap and be his little angel. Some days I could hang with Mom, and she would treat me like a grown up, making plans, and talking to me about love and things I wasn't ready for yet. I could let go, or I could hang on.

Sometimes I wanted to remind them I was smarter than they thought I was. The fact I knew more about the world than they thought, would scare them. If they knew how much I was aware of. Dad's job would, especially scare them...

And, sometimes I missed having a brother or sister to share things with. I was glad I had Richard and Sam. But there was no one I could really talk to about twelve-year- old girl things. Maybe that's why I wanted to write so much. It helped me understand things, and gave me an audience to share life with.

I was also glad I was a girl. Everyone said how tough it was being a girl. My body changing, and all of that. But, Mom said to take it in stride. So I did not dwell on it. Boys seem to have it easier - but do they?

They don't have the flexibility girls do. We can totally change our look and personalities. We have the prerogative to be anything, anytime. We are allowed to change our minds from moment to moment.

Aunt Susan's voice broke my rambling thoughts, and I turned away from the car window. I hadn't been paying attention to the scenery anyway.

"Zip. Are you there?" She was speaking into the handheld (that's agent talk for cell phone).

Zips' voice came back, "Yes, Susan. I am here. What would you like?"

I was still amazed at voice recognition technology, and decided Zip was male.

"The mission is hot. I repeat the mission is hot." Aunt Susan was talking in code, and I guessed we were moving to a new level of seriousness. I was not sure what it meant, but I sensed her tone. I wondered if Dad would be alerted.

Zip replied, "Okay, Susan. DEF CON 3 activated. Continue mission. Tracking enabled. I have your location. Steven's plan is in motion. Follow his lead. I will stay in voice touch with your personal COM link."

"Ten-four, Zip. Susan out."

Wow! This was cool! Like being in a movie! Too intense! I was already thinking of the Newsletter, and what I could - and could not - write about. I hoped there would be some things I could. I knew what the headline would be as Steven left the Long Island Expressway and announced, "Okay, ladies, next stop - Fifth Avenue!"

Chapter Nine

Steven took over. There was a change in his voice, as he became part cab driver/tour guide, and secret agent in charge. He looked into the rearview mirror, and said, "The tail is still on the dog." I knew we were being logged by Zip and The Agency. Aunt Susan seemed content to follow his lead, and I decided to follow hers.

"We are headed to the Rockefeller Center," he continued. But first we are going to look like tourists. Well, you are anyway. We are going down Fifth Avenue instead of Sixth. I'm turning south on Fifth, and we'll drive by the Empire State Building. We don't have time to actually see these places, but you can look them up later.

"Our destination is on Fifth Avenue and 59th St. A La Vieille Russie. At the corner of Central Park across from the Pond. I know you are familiar with it, Susan. Now, we can't go there directly, so after we pass the New York Library; we'll go to Times Square. Then we'll pick up Broadway, go east on 57th past Carnegie Hall, right again on Fifth, past the Museum of Modern Art, and then to the Rockefeller Center."

Sheesh! I felt like we had already had the tour! But I surmised he was speaking the directions in case we disappeared... I did not want to think about that! I sat back to enjoy our five-dollar tour of New York.

Steven checked the rear view mirror from time to time to see if "the tail was still on the dog". He talked as he drove, and soon we were in front of the Empire State Building. I could not see the top, and my neck was sore from trying.

Steven began his tour guide talk:

"Unfortunately, we do not have time to give you a real tour, but I can give you some quick facts as we drive. The Empire State Building is a National Historic Landmark. No surprise there. It stands a quarter of a mile high. The observatory, on the 86th floor, is open 365 days a year in any kind of weather. More than three million people a year visit it. Of course, it is one of the main attractions in New York. You'll have to come back some time and see it."

I was impressed. The size of the building alone would impress anybody. I remembered the movie King Kong. I made a note that the Empire State Building would make a good story for an upcoming Newsletter.

The next "stop" on our tour was The New York Library. Steven did not have a lot of information on it, though. We made note of it as we drove by. Aunt Susan, it seemed, was already familiar with New York. But she acted like a tourist anyway for the benefit of our "tail". She craned her neck to look at the architecture of the building as we drove by.

"It's too bad we can't see Times Square at night," Steven continued. "It's quite a place. And, as you can see, the traffic is too. I see we still have the tail. So far the plan is working!"

Steven turned on Broadway, and said, "Give my regards to Broadway…remember me to Harold Square!" I thought he was going to start singing any minute! He talked about George M. Cohan, and I made a note to look that up when I got home. Soon we were at Carnegie Hall. Steven must have been more familiar with it, because he had a lot more information about it.

"Carnegie Hall held it's first concerts in 1891. It began with a man named Leopold Damrosch, who left Germany in 1871, and came to America. Within two years he had organized the Oratorio Society, and by 1877 he had founded the New York Symphony Society. Since the new organizations did not have a home, he began to search for money, and a location for a building. He died in 1885, leaving the organizations and his dream of a large concert hall to his son, Walter. Walter found the backing in Andrew Carnegie."

Aunt Susan listened intently as Steven talked. She was impressed with his knowledge of Carnegie Hall. I was busy taking notes. I had always wanted my Newsletter to be more than just fluffy girl's school stuff. I wanted it to be interesting and educational too. I felt like I was on a field trip.

"Steven," Aunt Susan said, "I had no idea you were so passionate about New York."

"It's not just New York, Susan. I have a passion for history and music. I love old movies about people like Benny Goodman - did you know they have his clarinet in the Rose Museum in Carnegie Hall?"

He looked at me when he said that. I thought the Rose Museum was a great name for it! This one I would have to see. Did they have roses everywhere? Anyway, I gathered that many famous concerts were held there. I made notes to look up Carnegie Hall, and also promised myself to come back and see it. Steven's passion was contagious, and as he talked I became curious about the history of music in the United States. My mind was ramblin' as Steven went on.

"Coming up is the Museum of Modern Art. It was founded in 1929 by three private citizens; Lillie P. Bliss, Mary Quinn Sullivan, and Abby Aldrich Rockefeller. Their mission was to make modern and contemporary art available to the public. It was the first museum devoted entirely to the modern movement. Today it houses more than 100,000 works dating from the 1840s to the present."

I caught the name Rockefeller as we pulled into the Rockefeller Center. I was just going to ask Steven about the connection, but he stopped me with a look in the mirror. His job as tour guide was over.

"No time to answer your question, Rose. When this is over I would love to escort the two of you on a real tour of New York. Now here is the plan..."

Chapter Ten

A few minutes later Aunt Susan and I were walking into the Rockefeller Center. I had no idea what it might be like. I wished Steven was with us to be a tour guide, but he was waiting in the cab. It was all part of the plan.

The tail was still on the dog. Vladimir Petchenko was sitting in his car, also. He was waiting for us to come back out. I guess he did not want to take a chance on losing us inside the Rockefeller Center. Inside or outside, that is. It was an indoor-outdoor complex consisting of four-teen different buildings.

Our part of the plan was to act like tourists, look around, have some lunch and shop. Pretty easy, huh?

Unless, of course, Vladimir had called ahead, and someone was waiting for us inside. I guess that's why we supposed to act like tourists. My heart was racing from both the excitement of our "mission", and seeing the Rockefeller Center. I did not know if I could ever sit still in school again!

Time was short. We were to leave here in an hour. We still had to get back to the hotel and the airport. Our flight left JFK at 4 p.m., New York time, and arrived in Minneapolis at approximately 9 p.m. central time. We still had to pick up the plate. It was already 10 a.m. We would be eating lunch early. If we left here at 11 a.m., picked up the plate at noon, returned to our hotel, and packed by 2 p.m., we could be at the air-port at 3 p.m.

If all went well, we would be home tonight in our own beds. I hugged my jacket again, lonesome for Sam.

The architecture and art here was fabulous, but Aunt Susan reminded me we did not have time to explore it. We were searching out the restaurant Steven had told us to go to. We were a little hungry after our "continental" breakfast. A sandwich would do fine. Of course, I would have settled for ice cream as we passed the Ben and Jerry's on the Plaza. Aunt Susan pulled me away.

After "browsing" along the way, we came to Dean (Deluca's. We ordered a quick sandwich for me, and a salad for Aunt Susan. I wasn't so sure I was going to like growing up if you had to eat like a rabbit all of the time to keep your figure! But, we were there for a reason. To be seen by our contacts.

We ate quickly, and Aunt Susan turned to me and said, "Rose, you need a new jacket!"

I did not like the next part of the plan. I liked my old faded, denim jacket; it was my security blanket and trademark. There were special things in each pocket - and Mom had been trying to get me to throw it out for the whole last year. I knew I was outgrowing it anyway, but still did not want to part with it.

That was exactly what the plan was.

We headed to the ladies room and ran smack dab into ourselves!

Standing in front of the mirror was a woman and a girl that looked just like us. They were dressed a little different though.

The woman looked at Aunt Susan, and said, "The suitcase is open."

Aunt Susan replied, "Yes, but the bag is zipped."

"No time to talk," said the woman. "I'm Kate, and this is Doe."

I could not believe the resemblance! Doe was about my height, age and size. She was wearing blue jeans, Reeboks, and a New York jacket. Her hair was thrown in a quick ponytail under her baseball cap, and was the same color as mine. While Aunt Susan and Kate exchanged jackets, Doe and I reluctantly swapped ours.

Doe had a "yuck!" look on her face as she eyed my favorite jacket. I was not eager to wear her jacket either. Aunt Susan knew how attached I was to mine.

"Come on, Rose. You'll get it back," Kate said.

"Yeah, don't worry," said Doe. "I'll take care of it for you. The Agency will send it back. Your Dad is a friend of ours. Kate's my mom, and we help out when we can."

I smiled at Doe, thanking her for understanding, and switched the jackets. Hers felt kind of good. I finally had my new jacket, but somehow felt disloyal to my old one. But it was for a good cause, and parting with it made me feel a little more grown up.

"Okay, time's up," said Kate. She was now wearing Aunt Susan's suit jacket, and Susan was wearing hers.

"Remember the plan," she said as they left the restroom.

I put on the Yankee's cap.

We left a minute later headed in the opposite direction. We would not be getting in the cab with Steven. Instead we were to pick up Kate's car, and drive directly to the A La Vieille Russie shop. Kate and Doe would get into the cab with Steven, and drag the tail with them back to our hotel room. There they would pick up our luggage, and Steven would take it to the airport with the two decoys.

We found Kate's old Voyager van, and headed across Central Park in search of the Russian shop.

So far the plan was going perfect!

Aunt Susan knew the way, and in a short time we were at the corner of 59th Street and Fifth Avenue. We were looking at a shop called A La Vieille Russie. Aunt Susan was familiar with it, and gave me the tourist talk on it.

"A La Vieille Russie has been in business since 1851. It was founded in Kiev. During the Revolution it was re-established in Paris around 1921. The New York branch was opened in 1941 by the late Alexander Schaeffer. They deal in fine art and antiques.

Carl Faberge was a client. He was a famous goldsmith and jeweler. They are known worldwide for their collection of Russian Imperial treasures. And, of course Russian porcelain. They hold exhibitions around the world. And that's where I had the backup plate sent."

"Do they know what's on the plate?" I asked.

"No, they are not involved. They are simply performing a service for a customer. The package has my name on it, and instructions that if it was not picked up in thirty days they could sell the plate for their trouble. I really did not think it would be needed."

"Ouch!" I said as Aunt Susan reminded me of how we got into this situation. "Shouldn't we go in now?"

"Yes, we have been standing here for a few minutes. Let's go!" Aunt Susan smiled as we walked through the door.

I was impressed with Aunt Susan's knowledge of this shop. Of course, she had grown up traveling with her father, and now traveled around the world as a consultant for his company. They were familiar with importing and exporting. I felt the family tradition in my blood, and was more at home among the treasures and antiques than I expected.

"Hello Susan! So good to see you!" The man behind the counter greeted us with a warm smile.

"Hello, Dr. Schaeffer! It's good to see you also. May I introduce my niece, Rose?"

"A pleasure to meet you, Rose." Dr. Schaeffer replied, and gave me a warm smile. He was very sincere, and did not treat me like a kid, although I was wearing a baseball cap and jacket. Not the sort of thing one would wear in a shop like this.

"Mark," Susan, said, less formal now, "did the package arrive?"

"Yes, it did, Susan. I have it in my office with your instructions. If you would like to follow me..."

While Aunt Susan and Dr. Schaeffer went to get the package, I looked around at all the "treasures". Mom would love this place! I thought about porcelain and art as I looked at the pieces, and imagined the prices. It seemed to me a lot of "art" had its' beginnings in necessity. Like the porcelain. People needed plates and cups, and they also needed to express themselves. They needed to brighten up their world. They needed to feel important. There had to be more to life than just survival and bare necessity. I thought about all the everyday things we take for granted, and tried to imagine a world with no art. No color or variety. Everything the same. Everybody the same.

I shuddered. Suddenly art seemed very important, and I began to understand why people put such a value on it. Look at all the trouble caused by it. I wanted to go see some museums, but knew we didn't have time. We had to get that plate back in time for the party! Mom had to get the information on it to the Russian couple going into business in Minnesota!

I don't know what Aunt Susan and Dr. Schaeffer talked about, but they finally returned with the package. Aunt Susan smiled at me, and said, "Did you see anything you liked?"

"I wish we had time to talk to Dr. Schaeffer. There are a lot of questions I would like to ask about the beautiful things here. It would be great for my newsletter!"

"Unfortunately, we have a schedule to keep," Aunt Susan reminded me, looking at Dr. Schaeffer. "Thank you for your assistance, Mark. I'm sure we will be seeing you soon. Rose and I will have to come back on a vacation, and see New York again."

As Aunt Susan talked, an official-looking car pulled up in front of the store. We said goodbye to Dr.Schaeffer, and went through the door. It was like leaving a different world. The atmosphere stayed with me and I thought about what it must be like in Russia.

As the door closed behind us, a man in a dark suit got out of the waiting car. I was suddenly back in New York, and very scared. He walked right up to us. I was sure he was an enemy agent, and got ready to run - but Aunt Susan just stood there! I looked at her wondering what to do as she smiled, and handed him the package.

"Don't worry, Susan. We'll get it there." The man smiled at us, and I realized Aunt Susan knew him. I had thought we were going to bring the plate back with us, but Aunt Susan explained she had called from Dr. Schaeffer's office, and arranged to have the plate sent back by courier. I guess it made sense. At least I wouldn't break this one! I could relax now! The plate was on its way, and everything would be fine!

The man did not introduce himself. Instead, he took the package from Aunt Susan, got back into the car and drove off.

All we had to do now was get to the airport, then find Kate, Doe, and Steven. The plan had worked! No one had seen us here. The bad guys were following the decoys, and still did not know why we were here! It was a little like Mission Impossible!

If I had known what was happening at the hotel I wouldn't have been so smug!

Chapter Eleven

But I didn't know what was happening. As Aunt Susan drove the old van, I looked out the window at the autumn day in New York without really seeing anything. I was excited to be going home. The mission was complete! It had been a fun adventure, yet I was sad about the opportunities I had missed to see more of life outside my humdrum world.

So much had happened in these last 24 hours! My little girl world would never be the same. I felt more grown up now. Already I longed for the familiar life I knew I was leaving behind. I was anxious to get home before it changed any more.

With my thoughts still rambling, I looked over at Aunt Susan. She was driving the old van confidently; apparently satisfied things had gone so well. The plate was on its way to the party, Steven was waiting at the airport, we were on our way home, and everything seemed to be falling into place. But why was her forehead wrinkled? It was as if things were going too smooth...

"What's wrong, Aunt Susan?" I asked, picking up on the worried look. "Aren't you happy with the way things went?"

Aunt Susan looked over at me and smiled, "Yes, Rose," she nodded. "Things went great. It was a lot of fun, too. Still, I can't shake this feeling it's not over yet. Maybe it's just I've been on too many of these "missions". Experience tells me when things go too well there's something we're not seeing. Life is seldom as simple as it seems."

"Well," I replied, "nobody is following us. All we have to do is get to the airport, and get on the plane! I can't think of anything we forgot. Mom will be happy to have the plate, the party will be a success, the Russian couple will have the information they will need to start their business, and I won't get grounded! Of course, now I know about Mom from that page you had Zip print for me...oh, Mi'Gosh!"

When Aunt Susan heard the alarm in my voice, she turned to me again. "What is it, Rose? What did you just remember?"

"The paper, Aunt Susan! The one I tried to get rid of on the plane! I could not think of what to do with it, so I shoved it in my back pocket! When we got to the hotel, I forgot about it. I wore my other jeans today. It's still in the pocket of my dirty jeans back at the hotel! What if someone finds it! Vladimir knows where we were staying..."

"Relax, Rose. The Agency uses that hotel a lot. Steven said it was secure. I'm sure Kate and Doe have been there already, and packed our bags. The note is probably in the trunk of Steven's cab on the way to the airport now. We'll find it when we get back home."

"I didn't want to screw things up, Aunt Susan. I wanted to be a good agent. The plane was getting ready to land, and I was afraid someone was watching us. It seemed like the right thing to do at the time. I hope you are right. It was me who started all of this anyway."

"Hey," Aunt Susan said. "Don't be so hard on yourself. Even the best agents make mistakes. That's life."

"I'll bet Dad doesn't make mistakes! Where is he anyway? I've known he works for the Government, and is not supposed to tell us where he is sometimes, and now I understand why. It's to keep us safe. It must be hard for him not to talk about his work, like other men can, to worry about putting his family in jeopardy. Still, I used to wonder if he had a secret life with another family..."

Aunt Susan looked over at me again, sadness in her eyes. I could see the thoughts behind her face. She was thinking of the price we paid for being who we were. There was more to this than just a career. What they did was important. Having a normal life was not always possible.

Aunt Susan heard the hurt in my voice. It was a childish resentment. I wanted my Dad around me all of the time. Sometimes it seemed like Mom and I competed for his attention. There was never enough time, and we cherished the moments we spent together as a family, and with each one. I repeated my question to Susan.

Aunt Susan answered as we pulled the van into the parking ramp at JFK.

"Your Dad is working on the same mission we are, Rose. He is heading up security for the international meeting-taking place in Gzhel, Russia. The United Sates and Russia are working on trade agreements for importing porcelain and other products from Russia to the United States. That is probably why Vladimir was following us. He deals in porcelain, and his hard-line backers want to be included in the negotiations. They were not invited, and have to get past your Dad to get in. Free trade in Russia is like a new baby, and must be protected."

"Wow! This is too intense! I had no idea breaking that plate was so big!

I'm actually working on the same project as Dad!"

"In a sense, yes. It is all connected. We need to get you and me home safe so your Dad does not have to worry about us. There is always a chance we could be used as a bargaining chip to make him let the hard-liners in."

As we walked into the airport I knew why Aunt Susan had that worried look.

We looked around for Steven, and sighed with relief when he met us - smiling.

"The suitcase is closed, and the bag is zipped," he told us. "Glad to see you two! Kate and Doe packed your bags, and they are loaded on the plane. I'll escort you to the gate, and see you off. I'm gonna' miss you two!"

Yep. Everything looked great. But like I said before, if I had known what went on at the hotel...

We found out later, while we were driving Kate's van, Kate and Doe had gone to our room. They were to pack our bags and get in the cab with Steven, while still pretending to be us. Vladimir, who had followed them just like Steven had planned, watched them the whole time. He waited outside in his car - just like at the Rockefeller Center.

But before they got there, the maid had come in to make the beds. She had picked up the jeans I had tossed on the chair, and noticed a crumpled piece of paper in the back pocket. She took it out and read it, then carefully smoothed it out, and slipped it into the pocket of her apron. Then she took out her cell phone, and called Vladimir.

It was a hotel The Agency used often. It was secure as far as they knew. But there was a lot of money at stake in porcelain - and money talks. The maid was listening.

Still, we weren't aware of all of this as we walked to the gate to board our plane.

When Steven's cell phone rang, and he stopped to answer it, we walked on ahead. I turned around to see if he was still behind us. He wasn't.

Aunt Susan realized it at the same time and just as our hearts started pumping louder, two men in suits walked up to us, and took our arms, escorting us in another direction.

They did not look American. I shot a look of panic at Aunt Susan, ready to run, but she shook her head. Her eyes told me to stay put, and go along with them. We walked across the airport to another gate. There was a plane leaving for Russia. And there was Vladimir, smiling as we approached!

I wondered what happened to Steven...

Chapter Twelve

I wondered about a lot of things just then. Steven, Kate, Doe, Mom, Dad, Aunt Susan, school, Sam, the newsletter, Richard - and of course, myself.

Vladimir was still smiling as we approached. He moved toward us, and said, "Susan! And this must be little Rosie..."

That did it! Now I was mad! I hated being called "Rosie"! I could be tough too! Rose was a name you had to defend sometimes. My mother was ashamed to say how many times I had been sent home for fighting over it. But I think Dad was proud of me. Old Vlad was a little too big for me to take on; but if I started a fight, maybe Security would come and rescue us.

Vlad must have known what I was thinking because he looked at Aunt Susan and said, "One outburst, and her father is a dead man."

Aunt Susan looked at me and said, "Now, Rose, I think we should listen to what "Uncle" Vladimir has to say."

Uncle? Was this surprise? Another skeleton in the family closet? I had enough surprises already this trip! Sheesh! But I caught on. This was not a good time for any ramblin'...

I sighed, and everyone relaxed.

Like "pickles in the middle" we followed "Uncle Vladimir" to the gate while his "assistants" followed us. Of course, he had boarding passes, and we were escorted onto the plane.

Kidnapped! Boy, somebody was going to pay for this one! It looked like we were going to Russia.

I was curious, but not that curious! I had already taken one unscheduled trip. I was not anxious to take another!

"Aeroflot. Non-stop, fifteen hours." Vladimir said, as one of his "assistants" took Susan's purse; I hadn't brought one, but the other assistant checked the pockets on my New York jacket.

There were no guns allowed in the gate area, but they knew an agent like Aunt Susan might have other weapons. They found her cell phone (our link to Zip), and her mace, checked her cosmetics, and finally returned the purse to her with a warning look.

The luggage we thought was bound for Minnesota was transferred to this plane we were told. Old Vlad had connections; or rather he had paid some baggage handler.

Fat lot of good our luggage would do anyway! We had hardly brought anything at all - and some of it was dirty.

"You will be provided with clothes when we reach Moscow," Vlad said.

He had dropped his phony salesman accent, and now sounded cold and hard. My anger was turning to fear as I realized there was no turning back.

"What happened to Steven?" I demanded, trying to hold on to it.

"Steven is sleeping peacefully in the airport restroom. Chloroform might be outdated, but it still works. We have no wish to kill anyone or cause an international incident. When we are seated, I will answer all of your questions."

I looked around the plane as we walked on. There weren't a lot of people. Mostly businessmen, I guessed from the way they were dressed. They all seemed to have open briefcases, and were quietly shuffling papers. There were also some average citizens returning home from visiting relatives in the U.S., - all adults - and no kids except me. Sheesh!

We were escorted to three seats on the right in coach. No first class this trip! I groaned when I realized Aunt Susan would have the window seat, and I would be stuck next to fatso himself.

"What about my Dad?" I asked defiantly. By now I knew he was out of the country again.

"Your Dad is being watched. One word from me, and our assassin will strike. At this moment a message is on it's way informing him of the situation, and his need to co-operate if he ever wants to see his family again. He is being told you and your Aunt will be killed if he contacts anyone. If he meets our demands you will live."

"And what are those demands?" Aunt Susan asked as she made her way to her "assigned" seat.

"It is very simple," Vlad answered. "All we want is to attend the trade meeting being held in Gzhel on Monday." He looked at me, and continued. "Your Dad is in charge of the security for the trade talks concerning porcelain. My employers wish to attend that meeting, and be a part of the negotiations. There are several points of the agreement that are important to them. Your father has barred our attendance on "security" grounds. The real reason we are barred is the U.S. favors its "free market" program. We are a part of the economy also. Porcelain has long been a leading export. Russian art is in demand, and the profits fund a large part of our political operations."

Wow! And I thought I could ramble!

As Aunt Susan sat down, she tugged at her purse, pressing it against her chest

"Darn! The zipper is stuck!"

Somehow I knew she had activated her hidden COM link to Zip. It wasn't in her purse, though. It was voice-activated and hidden in her bra. They would never know it was there! I felt better now, knowing Zip was tracking us.

"It's hot in here!" Aunt Susan said as she unbuttoned her jacket. Another signal!

As the plane took off, Vladimir, a.k.a., John Henry in the United States, got quiet. I thought about the plate that had started all of this, and realized how important the information on it was. It named the hard-line sympathizers for our Russian friends to avoid doing business with. People in our own country, too. Double agents perhaps, who for some reason were sympathetic to the old hard-line cause. Enemies within!

We had more questions, but settled on one as the runway dropped away, and we headed east into the darkening sky.

"What happens if you don't get your way?"

Chapter Thirteen

Vladimir was silent, not wanting to answer the question. Aunt Susan spoke up again, "You know The Agency won't let you get away with this. They know where we are. Rose's mother will miss us when we don't return on time. They'll be there when we land. Fifteen hours is a long time. At the very least, they will cancel the meeting you are trying to attend."

"Why of course, dear Susan! If we cannot attend, and get our way, the meeting will be canceled, and the trade agreement will remain the same! We can operate as we have been. As to getting away with this, we have people in high places...you see I am not worried. You should be worried!"

Aunt Susan countered, "I suppose you are just going to let us walk away when we land?"

"Ah, my dear Susan, I have seen enough American movies to know better than reveal all the details of my plan. You may as well relax. Trust your Agency and sleep. You may need your rest!"

The "Fasten Seat Belts" sign went dark. Vladimir stood up and walked to the front of the plane. I wondered who was riding in first class.

"Aunt Susan! He's gone! Now we can talk!"

"Shh! That's what he wants us to do. My zipper is still stuck. The Agency can hear us. We'll just have to trust them. We'll try not to sleep at the same time."

"But what can we do?" I asked. My heart was pounding. I did not feel so tough anymore. We were thousands of feet in the air, headed for Russia with three ruthless men watching us. If we tried anything, my father would be killed! Unless they were bluffing. I didn't want to take that chance!

Suddenly I felt like a little kid again. I needed to fight that feeling, and be more like Aunt Susan. Confident! My Dad was depending on me!

I looked past Aunt Susan out the window, and said, "Okay, I'll take the first shift! Wake me up when you get tired."

Looking across the aisle, I saw pillows tucked up on the shelf above the seats. I decided to risk getting one. I unbuckled my seat belt and stood up. Just then the curtain opened, and Vladimir appeared.

"What are you doing?" He asked. He gave me a stern look as he approached.

I wanted to kick him in the shins, but instead pointed to the pillows. He smiled with relief, and took one down. He handed it to me, and said, "Ah, now that's a smart girl."

I took the pillow, and looked at Aunt Susan. Her tense look broke into a smile as I winked at her, confidently.

While I was fluffing the pillow, I looked around at the other passengers. No one was paying any attention to us. Some were reading, some were writing, and some of them were sleeping. Vladimir's' goons were busy playing a card game on the seat tray in front of them. They turned when Vlad had asked me what I was doing, but seeing he had things under control, went back to their game.

I sighed and zipped my new jacket. I missed my old one, though this one was warmer. I was lonesome for home. We would be there about now if not for "Vlad". I missed Samson the Great, Mom, Dad, and Richard.

Holding back tears, I settled into the seat, not wanting to look at anybody. I buried my head in the pillow facing Aunt Susan, and closed my eyes before she could see me. I did not care how long I slept.

Aunt Susan was holding back her tears as she watched me. She did not think I noticed. I was glad that being an Agent did not mean losing your heart. She turned her head to the window, and looked out at the darkness.

Back at home things were really popping! Zip had alerted The Agency to our location and situation. Aunt Susan's COM link was open and broadcasting. Zip's remote locations kept track of us as we passed from one zone into another, our signal being picked up by The Agency's satellites.

It was Friday night and Mom and Richard were just about to leave for the airport to pick us up. Sam was lying on the kitchen floor with his head on his front paws, whining softly.

Mom's pager beeped, showing her a special number. The number was a secure connection to The Agency. Richard's pager beeped also, but he waited to respond, guessing that Mom's call was for the same reason.

Mom grabbed her cell phone and dialed the number, sitting down and looking at Richard as she heard the news. She listened carefully to the voice on the other end, nodding as she got instructions. Richard watched her, worried. He fidgeted with his hands, wanting to take action.

Finally, Mom hung up the phone, and filled him in. Sam raised his head from his paws, and cocked it to one side, his tail pounding the floor.

Elsewhere, Steven's pager also beeped. He had found himself in the restroom at JFK, sitting in a stall with his pants still up. When he woke up, he washed his face with cold water, and stumbled out to look for us. By then we were already gone, and he tried to remember what had happened. He went to the gate, and was told the Minneapolis flight had left an hour before. He called airport security to check if we were on that plane. No, he was told; we were not.

He was sitting in his cab, pondering his next move when the beeper went off.

Kate and Doe had left the airport after changing their wigs and jackets. They had picked up the van and driven back to Manhattan, stopping to eat along the way. Doe had packed my old jacket into the luggage. She still did not know why I was so attached to it.

When Kate's beeper went off, Doe knew something had gone wrong.

In Gzhel, my Dad was sitting in his room at the Inn. He had planned on being home Thursday night, but a call from The Agency had sent him to Gzhel two days early. He hoped I wasn't mad at him for not being home. He missed his family. Even Samson.

As he worked on his laptop, Zip appeared. He sat frozen, as The Agency filled him in on the situation. As he was listening, an envelope slid silently under the door. He retrieved it, and returned to his chair - ripping it open on the way. He read the note inside, and listened to Zip simultaneously.

The Crisis Team at The Agency had pieced together the situation and developed a plan. Things happened fast at The Agency. The race was on to salvage the two events; the trade talks and the party, and to save Susan and me. There was no way for us to know this, as Aunt Susan's COM link was one way. Fortunately, it transmitted voices around her and Vladimir's conversation with us was digitized and analyzed by several computers. All kinds of data were being collected and all aspects of the situation were being studied.

Dad was pacing nervously. He was used to pressure, but so far his family had not been directly in danger. He thought about his career, guilt building up for being married in such a dangerous occupation. But many men worked in professions that placed them in harm's way, risking their lives to help others.

His training kept him from breaking down, and with an effort he became calm again. Talking to Zip on his laptop, he relayed a message to Mom and then began to implement the plan the Crisis Team had put together. Old John Henry was going to get a surprise when that plane landed in Moscow!

Chapter Fourteen

I stood up slowly and tried to stretch. I had been asleep for several hours. Now it seemed like I was the only one awake on the plane. I wondered how the pilots stayed awake. Did they sleep in shifts? In their seats like us? Were we on autopilot now? I realized my thoughts were starting to ramble again. I was just curious, but I remembered what they said about curiosity killing the cat, and decided to concentrate on the current mission. It was becoming urgent.

It was hard to see in the dim light. Aunt Susan, Vlad, and his goons were asleep, as were the people in front and back of us. Their seats were reclined, making it hard to move without waking "Uncle Vlad".

I was glad I was a kid. I was short and small enough to climb over our "Sleeping Beauty". But, I had to face him to do it. Facing my seat, I leaned forward, and placed my hands on the headrest. Finding my balance, I moved my right hand to the aisle seat. I did it slow and quiet so it would not disturb Vladimir.

So far, so good! I looked at my feet; if I was careful I could step over his outstretched legs. His feet were spread apart and I picked up my right foot, setting it down between his size twelve shoes.

Well, they looked like size twelve. Now I had to move my right hand to the other side of his head, then my left one to his seat so that now I was leaning right over him.

Yuck! How did I get myself in this mess? I hurried over him, not caring if he woke up or not. What could he do to us anyway? We were on a plane full of people. One scream from a young girl would bring everybody running. Maybe that's what I needed to do! We could end this right now...

Except for Dad. How could I take the risk that they might really kill him? I thought about passing a note to somebody as I made my way to the rest room. I remembered trying to pass a note in class one day. It was a simple note about the boy down the block from me, but both me and the girl I was passing it to get in trouble. Both of us had to stay after school because we were not doing what we were supposed to be doing.

They even told my parents about it.

Now I thought of Aunt Susan. I decided to follow her lead, and stay cool.

I found the stewardess in the back of the plane. Now that I wasn't under pressure, I could think about my stomach.

She was a tall, dark-haired lady, about twenty-five, I would guess. I couldn't recognize her accent; but she spoke in English. "How can I help you?"

"I'm really hungry. Will you be serving anything soon?" I asked.

"Not until breakfast, but we do have some sandwiches. Would you like me to bring you one?"

"Yes, whatever you have. I don't want to wake up my friends, though. Can I have it in one of the empty seats?"

There were some empty seats at the rear of the plane. We were not assigned to them, she told me, but she would make an exception for me, and let me eat in one anyway. I thanked her, and asked when we would be landing.

"In about eight hours. We will be refueled soon, but won't be getting off the plane. We should reach Moscow about 9 a.m. this morning. We will start serving breakfast about six."

I thanked her, and sat down to wait. She brought me a ham sandwich, a Coke, and a bag of chips. While I ate, I wondered what The Agency was doing about all of this.

I knew they must have a plan. I tried to imagine a rescue. Would they come and get us at the refueling stop, or wait until we landed in Moscow? What was Vlad's plan?

And who was sitting in First Class? I decided to see for myself as I finished the sandwich.

My stomach growled in thanks. We had not eaten since the evening meal on the plane. Before that we had just a sandwich at The Rockefeller Center. It seemed so long ago. I used to be bored on the weekends. I had no idea how much a person could do in such a short amount of time. I was a kid; what did time mean to me anyway? I had all the time in the world, and knew I was going to live forever! Look at Peter Pan! Part of me wondered if there was such a place as Never-

Never Land. My grandfather always said every story has some basis in fact...

I was suddenly lonesome for him. I wished I were a little girl again, sitting in his lap, listening to his stories and adventures. I wanted to let him know how much they meant to me. That he had stretched my world, and made it bigger. That he had put this curiosity in me. That thanks to him, I would see the world - and not have just an ordinary life.

But what was wrong with an ordinary life? I was glad to be alive. I could not imagine not being here. Whatever kind of life it was.

The sandwich and the memories brought my spirit back, and I decided to see what I could do to help. It was nice to have people that cared about you, and I knew my parents would do anything to bring us home safe. I was not afraid of Vladimir and his goons anymore! If my whole family was in The Agency, then I was too! I was going to act like it!

I began to understand where Aunt Susan got her confidence.

I got up from my seat and approached the stewardess again, carrying my empty tray, and turning on the little girl charm that worked so well on my Dad and Mom...

"Thank you for the sandwich. You know, I've never been on a plane this big. Do you think I could meet the Captain? I would love to see the cockpit."

The innocent look in my eyes, and the smile I gave her must have worked. She smiled back at me and picked up a phone. Before long we were walking to the front of the plane, right past Vladimir and his "assistants". Now I would see who was in First Class!

What a surprise to see Dr. Schaeffer from the A La Vie Russie shop!

He was asleep. I did not want to wake him up. But my mind was rambling with questions. Was he working with Vladimir - a.k.a. John Henry? Did he know we were on the plane? Why was he here?

Of course it would not be unusual for him to be going to Russia. That was his business. Vladimir posed as a salesman for porcelain in the U.S. It would not be out of the ordinary for them to talk. But did he have political or business ties to the hard liners? I thought about my grandfather who helped the Allies in WWII. He dealt with both sides - sort of a double agent on the good side. I thought about the Swiss people too, remaining neutral.

I was finding out that nothing was what it seemed sometimes, and that sometimes things were exactly what they seemed. I decided to think of Dr. Schaeffer as just what he was, an honest businessman. Aunt Susan knew and liked him, and I would follow her lead.

But what was going on in Russia? I knew about the Trade Meeting on Monday. Perhaps he was here to attend it. He must be an important part of the distribution process. A La Vie Russie was a 150-year-old business. It had survived every change over those years. It would not be unusual for them to be here for the talks. I would have to find out in the morning.

But here we were at the door, and I went in to meet the Captain. Now I was a reporter again. This would be great for a future newsletter!

The stewardess knocked softly on the door, and opened it slowly. I could see the captain and co-pilot – with all the controls and gauges. Up here I was more aware of the high-pitched sound of the plane cutting through the wind. The windows in front showed only the blackness of the sky.

The captain turned his head as we approached. "Yes, Irina? Is this our American guest?"

"Yes, captain, this is Rose. Rose, this is Captain Yuri Ivanovich and our co-pilot, Ivan."

"Hi! It's nice to meet you! Wow, I've never seen the cockpit of a plane before!"

Captain Yuri smiled. " We are proud of our plane. Aeroflot is the fourth largest airline in the world today. We fly to 140 destinations in 94 countries!" The captain beamed at me, obviously pleased with his attempt to impress me.

"Wow!" I said, looking impressed. I was. I turned on the little girl charm, and blinked my eyes. "I write a newsletter for my school back in Minnesota. Do you have some information I could take back with me?"

Captain Yuri sat up a little straighter. "I'm sorry, we do not. If I had the time I would answer all of your questions for you. But, unfortunately I must return to my duties. Regulations don't permit you to be up here. May I suggest you return to your seat, and take a copy of our in-flight magazine? You really should get some sleep, as we will be landing in about seven hours, and you don't want to be tired when we land in Russia. It is a new country again, and there is much to see."

The co-pilot turned and smiled at me also. They must get bored on these long flights. I thought about telling them about what was going on with "Uncle Vladimir", and asking them to use their radio to call for help.

Just then, two big hands landed on my shoulders. Oh, no! It was old Vlad himself!

"There you are Rose! I wondered where you had got off to! So sorry if my niece has disturbed you, gentlemen. She is restless sometimes."

"Not at all. She is a very pleasant girl, and we enjoyed meeting her. We will say good night, Rose. Good luck with your newsletter!"

I wished he hadn't said that! "Uncle Vladimir" turned me around with his big paws and we left the cockpit.

"Get your hands off me!" I said as the door closed, leaving Irina, the stewardess with the crew.

"What have you told them?" Vlad demanded.

"Nothing. Do you think I would risk my father's life?" I retorted.

"What is this newsletter they refer to?" He asked, worried.

"Just a dumb girl's school newsletter. I am the Editor this year. I wanted to write about the plane instead of the usual girls stuff." The anger was still in my voice. Now I took on a pouting sound; that wasn't all faked. We talked in whispers so we would not wake anyone.

"You kidnap us and take us to Russia! I miss my dog, I miss my mother and I miss my bed! Who do you think you are anyway?" Tears were now streaming down my face.

Vlad softened a little, and looked more like his John Henry identity. "Don't cry. I am sorry we had to take such drastic measures. I too have missed my home. Also, will I miss the United States. I will never be allowed to return again. I have enjoyed seeing your country, though I do not agree with your democracy. If all goes well, you will return to your home with your Aunt Susan. We know your whole family works for The Agency. It is a chess game, you see. No one will ever know what really happened here. Think of this as an unexpected trip to a far away country. Mind your manners and sleep. All will be well."

I wished I could trust his smile. I wiped my tears, and walked back to my "assigned" seat.

Vladimir seemed satisfied with my explanation of the newsletter as the reason to see the Captain. Neither of us noticed how while we were talking, Dr. Schaeffer had opened an eye, and heard our conversation. He appeared to be sleeping as we passed him.

Aunt Susan stirred a bit, but continued sleeping as I sat down. I wished she were awake. I was really homesick now.

I looked for the magazine the captain had mentioned, and stifled a yawn as Vladimir woke his two assistants and chided them for not watching me. Though I was tired, I wanted to stay awake and get Vlad to talk some more in range of Aunt Susan's hidden link to Zip.

The magazine slipped from my hands as sleep crept up on me.

Chapter Fifiteen

When I woke up again we were in daylight. Aunt Susan and Vlad were talking. I kept my eyes shut, and pretended I was still sleeping. I did not want Vladimir to stop talking. Aunt Susan was trying to get him to reveal as much of the plan as possible without letting him get suspicious. She had to keep her questions natural or he might suspect the COM link.

"Why don't you let Rose go when we reach Moscow? I'll stay and be your hostage," Aunt Susan volunteered.

"That is very noble of you, my dear, but we both know Rose carries more weight with her father. Our whole purpose is to give him a reason to allow our presence at the trade meeting," Vlad replied.

"Yes, but you must know the meeting will be called off because of what you have done. And The Agency will be waiting when we land." Aunt Susan was defiant.

"You are making me repeat myself, Susan. If the meeting is called off, we still achieve a goal. If the trade agreement cannot be changed, then we will continue to operate as we have been. If it is re-scheduled, then we still have time - and leverage - to attend or at least have, our proposals presented, Vladimir was cocky, as if he had just moved a chess piece. "Checkmate."

"The Agency will file charges of kidnapping against you and your associates. Both of our governments will be upset about the damage to the free enterprise movement. You will be arrested." Aunt Susan would not concede the game yet.

"I think not," Vladimir replied, holding his position. "A great many interests in both of our countries want to avoid scandal. As long as you and Rose are returned safe, the charges will be dropped - and the incident will be swept under the rug. The "New Russia" is busy promoting tourism, and good will in America. Many companies in the U.S. have millions of dollars invested here. Both of our governments have people in high places who have wagered their careers on the new relationship between Russia and the United States. I will not be returning to your country at any rate. When we land in Moscow, your Agency will not be the only one watching." Vlad smiled, convinced of his checkmate.

I hoped that Zip had gotten all of this, and thought now was a good time to "wake up".

"What time is it?" I said, groggily.

"Almost breakfast," Aunt Susan replied. "Did you sleep okay?

"Well, it's kind of hard to sleep in these conditions, but yeah, it was okay. I wanted to tell Aunt Susan all about last night, and Dr. Schaeffer. I wished we could talk alone. Zip would be interested, too.

"Well, our Rambling Rose is awake!" Vlad said, referring to my "midnight romp". I will leave you two to your breakfast. We will be landing in a couple of hours. After we are safely off of the plane without interference, you will be provided with fresh clothes and accommodations."

"Are we staying in Moscow?" I asked.

"What does it matter?" Vlad answered." You will not be sightseeing anyway."

"If we cooperate, couldn't we be treated as guests instead of hostages? Since I will be missing school this week; at least I could be learning something. This would be like a field trip. I could write about it..."

Vlad's anger was rising. "I am not a babysitter - and this is not a field trip! You will not write about any of this! This is serious international business. When we get to Gzhel you can write about porcelain!" When he realized what he had just said, he stopped. Composing himself, he continued. "Forgive me, ladies. Of course you are guests here. Unfortunately, our schedule does not allow us to give you a guided tour. If all goes well, you will return to your homes by the end of the week."

He was smiling again. I wished I could trust his smile.

Aunt Susan was smiling too. Zip knew where we were going, and we both knew The Agency would have a plan to rescue us. I was fairly sure we would not be harmed, but could not help but wonder what would happen when we landed.

And what was Dad doing? Surely his bosses were aware of the situation. Would they try to save the meeting? What were Mom and Richard doing now? Would the party still go on? Could the whole operation be saved? This was Saturday morning in Minnesota, or was it afternoon? I would have to get Aunt Susan to explain the time zone to me.

My mind was rambling again. What was this week going to be like? What would the kids in school think if they knew where I was right now?

As I walked to the restroom to wash up, there was another unanswered question...

What were we having for breakfast?

Chapter Sixteen

It's amazing how hungry you can get when you are traveling. Even the frozen scrambled eggs looked good. I remember Dad telling me when he was in the Navy they had to eat four times a day on the ship. He said just traveling took more energy than we realized. Aunt Susan and I had not eaten much over the last forty-eight hours.

Wow! So much had happened in these last two days!

While I was eating, I thought about Vlad's two "assistants". So far they had not been much help to him. He was doing all of the "babysitting". Neither of them had said a word to Aunt Susan and I. This was very curious!

I wondered if they would talk to me. I was sure they spoke English, as they traveled with Vlad in the U.S. Or did they? Maybe they joined him in New York. Maybe they hadn't come for Aunt Susan and me. Of course not! Unless they were already in New York, they would not have had time to get there from Russia. Maybe they had come for Vlad! How many times had he said he would not be returning to the United States?

I remembered something else that Dad always said: "The answer is always in the question." I never quite understood it before, but now it was making sense. Then there were Grandfather's stories. I was learning there was some truth in every story! There really were porcelain mines in Russia! They did not chisel plates out of them - but they did dig the clay from them they used to make them. Also, like a gold mine, there was a lot of money in it!

Maybe we just needed to ask the right questions!

Aunt Susan interrupted my ramblin' thoughts. "You're awfully quiet, Rose. Is everything okay?

What a question! Just about everything was not okay. Sheesh! I guess Aunt Susan was used to me ramblin' on when we talked. She did not realize when I was not talking a mile a minute, my brain was.

Vlad finished his breakfast, and excused himself. Finally, we could talk. The "assistants" were two rows up across the aisle. I hoped Aunt Susan's link with Zip was still open.

"Aunt Susan, I've been thinking. I don't think Vlad is playing chess, I think he is playing poker! Or better yet, Russian roulette!"

I filled Aunt Susan in on last night's events, Dr. Schaeffer, and my suspicions about Vladimir's "assistants". Who had kidnapped whom?

"Rose, that's great thinking! But I wonder if it makes our situation any better. Maybe Vladimir's organization was not happy with him and this kidnapping is a desperate measure on his part. That would explain why the other two have seemed reluctant and have not talked to us! I hope the Agency is checking this out right now as we speak." Aunt Susan sounded more optimistic than she had since we left our "five dollar" tour of New York.

Before I could start ramblin' again, Vlad appeared and sat down next to us.

"We will be landing soon. You will do exactly as I say, or Rose's father will die."

He said it so matter-of-factly chills ran down my spine. He sounded like a man with nothing to lose. It seemed that the closer we got to Russia, the colder he got.

The chills in my spine turned to anger as he threatened my Dad again. I was very protective of my family. I began to realize how Mom and Dad felt about me all of those times when I wanted to do things that might not be good for me. And how they had felt after I had done some of the things they found out about later.

I felt butterflies in my stomach now. A lot of them. My thoughts were mixed up with excitement at going to a foreign country, especially Russia, and anxiety about what would happen next. Not to mention what was happening back home, and at The Agency.

What was Dad going through right now? And Mom. And Richard. And Steven?

Vlad continued to talk while I wondered about all of that, and I missed most of what he said. Oh, great! I did not want him to know I hadn't paid attention. I would just have to wing it. Fortunately, he did not know about Aunt Susan's link with Zip.

I looked at Aunt Susan. She was listening intently and nodding. I could almost see her mentally channeling the information to her COM link. I could still see her confidence. She was a pro! Old Vladimir did not know who he was dealing with! I knew Aunt Susan and I made a great team, and somehow we would come through this all right.

Vladimir's "assistants" turned and looked at us. I wondered if he had briefed them the same way. Somehow the three of them did not seem like a team. Now that I thought of them differently, I could see it.

As the plane was approaching Moscow, the captain's voice cut through our thoughts, and I braced myself for the coming events. If I had known the plans in motion back home and at The Agency I probably would not have been so nervous.

But we had no way of knowing. The link with Zip was one way. We could only hope Dad was okay, and would be at the Moscow airport to pick us up. Surely The Agency would be there to arrest Vladimir and his "assistants". We'd show him what happens when you kidnap Americans!

As we approached Moscow, my feelings alternated between hope and anger. Aunt Susan was calm on the outside, but inside she must be having the same thoughts. I decided to look confident, and not give Vlad the satisfaction of knowing we were afraid.

At last we were in the final approach and Aunt Susan leaned back so I could look out of the window at Moscow from up here. Unfortunately, the sky was overcast, and a haze surrounded the city. Being daylight, there were no lights to see. I settled back in my seat, and tried to imagine the Russian city. Anything to keep my mind off the coming events.

I wanted to be home. I missed my computer, and the secure little world I had known.

Back at home, the plate had been delivered. Mom and Richard had been instructed to carry on with Saturday night's party. There was nothing they could do about our situation. The Agency had informed them of our whereabouts, and their plan for rescuing us. We had no way of knowing that as we followed Vlad off of the plane, followed by "Huey and Louie". We looked around anxiously as we entered the waiting area, and were surprised to see...

No one! A few people meeting the businessmen and relatives as they disembarked, but no Dad. No contingent of agents. No one to rescue us. I was heartbroken. My mask of confidence was gone. My heart was beating so loud I was sure everyone could hear it.

Vlad called a halt, and turned to face us. He was smiling. "It seems your Dad was wise, and would not risk your lives! Wipe your tears, Little Rose. He must care about you very much!"

Then he turned to his assistants, and confidently gave them instructions. There went my other theory! For the first time he called them by their names.

"Peter, take Susan to the car. You know where to go from there. Victor, bring the other car for Rose and I."

We were shocked. Was he splitting us up? Or was he taking precautions? Would The Agency try to rescue us outside of the airport?

"Where are you taking us?" Aunt Susan demanded. "Why are we going in separate cars? What about the shopping you promised us?"

Panic held my mouth shut. For once I didn't feel like talking. What would I do without Aunt Susan? We were in a strange country. Maybe I should shout for help! Where was Dr. Schaeffer? Of course, he was in first class, and had gotten off before us. I could not see him anywhere. If I could get away, call Dad...

Vladimir must have seen my darting looks. "Remember your Dad, Rose. Any outburst could be fatal to him. The best thing you can do for all of you now is to come along quietly. I will try to make this as comfortable as possible for you both."

So I watched Aunt Susan walk away, trying to hold her shoulders straight.

I didn't see much of the Moscow airport, nor did I care. We climbed into a big, black limousine, and drove away in the opposite direction from the one Aunt Susan had gotten into.

I already did not like Russia.

Chapter Seventeen

The limousine had slippery black leather seats. It was as cold and dark as the gloomy Moscow sky. Just like the way I felt.

But my shock was turning to anger now. Why wasn't Dad there to meet us, and take us home? Did Aunt Susan's COM link not work? What was that comment about agents never being alone? I never felt so alone in my life! How could Aunt Susan walk away like that - without saying goodbye? Here I was, kidnapped, halfway around the world, twelve years old...

I could not believe this was happening. I thought I had grown up a little in New York - but that was kid's stuff! I loosed my anger on Vlad, who was sitting next to me, and saying nothing.

"Where are you taking me?" I demanded, not worried about making a scene now.

I knew if I was alive, then Dad was, too. "And where have you taken Aunt Susan!" My tears were hot, and I felt them burning tracks in my cheeks. I was embarrassed about crying in front of strangers.

"She is safe, and you will be too if you quiet down! I know you must feel very alone. For the next two days all will depend on your father. If he is successful, and we are represented at the trade meeting on Monday, you will be re-united with him unharmed. As to where we are going, well, you will find out soon enough."

"My father would never co-operate with you!" I said as I wiped my tears on the sleeve of the New York jacket. At least the jacket was a piece of America. Of freedom. I thought Russia was a free country now, too. It sure did not feel like it to me.

Vlad replied, "Your father would never abandon you, either. Am I not right? Then why was he not at the airport? You should think about that!"

I hated him for saying that. *John E. Carson*

As he turned, and stared out the window at his homeland, I tried not to think about mine. Vlad had a point. I should think. The answer was always in the question. If Dad was not there, then there were two possibilities. One: Aunt Susan's COM link with Zip was not working on the plane, or, two: The Agency had a plan Dad felt better about. Maybe they did not want to risk my safety, and Aunt Susan's for that matter, by creating a scene or shooting. On the plane, Vlad had slipped and mentioned Gzhel. If the meeting were being held there, that would seem a logical place to take us. But why split us up?

Again, the answer must be in the question. By splitting us up, Vlad would be sure of having at least one "safe" hostage. If The Agency tried to rescue us in Gzhel - and it seemed likely since it would be full of agents - Aunt Susan would be held somewhere else. Maybe she had not said anything, so they would still think we were in the same place! That way, if Vlad tried to spoil a rescue plan by telling The Agency Aunt Susan was somewhere else, they would not believe him. Maybe Aunt Susan hadn't abandoned me!

My ramblin' thoughts were drying my tears. I was growing up now. It was up to me to be strong. I could not run to my safe bed, or my favorite jacket, or hug Sam. My parents were not in the other room. I suddenly realized it was up to me to get back home - and nothing would be the same when I did.

Instead of crying like a baby, I had to think my way out of this. Grandpa, sometimes I wished you had not told me so many stories!

I sat quietly in the big limo, looking out the window as the country-side changed. The fog was clearing now, and the world was looking brighter. I glanced at the rearview mirror from time to time at Vlad's assistant. His eyes were blank, and told me nothing. He did not talk the whole way. After about an hour we saw the village of Gzhel.

It looked like a storybook. The houses were all like the gingerbread house in Hansel and Gretel. The trees were beautiful and reminded me of Minnesota. I felt better already! I remembered the shopping, and thought about buying clean clothes.

"Vlad, what about the clothes and shopping you promised? I need a shower and some food - I'm hungry!" I tried to sound sweeter as I said it, hoping it would speed up the results.

Vlad did not reply right away, but continued looking out the window. The village was full of official-looking cars, limousines, and U.N. guards. He seemed to be counting them.

"We have not arrived at our destination. When we do, you will be provided with all of those things."

"What is our destination?" I asked. I was not surprised he would not stay in Gzhel, with The Agency all over the place. Somehow I felt Dad was near.

He was nearer than I thought. Overseeing the security for the trade meeting, he was naturally in Gzhel. The limousines and security cars were everywhere! What I did not know was they were there for Vlad's benefit. Upon learning of our kidnapping, The Agency contacted Dad, Mom, Richard, Steven, Kate, and Doe. The "Crisis Team" had worked out the scenario based on the information relayed through Aunt Susan's COM link.

Using Zip's security, a decoy meeting had been set up. The Agency felt confident the safest situation for Aunt Susan and I was to act like it knew nothing of the kidnapping. Dad agreed, and set up a trap for Vlad. The meeting was delayed a day, and an invitation would be sent by Dad to Vladimir to attend Monday's meeting, with the stipulation Aunt Susan and I be brought to Gzhel, and be placed in safe hands prior to the meeting.

Back at home, Mom and Richard were to carry on with the party. The plate had arrived, and they were informed of the plan to rescue us. That phase of the original operation had gone well, with excuses given for Dad and I not being there.

The Brookhaven School for girls was contacted by The Agency, and told I would be returning next week. The school's reputation for discretion was called upon. Meaning they couldn't compromise my family's security.

Of course, I knew nothing of all of this; there was no way to contact Susan or me without a handheld unit or cell phone.

So I was very surprised when the limo's cell phone beeped, and Vlad picked it up and listened, then told Victor to turn the car around. Were we going back to Gzhel?

Vlad was smiling as he picked up the phone again and spoke in Russian. I could not understand a word of it! Finally, he turned around to look at me.

"Well, Rose, your father is a smart man after all! Our demands have been met! We will be attending the trade meeting on Monday! You will be our guest until then. If you cooperate, you will be re-united with your father after the meeting. Your Aunt Susan also will be returned unharmed. However, should anything go wrong, you will never see home again!"

I wanted to jump for joy! Dad! Home! Everything back to normal! Tears were streaming down my face, and I turned away to look out the window and keep this moment private.

I watched the gingerbread houses of Gzhel go by as we drove right back in and out of the village.

"Where are we going now?" I demanded, wanting to get out of this car.

"Well, we can't very well hand you over today, and risk losing our invitation, can we? We will return to Moscow, and wait for the meeting. Had the call not come in you would have been held prisoner in a nearby village. As it is, we can now return to a proper hotel; provided you will be good."

There was nothing I would do to mess this up! All I could think about was going home. I shuddered to think of what could have happened! Now I hoped nothing would go wrong somewhere else along the line...

Chapter Eighteen

I was tired. I tried to stay awake, but the long ride in the quiet car, and the emotional strain of the last two days was too much to fight. I don't know who carried me, but I woke up in a strange bed still wearing my clothes, and the New York jacket. I thought it all might have been a bad dream until my eyes adjusted to the darkness, and I realized I was in a hotel room.

I looked around for Aunt Susan, but she was not there. Lying quietly, I held back the panic that was building inside me. Now I felt more alone than I had in the limo. Could I trust Vlad? How could you trust an enemy spy and kidnapper? Still, the fact I was alive and unharmed told me something.

This spy business was no fun anymore! Without Aunt Susan to give me confidence it was very scary. I wanted to be good ol' Ramblin' Rose again. I found out I liked myself. It was fun being me!

I remembered sitting on Grandpa's lap, and laughing at his stories. "Oh, Grandpa!" I would say as he told me some wild tale I just had to repeat to my parents, and Richard the next day. At night, I would dream the stories he had told, and I was filled with curiosity about the world.

The memories made me feel better. I wasn't as scared anymore. I felt that Grandpa was watching over me. He was surely an angel by now!

"Okay, Rose. Get a hold on it now," he would say. I could almost hear him. "Wake up, Rose! Find out what's goin' on!"

"Okay, Grandpa…" I replied, more asleep than awake. "I'll get up now…"

But for some reason I could not wake up, and fell back into sleep as the muffled voices in the next room behind the double doors reached my ears.

"Are you sure we didn't give her too much?"

Too much what? I thought, as I joined Grandpa in another wild adventure which lasted until morning.

Sunday morning! I woke up facing the digital alarm clock next to the hotel bed. I was too groggy to figure out what time it might be back home. I had no idea how long I had slept - or what had happened after we left Gzhel. I vaguely remembered waking up last night, and hearing voices through the doors of the suite. I suspected Vlad had given me something to keep me quiet, though I didn't know what. He would not have had to do that. I would not have done anything to screw things up!

My anger was starting to rise, and I sat up. I needed a shower and a change of clothes. I looked around and was surprised to see my suitcase on the chair, and my other clothes cleaned and folded with a note saying "Compliments of Hotel Services".

I knew we were not going shopping! I didn't care about shopping anyway. All I wanted was to be home, and here was a piece of home. I was happy to see my old jacket too. My anger was softening a bit, and I looked around for the bathroom. Thank goodness this room had one. And a shower!

After checking to see that the door was locked, and not spotting any cameras, I went into the bathroom, and locked the door. I stripped out of the clothes I had slept in, and stepped into the shower.

The warm water felt good, and as I stood there I cried like a baby. How could this be happening? I thought about a recent newspaper story I had read about kidnapping. It was not a crime that only happened to rich people. Children, kids and adults all over the world are kidnapped every day for far less important things than this. It is sad anyone thinks they have the right to take a person out of their life for any reason. Often they are often beaten, raped - or worse!

The tears washed away a lot of tension and frustration, and as I dried myself, my courage came back somewhat. I remembered what Aunt Susan had said, and I repeated to myself, "Buck up kid! If you are going to get out of this; it's up to you!"

It was time to stop being a victim, and start taking action! I would play along, and hope things went as planned; but if not, I would make a plan of my own! Everyone else seemed to have one! I was tired of being in the dark!

As I was dressing, there was a knock on the bedroom door. It was Victor. "Breakfast in five minutes!" He called out.

"I'll be ready!" I shouted back. I was hungry! My immediate plan was to eat as much as possible! I would need the energy, and I had to be ready for anything! Overeating had not been a problem on this trip!

I brushed my hair, threw it in a quick ponytail, and packed my dirty clothes in the suitcase. I kept the New York Jacket out, laying it on the bed. Feeling better than I had for a long time, I opened the bedroom door, and walked to the living room, where a table had been set up with breakfast.

There sat Vlad and Victor. "Good morning, Rose! Please join us!" Vlad was smiling, and being extra nice. I gave a half smile, and looked immediately at the food like a hungry dog. Pancakes! A big stack - and bacon! Orange slices and juice. And Scrambled eggs!

Looking at Vladimir's big belly, I knew I would have to eat fast to get enough! I didn't know if this was a typical Russian breakfast or not. The reporter in me was too busy eating to care.

While we ate, Vlad talked. "This is a big day for all of us! We will collect your Aunt Susan after breakfast, and drive to Gzhel! I understand your Dad is a man of his word, and so I will bring you both to him at the same time. I had separated you for a little extra insurance, but the conditions of the agreement demand you both be returned at the same time!"

"Where is Aunt Susan?" I asked, as I grabbed the last pancake from the platter.

"She is safe, nearby," Victor replied.

I had not heard Victor speak up much. I was getting the impression he was trying to reassure me things would be okay. It seemed he was not comfortable with the kidnapping. Neither was I.

Vlad shot him a look. Not to tell too much? Old Vlad was still being cautious. So! He was not that sure of the outcome! That told me a lot!

"What time will we get to Gzhel?" I asked, excitement showing through.

"If all goes as planned, we will arrive early this afternoon. The exchange is set for…"

Vlad stopped in mid-sentence. This was curious! Had he said "exchange"? What "exchange"? I had thought it was a matter of trust. He was to hand over Aunt Susan and I, and in exchange his hard liners would be allowed to attend this all important trade meeting. My heart started beating a little faster. Something was not right! What was it I did not know? It was clear he wasn't going to tell me, so I thought it wise not to ask.

Everyone did have a plan, and what we didn't know was what caused the problems. What happened next was definitely not in the plans!

Vlad picked up the hotel phone, and dialed a room number. After hearing several rings he shot a worried look at Victor. Then he looked at him, and motioned with his head toward the door. Victor got up and left the room.

Vlad continued his ramblin' while he waited for some news. Had something gone wrong already? Was Aunt Susan okay? I did not like this feeling, and forced myself to stay calm as I listened to Vlad.

"You will like Gzhel! There the children learn the art of the famous Gzhel porcelain from the time they are in kindergarten! Then they are sent to the university here in Moscow for graduate studies in art. It is a way of life here. So many people in your country have no appreciation for art. Oh, some do, but many just collect things without a real appreciation for the history and beauty of it."

He must have seen the look on my face. I was surprised he had any appreciation for art. I, myself was not into art all that much. I was not one of the debutantes at school. Yes, there were girls there who only seemed to appreciate snobbery, and being in society circles.

"You think I do not appreciate such things?" Vlad defended himself from my look. "Russia is famous for art! I have not appreciated warehousing the cheap porcelain to the discount stores in the United States! But it has been my assignment as an agent."

"But why kidnap me and Aunt Susan?" I asked.

"That was a desperate act on my part! Word was sent to me that my bosses were not happy with the returns from my sales. There was talk of "retiring" me. Permanently! I had to do something to stay in their graces or face a life in Siberia, if I lived!"

"But is there really that much money in porcelain?" I wanted to keep his mind off of Victor and Aunt Susan. I wanted to keep my mind off of it as well. I was afraid of what might happen next.

"Money in porcelain? Why, child, it is a gold mine! Just this year your Secretary of State signed a contract for six tons of fine, gold-trimmed porcelain for Air Force One, Camp David, and U.S. posts overseas! Then consider the population of your country; who must all eat - and they use plates. Then the world! Then the porcelain art such as produced in Gzhel! Oh yes, there are porcelain mines in Russia! Which used to be under government control!"

Wow! Vlad was getting too intense! I really hit his hot button! I was surprised to hear him answer the question! Unfortunately, he looked at his watch, and we both dreaded the time. Victor had been gone too long. What had happened?

Just then Victor opened the door, and next to him was a nervous and rumpled Peter. Peter, who had been assigned to watch Aunt Susan. They motioned Vlad into the hallway outside. Vlad told me to stay put, and went to talk to them.

What had happened to Aunt Susan? I ran up to the door, and tried to hear what they were saying. I could not hear much, but gathered that Aunt Susan had escaped!

My heart was really beating now. I heard the words, "We'll all be killed! The plan is ruined! Get the girl!"

That was all I needed to hear! I ran to the bedroom and grabbed my suitcase and a sheet off of the bed. I ran back to the living room and went to the French doors, to the little balcony overlooking the street. It was about thirty feet to the ground. The ceilings were about ten feet high, I guessed. I stepped out onto the balcony. The wrought iron railing was as high as my chest.

If I fell...

I did not have time to think about it. Now I had a plan; to escape and call Dad! If Aunt Susan was gone, then the deal was off! Vlad would be angry and desperate! We might never get home!

What I did not know was that Peter and Victor were double agents. They were loyal to The Agency. They had been sent by The Agency to pick up Vlad after he had started following us in New York. They were to tell him the "Home Office" was not happy, and he must return to face reassignment. He did not want to leave the United States, and concocted his desperate plan after the hotel maid had found Aunt Susan's crumpled printout in my back pocket and called Vladimir; a.k.a. John Henry, who had paid her for any information she could find.

It was his normal spy business. Peter and Victor did not want to risk blowing their cover, and after Vlad kidnapped us, they went along on Agency orders to protect us, and set a trap for Vlad. They were afraid to stop him at the airport for fear he might harm us.

When Peter took Aunt Susan to the hotel, he told her who he was, and Aunt Susan made a plan to escape. To protect Peter's cover, she tied him up just out of reach of the phone, and left for Gzhel to find me.

Of course, I did not know this as I tied the sheet around the base of the railing. I threw my suitcase on the ground, knowing I had only minutes to get away.

To where? I did not know Moscow! But any place was better than here! It was too late to stop now, and I climbed over the railing, holding onto the sheet for dear life. I wrapped my legs around it, and slid down as far as I could, a few feet above the next balcony on the second floor.

It was still too far to drop to the ground, so I began to swing outward, like Bruce Willis in the movie Die-Hard. I'm glad Dad let me watch it with him! I remembered how he crashed through the window on the fire hose, and hoped I would not crash through the French doors! I was afraid Vlad would lean over the balcony any second now and haul me back up!

"Here goes everything!" I said as I swung in and let go, landing like a parachutist in a crouched position on my toes, and bonking my head on the French doors. I could only hope Vlad had not seen the sheet!

Through the lace curtains I could see a man coming toward me. I was surprised when I stood up, and he opened the door.

"Dr. Schaeffer! What are you doing here?" I asked as I stood up and tried not to look like a mischievous kid.

Chapter Nineteen

"I might ask you the same thing, Rose!" He replied as he swung the door open and motioned me in.

I should not have been surprised to see him. He was on the plane. And his business was Russian art and porcelain.

"I really don't have time to talk," I said as he closed the French doors and turned around, "I've been kidnapped, and there are Russian agents chasing me…"

I expected a look of unbelief. It sounded like a kid's imagination to me, too. But, I was surprised when he held up his hand and stopped me, and put a finger to his lips.

"Shh! I saw you with John Henry on the plane the other night. I pretended to be asleep but heard everything said as you left the cockpit. I have never liked John Henry. He deals in cheap sweat house porcelain…"

"We, er, I, don't have much time. I escaped off the balcony, he's bound to see the sheet - and will be coming after me! I've got to get to a phone and call my Dad."

"You could use mine, but I'm afraid if he is looking for you, you will not have time. Where is Susan? Is she all right?"

"I think Aunt Susan is in Gzhel, looking for me. She escaped also. Can you take me there? We have to hurry!"

"Yes, I can take you there, but I am waiting for someone. I'll have to leave him a note…"

Just then we noticed the sheet being hauled up as we looked out the French doors. I wondered if Vlad had seen my suitcase lying on the ground…

"Let's go!" I said as I ran to the door of the room. Dr. Schaeffer followed, grabbing his coat and keys, and forgetting about the note.

I swung the room door open just as a hand was about to knock. It almost hit me on the head!

There was a boy about my age, holding my suitcase with a puzzled look on his face.

"Dimitri! I'm sorry about our meeting, but I must run now, and take this young lady to Gzhel."

I was getting more anxious by the second! "C'mon, let's go! We can talk later..."

Just then we heard several footsteps running down the hall.

"Dimitri, how did you get here?" Dr. Schaeffer asked.

"On my scooter..." he replied as Dr. Schaeffer stopped his explanation.

"Take Rose to Gzhel! I'll join you later at your house."

Dimitri didn't argue, and neither did I. We pushed the button on the elevator, and waited for the doors to open. Why did it always take so long when you were in a hurry?

We heard the soft "Ding", and ran through the still-opening doors just as Vlad's feet turned the corner of the corridor.

As the elevator descended to the garage, Vlad turned to Dr. Schaeffer.

"Why, Dr. Schaeffer! What a nice surprise! But there is no time for pleasantries, where is Rose?"

Dr. Schaeffer looked at Vlad, a.k.a. John Henry, Peter, and Victor who were just returning from searching the other corridors of the hotel.

"Who is Rose?" He asked.

When the elevator doors opened into the garage, we ran to Dimitri's scooter. I had to hold the suitcase with one hand, and the seat with the other as Dimtri started the engine, and we took off through the parking garage. He did not know why we were in such a hurry, but he sensed the danger - and we drove into the daylight, out on the street as if the devil himself were chasing us!

It was too hard to talk as we drove through the streets of Moscow. I was relieved to be away from Vlad; it had been a close call! This was definitely too intense!

I wondered about Dimitri. He had spoken English, but was clearly Russian. He must be older than me, but not by much. Why was he seeing Dr. Schaeffer? He must have seen my suitcase as he drove up, and picked it up. I hoped Vlad had not seen it on the ground, but he would know I would have it with me. I hoped he would search the hotel before figuring out I was on the way to Gzhel.

As usual, I did not see much of Moscow as my mind rambled on.

Before long we were out of the city, and Dimitri asked if I wanted to stop.

My arms were tired from holding the seat, and the suitcase. I knew I could not go the whole way like this. I hollered, "Yes!"

Dimitri pulled into a park-like area, and stopped in a small grove of trees where we would be somewhat hidden.

We got off the scooter, and he tried to think of a way to secure the suitcase. It wasn't too hard as it was a small, soft-sided one, and there was a little rack behind the seat over the rear fender. He unfastened the elastic strap, and stretched it around the suitcase and undid the whole thing again!

"Your jacket," he said. "Take it off. You will be recognized too easily. Do you have another?"

"Yes, in the suitcase." I was happy to see my old jacket again, and put it on, stuffing the New York jacket into the suitcase.

"I have a sister about your age. You could almost pass for her."

"What's her name?" I asked.

"Anna. She is my youngest sister; she is twelve. I have three older sisters also."

"You are the only boy?"

"Yes, my father and I are the only men in the house," he said proudly.

"My name is Rose," I said as I stuck my hand out. "We were not properly introduced."

"Dimirti Petronova, at your service," he bowed gallantly. I was impressed with his manners.

"Well, Dimitri, it's nice to meet you, but I'm afraid we don't have much time. I must get to Gzhel before Vladimir catches up with us," I smiled and climbed on the back of the scooter. "I'll tell you everything later. I'm afraid you are in danger now, also!"

Dimitri climbed on the scooter, and started it up. "Any friend of Dr. Schaeffer is a friend of mine!" He said as we wove back through the trees, and out onto the road.

I wondered what Dad would say if he knew I had a crush on this cute, dark haired boy.

I decided not to tell him.

Chapter Twenty

It wasn't long before a car approached us on the road. We couldn't take a chance on who might be in it, so I tugged on Dimitri's jacket and he pulled the scooter off the road.

Finding some nearby trees to hide us, we waited for the car to pass. Had we had known who was in that car; we would have flagged it down!

Aunt Susan had left the hotel early that morning, not knowing I was there. Vlad and Victor had not contacted Peter when we returned the night before. It was natural for Aunt Susan to assume we were in Gzhel.

Not finding us there, she contacted The Agency, and Dad. But we didn't know. So we waited until the coast was clear.

We sat on the ground, leaning on two trees, and I asked Dimitri what he was doing at Dr. Schaeffer's.

"I was to meet Dr. Schaeffer, and plan our trip to New York. My sister Anna and I were chosen to represent Gzhel at the show in New York this coming weekend. Several children and teenagers from the nearby villages will be going also. The Association is sponsoring the show."

"New York! I just came from there!" I said, amazed at the timing of things. "But, why drive to Moscow to see Dr. Schaeffer? Wasn't he going to Gzhel?"

"I attend classes at the University in Moscow. All of my life I have studied the Gzhel art. At fourteen I was advanced enough to go to University. I go home on Sundays. I cannot afford to drive there every day. I was on my way home."

"Wow! You've studied art all of your life?"

"Yes, in addition to my regular school. Art is very important!"

Dimitri's enthusiasm was building. His eyes were alive with his passion for art.

"But don't you get tired of it?" I asked, thinking of how I got tired of school sometimes. Maybe it was because I did not have a passion for anything. Except the curiosity in me. I was excited about the newsletter!

"Tired of it? No! It gives me pride! It gives me a heritage and opportunities! Why, the ability to express oneself is the universal craving! People express themselves in countless ways, from needlepoint to writing; in how they live, talk, and work. Art in its many forms brightens our world, takes us beyond oppression and survival; it gives us hope! Being free, as we now are, has brought a new confidence to our country!"

Wow! I could see the confidence in Dimitri! He was mature for his age, yet still enjoying being a kid.

Dimitri looked at me, "And what brought you to the other side of the world, Rose?"

"Art." I said and told him the whole story. He listened with expressions of excitement and sadness. Yet, I could see his mind working behind his dark eyes.

"I have a plan," he announced, jumping to his feet, and turning the scooter towards Gzhel.

I climbed on, and we hit the road again, a new excitement in us. Even the scooter's little motor seemed to have more life in it!

The early afternoon sun had burned away the fog, and the bright fall colors turned the landscape into a beautiful picture.

Dimitri's enthusiasm had caught me, and I began to have a different view of Russia. It wasn't the gloomy place I had thought. Now I saw a warm country, and people with a heart.

For the first time since this whole trip started I noticed the scenery around me. Looking in the mirror of the scooter, I also noticed a car coming up behind us.

This time there was no time to hide!

Dimitri saw the car in his mirror, too. His first thought was to speed up, but the scooter was no match for the black limo.

As it pulled up next to us, we could see three men; Victor was driving, and Peter was in the back seat with Vlad.

At first it looked like they were going to pass us; racing to Gzhel to find me, no doubt. But Victor recognized me, slowing down enough to cause Vlad and Peter to look closer.

While Dimitri tried to think of what to do, Victor did also. When we sped up, so did the limo. When we slowed down, they did too.

The scooter was not made for off-road. And while the road we were on wasn't the greatest, we had to stay on it.

Vlad was motioning us to pull over to the side, but Dimitri kept going. There was a crossroad coming up, and I expected Dimitri to slow down and take it. Instead, he pushed the little scooter to the limit!

The limo stayed alongside of us as we ignored the hand signals to stop. Victor and Peter lowered their windows and pleaded with us to pull over. We kept on racing for the finish.

Up ahead, an old farm truck loaded with hay was approaching from the right. Victor was so preoccupied with not running into us he didn't see it.

Dimitri pushed the little scooter for all it had, and buzzed through the intersection just ahead of the oncoming truck. The old farmer must have had a heart attack!

At the last second, Victor saw the truck, and with both the trucks and the limo's horn blaring, Victor slammed on his brakes as we shot through the crossing.

Watching in the scooter's mirrors, we heard the squeal of tires and a SLAM and CRASH! The limo slid sideways into the side of the truck, knocking the sideboards loose and dumping bales of hay everywhere!

Hoping no one was hurt too badly, we pressed on toward Gzhel. It wasn't far now, and Dimitri knew he could hide us once we were there.

I let out a sigh of relief, and a prayer of thanks for being alive!

The scooter finally began to wind down as we approached the village. I looked around for all of the security and cars that had been here the day before. There wasn't a one in sight!

It was too intense! Where had they gone? Where was Dad? What about the "exchange"?

Gzhel looked empty, as if nothing had ever happened here. I could hear my heart beating. This was like The Twilight Zone.

Finally, we drove up into Dimitri's yard. "We are home!" He announced, as he stepped off the scooter, which was now cracking and popping from the heat of the motor cooling down.

We un-strapped the suitcase from the back, and hid the scooter behind a woodpile. I helped Dimitri throw a tarp over it to hide it.

I turned to look at the old, farm-style house, and was still puzzled by the lack of activity. Standing on the porch was a girl about my age.

"Hello, Anna!" Dimitri said as we climbed the steps, "This is Rose."

Anna smiled and waved us in. "Dr. Schaeffer called. He said you were bringing a girl home with you. Momma thought you got married!"

Sheesh! I might have had a crush on Dimitri, but this was ridiculous!

It was the perfect ending to all that had happened, and we all stood there laughing, instant friends.

Chapter Twenty-One

It was nice to be around kids my own age. I mean, I like adults, but I needed a break! Dimitri said he had a plan. Right now I didn't want to hear it.

I was not used to having many friends, outside of school and summer camp. I kept in touch with people on my computer and when I saw them again. I wanted to enjoy some time with my newfound pals. Even though I was far away from home, and in a foreign country, they made me feel right at home. They were so real, just being themselves, and let me be myself, too.

For the first time on this whole adventure, I forgot about home. Oh, I still wanted to go home - and still had questions, but they could wait.

Dimitri's mother heard the laughing going on by the front door, and came out of the kitchen. She had a smile and a questioning look at Dimitri as she approached us.

"Vat is all the laughter about?" She said in English, knowing I was from the United States. "Dimitri, who is your friend?"

I liked her instantly! Even though she was different from my Mom, they had a lot in common. I think there are some universal things about moms - no matter what they do, or where they live. And I think they feel the same way about kids!

"Mother," Dimitri said, being more formal, "This is Rose. She is from the United States. Rose, this is my mother, Svetlana Petronova."

"A pleasure to meet you, Rose. Come into the kitchen, and have some dinner with us, and tell us about yourself. Alexander, my husband, will join us soon. Dr. Schaeffer will join us later for uzhin, supper."

I followed them into the kitchen, taking note of the porcelain plates, Samovars, and the Gzhel style of the decoration. The house had a warm country atmosphere, and though my home was different, I felt at home here.

Dimitri's father, Alexander, came in through the back door, and sat at the head of the table. A handsome, hard-working man, he led us in prayer (in English for my benefit), and asked to be introduced to Dimitri's new girlfriend (with a wink at me, while Dimitri blushed at the teasing, and pretended to be angry).

For the next hour we all sat around the big table exchanging stories, and family backgrounds. We finally got around to why I was here. I told them what I thought I could without giving away any secrets.

Along the way, I learned something about Russian mealtimes and food. Breakfast was called zavtrak, and was not the bowl of cold cereal many Americans started the day with. In fact, cold cereal wasn't known here until the early 1990's. Lunch is not a meal in Russia. It was what we were having now, dinner or obyed. This was the main meal of the day.

We had zakuski or appetizers. There were caviar, pickles, smoked fish, and vegetables. There was also my favorite for the main course, roast beef and potatoes. The main course was called vtoroye. We also had tretye; dessert, which today was cake.

There were a lot of things I normally did not eat, like caviar, smoked fish, and vegetables! But I found myself eating without thinking as we talked, and enjoyed the family atmosphere.

But when the conversation lagged, I felt sad again. Where was Dad? I missed my home, my mother, Richard, Sam, and Aunt Susan. It's funny how when you are away from home, you look for familiar things.

It was times like this I remembered my age, and longed to be around my own family. I looked at Dimitri. He saw the sadness on my face.

"Rose, remember I told you I have a plan? Let us go to Anna's room, and I will tell you about it!"

Anna was excited to have an American guest in her room, and jumped up from the table, asking to be excused from her after-dinner chores. Her mother smiled, and looked at Alexander.

"Only if you agree to tell us what it is, and get our approval," he said.

"Yes, Father. We will need Dr. Schaeffer's help also."

We followed Anna to her room, climbing the narrow wooden stairs. The whole house was in remarkable condition, and Dimitri explained many tourists came to Gzhel to see the porcelain, and the village.

Besides, like his parents it was very traditional. They respected tradition, and their possessions.

Anna was proud of her room. Like me, this was her private world. Along with the beautiful antique furniture and the hand-made quilts, and of course, Gzhel figurines were posters of the outside world. I noticed New York on the wall, and a couple American rock groups. She explained she had to convince her parents to let her put the posters up.

She did not have a computer, but Dimitri did. She had a desk by the window, and it was where she studied. She parted the curtains to see who was coming and going, as her room looked out on the front yard.

Moving a couple of her dolls, we sat on the bed. Dimitri sat at Anna's desk, waiting to finally reveal his plan.

I was anxious to hear it!

Chapter Twenty-Two

Dimitri's plan was simple; I liked that. He had formed the plan back on the road. When I had told him about Kate and Doe, and how we had pulled a switch to shake Vladimir off our tail in New York, he thought of Anna.

We were about the same age, height, and hair color; why wouldn't it work twice?

"Anna and I have the week off from school for the Gzhel show in New York," he explained. "You could take her place while she visits her cousins. Vladimir does not know us, and he would have no reason to expect the same deception again. He thinks you are on your own now."

"But why not just call my Dad?" I asked.

"We can't trust our phone. Also, Vlad is on his way here to find you now. We don't have much time. He will be like an angry bee... and where is your Dad?"

That was a question we couldn't answer. All week long, Gzhel had been filled with security, and visiting dignitaries. It was like a ghost town now. The big trade meeting must have been moved. Dad and Aunt Susan were probably searching for me now.

What we didn't know was that Aunt Susan had pulled into town very early this morning. When Vlad split us up, she saw us drive the other way and heard Vladimir say "Gzhel". She naturally assumed we would be here, at the meeting site.

Peter had told her he and Victor were really double agents, sent to watch Vladimir, and keep us safe. They were told to tell Vladimir it was time to come home. They did not have COM links, as it was too dangerous for them if they should be caught.

So, when Vlad got the call for the exchange, and we headed back to Moscow, there was no way for anyone but Victor to know.

When Aunt Susan escaped she came here to find me.

But most of the cars were gone. Only a couple of security guards stayed behind with Dad. The meeting had been moved to Moscow, and a trap had been set. Vlad was supposed to walk right into it!

Aunt Susan's arrival had changed things, again.

"Susan! Where's Rose?" Dad had said, almost frantic with worry. "What happened? The last signal we got from her was from Moscow last night."

Another thing we didn't know was the New York jacket was equipped with a COM link! Doe was supposed to activate it when she handed it to me in the ladies room. That is why Kate's cell phone went off when they had returned home that night. The Agency had not gotten a signal from it yet. Doe had activated it by pulling on the "Made In USA" tag on the collar. But it must have been defective.

No one had told me about the link, because they worried I would not act natural knowing it was there. Also, Aunt Susan and I were not supposed to be separated. We were supposed to get on the plane and be back in Minnesota in a few hours.

Sheesh! Talk about a failure to communicate!

So, Aunt Susan told Dad everything she knew. Dad told her everything he knew, and they headed off to Moscow to find me! Leaving Gzhel as if nothing had happened!

We could only operate on what we knew then. Dimitri continued explaining his plan. There were more surprises to come!

"We can get you home, Rose! You could take Anna's place in the show. Dr. Schaeffer can help us."

I looked at Anna. Tears were forming in her eyes. I could see how much she wanted to go to New York.

"No! I won't take away Anna's trip! I will wait for my Dad to pick me up. I will hide out until Vlad goes away!"

"But don't you see you are placing my family in danger too?" Dimitri said.

He was right. How could I do that? Before I could open my mouth, Anna spoke up.

"Yes, Rose. You must! I can go to the next one! I will stay with my cousins all week. On Thursday you will take my place on the plane. You will return to your home. Your mother must be terribly worried! My cousins are alone also. They will like the company of my mother and I."

"Why are they alone?" I asked.

"Their parents, my Aunt and Uncle, have gone to the United States to open a distribution center in Minnesota for Gzhel porcelain."

This was too intense! More surprises! I had no idea when I broke that plate what a Pandora's box I had opened.

"We must hurry, girls!" Dimitri said. "I will tell Father and Mother the plan while you two change!"

Dimitri left the room, and I unzipped my bag. I took out the New York jacket, and gave it to Anna, holding it by the "Made In USA" tag.

"This is yours, now," I said as I handed it to her.

She smiled, and said, "Thank You! I have always wanted to see New York!"

Anna's hair was longer than mine. I didn't know what to do about that. But she did!

Her hair was braided and curled around her ears. She had done it herself and wore it this way often. She braided mine, and fixed it the same way. Curled like that it looked pretty much the same!

We walked down the steps, side by side, like two twins! Dimitri's parents stared in amazement, and Dimitri groaned; "Now I have another sister!"

Just then, a car pulled into the driveway.

Chapter Twenty-Three

While we were standing on the steps, wondering who was in the car, Dad and Aunt Susan were in a hotel in Moscow. After questioning the hotel manager - and everyone else they could find - they decided to take two rooms and set up a headquarters for their search.

"I don't understand it!" Susan said, blaming herself for my disappearance. "Why didn't I stop Vlad? Why did I let him separate us?"

"Susan, stop blaming yourself. The crisis team had a plan, and there was no way you could have known it. Peter and Victor never had the opportunity to tell you who they really were. They did not expect Vladimir to go off the deep end and kidnap you two.

All they were supposed to do was get him off your tail so you could return to Minnesota safely. Thanks to you and Rose, the plate was delivered, and that part of the plan was salvaged. You could not have known Rose's COM link was defective. As long as she was with you and Peter and Victor we knew she was safe. We did not anticipate Vlad's "insurance policy" move. At least we can assume that Rose is with Peter and Victor, and even if it means blowing their cover, they will protect her."

Dad did his best to make Aunt Susan feel better, but he knew what they both needed to do was to take action!

"Susan, get in touch with Zip on a two-way and let The Agency know what we are doing. Tell them my assistant will oversee the trade meeting tomorrow and you and I will continue our search for Rose."

"What are you going to do?" Susan asked as she opened the door, and started for her room.

"I'm going to call home, and then I'm going to call in every favor from every agent in Moscow - including Vladimir's boss. If we find Vlad, we'll find Rose."

They spent the rest of the night on their phones, and Dad's laptop talking to Zip and setting up an extensive search for me. Then they laid out a scientific plan to pinpoint me while Zip scanned for a signal from the COM link I was supposed to be wearing.

Vladimir's boss agreed to co-operate. He had not sanctioned Vladimir's actions, and he was not anxious to have a political crisis. As long as the media was kept out of things, he was happy to co-operate in the search.

Late that night Susan retired to her room, and Dad knelt by the side of his bed and prayed for my safe return.

Back at home, Mom and Richard said prayers also. Samson The Great lay on my bed and refused to be moved. Eventually Mom gave up and lay down by him. She fell asleep on his warm soft fur.

Of course, the time zones were opposite. I still haven't figured them out exactly, but at least Dad and Aunt Susan were in the same time zone I was.

And that brings me back to where we were. Standing on the steps in Dimitri's house, looking like sisters. We exchanged clothes and Dimitri's parents were looking back and forth making sure who was who. If we could do that, we could sure fool Vlad!

A car pulled into the driveway and broke the spell. Dimitri and his parents looked nervously at each other, and my heart began to race. Who was it? Dr. Schaeffer? Vladimir? Aunt Susan? Dad?

Before we could move, there was a knock at the door. Alexander spoke up, "Back to your rooms, children!"

While he started for the door, we turned around and scrambled up the stairs. Dimitri was right on our heels, and we dived into Anna's room shutting the door behind us.

Looking out Anna's window we could see the car, a newer model, expensive, but not too expensive, Dimitri said. I was relieved it was not the limo Vlad, Peter, and Victor had been in. Were they okay? I wondered.

We could not see who was at the door though, so we put our ears to Anna's door and listened. Dimitri was taller, so he got the top, I was in the middle, and Anna was at the bottom. We must have looked like a Norman Rockwell painting!

We could hear voices, and heard Dr. Schaeffer! I was happy about that. Dimitri's mother had said he was coming later for supper. What a relief! I tried to stand up, ready to go downstairs, but Dimitri stopped me.

"Shhh!" he said. There was another voice; it was Vladimir! He was speaking in Russian, so I couldn't understand what he was saying, but Dimitri and Anna told me later.

"Forgive our intrusion. We had some car trouble down the road, and this nice gentleman; Dr. Schaeffer, offered us a ride. If you would be so kind as to let us use your telephone, we will call for a repair truck and be on our way."

Vladimir had a cell phone! The real reason he was here was to look for me!

What really happened was the limo had slid sideways into the farm truck, and the three of them had gotten out of the car. They were unhurt, but the car was not drivable. After Vlad had argued with the farmer - who drove away angrily - he saw a car coming down the road behind them.

It was Dr. Schaeffer. After Vladimir questioned him at the hotel, he went into his room and called Dimitri's house. He told Dimitri's mother Dimitri was on his way home, and he was bringing a girl with him!

Looking out his window, he could see Vlad, Peter, and Victor pulling out of the parking garage in the limo. He knew they were looking for us!

Jumping up, he went to the garage, and got in his rented car in pursuit of the limo and us! He did not take the time to call The Agency.

Now he was approaching the wrecked limo, and Vladimir flagged him down.

Dr. Schaeffer rolled down his window as Vladimir approached him.

"Dr. Schaeffer! We meet again! This is a surprise! And on the road to Gzhel! Tell me again you do not know this girl, Rose!" Then he drew his gun!

Peter and Victor looked at each other. They did not want to blow their cover! Going along with Vlad, they put menacing looks on their faces, and approached the car.

"I told you once before, Vladimir, I am going to Gzhel to escort the porcelain show to New York on Thursday. I am here on business, like you."

"You are trying to delay us, Doctor! We will ride with you and you will take us to Rose!"

Vladimir took out his cell phone while Peter and Victor climbed into the back seat. He called for a repair truck to tow the limousine. Dr.

Schaeffer was in no hurry to go anywhere. He waited until Vladimir prompted him to drive on. He knew every minute he bought us was important.

Trying not to incur the "Wrath of Vlad", he drove as slowly as he could. Vladimir's patience was wearing thin, and when Dr. Schaeffer drove into Gzhel, he turned toward the porcelain factory.

"I must stop and pick something up here," he said as he parked the car in front of the building.

Vladimir thought we might be here, and he sent Victor with Dr. Schaeffer. They stood at the door, knocking.

It was Sunday in Gzhel, and suppertime was approaching. No one answered the door. Dr. Schaeffer was getting nervous. If no one came, Vlad would know he was stalling. Peter and Victor made him nervous also.

As the sweat began to form on his brow, the door opened. A kindly old gentleman appeared. The janitor! He recognized Dr. Schaeffer.

"Why, Dr. Schaeffer! What brings you here tonight? We thought you would be here tomorrow..."

"Shh! Old friend! I would like to introduce you to my associate, Peter."

"How do you do, sir? My name is Boris.

Now, Peter knew what Dr. Schaeffer was up to. He went along with the game.

"A pleasure to meet you, sir. Dr. Schaeffer was kind enough to offer my friends and I a tour of your factory this evening. May we come in?"

"Well, we have had tours here all week long. Certainly, one more will not do any harm." And, smiling, he waved Vladimir and Victor to come in also.

Vladimir was anxious to find out what was happening. He was also curious, having never seen the facilities in Gzhel before. Hoping to find me hiding inside, he entered the building, Victor following behind.

Boris was used to escorting tours. He took them through the studios one by one, switching on the lights as he went. He explained what each was and showed them samples of the work in progress.

As they went, all four men looked around, each trying to see a glimpse of Dimitri or me. They heard little of what Boris was telling them. Dr. Schaeffer of course, had been here before, and was able to listen to Boris - and search at the same time. Vlad watched Dr. Schaeffer, and noticed him looking for us also. This kept him thinking we might be there.

Eventually, Boris came to the end of the tour, and as they approached the front door again, began to tell the men of Dr. Schaeffer's contribution to the advancement of Gzhel art, and how he had helped the children of the Gzhel Association win the opportunities of advanced schooling and trips to the United States, and other countries.

Why, there was one coming up this week!

Dr. Schaeffer stopped him. "Thank you, Boris. We must be going now. Oh, by the way, do you have the schedule I was to pick up?"

"The schedule! Of course! It is in the office, but I thought you would pick it up tomorrow..."

"A change of schedule for me, Boris. I need to get it tonight."

"Of course, Doctor! I will be back presently!"

"Very clever, Dr. Schaeffer! Do you think I am a fool?" Vladimir said while they waited for Boris to return. "Now, you will take us to your real destination!"

So here they were.

"Mother has invited them to stay for supper," Dimitri said. "We cannot go down, Rose. Anna, you go to supper, but leave the jacket here. Rose and I will have to eat later!"

Anna opened the door, and started down the steps as her mother was coming up.

"Anna, Dr. Schaeffer, and his friends are here. They will be staying for supper tonight. I think you should change your clothes, come and meet them. Remember, tonight we are going to visit your cousins in Vladimir. We will leave after we eat."

"Yes, Mother. I will change, pack, and be down shortly."

Anna returned to the room, and asked if we had heard.

"Yes," Dimitri said. "I will go to my room. Rose, you can come too, if you like, or you can stay with Anna."

"I think I will stay and talk to Anna for a while."

Dimitri nodded, and quietly opened the door. Tiptoeing down the hallway, he ducked into his room.

"Rose, you can stay in my room while I am gone. Dimitri will show you the pieces I have made for the show."

"Anna, I will make this up to you! After I get back home, you will have your trip! Now, tell me about your uncle and aunt."

With the enemy downstairs - and not daring to talk too loud, we felt like secret agents!

This was too intense!

Chapter Twenty-Four

As I sat on Anna's bed, my mind was wandering; little thoughts were coming to me.

"Rose! Go to your room!" Mother shouted, hurt and angry.

I jumped up from my chair at the table, just as angry, and stomped up the stairs, trying to crash my feet through each one. Finally reaching the top, I continued stomping, making my exact whereabouts known every step of the way.

I grabbed the door, and slammed it to drive my point home.

I did not eat supper that night. I was ten years old and upset! Dad had promised to take me to see David Copperfield, the magician. Then he was called to work and had to leave.

I took it personal. Being an only child is not easy. You get used to all the attention. Dad was gone a lot, and when he was home everyone, including Samson The Great wanted his attention.

Did Dad love his job more than me?

Here I was again, thinking the same thoughts. Confined to a strangers room, missing supper and. missing home, missing Dad.

I was being punished for breaking that plate!

What I didn't know then, was that Dad was just as hurt and angry. He was mad at himself for breaking his promise to me. Guilt was piling up on him. Why must his job come between him and his family? Why hadn't he made other choices with his life?

But, who had a crystal ball? When he had chosen his career, he couldn't foresee the future. Oh, he knew how he wanted things to be, but life did not always co-operate. Sometimes he felt like he was in a maze that kept changing. Every wrong turn added to his frustration, and he piled bricks of guilt on himself for not being perfect.

Why was it other men seemed to breeze to their goals, confident and balanced every step of the way?

The Agency had given him no choice. They had said he was the only one for the job. He would have to put his personal life aside one more time.

Duty-bound, he tried to explain, he needed me to understand.

I did not give him a hug as he left.

Now, lying on Anna's bed, remembering all of this, I wanted to tell him I was sorry, that I did understand, and it was okay.

Sixty kilometers away, in the hotel in Moscow, Dad was remembering too.

Chapter Twenty-Five

"What do you mean you don't know where she is? How could this happen?"

Mother was angry when Dad called.

Feeling powerless, waiting at home, she couldn't hold back anymore. There was no one she could talk to, except Richard and Sam.

She couldn't tell Richard the things in her deepest heart. Her dreams. The little big things playing in her mind like a movie. She and Dad had nothing between them. The three of us doing things together. Rainy days spent reading, everyone home under her loving protection. A fortress. No jobs, no school, no world to save.

But Richard knew. He worried, too.

He remembered the things we had done. How we had been the family he never had for himself, and knew he never would.

Richard had been Dad's partner, and Dad had saved his life, pushing him out of the way of an enemy agent's bullet, stepping into it himself as he did. The bullet tore his left shoulder, and it was never the same.

They had stayed partners, each like the brother they never had.

When I came along, Dad was torn again. He considered leaving The Agency, wanting to be with his family - and keeping us safe.

But he had seen too much. He knew someone had to do something about the evil threatening every family. He thought of all the soldiers who had died protecting their ideals from the sick minds who wanted to rule the world.

He asked for a bodyguard for Mom and I. The Agency said they could not afford one.

Richard offered a solution. Giving up his personal freedom, he volunteered. The Agency would pay half and Dad would pay the other half.

So we adopted each other, and Richard repaid the debt he felt he owed to Dad. And he gained a family in return, watching me grow up; stepping in to be the father he never would have been otherwise.

My adventure had been a roller coaster for him, too. He was an agent, used to action! He wanted to be in Moscow, hunting down Vladimir and bringing me home!

But, orders and duty prevailed, and he waited, watching over Mom and helping her cope.

Deep inside, they both knew it would all work out. It always did.

Chapter Twenty-Six

"Rose! You are not listening!" Anna was shaking my shoulder.

She had been trying to tell me about her aunt and uncle. Somewhere along the way I had drifted off, thinking of all those things back home.

I was still drifting. Now I was thinking of all those times when I wished I had a brother or sister.

And in a strange way, now I did. But what was so strange about that? I came from a strange family anyway.

"Rose! Are you okay?" Anna finally broke the spell and I returned to the present.

"Mom and I will be leaving soon. We have eaten supper. Dr. Schaeffer has left. Vladimir and Peter and Victor have taken rooms at the bed and breakfast here in Gzhel.

They have all left. My father is out taking a walk, telling the neighbors the story, and explaining to them to call you Anna for the next few days. They will help protect you from Vladimir until you leave on Thursday with Dr. Schaeffer."

Anna continued telling me the plan. Soon, her mother knocked on the door, calling Dimitri and I to come down to the table and eat. It was getting dark; she and Anna would be leaving soon.

When everyone was gone, Dimitri and I sat across from each other at the table, eating the warmed-up food.

Still drifting a little, I was confused about my feelings. I liked Dimitri, and even had a crush on him, but now he seemed more like a brother. The brother I never had.

I looked around, avoiding his eyes. I saw the carved wooden shelves on the wall, each one holding the white and blue pieces of Gzhel art.

Here was a porcelain knight on horseback, holding a lance in front of him, the horse rearing slightly, charging forward.

"That one is mine," Dimitri said.

"You made that?" I asked, amazed at his talent.

"Yes. I will show you how. Tomorrow we will go to the factory, and I will give you a tour. I will show you Anna's things also. You must see the frolicking sea serpent she designed and made!"

I was grateful Dimitri had taken my mind off of my thoughts. I had something to look forward to. I had a chance to repay the kindness they had shown me by being interested in their creations. I no longer felt helpless. Here was something I could do!

We finished eating, and Dimitri took me around the house, showing me where things were - the bathroom, the towels, the dishes. He also showed me the pictures on the wall. His Grandparents, his sisters, and told me a little about each one, and what they were doing now.

He told me he was named after the man who had discovered Gzhel clay, and developed porcelain independent of China and Europe. He was responsible for the heritage and opportunities the Gzhel area enjoyed today. His name was Dmitry, and even though it was spelled differently, he was proud of it.

When his mother named him, she set him on a path of life, embedding in his mind a desire to be a great artist for Gzhel.

I understood what it was like to want to be part of a family tradition.

Though it felt strange to me to be in someone else's home, Dimitri had made me feel like part of the family.

As I got ready for bed, I wondered where Anna and her mother were now. I took a hot bath, and borrowed Anna's pajamas. I felt safe, and did not worry about being alone with Dimitri. We both felt grown up.

Dimitri knocked on the door. I opened it, and I could see the conflict on his face. His feelings were mixed up, too.

Though I was a year and two months younger, he liked me. But I was more like a sister to him, and he had enough sisters already!

We decided not to talk about our feelings, and just remain friends.

Later that night, Anna and her mother arrived in Moscow. They would stay at the hotel, and do some shopping Monday morning. Then they would continue on to Vladimir.

They had no idea the confusion they would cause!

Chapter Twenty-Seven

Aunt Susan woke up first. She stretched yawned, and looked at the clock. Eight a.m., Moscow time. That would be 11 p.m. Sunday night back in the States. Even after all of her travels, she still had to stop and figure out the time zones. She was still too sleepy to calculate the exact time for Minnesota. Close enough, she thought, whatever it was!

She had stayed up late last night, monitoring the handheld, checking with Zip to see if they were picking her up. The COM link was still not transmitting from the jacket they had given her. Aunt Susan was still mad at herself for not telling me about it when I got the jacket.

Rising from the bed she walked to the shower, stretching on the way. The people in the neighboring room were already running theirs. Early risers, she thought, hope they don't use all the hot water...

In the neighboring room, Anna and her mother were getting ready for their big day.

Dad woke up to Zip's high-pitched sleep alarm. Nice thing about these handhelds is they were a phone, computer, link to The Agency, and alarm clock! Too bad Rose didn't have one!

While he was doing his stretches and morning exercises, he brought up Zip.

"Any contact with Rose, Zip?" He asked as he did his sit ups.

"Nothing since you signed off at two a.m., sir."

"Also, no reports from Russian spotters," Zip remained in the background on the little screen, displaying "For Your Eyes Only" information; readouts from The Agency relating to the current case.

Dad finished his exercises and headed for the showers, thinking about breakfast. He wanted to keep his strength up for his hoped for confrontation with the man who had kidnapped his daughter.

While he was eating breakfast, a blip from Zip told him a signal had come in. And it was close, too!

Susan's hand held went off, too. Running across the hall, wiping the eggs from her mouth, she knocked on Dad's door.

While Dad was jumping up to answer the knock, he did not see the Citroen pulling out of the garage below.

Svetlana Petronova looked over at her daughter as she piloted the Citroen down the early morning Moscow street. It was not often they had an outing like this. As close as Moscow was, they could not afford to come here often. And then to visit family! This was a big day indeed!

She was so proud of Anna! Not only for making such beautiful porcelain pieces, and making it to the show in New York, but then giving it up to help the American girl, Rose.

She would reward her with a stop at the department store! Maybe she could find a pair of American jeans for her. She would have to use more of her savings. The hotel was expensive enough for a secretary and farmer's wife!

But working for the Gzhel Association had brought them opportunities! Her two youngest children had a promising future!

She was still smiling as she parked the car, not noticing the man across the way.

The man across the way had gotten up at six. He was a Russian agent. He had no idea why they were co-operating with the Americans, but it was a simple enough task. All he had to do was watch for a young girl in a New York jacket.

As he bent to light his cigarette, Anna and her mother entered the store. He never saw them go in.

"What a glorious time we'll have today, Anna!" Svetlana said as they entered the store.

"Yes, it is a glorious day, Mother!" It would be even more glorious if she could buy a pair of Levi's! She hadn't told her mother she had brought her savings with her also!

The store had opened at nine a.m., and there was a long line. Anna and her Mother were near the front. There was one table in the girl's department with jeans. They were arranged by size, neatly folded.

"Oh, please let them have my size!" Anna said as they headed for the table. She was the only girl so far, but other mothers knew their children's sizes too.

She knew they could only buy one thing today. She felt selfish for wanting the jeans so bad. She had planned to wear them in New York, when she was not wearing the traditional dress for the show. But now she wasn't going. She would have to wait for the next show.

As they reached the table, and her mother was reaching for the last pair, Anna pulled her away. She knew her mother needed a new purse, and there was a table right across from the girl's department.

With a smile on her face, she dragged her mother to the purses and helped her pick one out.

About ten o'clock, a teary eyed Svetlana and her l daughter left the store, and drove away in the aging Citroen.

This time the Agent spotted them, and reached for his cell phone. Looking down to dial, he did not see which way the car turned at the intersection. East or West?

Of course, I found out about all of this later. Back at Dimitri's house we were having breakfast with Alexander.

It was going to be a big day for us, too!

Chapter Twenty-Eight

This was the first Monday, except for summer vacation; I had ever looked forward to. After breakfast, Dimitri was going to take me to the porcelain factory! I was still not a big fan of porcelain, but I was anxious to get on with the plan. I did not mind spending some time with Dimitri, either.

Alexander had gone to the neighbors' the night before and spread the word about Vladimir. By nine o'clock in the morning, everyone in Gzhel would be watching for him and his two "assistants". They would also be curious to meet the new "Anna". Me.

The early morning rain had stopped, and the clouds were breaking into a beautiful fall morning. The streets were still shiny with water. The whole day smelled clean and fresh as I walked alongside of Dimitri, only half-hearing him as he talked.

Finally at the door of the factory, Dimitri turned to me and said, "You did not hear a thing of what I was saying, did you?"

"I'm sorry, Dimitri, I was too busy sightseeing. What a beautiful town."

"That's okay. I was trying to explain the process of making the Gzhel porcelain. I will show you inside."

At exactly nine o'clock the door to the factory opened and a white-haired man wearing little glasses greeted us. He looked like a janitor.

"Good morning, Dimitri!" he said in a friendly tone.

"Good morning, Boris. And of course you know my "sister" Anna?"

"Of course. Good morning, Anna. A pleasure to see you again," he said with a wink.

Catching on quickly, I replied, "Good morning, Boris. It is nice to see you, too."

Boris opened the door and we stepped inside the famous factory. I went into "reporter" mode, determined to learn something today. Everyone had heard the news, and as I followed Dimitri from place to place, they turned and smiled. I was sure he would get some teasing when this was all over.

"The first thing I would like to do is introduce you to some of the artists. There are about twelve hundred people working in six different production facilities. Don't worry - we will not meet them all."

As we walked from station to station, I met Ludmilla, Gennadiy, Tatiana, Victor, and Alexander. Each one was a master artist with degrees, and awards. I knew I would not be able to spell their names, so Dimitri brought me a brochure in English. They were all very polite and eager to show me their work. As we went on, I became more interested in porcelain, and the process of creating it.

Dimitri could see my interest growing. He smiled and stood taller, enjoying his role as a tour guide.

"I have an idea," he said, "the best way to learn something is to do it! You will make a piece to take home!"

"Oh, no, I couldn't make something like this! I've never been good at art..." I started to protest nervously.

"Of course you can! I was twelve when I made my first piece. I knew if someone else could do it, I could too. I will guide you through the process. We will choose a simple piece that has already been designed. A candy dish, or sugar bowl, perhaps."

And before I could protest anymore, we were off!

Dimitri took me to the shapers, first. They were very experienced, he told me.

"We will let them do the first part."

We chose a stock bowl with no top. We watched the shaper cast a plaster model of a potter's wheel with two uprights, where he placed a wooden support for his hand.

Using a steel cutter with a long wooden handle, he scraped off the extra plaster. Then he made a work mold. Next, china paste was poured into the mold.

"Now, when it's dry," Dimitri said, "We will cut away the mold, and finish processing it. Then you can fire it, and paint it yourself!"

I was anxious to finish it! What a fine present for Mother! I would replace the plate I had broken with a bowl I had made! Truly an original. I would sign it Ramblin' Rose!

We would not get to fire it until tomorrow. In the meantime, Dimitri finished the tour of the factory.

"When do I get to see your pieces, Dimitri? And Anna's?"

"Later this evening, when Dr. Schaeffer comes to prepare them for transport to the show."

Dr. Schaeffer! Of course! He would be responsible to escort the children and the exhibit! I looked at Dimitri, with excitement on my face. Thoughts of Mother, and home had been ramblin' around as we took our tour of the factory.

Since Vladimir had kidnapped Aunt Susan and I in New York, I had been fighting homesickness. Now we needed Dr. Schaeffer to contact The Agency, and let my family know I was safe.

Safe, if Vlad didn't find me!

"What time is Dr. Schaeffer supposed to be here?" I asked.

"About five p.m. Boris said he stopped here last night to pick up the schedule. I am sure Vladimir had forced him to bring him over to the house. He would probably be watching him now. He may even be in town. We would stay in the factory until tonight. You will be safe here. We can leave with friends if Dr. Schaeffer is detained."

Though Dimitri tried to reassure me, I could not shake off the feeling Vladimir was nearby. As we watched the painters work, I kept looking over my shoulder.

Outside, it had begun to rain again, and I wondered what Dad and Aunt Susan were doing now.

Chapter Twenty-Nine

Vladimir and Company were nearby. They had not left Monday morning. I was the reason. Vladimir had seen me on the back of Dimitri's scooter. He knew I was here somewhere. He even deduced I might be returning to New York with Dr. Schaeffer and the children from the Gzhel Association. Each village was sending two kids ranging in age from twelve to eighteen. If he could not find me, and use me as a bargaining chip, he would find a way to get on the plane and escape to the United States. He had enough money in his Swiss bank account to live in comfort somewhere in the world. If he had to live in disgrace; at least he would eat well.

Sure, he could escape in Russia. He had many friends and contacts. But he would never be safe. His plan had gone bad, and he had embarrassed his bosses. Now they wanted him to pay. But they didn't want a scandal. They could not just let him walk away either.

So, Vlad was more dangerous than ever! He had little to lose! That's why he was still bent on finding me. I had ruined his plan! Plus, I could still be his ticket out! So, just like in New York, he had bribed the maid, actually the owner of the bed and breakfast, to tell him when she spotted us - or relay any information she might have.

Natasha took his money, knowing the whole town was protecting me!

But it was Tuesday morning now. Dimitri and I were eating breakfast, getting ready for Day Two. I had no idea Vlad and Company were still here. I thought they had left Monday morning in a new car, but I should have known better! Aunt Susan would be ashamed of me! I was blissfully unaware, looking forward to the distraction of spending the day with Dimitri, and working on the piece I had started.

Today I would get to fire it, and tomorrow we would paint it and have it ready in time for the show. Dr. Schaeffer said I could not show it because I was not a member of the Association, but he would approach them with the theme I was a cultural exchange student - and maybe we could show it after all!

He had come by the factory Monday night as Dimitri said to pack the exhibit, and make preparations for the trip. The bus had been hired, and would arrive Thursday morning to take us to the airport in Moscow. The other participants from the nearby villages would gather in Gzhel on Wednesday night for a dinner and dance celebration. The bus would leave early Thursday morning to arrive at the Moscow airport by eight a.m.

Dr. Schaeffer arrived at the factory at five p.m. Monday night. Most of the workers were leaving. Only the artists, Dimitri, and I stayed to talk. Dr. Schaeffer had already talked to the dignitaries from the Association, and would see them again on Wednesday.

After the other artists had left, we had the chance to talk to him as he worked.

"Dr. Schaeffer!" I said, "Have you talked to my parents?" I still could not trust the phones in Gzhel - as Vlad might have had them tapped.

"No. After I left last night, I was afraid Vladimir or one of his agents would follow me. I was afraid to use my phone when I returned to the hotel."

With so many preparations already on his mind, I felt bad for complicating his life even more.

"We have a plan," Dimitri said, and his enthusiasm put a spark of hope on the Doctor's face.

Dimitri laid out the plan, and Dr. Schaeffer smiled. "Yes, you do look like Anna, Rose! I have a laptop computer with me, when I return to the hotel tonight, I will contact your Agency. You will take Anna's place in the show, and return safely to New York! There your parents can pick you up! You are very talented children indeed!"

And Dr. Schaeffer returned to packing the exhibit, taking time to explain the artistic points of each one. I learned quite a bit that night.

Anna had six pieces. Dimitri was right to be excited about them. They made me smile. Her work reflected a young girl, and consisted of whimsical sea serpents, dolphins, and seahorses, perhaps also reflecting her desire to travel across the ocean to her dream of seeing New York.

Dimitri's art reflected him as well. A young knight, proud and independent, yet defending his heritage and family. There were also six pieces in his collection. A knight, standing; a knight on horseback; a jester; a rectangular covered dish with a coat of arms, and two traditional pieces- a creamer and a sugar bowl.

"You are a natural born artist, Dimitri! Where did you learn how to do this?" I asked.

"I watched. I believe that I can do anything that someone else can do. So I watched the artists work and copied them. I learned the basics and developed my skills. This is all I have done for two years except for my studies. I knew that if I scored high enough in my schoolwork, I would have the opportunity to go to the University for advance studies. Thanks to Doctor Schaeffer I have done it."

"Yes, I am very proud of Dimitri and Anna. They have both helped bring this art to a new generation. Now, in New York they have the opportunity to reach young people everywhere and bring the message of art to them. The program has been a success! But, go along now children. I will finish up here and see you on Wednesday. We all have a lot to do tomorrow! And Rose, your piece looks quite good also! I look forward to seeing it finished!"

So, Dimitri and I said goodnight to the good Doctor and Boris watched as we left the factory. It was just beginning to get dark. We made it safely to Dimitri's house in time for supper with Alexander.

That night I lay on Anna's bed, praying for all of us. As I drifted off to sleep I thought I felt Samson next to me. I could almost see Grandpa standing in the doorway, smiling as he turned off the light.

Chapter Thirty

It was Tuesday morning in Vladimir, Russia also. Sheesh! Vladimir, of all places! What a place for Dimitri and Anna's cousins to be from! The coincidence was amazing! But then, this whole trip was, too.

Monday had been busy there also. Dad and Aunt Susan had finally got a visual from Zip, and were hot on what they thought was my trail! So they thought.

When Anna and her mother left the Department Store, they had been spotted by the Russian agent across the street. As they drove off down the street he'd lost sight of which way they had gone.

He had looked down to dial his cell phone, and when he looked up again for the license plate number the car was gone! But he reported the Citroen and the Russian Agency took over, using their tracking satellites to pinpoint the car. Once they had the car in their sights, they called Dad.

Dad and Aunt Susan had just finished breakfast when the phone rang. The Russians were cooperating with the Americans. But they still did not have access to Zip. Nor would they get it. It was one of the reasons they were inclined to help. They hoped they would.

In the meantime they used the phone.

Dad was excited. He wrote down the description of the car, the time, and place. Susan's heart started beating faster; she knew they had a sighting. The Russians said they could not afford to continue tracking the car, and that Dad would have to take it from there.

Dad thanked them, then hung up the phone, and opened his laptop. Zip took over while they left the room, and went to the garage.

Susan watched the laptop as Dad drove out of the garage. She had to tell him to slow down! He was anxious to catch that car!

The car's tires squealed as they hit the street. Dad and Susan were both buckled up, anticipating a possible chase. The computer almost slid off Susan's lap, and she shot Dad an angry look.

"Hey! We can't help Rose if we can't find her! How can I monitor Zip if you keep driving like that?"

"You're right, Susan. I'll be more careful. It's just that ..."

"I know," Susan broke in, "I want to catch Vladimir too! But we need to be professional to do it."

Dad settled down a little, and Susan asked Zip where the Citroen was now.

"The car is headed northeast - just leaving Moscow," Zip answered.

"Where will that road take them, Zip?"

"Through Elektrostal, past Orekhova-Zuyevo, and on to the probable destination of Vladimir, Russia."

Zip had brought up a map, and showed the car moving up the road. The town of Vladimir was flashing on and off in red letters.

"Vladimir! Of course! Where else would he take her?" Dad's foot got a little heavier on the pedal as his fatherly instincts kicked in again.

"Wait a minute," Susan said, "wouldn't that be a little obvious? Vlad might not be the smartest duck in the pond, but he's eluded us so far."

"Yes, it would be a little obvious," Dad replied, "But maybe that is exactly what he is counting on."

"Yes, but the Russian Agency said Rose was with a woman..." Susan was thoughtful now.

"She could be working for Vlad. He has friends and accomplices all over Russia. He has never been afraid to pay for what he wants."

Every time Dad made a point about Vlad, the car lurched forward as his foot got heavier.

"I wish you would stop doing that! Why don't you let me drive?" Susan suggested.

"No way! We are going to catch them, and I'm going to..."

"Whoa, Dad. Let's not kill Rose in the process! Why don't we just follow them from a distance? Why tip them off, and risk a high-speed chase? They won't escape Zip. Let's see where they are going - they may lead us to Vladimir."

Dad knew that Susan was right. That is exactly what he would have said if he had been in her seat. Since word had come in about the kidnapping, Dad had kept his cool. He had handled everything as professional as possible. But now that Vlad was in his sights, he could not contain himself any longer.

But Susan's words sunk in. "You are right again, Susan. We'll just follow them. That will give me time to settle down so I won't do anything that might endanger Rose when we catch up with them."

Just as Dad was calming down, and his foot was easing off the accelerator, the Citroen came into view.

Svetlana Petronova looked into the rearview mirror. A black car had just come over the hill behind them. At first it had been traveling very fast, and then it slowed down suddenly. They had just passed the sign for Elektrostal.

"Vladimir!" She said out loud. "He must still be after Rose. And he thinks you are her!" She looked over at Anna, as her foot pushed the pedal down, and the car picked up speed.

Anna was as nervous as her mother. The old Citroen did not look like much but the motor was good. Still, it was no match for the black official-looking car she could see in the rearview mirror. Her mother was driving very fast now.

"Mother! Don't drive so fast. You are scaring me. What if it's just another car?"

"Of course. You are correct, Anna. I should not panic. We should think."

The car slowed slightly. Svetlana looked into the mirror. The black car was still behind them, but it was gaining.

When Dad saw the Citroen speed up, he did too. Susan had just got him settled down when the Citroen took off. Dad did not like anyone playing games with him.

"That does it! We are going to catch that car!"

Susan was thrown back on the seat as the pedal hit the floor. She hung onto the laptop and asked Zip for a course of action.

"Insufficient information available to advise. Suggest agent discretion, and refer to training manual." Zip did not want to incur Dad's wrath, either.

The sign for Orekhova-Zuyevo flew past. They were almost half way to Vladimir now. Zip informed them of this fact, but it had no effect on the speed of the car.

The Citroen was very close now. Dad smiled in anticipation.

Svetlana looked into the mirror again. The black car was very close. She thought fast and hard. If it was Vlad, she couldn't risk getting caught. He might take them hostage. If it wasn't him, it might be one of his agents... if they continued to follow them they would lead them right to her sister's house, and endanger her family.

She should have known her brother-in-law's plan to open a porcelain distribution center in the United States would bring on scrutiny. So in a way, this was his entire fault!

But, free enterprise was important. Here was an opportunity for Gzhel, and future generations. The world was changing, whether they liked it or not. The Russians were used to change. They were survivors. This change might be the best one of all.

Calm now, Svetlana eased the car to the side of the road, coming to a stop.

"Mother, what are you doing?" Anna asked.

"Shhh," was all she said. They sat very still, with the motor still running.

Dad kept his distance. He had not expected the car to pull over. With his heart pounding, and questions on his mind, he eased the car over some distance behind the Citroen.

"What do you think they are doing?" Susan asked.

"I was just going to ask you the same thing! We can't just sit here and wait. Maybe it's a trap. They might have called another car to help, and they are waiting for it to catch up... or, they might not be sure of who we are, and want to find out. For that matter, we are not even sure Rose is in that car. We have not seen her for ourselves. We've got to find out for sure."

"You are not going out there!" Susan was also worried this might be a trap.

"Relax. I'll pretend we are lost. If Rose is in the car, you'll know. I need you to watch my back!"

And over Susan's protests, Dad got out of the car, reaching into his pocket, taking the safety off his gun as he walked. There was no movement in the Citroen. The two figures in the front seat sat as still as mannequins. This puzzled Dad even more.

Susan was relaying information about the car into Zip as she watched Dad. The Agency would identify it for them. He was getting close now, her heart started beating in anticipation.

Just as Dad was close enough to see who was in the car, the tires spun on the dirt, shooting rocks and gravel at his legs. He turned sideways to avoid the spray while the car sped away.

By the time the dust settled, Anna and her mother had quite a head start. Dad ran back to his car and jumped - in throwing the car into gear, and burning the rubber on the tires. He was sure he could catch them again!

"Whoa, Hoss!" Susan said. "Zip just ID'd the car. You'll never guess who it's registered to…"

"Tell me later!" Dad said. "That could have been Rose in that car!"

Susan gave up. She closed the laptop, and looked out the window. She was thinking as they sped along. A woman and a girl…

There was something familiar about all of this…

Chapter Thirty-One

Tuesday morning! One day closer to home. I appreciated what Dimitri was doing for me. I know he suggested me making a porcelain piece to take home partly to keep my mind off of the situation.

As we walked along the village street, I thanked him for being so nice to me. He blushed and said, "That's what friends do."

We passed the bed and b breakfast hardly noticing it. Inside, Vladimir had been looking out the front window. His mind was ramblin' as he stood there. The trade meeting had been moved to a secret location. Vlad and his hard-liners had been kept out. His plan had failed, and now he knew he was in trouble. The American had set a trap for him! He was angry, but professional, too.

It was all part of the game. If he could escape Russia he could live in comfort. If he could get his hands on that girl, Rose, he could use her for a ticket out. Where was she?

Natasha entered the room behind Vladimir. Looking past him through the window she saw Dimitri and I approaching. Vlad would spot us for sure! She had taken Vlad's money, and now came the moment of truth. Would she point us out?

Behind Natasha came Peter and Victor. They entered the room, asking about breakfast, and Vlad turned to talk to them. Natasha was spared from her decision.

When we arrived at the factory, Boris greeted us at the door.

"Good morning, children! What a beautiful day! Come in, come in!"

The factory was alive with excitement! Artists and painters were busy with the days work. Everyone was talking in Russian, and Dimitri translated for me.

"What are they so excited about?" I asked him.

"They are all talking about the events this week. The trade meeting was very important to them. Tomorrow night at the dinner and dance the President of the Gzhel Association will make an announcement about the results of the meeting."

"Of course! I almost forgot about the meeting!"

"Yes, and the show in New York! The bus will arrive Thursday morning to take us to the airport! We must finish your piece!"

I followed Dimitri to the workstation where my piece had been drying. Now it could be fired. Dimitri told me what to do, and I followed his instructions while an experienced craftsman stood by with a watchful eye. He smiled and nodded each time I did something right.

When the piece was fired, I was quite proud of myself. I could see the finished product taking shape.

"Tomorrow we will paint it" Dimitri said, proud of his student.

We stayed at the factory for a while, watching the painters work. Like Dimitri, I made mental notes about the process. Soon it was dinnertime, and as we started to leave, Boris approached us. His cheerful look was gone.

"What is it, Boris? Why do you look so worried?"

"There is a man here to see you; the same man who came with Doctor Schaeffer Sunday night. I think he is not good. I think he is working for Vladimir!"

My heart was pounding now! Was it Peter? Victor? Could we trust him? If he was here Vlad was not far away. I did not want to see him!

"Dimitri, is there another way out?" I asked, my voice shaking.

"Yes, follow me! Boris, delay him until we get a head start!"

"Should I call the authorities?" Boris asked.

"No. We don't want to tip off Vlad. He has friends in high places. Friends we might not like. Just tell him we will be there shortly. We'll go out the back."

And off we went, slowly at first, then walking faster and faster through the factory to the back door. We jumped off the loading dock and headed for the trees, circling around the town back to Dimitri's house.

If we could get to Dimitri's scooter we could get away!

Boris detained Peter as long as he could. Finally Peter stood up from the old wooden bench, and shook his head. He looked at Boris.

"I know you have reason not to trust me, Boris. If I were you, I would feel the same way. It is quite obvious the children have gotten away now. My partner, Victor, is looking for them also. We know that Rose is here somewhere. We came to give her a message. To help.

"Why should I believe you?" Boris asked.

"Tomorrow night Gzhel is celebrating with a dinner and dance, is it not?" Peter asked.

"Yes, but that is public knowledge," Boris responded defensively.

"Of course; that is not the point. The point is that Vladimir knows about it also. He will be there looking for Rose. His plan has failed, and now he is looking to escape Russia. He will seek out Rose for a hostage. Victor and I are double agents. We work for the same Agency as Rose's father. We have actually been protecting her by staying with Vladimir. We cannot contact the Agency because it may tip off Vladimir and he would have us arrested or killed! Then we could not help Rose at all."

"Why should I believe a double agent?" Boris was not easily convinced.

"It was a chance I had to take. Tell Rose the suitcase is open... she will know what it means. And tell her not to be at the celebration tomorrow."

Without another word, Peter opened the door, and left the building.

Dimitri and I reached the edge of the field behind his house. Leaving the cover of the trees, we sprinted into the recently harvested open land. There was a stand of trees behind his house, and we hoped no one would see us as we crossed.

The crisp fall air and the clear blue sky made the whole thing seem ridiculous. It had turned into such a pretty day. We could have been on a farm in Minnesota. My mind wanted to wander there, but I forced myself to face the situation. We reached the other side without being seen, our hearts pumping from the running, racing with fear.

We crouched low by the base of a big old tree and Dimitri stood up, holding his hand flat to tell me to stay low. He boldly walked to the back of the house and edged his way around, listening under every window as he went.

I waited for the sound of the scooter, but it never came. Dimitri did not come back into view, and I couldn't wait any longer. I sprinted for the house, tracing his steps.

I listened carefully as I edged around the corners of the house, finally reaching the front. There was Dimitri, and he wasn't alone!

Just like in the movies, I stepped on an old dry twig - and it snapped loudly, giving my position away.

"Come on out, Rose!" I recognized Victor's voice, and expected to see Vladimir at any moment. I stepped out to face him - but not too close.

Victor had one hand on Dimitri's shoulder, holding him lightly. Both of us were ready to run. Alexander was nowhere to be seen, and must not have been home. I kept my eyes from going to the covered up scooter, and thought furiously of escape.

But Victor knew what I was thinking. "The suitcase is open, Rose," he said.

At first I thought the Russians had compromised Zip. That was a phrase I heard from my Dad and Aunt Susan. But then I remembered my thoughts on the plane about Vlad's "assistants". I decided to test my hunch.

"But the bag is Zipped," I replied.

Victor let go of Dimitri's shoulder. "Thank God!" Victor said. "I have been trying to let you know we are on your side! We are here to help you."

"Who is "we"?" I asked.

"Peter and I; we are double agents, under cover for The Agency. We were sent to New York to get Vladimir off your tail. When he kidnapped you and Susan, we had no choice but to stay with him and keep you safe."

"Then why didn't you stop him at the airport?" I was not convinced of his story.

"We told Vladimir he was to return to Russia. We were to escort him to his plane. The Agency arranged for him to board. The maid at your hotel found a note in your pocket, and tipped Vladimir off about your decoys. In the restroom, he encountered Steven, and used the chloroform in his pocket. We were told to avoid an international incident, to stay low key. When Vlad left the restroom, he threatened to have your parents killed if anyone interfered with is plan. He was desperate to save face with his bosses, and had already decided to kidnap you and Susan - and sway your father to let the hard-liners attend the trade meeting. We were afraid to stop him for fear of his threat."

"Then why haven't you contacted my father, or The Agency and sent me home?"

"Unlike you and Susan, we do not wear COM links. Also, if our cover was blown, we could be arrested or killed - and it would not help you or Susan. Or us."

"COM links? I don't have one," I said, a questioning look on my face.

"You did. It was in the jacket Doe gave you."

The jacket! Oh no! Dimitri and I looked at each other. Anna was wearing it now! I wondered where they were. And was the COM link working? Why hadn't anyone come to get me?

Something in Victor's face told me we could trust him, and we all relaxed. Sitting on the steps of the old front porch I looked at Victor and told him our plan.

He smiled and nodded, impressed. I asked him what he thought we should do.

"Carry out your plan," he said. "We will watch Vladimir, and keep you safe until you leave.

"Peter and I came today to tell you not to go to the celebration tomorrow night. Vladimir still plans to use you as a hostage to escape Russia. We believe he will be on the bus when you leave Gzhel. He plans to convince Doctor Schaeffer to let him accompany you to New York. He is using threats to Doctor Schaeffer's business; – you, Susan, and your family.

"There is nothing more dangerous than a cornered rat. Vladimir still has many loyal contacts, and could make good on his threats. The safest thing to do is let him escape, and arrest him in New York. Your father must be looking for you now. Informants of the Russian Agency have told Vlad your father and Susan are attempting to locate you. He will catch up with you shortly."

"Then we must go to the dance!" I said, standing up, "We can't make Vlad suspicious."

"My father can accompany us, Rose. He is planning on being there. The whole town is watching you and Vlad. They will not let any harm come to you."

"It's not just me I'm thinking of. I don't want anyone to get hurt!" Especially Dimitri and his family, I thought.

Victor stood up. "Do not worry, Rose. We will get you home. I must go now. When you see us at the celebration, you must pretend you don't know us. You are Anna, and Anna does not know us. Be careful in the meantime that Vladimir does not find you, for he does not care how he gets results. We must let him get on that bus."

We watched him walk away. He had come on foot, walking across town so Vlad would not be suspicious.

Dimitri and I went into the house to wait for his father. If we had followed Victor down the road, we would have seen him getting into Vladimir's car...

Chapter Thirty-Two

I was worried about Anna. I had no idea there was a COM in my new jacket! Vlad was here in Gzhel, but what if had sent someone else to intercept her and Svetlana?

We decided to risk a phone call to Dimitri's cousins in Vladimir. After all, it would not be unusual for Dimitri to call. In fact it would be expected! We were both nervous as we dialed the phone.

It was late afternoon, and Alexander would be coming home soon. Anna and her mother should have arrived. I realized they would miss the celebration also. I told Dimitri how bad I felt about all of this.

"They knew they would miss this, Rose. They went at the request of my Aunt and Uncle. What a strange circle! They are in Minnesota and you are here!"

The operator came on, and helped Dimitri with the call. Finally we were able to connect. Dimitri asked for Vassily, the oldest boy.

"Yes, they are here," he said. "I will put them on."

Dimitri smiled with relief as he waited.

"Hello, Dimitri," his mother said. "Yes, we arrived safely. Everything is fine but we found our suitcase was open and there were extras in the bag..."

Dimitri relayed this comment to me, and my heart started beating rapidly! Was it Dad and Aunt Susan, or Vlad and Company?

I knew they could not trust the phone. Dimitri thought carefully before answering.

"Were our surprises welcome?" He asked.

"Well, at first we did not know what they were. But we discovered they were a pleasant surprise, and were very welcome."

"Is your trip on schedule?" Dimitri again was very clever on the phone.

"Yes, all is according to plan. They were the approved editions."

"And how are the flowers?" Dimitri said, smiling.

"The Roses are well. But they cannot be in the sun too long, so we cannot stand and talk now. There will be time for that later. The Lazy Susans look well, also. All of the children are accounted for. We must be patient until they are reunited with their parents. We must go now. There is love sent to all. Your father will be home soon. Be sure to tell him of my love, and watch my Ramblin' Rose."

Dimitri and I were both crying as he relayed my father's message. I went up to Anna's room, and laid on her bed. I cried myself to sleep, and Dimitri woke me later for dinner.

We sat at the table with Alexander that evening, recounting all the events of the day, and making plans for the next day. His face showed anger at the danger we had been placed in, and frustration at the necessity of our plan.

"This is not right! No child or family should be the pawn of politics! Lord, will the world ever be free from this?" He stood and sat again and stood and paced and finally settled down. He was angry at not being able to march up to his enemy and face him. Just like my Dad, I thought.

"Father, you must be calm. Tomorrow at the celebration you must control your anger. Vladimir must not get away! If he escapes in Russia we may never be free of him or his kind. And if he is arrested, he may escape. Rose's family must meet her in New York where they will be safe from any assassins near their home. Our governments must continue to work together to promote free enterprise." Dimitri was passionate and once again surprised me with his level of understanding.

"Ah, Dimitri, you are a smart boy." Pride showed on Alexander's face as he looked at his son. "Yes, sometimes we must fight with our brains. I will talk to people tomorrow, and we will watch Vladimir like hawks!"

"Now I know where Dad and Aunt Susan were all this time," I said, changing the subject. "They were after the COM link in the jacket I gave Anna! At least they were being watched, also! I guess you and my Dad have traded places…"

"It is a fair exchange," Alexander smiled.

Later, we heard the story of my rescue on the road to Vladimir.

Chapter Thirty-Three

Svetlana looked into the mirror. The black car was nowhere in sight. They had gotten a good head start when the man had approached them. Anna was proud of her mother's driving skills.

If they could just get to the house before he caught them, they could hide the car and be safe. It looked like they were going to make it.

Susan was staring out the window. What was it that that seemed so familiar? Thinking back to New York, she remembered Kate and Doe. A woman and a girl! Of course! Rose was probably not in the car! She tried to tell Dad, but he wouldn't listen. He had felt helpless the whole time, and now he was in action!

The speedometer climbed higher as Susan put more pieces into place. Rose must have escaped, and gone to Gzhel looking for us. We had probably just left. Using her wits, she would have remembered what Steven had done in New York. Zip had brought up a list of Alexander and Svetlana's children. They had a twelve-year-old daughter named Anna. A description of the girl matched Rose close enough to have inspired the same plan! Add to this the relationship of Anna's uncle and aunt, the very same people who had gone to Minnesota! Could there be any other explanation? Since there was no stopping Dad, she might just as well wait until they caught up with them. Everything would fall into place.

Dad drove like a maniac, pushing the car to its limit. They finally spotted the Citroen, and followed it down a rural road outside of town.

Just when Svetlana thought they were clear of the black car and made the turn down the dirt road to her sister's house, she caught a glimpse of it in her side mirror. There was no escaping now. They would run out of fuel if they kept driving.

Dad watched the Citroen pull over again, but this time he did not pull in behind it. Instead he pulled up alongside of it, trapping the driver inside. He rolled down the power window, and shouted past Susan.

"Identify yourselves!" He ordered.

"Identify yourself!" Svetlana shouted back.

Susan said, "Hold it! Stop! I will not be in the middle of this! Rose, is that you in there?"

"My name is not Rose, it is Anna!" The girl said. "And this is my mother. We are on the way to visit my cousins, and I have had enough of adults! I am missing everything because of stupid adults!"

Dad spoke up, smiling now at Anna's temperament. "That could be my Rose! Sometimes she's a little thorny too!"

Dad introduced us, and said, "We are friends. Vladimir has kidnapped my daughter, Rose, and we are trying to find her. Anna looks a lot like her. And that is her jacket, isn't it?"

"Rose gave it to me. We are working with her. She is trying to get home, and we have a plan." Anna was proud to be helping me.

"I think we should drive to the house, and we will start again," Svetlana said.

The farmhouse reminded Dad of Minnesota, too. He was as homesick as I was. He had been in Russia long enough! Away from his wife and family. And now running all over Russia in search of me! He was tired. Tired of his job, tired of Vladimir, and tired of saving the world. There was a new crop of young agents at The Agency. Maybe it was time to let them take over. His assistant had finished the job he had started, and Zip reported all had gone well with the trade meeting. Maybe it was time to move into the private sector...

Susan brought him back to the present. His mind had been ramblin', and he hadn't heard the introductions.

"Hey! Are you okay?" She asked him. "Svetlana has been trying to introduce you to her nephews and niece."

Dad looked at the lineup. There was Vassily, about fourteen, he guessed. Sergei, about ten, Yuri was eight, and little sister Katarina about six. She was hiding behind Vassily, peeking out from his legs shyly.

And Anna, who looked a lot like me.

His heart ached for his daughter, and home.

Finally he regained his composure and introduced himself to the children, smiling, and happy to be around a family again.

Svetlana invited him into the kitchen for some tea or coffee with Susan and Anna. The rest of the children followed, excited to have visitors.

As they crowded around the table, Dad asked Anna about the plan she had mentioned.

Anna repeated the plan as best as she could and Svetlana corrected her when necessary. Finally they looked at Dad and Susan for confirmation.

Dad smiled. He was happy to hear that I was safe. He was also impressed with the plan we had put together. He looked up at Susan, who nodded .

"I think it's a good plan, and we should let the children carry it out. When Peter let me escape he told me he and Victor would watch out for Rose, and keep her safe from Vladimir. Now we know where she is, and she is surrounded by friends!"

"Susan, contact The Agency, and let them know what the plan is. We have some calls to make tonight, but we'll have to use Zip.

"Okay, Boss!" Susan replied, smiling.

"Anna, may I see your jacket?" Dad wanted to check the COM.

There was no way for Dad to get a message to me. Not trusting the Russian Agency fully, he did not want to risk using the phone. Since it was late, Svetlana suggested they stay overnight, and wait until the next day to try to contact us.

"Perhaps Dimitri and Rose will call us," she said, as she finished her tea.

Chapter Thirty-Four

Back at home; Mom was just pouring herself a cup of tea. She was sitting alone at the kitchen table. It was early morning, and Richard had not come in yet. Sam was still asleep on Rose's bed. Mom was tired.

She was tired of keeping busy by herself. She was tired of Dad being gone all the time, off saving the world. She was tired of being strong. Her daughter was missing, and the world seemed no better off than when they had started all of this.

She was tired of keeping her secret life from me, too. Maybe when this was all over they could retire; or at least move into the private sector. She had already established that with her consulting firm.

Why didn't someone call? What was happening? The soothing herbal tea did not seem to be working. She could not concentrate on anything today. Her secretary was running everything through this whole crisis. Maybe it was time to stop trying to be everything; to let the younger generation have their turn. Maybe it was time to let go a little of the world they thought they had built. "But we did move it along a little, didn't we?" She asked herself.

Sam had finally awakened. He seemed to have the doldrums too. Usually he bounded down the steps, as if he suddenly remembered he had to go out. Now, it seemed half of his spirit was gone. He seemed resigned to the fact of another day without his friend. He walked into the kitchen, head hung low, and stood with his nose to the back door. He did not even look at Mom.

Automatically, Mom got up and opened the back door. She suddenly felt old. Was this what her life would be like? An old lady with an old dog? No life, no hope, no family? Nothing to do but get through the day?

She resolved when her family was back home, things would change. She would home-school Rose, she thought. And any assignments we take will be as a husband and wife team! If we travel, we'll all travel!

Making a new plan brought her spirits up. She was not old, and refused to go quietly, as she often had said. Determination marched back into her eyes. It was time to stop acting like a victim, and start living! They would take charge from now on, refusing to be dictated to!

Samson The Great returned to the door, and Mom opened it to let him in.

"Wake up you lazy mutt! How are you going to protect Rose with that attitude?"

She said it lovingly, but sternly. At the mention of my name Samson perked up. His tail started to wag, and he looked around expectantly, as if I might be there. He started running around the house, sniffing corners, barking and working himself into a frenzy.

Mom laughed, and the whole day seemed to brighten up. Hope came back into her eyes, and by the time Richard knocked on the back door things were pretty much back to normal.

Richard looked terrible! Mom realized for the first time how important I was to him. Many times she had resented sharing me with Richard, but she was grateful he was there. He had filled in for both her and Dad many times. He was part of the family after all. Now he was sharing the frustration and waiting.

Looking into each other's eyes, they could see all the unsaid things, and admit in their own ways how much they loved me. Hearing about all this later, I realized how lucky I was to have the family I had.

"Would you like some breakfast, Richard?" Mom asked and went about making it before he answered. Richard sat at the table petting Sam while the smell of sizzling bacon and eggs filled the room.

"Do you remember when Rose was six, and her grandfather would put her on his knee, and tell those wild stories?" He asked. "I always thought someday I would have a child to tell my stories to."

"Richard, we'll have to be glad for what we have. Rose will be back. In many ways she is your daughter too! Susan and her Dad are looking for her now. Any minute now the phone will ring, and we'll find out when she's coming home. And when she does, there will be some changes around here!"

"What kind of changes?" Richard asked. He had also grown tired of the routine. As a bodyguard, he did not like the family being scattered so much. One person could not cover them all. Even with his connections in The Agency, like the stewardess at the airline who had watched

Susan and Rose get off the plane, and Zip, it was too much. At least until Rose was grown they needed a better operation.

"We are going to start a family business! Rose will be home-schooled, and we'll move into the private sector as a team. We can all be partners. What do you think?"

"I like the idea! At least until we all get rich and retire! There is danger in the private sector too," he reminded her.

"I know, but we will be able to control it better. We'll have more choice in the assignments we take. We can still take contract work for The Agency, and have access to Zip! We won't have to keep any secrets from Rose anymore."

"There are two more people we have to talk to first," he reminded Mom.

"Of course, but my mother's intuition tells me they are thinking similar thoughts right about now."

Richard smiled and nodded. His connection with the family told him she was right. He changed the subject. "How are our Russian friends doing?"

"They opened in the Mega Mall this weekend. So far they have had many customers. People who had never seen Russian art before. A lot of them were impressed with the quality of it. I think their business will be a success, and eventually they will move their family here. I wonder how the children are getting along. They are on holiday from school this week.

Their Aunt Svetlana and her daughter were going to stay with them until their mother returns next week. Their father is going to stay here, and oversee the business until spring. If all goes well they will move here in the spring."

"What a strange twist," Richard said, "They are over here and Rose is over there! I wonder what is going to happen next!"

Just then the phone rang. Mom picked it up and started to cry. It was Dad.

"You'll never guess where he's calling from!" Mom said to Richard.

"Is Rose safe?" He asked.

"Yes, and she's coming home!" Mom waved his questions aside and listened to Dad.

At the same time, both of their pagers went off. It was The Agency.

"Richard, call the airlines! We're going to New York!"

Chapter Thirty-Five

Wednesday was finally here! Tomorrow morning I would be on the plane going back to the good ol' USA! This was the best day on this crazy adventure yet! I never realized how homesick I could get. This was worse than summer camp last year. The first few days were exciting, and then I started thinking of home. Maybe that's why we look for the familiar things when we travel.

Anna's room was nice, small, and cozy, and I liked her posters. Her bed was covered with handmade quilts and pillowcases her mother and grandmother had embroidered. But it wasn't my room. Dimitri and his father did not see me cry myself to sleep every night. They thought I was so brave. It's not hard to be brave when you don't have a choice.

Dimitri was so excited about today! First we were going to the factory and finish the piece I was making for my mother. I hoped she wasn't too worried about me. I hope Aunt Susan had contacted her and told her the situation. Doctor Schaeffer said he was going to contact The Agency. Surely, Dad would show up soon...

Sheesh! There I go, ramblin' again! We had a plan at least, and we were following it!

But back to the porcelain. I wanted to bring Mother something special for all she had gone through this past week. That's why I told Dimitri at breakfast I did not want to paint it myself. I had watched the artists and master craftsmen at work, painting the delicate little blue designs on the porcelain, and knew I did not have enough practice to do it well.

Dimitri finally gave up and said he'd have one of the masters paint it for me. I was happy with the finished work! Mother would still be proud!

We had spent the morning at the factory, after a careful walk watching for Vladimir. But today I felt defiant, and we boldly walked right past the bed and breakfast, almost daring him to try something!

What we didn't know was Vlad had been watching out the window and again, Natasha had seen us coming. She had stepped in front of Vlad so he would not see us! She may have taken his money, but she wasn't going to rat on a couple of kids!

Boris had looked around nervously when he opened the door. He told us about Peter's message, and we told him what had happened after we went out the back door. We asked him to keep an eye out for any of Vlad and Company today.

Word had gotten around the factory quickly, and several people came up to us, and told us not to worry. They would be watching out for us at the dinner and dance tonight! Just let Vlad try something now!

At dinnertime we went back to Dimitri's house. Doctor Schaeffer had called and said he would see us at the dinner. He was going to introduce us to the President of the Gzhel Association.

He also said he would be staying at the bed and breakfast tonight, as his business in Moscow was complete, and he would be on the bus with us Thursday morning. He was in charge from then on.

Back at Dimitri's house, I looked through Anna's things. She had a traditional Russian dress she said I could wear tonight. I looked for it in her closet and found it in a box, wrapped in tissue paper. It must have been very special. I felt bad again for her not being here. I did not want to steal her moment. I swore I would make this up to her!

"Have fun," she'd said, "or none of this will be worth anything!"

So, I decided to just that!

I tried the dress on, and asked Dimitri to come and look.

He had never seen me in a dress.

"Wow!" You look like a girl..." he stopped when he saw my hurt look. I know I am only twelve, and something of a tomboy, but I am a girl - and like to be treated like one!

I forgave him, and took his comment as a compliment. I felt like a girl. No, a princess! A Russian princess like Katarina! And here was my prince!

Now, to go downstairs and get the approval of the King...

Alexander broke into tears when he saw me in Anna's dress. He didn't sob; the tears just kind of kind of leaked out of the corners of his eyes. He missed his wife and daughter. I missed my Dad and Mom, so I guess things evened out. We would have to make do.

120

Still, it was pretty intense!

The dance was held at the Grand Hotel, the original site of the trade meeting.

The ballroom was filled with tables, decorated in white linen with Gzhel porcelain and flowers. It was beautiful!

Alexander watched his young son and I. He saw him growing up. He was a chaperone tonight! And he watched for Vladimir.

Dimitri tried to explain the history of the traditional Russian dancers we would see after dinner, but I wasn't taking any notes. Tonight I did not want to be a reporter. I just wanted to have fun.

We ate a beautiful catered dinner with Dimitri playing the distinguished gentleman, being very careful not to spill anything on his suit. He was nervous, probably because he was with a girl who was not his sister.

Before going up on stage after dinner, Doctor Schaeffer came and sat at our table. He gave us a brief description of what the president would say, and congratulated us all. We would talk again after the dance.

Vladimir did not make an appearance until the dance had started.

When dinner was over, Doctor Schaeffer left our table, and went up onstage. He introduced himself to the audience, most of whom knew him anyway. Then he gave a brief history of the upcoming trip. He mentioned all the participants, and asked them to stand and bow. Each was applauded heartily. I got my first look at the kids from the other villages that would be on the plane tomorrow.

As the festivities went on, I felt more and more like an imposter. I did not belong there. But it was the only way I had of getting home.

I wanted to quit right there and call my Dad - bugged phones or not! I wanted Anna to be in her rightful place! I would have quit, too! But Vladimir wouldn't let me!

Chapter Thirty-Six

There was a lot going on that I did not know about. While we were watching the Russian dancers in their white flowing sleeves and bright red sashes, several unexpected guests arrived.

In spite of all the people who said they would watch out for me, Vladimir walked right up to our table. He looked at me searchingly as he asked Alexander where he might find Doctor Schaeffer.

Before Alexander could respond, Vladimir said, "What a handsome family you have! Perhaps you will introduce me..."

Alexander kept his cool. "This is my son, Dimitri, and his sister, Anna."

"A pleasure to meet you, both," Vlad said with a slight bow. He looked at me quizzically, as if he might know me from somewhere else. Then he turned and left.

I was afraid to look around for Peter and Victor until Vlad had walked away. I did not see them anywhere. We watched as Vlad stopped at Natasha's table, and after a brief exchange he moved on.

Our attention turned to the stage as Doctor Schaeffer tapped on the microphone.

"Applaud for our wonderful dancers! They will return after a short rest. In the interim, I would like to present Illya Federovsky, President of the Gzhel Association!"

It was the same man Aunt Susan had talked to on Zip, in my room!

Applause erupted from all of the tables. Everyone in Gzhel was proud of what the Association was doing. This was their life.

Illya thanked Doctor Schaeffer. "A big thank you, Doctor, to you! You have done so much to bring our art to the world! And opportunities to our children, we are so proud!"

I joined in the applause for Doctor Schaeffer, who bowed humbly and smiled. He walked off behind the stage.

The president continued his speech. "As you know, the trade meeting was moved to a secret location in Moscow. I am happy to report to you the interests of the Gzhel Association were expanded. We have more freedom to export our work to the United States with fewer tariffs. Also, we have new retail outlets, such as the one being established in Minnesota, increasing demand and production. This will bring more work and financial benefits to our community!"

Dimitri translated for me as the people broke into thunderous applause. I was happy and surprised to hear about Minnesota. When the noise settled down, the president continued his report.

"Also there was a decision to increase tariffs on "non-artistic" porcelain. This will encourage and subsidize the efforts of our artists as well as limit the cheap "sweat shop" products that continue to suppress our people. Many of these products help fund the enemies of free enterprise."

Again there was much applause as Dimitri tried to translate over the noise. The president raised his hand, quieting the crowd, as he concluded his speech.

"So, my friends, as we celebrate the upcoming show in New York, and our artists, and children, who will be attending, let us also celebrate our victory at the trade meeting!"

As the room once more exploded with applause, Illya left the stage.

Alexander and Dimitri smiled, and I looked around for Peter and Victor. They were still nowhere to be seen.

Backstage, the three men I had been looking for had confronted Doctor Schaeffer.

"Congratulations, Doctor. Things seem to be going your way. Let us find a place where we can talk," Vlad said as he drew his gun from his suit pocket.

"What could there be for us to talk about, Vladimir?" He answered defiantly.

"A simple request, Doctor. We will be on that plane with you tomorrow."

"The arrangements have already been made, I cannot get you on that plane!"

"Let us step into this dressing room, and I will explain. If you refuse, you will be endangering many friends…"

Vladimir smiled menacingly. He might have lost with his plan, but his escape seemed certain.

Peter and Victor followed silently.

Out front, the dancers took the stage again, performing a lively dance of celebration.

We watched from our table, entranced.

As the dance was ending, I was surprised by Vlad's sudden appearance.

"Well, "Anna", it appears you and Dimitri will be on the plane tomorrow! My congratulations! It will be well for the people you care about to see you are there."

My heart was pounding with fear. If I had any thoughts about quitting, they were gone now!

Before I could answer, he was gone! Dimitri and Alexander had hardly noticed! They had been busy watching the stage.

Things were getting intense! Not only had Vlad slipped in and out without being noticed, but also Peter and Victor were nowhere to be seen! I gave up looking for them.

What other surprises were in store tonight? I knew after the dancers had finished their final performance, all of the participants of the New York exhibit were to line up on stage and take a bow. Doctor Schaeffer had already presented us at our tables, but wanted us to be honored together. I did not want to take Anna's place. I also was nervous about being in front of so many people!

"Dimitri, do I have to go on stage with you?" I asked.

A voice from behind me answered, "Only if Anna is not here!"

I turned around to see Anna and her mother!

Svetlana pulled out the chair next to her husband and sat down. She was smiling at the surprise on our faces. "I will explain everything!"

Anna sat next to me, smiling. She was wearing one of her other dresses.

"We stopped at the house on the way over so I could change. Rose, when we go onstage and line up, you are to slip behind the curtains. There is someone who wants to see you."

Tears formed in my eyes, and butterflies invaded my stomach. I was too choked up to answer. I just nodded, crying. It must be Dad!

"We brought all of the children with us. We did not want to miss Anna's big night!" Svetlana smiled and hugged Alexander's arm.

I looked around to see Anna's cousins being seated at one of the remaining tables.

Doctor Schaeffer walked onto the stage. "Were not the dancers wonderful?"

More applause erupted as the dancers bowed one by one and exited the stage.

"And now I would like to honor all of the participants in the upcoming show! Would you all please come on stage, and take a bow!"

As the room continued to applaud, each of the New York participants made their way to the stage. I followed Anna, my heart beating in my ears. I couldn't wait to see Dad!

Anna, Dimitri, and I were going to be center stage! I stepped backward before the line was in place, slipping through the curtains with hardly a ripple. No one noticed.

As I backed through to the other side, a pair of strong arms grabbed my shoulders, and spun me around. I knew my Dad's grip and threw my arms around him, crying for joy! I saw Aunt Susan standing behind him. She was crying too!

"Shhh! Not a word," Dad said, "we must get out of here before Vlad sees us. Peter and Victor are keeping him occupied."

I was too busy sobbing to talk anyway. And not talking was rare for me!

While the festivities continued out front, we left through the backstage door.

Dad's black BMW was waiting, and we drove off without lights. I kept my head down as we drove to Dimitri's house, while Dad and Susan hid the car under a tarp from the trunk, behind the woodpile.

"Must have learned that one from Dimitri," I thought as we quietly entered the house.

Once inside, Dad quickly explained the plan.

"Vladimir must be on that plane tomorrow. It is important he be arrested in the United States. Peter and Victor must get home safely; it is dangerous for them here. They have been watching over you all along. Doctor Schaeffer is helping us - and both you, and Anna will be on the plane. Vlad has seen you, and may recognize that Anna is not you. He does not know all of the children from the other villages, and Anna will be in another group, posing as one of them. Susan and I will be on the plane also, but Vladimir must not see us. We will be traveling with the luggage...when we arrive in New York...well, we'll cross that bridge later."

I knew Dad wanted to tell me more, but I was happy just to see him and Aunt Susan.

Dad looked at me, "Well, Ramblin' Rose, don't you have anything to say?"

I looked at them and laughed, "Sheesh! I've heard of "Take Your Kids to Work Day" - but this is ridiculous!"

In a way, I was glad the plane ride would be so long, because no one was going to get much sleep tonight!

Chapter Thirty-Seven

No one got much sleep that night, especially me, I was so happy to see Dad and Aunt Susan. I knew everything would be okay again.

Everyone was excited about the trip to New York, about leaving home for the first time, and I was excited about going home. I couldn't wait to see Mom, Richard, and Samson! To get back to my real life again, where I was comfortable.

Still, everyone here had accepted me the way I was, even if I looked like someone else.

We had big breakfast in the Grand Hotel. The tables were filled just like the night before.

I sat with Dimitri, Anna, and their parents. We ate a hearty breakfast like Russians do, and talked about the events of the last week. We laughed and cried.

My thoughts were all jumbled up as we said goodbye to Dimitri's parents, and boarded the bus. I choked up when Alexander handed me my old suitcase, and said he felt like they were sending off three children...

Dimitri and I had to sit together on the bus. Anna was supposed to be from another village, and so she sat across the aisle from us. I was so happy Dad and Susan found a way for her not to have to miss this trip! When Dad heard the sacrifice she was willing to make for me, he said Anna was like his daughter too.

He thanked Alexander, Svetlana, and Dimitri - as well as the whole town - for looking out for me. Of course, Dad and Aunt Susan had to leave very early to carry out their part of the plan. They had to get to the airport before we did - without Vladimir seeing them!

Illya, Boris, and the other people from the factory were there to see us off. Illya winked at me, and I gave Boris a hug and a kiss on the cheek. He blushed and turned his head to wipe his eye.

When all the participants were finally on the bus, a black limousine with a Russian flag on each front fender pulled in front of it.

Vladimir! He was going to pose as an official from the government to get on that plane! Peter and Victor were in the car also. Our "escort"!

The people from the villages waved in the early morning fog, the driver put the bus in gear, and we were off! I watched out the side window as I left the town of Gzhel for the last time.

The motor growled and chugged as the bus picked up speed. The gears whined and finally settled into a high-pitched drone. The noise of the passengers increased though, as they buzzed and chatted about the big trip!

Doctor Schaeffer had gone ahead to supervise loading of the exhibit and our luggage, which was to be handled by Dad and Aunt Susan. Posing as luggage handlers, they would stay on board the plane in the cargo area when the plane took off.

Everything was in place. I checked my COM link and settled in, realizing how natural it had become to think like an agent. But there was nothing to do at the moment but be a kid and talk to Dimitri and Anna. We didn't have to worry about anyone hearing us.

"I just realized," I said, "I have not learned any Russian words the whole time I've been here! I'll have to study when I get home."

"We must practice our English," Dimitri said. "It is good you were here. It has helped prepare us for the show."

"Well, I guess I won't need it right now anyway. Dimitri, where is the piece I made for my mother?"

"Doctor Schaeffer packed it with the show. It is safe. Your mother must be proud of you. She must be a special lady," Dimitri was always the gentleman!

"I have missed her so much. I wish you could meet her!" I said, tears welling up in my eyes.

"Perhaps we will," Anna spoke up from across the aisle. "We are young, and have much time."

The noise on the bus quieted as we all looked at the Russian countryside, and kept to our own thoughts. The bus stayed quiet until we approached Moscow, and the hubbub began again.

It never stopped until we were all settled in on the plane, and the captain told us to buckle our seat belts.

I was happy to see that Vladimir was seated up front, where I could keep an eye on him. So far he had not noticed Anna. But it was a long flight, and a lot of people were on board.

Again, Dimitri and I were seated next to each other. Anna was farther up on the left with another group. She had friends from the other villages, and was busy talking to them. There was no reason for Vlad to notice her.

I thought about Dad and Aunt Susan as the plane left the ground. I cleared my throat to let them know my COM link was on.

Down below, Dad and Aunt Susan were making themselves as comfortable as possible. It was hard for them to hold on as the plane left the runway and climbed to cruising altitude. They had removed the coveralls they had used as a disguise, and when the plane leveled off they set up Zip on Dad's laptop. It was going to be a long flight, but they had a lot to do.

They agreed to sleep in shifts, and listen to the COM link to make sure I was safe. They knew Vlad would grab me as a hostage if he needed one. If he knew who I was! We couldn't be sure about that.

I felt really safe. Dad and Aunt Susan were below; Peter and Victor were watching Vlad, who still did not know they were double agents. Doctor Schaeffer was sitting across from Vlad, and Dimitri next to me.

What could Vlad do up here anyway? He was only interested in getting off the plane, and disappearing in New York.

Dimitri leaned over me to look out the window at the sight of Moscow dropping away. We had never been so close. Emotion welled up in his eyes as he watched his home fade into the distance. Now he was the one away from home.

When he sat back up, he turned to look at me. "Rose, I have just realized how much I…"

I held up my hand to stop him. I put a finger to my lips, and said silently, "Shhh!" Pointing to my chest I reminded him of the COM link. My dad was listening!

He nodded, frustrated we could not talk. I took a pad and pen from my bag. A journalist was always prepared! I knew what he was going to say, and was glad Dad was listening so I wouldn't have to face the same thoughts. I still had a crush on him, and now that we were going to part in New York, I was no longer like a sister to him. But we were too young to be serious.

As for Dimitri, I was the first girl he really knew outside of his sisters, and after the adventure we had both been involved in he felt a bond between us. He shook his head at the pad and pen at first, then took it and wrote, "I love you!"

Handing the pen back to me, he looked me in the eyes to emphasize his message.

Sheesh! This was too intense! I finally had a boyfriend, but he lived half way around the world!

I looked back at him, trying to tell him with my eyes the mixed-up emotions in me. I had been so busy trying to get back home I had not let myself think too much about the crush I had on him. It was just a schoolgirl crush, I hoped.

Down below, Dad wondered why it was so quiet up here. Some instinct told him there was a silent communication going on, and he thought he knew what it was.

Susan heard Dimitri's comment also. She looked over at Dad and smiled. Typical Dad! She thought, grateful some things never change. She remembered her own Dad, and missed how he would try to protect her heart.

The plane droned on, and Susan told Dad to sleep, that she would take the first shift, and not to worry about me. "Give them some time to themselves," she thought, but did not say out loud

Sitting so close to Dimitri, we both had trouble shielding our thoughts. It was going to be a long flight! I decided to sleep awhile to give us both some space.

I drifted off, thinking of home. Dimitri watched me with puppy-dog eyes until he too, finally fell asleep, his head dropping onto my shoulder.

In the luggage compartment, Susan smiled as she heard the sound of our breathing.

Chapter Thirty-Eight

When I woke up, most of the people on the plane were sleeping. I gently moved Dimitri's head back to his own seat, and sat up to look around. We were catching up with the sun, and it still looked like early morning to me. I looked at my watch, and realized I had been asleep for about two hours. The other people on the plane must have talked longer, and they were still zonked.

Most of them had been at the celebration the night before and stayed out late. They had been too excited to sleep. Now it was catching up with them, which was a blessing on this flight, I knew.

The meals helped to break up the monotony. The fifteen hours seemed to go faster when you ate, slept, ate, and slept. I am not a fan of airline meals, but they were sure welcome. The Russian meals were not that much different than American ones.

I thought about Dad and Aunt Susan. How would they use the bathroom? They had to be careful not to let Vlad see them. Doctor Schaeffer had arranged for food. They had roast beef sandwiches, beverages and fruit.

I found out later, there was an access panel to the rear restroom. Dad had to resist the temptation to arrest Vlad on the plane. He did not want anyone to get hurt, or risk the safety of the plane.

He also had to resist the temptation to spy on Dimitri and me; but I know he did.

Vladimir must have sensed my presence, as he woke up, turning his head to look across the sleeping people, and stare at me. He had a quizzical look on his face as our eyes met, and I could see his brain working. He stood up to stretch, and looked over the passengers on his side. That's when he spotted Anna. He looked back and forth, comparing us, and his eyes took on a knowing look.

He wasn't sure which of us was which, but he knew he had at least one hostage if things went bad. He sat down again, smugly, and I watched his shoulders sigh in contentment. I could imagine his smile of satisfaction. He settled in and went back to sleep. He had been on this flight before, too.

I stared out the window wondering what was happening back home.

Mom looked at her watch. It was 8:30 a.m., New York time. She was first to the table in the hotel's restaurant. Richard was to join her for breakfast. They had rooms at the same hotel Susan and I had stayed at.

Steven had picked them up at the airport the night before and drove them to the hotel in his cab. They had gone over the plan, and he would return this morning. Kate and Doe would be with him. Steven couldn't wait for the plane to land. He had felt responsible for Vlad kidnapping us, and had been worried the whole time for our safety. Seeing me with Susan, he'd had made up his mind he was not going to let her get away again. He was going to ask her to marry him! They could go into business for themselves working in the private sector. Maybe even start a family...

Kate and Doe were having breakfast in their apartment. They had been so happy when The Agency had called. Worried about our safety, they jumped at the news we were coming home and a chance to be a part of the plan to capture Vladimir! They took out wigs and costumes. Steven would be picking them up early this afternoon.

Vlad had no idea what was waiting for him in New York!

When Susan woke up, Dad was talking to The Agency. "Everything's in place then? That's right, no uniforms. Let Vlad think he's just going to walk away. We don't want to endanger Rose or the other children. He will be expecting an arrest, and will go for Rose or Anna as a hostage. We will surprise him like we did in Moscow, and keep him off balance. We will have eight agents on the scene as it is. And Vlad doesn't suspect a thing! When the kids are clear, we'll grab him. Are the decoys in the water?"

Susan propped herself up on a duffle bag, leaning on one elbow. She knew every good plan had a back up. Kate and Doe would be on the scene. Vlad was bound to be confused with three "Roses"! A slight hesitation was all they needed to cuff him!

The biggest surprise of all would be Peter and Victor! They had fooled him all along!

At least, that's what they thought. When Vlad stopped at Natasha's table, she had told him what she had overheard in their room. Vlad had paid her for information, and even though she wouldn't rat on a couple of kids, double agents were another thing!

She told Vlad about Peter and Victor, but not about where I was and she left out the parts of their conversation concerning Dimitri, Anna, and I. Silly agents! They should know more than anyone how the walls have ears...

So Vlad pretended not to know. Forewarned is forearmed! When the plane landed in New York, he would be ready for Peter and Victor, the traitors! With them there The Agency would probably not send anyone else. All he had to do was get away from them and he would be in the clear. He could always grab Rose for a hostage if he needed to. A well-paid contact would be waiting outside with a cab, just like the one Steven drove...

"Good Morning, Richard!" Mother said brightly. "Would you like some coffee?"

"Good morning! Yes, thank you. I just talked to Zip. Everything's in place. We'll have Rose safely back this afternoon!"

"Yes, I was on Zip earlier. I can't wait to see Rose again! I'm so glad the three of them are safe! Though I don't envy them that plane ride!"

"Anna's aunt and uncle will meet us at the show. We don't want them involved at the airport," Richard said, telling Mom what she already knew.

"I'm anxious to meet that girl! Think of all that family has done to help Rose! And I'm dying to meet this Dimitri boy."

"We'll see if his intentions are honorable..."Richard said, protectively.

"Really, Richard. They are just children! You sound like Father Hen!"

"I guess you're right," Richard said, smiling. It was the first time either had laughed in a week.

As they finished their breakfast, a cab pulled up outside of the door. They joined Steven and headed for the airport.

Mom had not seen Steven for some time, and they had a reunion of sorts. Steven apologized for us being kidnapped. It was important for him Mom forgave him.

"Oh, Steven! I don't blame you! That slippery Vlad! Anyway, they are all on their way home! Lets go get them!"

After picking up Kate and Doe, they headed to the airport.

Of course, I didn't know what the rest of the plan was. Maybe Dad did not want me to know. But it's what I didn't know that caused all of the trouble before. I had to trust him. This time it was what Vlad didn't know!

Chapter Thirty-Nine

I was never so glad to see anything in my life! There was the Statue of Liberty! Home. "E.T. Home…" I said to myself. Dimitri was stirring now, and all of the sleeping passengers were waking up. I couldn't stop looking out the window and smiling.

The whole plane was alive with excitement! My heart was beating a mile a minute! Dimitri tapped me on the shoulder. "Well, Rose, I've got to know!" He didn't care about the COM link. I didn't either, but I picked up the pad I had been writing the newsletter on. Dimitri's message was still on the top page.

I wrote "Ditto" on it, and handed it to him. "What is "Ditto"?" He asked.

"It means "me too"," I said smiling. At that moment I loved everybody!

"Oh! Ditto, I like ditto!" He smiled back, lovesick.

I decided not to worry about his definition of it as the plane touched down on the runway. The pilot made a perfect landing, and we rolled up to the gate. I wanted to run off the plane, but had to hold myself in check.

Down below, the plan was in motion. Dad and Aunt Susan had closed up Zip and checked their guns. Vladimir would not have one as far as they knew, but he may have friends waiting. Dad was ready! The combination of being a professional agent, and a father protecting his daughter was a powerful force. Susan was just as intense, and anxious to wrap this up. She had not appreciated a week being taken out of her life, and her niece being kidnapped!

The wrath of this family was going to be worse than anything the Russians would do to Vlad!

Vladimir waited to slip in behind Anna and I as we departed the plane. Dimitri went ahead of us, as Peter and Victor went behind Vlad. Doctor Schaeffer had gotten off first to pick up the exhibit, and herd the participants. He was escorted on a motorized cart by security and met with Dad and Aunt Susan, who were driven back to the gate by another cart. The airport had been alerted by The Agency and was co-operating in the capture.

We walked the short distance through the exit ramp, and out into the gate. I felt Vlad's hands on my shoulders, and tried to shrug him off with a disgusted look. He stayed close. When we entered the gate area he stopped in his tracks! There were "Aunt Susan" and "Rose" looking right at him!

When Vladimir saw Kate and Doe, dressed like Susan and I, he was shocked. He looked around and saw three of us! It took a few seconds to sink in - and just as Peter and Victor tried to grab him, he twisted away.

Then everything happened at once. There was Mom telling me to run to her, Richard beginning to charge, Steven coming from one side and Dad from the other!

As Vlad made a grab for me, Peter pushed him. Falling, he landed at Aunt Susan's feet. Two Susan's? Vlad was confused and struggled to his feet, taking a wooden knife from his stocking as he stood up and held it to Susan's throat!

The threat to Susan stopped Steven in mid-stride. Everyone froze.

"One move - and she dies!" Vlad said as he dragged her around like a rag doll, looking for a way out.

But he couldn't watch everybody.

Dad had been coming from the other side, and grabbed Vlad's arm. He wrestled the knife away from him, freeing Susan. Again Vladimir was knocked off his feet. Dad's gun had been knocked loose also and Vlad picked it up.

Waving the gun, he held everyone back and grabbed me again.

"This girl will die if I am not allowed to leave!" Vlad said coldly.

Well, enough was enough! I threw my arms above my head and slipped down between Vlads' arms. On the way I bent my left arm and used my elbow on his stomach! He doubled over as broke away.

When he stood up again, he was holding the gun high in the air.

Dad dove for him, but Vlad held him about five feet away with the gun.

Richard had been waiting for his chance! Standing on the side of Vlad, with no one in his line of fire, he drew his gun and fired!

The gun flew from Vlads' hand and Dad came up with a right hand, cracking into Vladimir's jaw. Vlad's head flew back from the blow.

"You will never touch my family again!" He said as Peter and Victor each took one of "John Henry's" arms, and held him for the security guards.

Dad looked over at Richard. "I guess we're even now," he said as he rubbed his left shoulder. There was a round of cheers and applause as Vlad was led away.

Epilogue

After many introductions we all headed over to set up the show.

Everything went great. The show was a success and we spent the weekend getting to know each other. Doctor Schaeffer presented my mother with the piece I made, and I apologized for breaking the plate.

"I'm so proud of you, Rose and by the way, you're grounded!" Mother said, then laughed at my shocked expression.

Then she turned her gaze on Susan! And smiled as she hugged her.

Steven and Aunt Susan gave Anna and Dimitri a tour of New York, and promised them another one next year. I went along for the ride, taking over the tourist guide part. I wanted to show Steven how much I remembered!

Along the way they decided to get married, and go into business with Mom and Dad in the private sector.

Maybe they would even have kids!

All of this did not help Dimitri's love-struck state! I had to keep turning his head to the buildings! Sheesh! But Anna was thrilled and really paid attention.

Dad declined any publicity at first, but then decided to use the story of Vlad's arrest to announce his retirement from the Agency. He was going to take a position in the private sector, he told the press.

Finally, Anna, Dimitri, and I were left alone to say goodbye.

"Goodbye, Rose!" Anna said tearfully as she handed back the New York jacket.

"You keep it, Anna. I still have my Levi jacket. You and Dimitri can use the COM link to keep in touch... at least I can hear you..."

I broke off the hug, sobbing, and turned to Dimitri.

"I will never forget you!" He said as we boarded the plane for Minnesota.

"Ditto!" I replied as I hugged him. I turned and ran into the plane. I did not want him to see me cry anymore.

I also did not want to get back on another plane! At least this would be a short flight compared to the one I had just taken!

Funny, all week long all I could think of was getting home, and now I did not want it to end...

We left New York Sunday afternoon, finally arriving home in the evening.

Samson was there to greet us as we opened the front door. Mom and Dad went in first and I was right behind them, carrying the little bowl I had made for Mom.

They got past him pretty easy, but he was waiting for me! Jumping up, he slobbered my face with wet kisses! I went flying backwards, and as I did the little porcelain bowl flew up in the air...

Oh no! Not again! I thought as I landed on my back under the giant dog. The last time I had come home was what had started all this!

But Mom's hand shot out, catching the irreplaceable little bowl like an outfielder!

We all laughed as I rolled around with Samson, who finally let me up.

I had finished writing the newsletter on the plane. It made the deadline, and I was given an award for journalism by the school newsletter association.

I was commended for "heightening awareness of the importance of art in society" and became very popular with the debutantes!

My parents, Uncle Richard, and Aunt Susan and Steven were there as I accepted the award.

Later, I was told that arrangements were being made to home school me. I could still write the newsletter on the Internet, though.

So that's the story of Ramblin' Rose, and my Internet Newsletter. I still wrestle with Samson The Great, every time I come through the door!

The "Distribution Store" opened in the Mall and was a big success! As far as we know, Vlad was put away for a long time! But even Dad could not get a straight answer when he asked about it. The whole thing was hushed up.

Dimitri and I still carry on a long distance romance. We gave each other code names, and now we use Zip's web cam. Dad stopped by my room last night when he heard voices coming from it.

"What are you doing, Rose?"

"Just talking to The Boy Next Door, Dad." I said, thinking he'd picture our neighbor, Steve.

"Oh, well don't stay up too late. We got a call from The Agency. They want us to look into something for them. We'll all be traveling."

"Where are we going this time?" I asked.

"I'll tell you tomorrow. I don't want you talking to Dimitri about it all night!" He said as he walked away.

I signed off the computer, shaking my head and smiling. "Sheesh! The lack of privacy in this world is just too intense! Don't you think so, Grandpa?"

"Oh, by the way, there really are porcelain mines in Russia!"

The End

The Wire Forests of Peru

Ramblin' Rose

Prologue

I remember Grandma and Grandpa's house. It was a big white house by the sea with a white picket fence and a "widows watch" where Grandma used to sit watching the ocean, waiting for Grandpa to come home.

"Just like the sailors in the old days," Mother said. "Of course Grandpa wasn't on an old sailing ship. He owned the shipping company. But Mother used to wait up there anyway. Sometimes we would sit with her, and watch her work, embroidering fancy quilts, table covers, and pillowcases. She still does beautiful work."

"I know," I said, thinking of the handmade pillowcases on my bed, and the quilt on my wall as we drove up to the old house. I was six years old, and it would be the first and last time I would see it, and the last time I would hear them both tell me a story.

We had come to spend the weekend, and as soon as the car stopped I ran inside. The servants were gone now. Grandpa preferred it that way. He was retired, and wanted nothing to interfere with time with Grandma.

I remember the smell of his workshop. Pipe tobacco, sawdust, and the smell of soldered wire. It was a mysterious and fascinating place.

"Grandpa! Where are you?" I hollered as I bolted through the big wooden door.

"In the basement, Rose! Come on down!"

I followed his voice as my parents unloaded the car.

The kitchen was in the back of the house, and I soon found the basement door.

The light was on, and I held the painted railing, carefully navigating the open steps.

"Grandpa! We're here!" I informed him again.

"Is that my favorite girl?" He called out as I approached.

"Depends," I said. "Is that my favorite Grandpa?"

"Well, why don't you come in and see for yourself?"

"Okay, I will!" I said, jumping through the doorway as if to surprise him.

"Well, I'll be darned! Sure looks like my Ramblin' Rose!"

"Sure looks like my Grandpa!" I said, hopping onto his lap as he sat on the stool in front of his workbench.

Hugs and kisses followed and Grandpa added a warning

"Careful, Rose. Don't touch the soldering iron, it's hot!"

"What are you doing, Grandpa?"

"Working on my ham radio."

"I didn't know radios were made out of ham!" I said.

"They're not. People just call them that because they ham it up when they talk to each other."

I didn't really understand, so I just said, "Oh."

I watched him solder a small wire into place. Looking around the bench, I noticed lots of different colored ones wrapped on little metal spools. There were yellow ones, blue ones, green, and red ones, too.

I looked above the workbench at a picture of a sailing ship.

"Grandpa," I asked, always curious, "where does wire come from? Do people make it? Why are there so many colors?"

He smiled and unplugged the hot iron. Setting it on a flat metal tray, he re-lit his pipe.

"Peru," he said. "Wire comes from Peru. It grows on trees in the wire forests just like bananas do. The different colors are for the different sizes, and only one size grows on each tree. It looks like a rainbow fell on the forest. The natives cut them down with big blades and roll them onto large wooden spools. Then they send them to the USA and other countries where people put them on smaller spools so I can use them to fix my radio!"

I laughed. "Oh, Grandpa! You're so silly!"

"Why Rose! You don't believe me?" He looked hurt. "Remember, there is always some truth to every story!"

"Okay, Grandpa, maybe I believe you about the wire but there is no ham in your radio!"

"Tell you what, come on upstairs and ask your Grandma about our adventures in the wire forests of Peru."

I slipped off his lap as he stood up, and we climbed the painted stairway into another world.

Chapter One

"Here we go again, Sam!" I said as I packed the open suitcase on the bed. The big, black Newfie sat in the doorway, watching his tail thumping. He had picked up on the excitement in the house, and had not quite realized what it meant.

"Doesn't seem like very long since I unpacked!" I continued. Sam thumped his tail again as I rambled on.

"But this time it's different! We're going as a family! A 'working vacation' as Mom calls it. Two weeks in Peru! Machu Picchu, The Andes Mountains, great stuff for my newsletter! Of course, there will be things I can't write about, like the real reason we're going!"

Sam whined at my tone. I think he was catching on. I wished Sam could go. But Mother said, "No. Sam is used to traveling for the dog shows, but the hotel won't allow him. Besides, your Aunt Susan and Uncle Steven have volunteered to watch him while we are gone."

That was another exciting thing about this trip. Aunt Susan and Uncle Steven were not only taking care of Sam, but they would be staying in our house while we were gone. Richard, our "chauffer" and bodyguard would be coming with us!

A lot had happened since I returned from Russia! I was home-schooled now with a private tutor The Agency had recommended. She was a nice lady who reminded me a lot of my grandmother. At least from the pictures and all the stories I had heard about her.

My Internet Newsletter went toward my English credits, and Mom and Dad had moved into the private sector, with Aunt Susan and Uncle Steven, who were married now.

After my kidnapping, my parents vowed we would work together as a family for all our sakes! I felt good about it because I was included with the adults!

I missed the kids at The Brookhaven School for Girls a little, though. But I was still able to participate in home school events and get-togethers.

As I zipped the bag shut I, smiled, remembering the passwords The Agency had used; "The suitcase is open, but the bag is zipped".

Zip would be coming with us again! We still had access to him and The Agency. Dad was excited about our first contract with them. So many senior agents had left or been cut they were contracting out assignments former agents and private agencies. Budget problems, they called it.

This trip was about computers. The new Office Of Homeland Security had called for The Agency's computers to be updated. They were at least fifteen years old and needed replacing.

Something had happened along the way, and the new computers were six months late. The Agency said there was a danger in terrorists may be planning another big strike! The problem had been traced to the wire needed for the computers. Power cords, mice, and other cords needed to run the computers for The Agency. A lot of wire was needed to replace every computer in The Agency.

What was holding up the wire? That's what we were being sent to find out! Aunt Susan and Uncle Steven would have gone, but Mother wanted this trip for us. It was a good way to get our feet wet, she had said.

I looked out my window as I lugged the big suitcase off of the bed, and set it on the floor. A car had pulled up and Aunt Susan and Uncle Steven stepped out. Aunt Susan looked up at my window, smiling and waving as Uncle Steven unloaded the bags.

Samson The Great cocked his head at the sound of the car in the drive. He thumped his tail twice, and started to make a run down the steps, but whined and sat back down.

He had figured it out!

This was going to be the hardest part, saying goodbye to my best friend! I bent down and hugged his neck, feeling the stinging of tears on my cheeks. I patted him a few times, and stood up.

"Now Sam, you know I'll be back soon! You'll have lots of fun with Aunt Susan and Uncle Steven.

And Grandpa will be watching too! Right Grandpa?"

I looked into the air, as if seeing him there. Wiping the tears from my eyes, I let the butterflies of excitement take over my stomach.

"Well, Grandpa, I guess I'll find out if there really are wire forests in Peru!"

Chapter Two

For a twelve-year-old girl I had traveled a lot! I felt like a veteran as we boarded the plane. I was anxious to show my mother how experienced I was! They would never know how important they made me feel by including me on this trip!

Richard was right behind me. I turned and smiled at him from time to time as we walked through the corridor to the plane. He smiled back, but his face was a mixture of emotions. All the time we had been waiting, his trained eyes were scanning the airport and passengers. He was on the job! I think he was feeling guilty too for what had happened to Susan and I the last time I had left.

I wanted to make him feel better, so I put on my most grown-up face and said, "Relax, Richard. I have flown before!"

It worked. This time his smile was real. Even his shoulders relaxed.

"Yes, I know," he said. "I was with you in New York. You handled yourself quite well!"

This was a high compliment, and I stood a little taller as we stepped into the plane.

Dad took the lead, shepherding his flock into first class. He was proud to be taking his family on a trip. He took the window seat, followed by Mom, then me, with Richard on the aisle seat. I felt very safe.

I had brought some reading material with me, a printout from Zip on Peru. Once we were in the air, I started reading.

Mom looked over and smiled, proud of her daughter, and happy to be working together as a family.

I pretended not to notice, and kept on reading, smiling on the inside. I read about Machu Picchu, the Andes mountains, the Incas and the Amazon. Nowhere did I see anything about wire forests! But I did find out there were copper mines in the Andes! And copper is used in making wire!

Thinking of wire brought back the memory of Grandma and Grandpa, and our visit to their house when I was six.

I drifted off with the memory.

"Grandpa, where is Grandma?" I asked, staring at her portrait above the fireplace.

"Grandma is on an adventure, a top secret mission!" He said, his eyes tearing up.

"When will she be back?"

"She is on the biggest adventure of them all. She won't be back but someday we will all join her and she will tell us all about it!"

I smiled and looked at the portrait again. Grandma was a beautiful woman. She stood in a long white dress that seemed to cling to her in the wind, a large white hat in her hand, on the "Widows Watch." Looking across the ocean, she seemed to be thinking of far- away places she had been, dark hair alive as it wisped in the breeze. She was holding an orchid.

She turned and smiled at me.

I woke up with a start. I had been dreaming. The printouts had slipped from my hands, and were scattered in my lap, and on the floor.

Richard was asleep, as were my Mom and Dad - and half the people on the plane. I did not want to disturb them, so I collected my papers as quietly as I could, and placed them in the pouch of the seat ahead of me.

The steady drone of the plane soon lulled me back to sleep. Before I drifted off I thought of Grandma. I wanted to know more about her. Maybe on this trip Mom and I would have time to talk.

I fell back asleep, my thoughts ramblin' from one thing to another, and I had the strangest dreams! Something about a rainbow forest...

"Rose, wake up!" Mother was gently nudging me. "It's time to eat."

I woke up slowly, groggy from my nap. It was dark outside. Dad and Richard were awake.

"How long was I asleep?" I asked.

"You were asleep when we woke up about two hours ago."

"Where are we?"

"About an hour from Florida, where we'll change planes for the rest of the trip," Mother answered.

Even though I had logged a lot of flight time, it was still hard for me to sit still! But on a plane, the only thing you could do was go to the bathroom!

I got up and made my way past Richard, who smiled and let me out.

"Don't go too far!" He joked.

"Sheesh!" I said, rolling my eyes, and looking incredulous. "Just be here when I get back!" I retaliated.

There is just no privacy on a plane!

I didn't know how right I was until I noticed the stewardess. She was not the same one who greeted us when we boarded the plane!

I took a chance, and when no one was looking I parted the curtains and peered into coach.

There was our stewardess. They must have switched places!

"No big deal," I told myself, feeling silly. They probably do it all the time. It would not have bothered me at all, except there was something very familiar about this one.

Of course! She was the same one who watched Aunt Susan and I on the flight to New York!

My heart began to beat faster. What should I do?

I closed the curtain and turned around, right into her!

"Can I help you, miss?" She said.

"Uh, no, I was just curious," I improvised.

"Well, the fasten seat belt sign just came on. Please take your seat," she smiled.

This time there were four of us! I was glad to take my seat. Richard and Dad would hear about this!

I started for my seat as she turned around, and walked toward the cockpit. She tapped lightly on the door and stepped inside. I followed close enough to hear her as she entered.

Just before the door closed again I heard her say, "I think she recognized me."

Now my heart was really pounding! I scrambled to sit back down, almost tripping over Richard.

"What's wrong, Rose?" He said, alerting Mom and Dad at the same time.

All three of them looked at me as I fell into my seat, face red, and breathing fast!

"The stewardess! I've seen her before! She was the one on the plane to New York!"

"Of course she was. She works for The Agency. They always watch us. Especially now," Dad said.

"She makes me nervous. Are you sure she's not a double agent?" I whispered.

"Well, I know better than to doubt a woman's intuition. We don't want to alarm the other passengers. We will be landing soon. In the meantime I'll turn on my COM link, and Richard, use your button cam. We'll check in with Susan and Steven and have them run a check for us."

I felt better, but I didn't know if I would ever get used to the life of an agent.

Mother looked disappointed. She had wanted a family vacation. Now she just sighed.

Richard went into alert mode, and the whole atmosphere of the flight changed.

There's nothing like a whisper to get peoples' attention! I could almost see the ears stretching as the other passengers started to lean into us.

I felt embarrassed. Susan would be disappointed in me for blurting things out. I decided to change the subject.

"Mom, what's the first thing on our agenda when we get to the hotel? Can we go shopping?"

"Oh, great! I can see the money flying away!" Dad said, jokingly.

The other passengers chuckled a little, and the spell was broken. My spy skills were redeemed, and we all relaxed. Even Richard.

If I had eyes in the back of my head I might have seen the man sitting behind us typing on his laptop as the stewardess left the cockpit, and walked right into Richard's camera.

The button cam was silent, and tied into Zip. Dad was typing a message into his cell phone. He couldn't risk talking on the plane, so he used text mail. True, it could have been monitored, but he was typing in code.

It was a clever code; one that looked like an ordinary message. On the other end, Susan's cell phone alerted them to an incoming call. Since the phone was tied into Zip, the message was encoded to keep prying eyes from deciphering it.

But Susan knew what it said: "On vacation, will send pictures. Let us know what you think."

"Steven, are you getting this?" Susan asked.

It's coming through on Zip now. Why don't you join me?

"On my way," Susan replied, leaving the kitchen with Sam. She hooked him to his chain out back and headed for Richard's living quarters.

Richard's 'quarters' were actually his house. A "mother-in-law's" apartment, Mom had called it. It was a small house in the back of the yard next to the garage. In it was Richard's 'Ready Room', where he monitored all the security in the house, and on the property. It was also our link to Zip and The Agency.

One of the things Susan and Steven were here for was to set up 'Ready Room' for private business. Since moving into the private Sector, certain links had to be removed from the system. Dads direct access to The Agency was now cut off, and he would have to deal through a liaison officer.

Mom's business had to be adjusted, too. Susan was to go to her office and monitor the activities of the consulting firm while she was gone. Even though Mom had a second-in-command, Susan was to be her link while she was on 'vacation', relaying any problems her second needed help with.

All of this was being done according to protocol. It was designed to look natural, and not arouse suspicion. The Agency still valued Mom and Dad's contribution. Aunt Susan and Uncle Steven were in business with Mom and Dad, so it was a working vacation for them as well. They were excited about our first contract with The Agency.

Besides all that, they were building a new house in Connecticut, and needed a place to stay.

More cover.

Susan opened the door of the Ready Room. "Anything yet?" She asked as she took the swivel chair next to Steven in front of the monitor.

"A picture of the stewardess from Richard's button cam. Very pretty."

Susan punched him in the arm!

"Ow! I was only kidding!"

"I wasn't!" Susan said.

"I've sent it to the liaison. Waiting for a response."

A minute later Zip began to talk. "Kathy Lee Swanson, a.k.a. Kathleen Swanson, nickname, Kathy Lee. Agency operative. Current assignment; notify airlines when operatives are on board, inform captains, and monitor passengers for suspicious behaviors. No prior suspicions or outside activities. Considered safe."

"Well, that's a relief!" Susan said.

"They are still in flight," Steven noted. "Zip, send a green light to inquirer."

Zip complied, and a small green light flashed in the corner of Dad's phone. He looked over and smiled.

I knew it was all right and we would all talk later.

"Nice work, Rose," he said, pretending to look at the airline magazine crossword I had started.

I smiled inside and out. This was high praise indeed!

I still hadn't noticed the businessman behind us who was still silently typing on his laptop.

Richard relaxed a little and looked over at the crossword puzzle I had started.

"I think that's 'lure' you're looking for. Four letters for attracting fish. I know that one! Looking forward to doing some of that on this trip!"

"Thanks, Richard, but I would have gotten it. Even a child could figure that one out.

Richard was a fisherman. He loved to camp, fish, and even hunt. I didn't like him when he hunted, so he never told me when he did. On this trip he was looking forward to fishing on the Amazon. He had heard of Red Tail Catfish who sometimes grow to one hundred pounds! There were guided fishing tours, and he was going to take one.

"Well, we all know you are not a child! It won't be long before you won't be open child-proof containers, or program VCRs," he kidded.

"Sheesh! I hope I never get like that! That's why people keep having kids, eh?"

"That's why some of us never grow up, either!" He smiled.

I liked Richard's smile. He was a big man, six-foot-two and about 220 lbs. With his short, dark hair and blue eyes I always wondered why he wasn't married. I used to tease him about Susan because I thought they made a good match.

"Then you could be my real uncle!" I'd say.

"And I'm not now?" He looked hurt

"Of course you are! I only have two!"

That was before Steven. Of course, he was only an uncle by marriage. But in the short time I had known him, he was close to Richard who now seemed threatened.

"Relax, Richard. No one could ever take your place!" I had told him after the wedding.

My other uncle was Dad's brother, Matt. He was a captain in the Coast Guard. He lived with my aunt Rebecca and my cousin Abigail in Fairbanks Alaska. We never got to see them much.

There I go ramblin' again! Any way, Richard liked to go the gym and work out. He stayed in shape. I knew he had girlfriends, though. One from the gym he would go jogging with, and one he liked to go fishing and hunting with when he had time off.

Richard said he was never interested in Susan, but I think he was.

"Fly," Richard said.

"What?" I asked.

"One type of fishing, three letters," he said, pointing to the puzzle

"Oh, thanks!" I said, shaking off my daze, and returning to the puzzle

"It's a theme," he said. "Every word relates to flying and fishing trips."

"Yes, that's what the title says." I said, pointing to the top of the page.

"Oh, thanks," he said, pretending to blush.

"See," I said, "what would grown-ups do without kids?"

"I do fine, besides, you are not a kid."

"And you are not a grown-up!" I reminded him.

Mother had been quiet the whole time. Now she laughed.

"Oh, you two! You both act like a couple of juveniles!"

I looked at Richard and smiled. He winked back.

Dad looked over at the two of us and sighed.

"We can't take you guys anywhere!" But his eyes were smiling.

Richard beamed at his only family.

High praise indeed!

Chapter Three

When the stewardess returned with the drinks, she handed them to Richard who passed them across. I got Seven-Up(. I felt better knowing the Agency had checked her out.

Each one had a napkin underneath. On one of the napkins was a note. It said, "The man behind you is using a laptop. Typing in your descriptions. We will be landing soon, suggest you check him before we close communications on board."

Richard passed the note to Dad who immediately hit the Zip button on his cell phone. Richard stood up to stretch and snapped a picture of the man. The picture went straight to Aunt Susan and Uncle Steven who ran it through the liaison at The Agency.

Dad's phone showed a text message. "Might take you time. Call you later."

I had read the note as it went across, and was dying to turn around and look at the man. I knew I could not act suspicious, so I fought the urge. But suddenly I had to go to the bathroom again!

"Richard, let me out. I gotta go again!"

"Kids on planes!" He pretended to grumble. He knew exactly what I was doing!

When I returned I stole a glance at the man. He looked like any other businessman. Older than my parents, though. He had brown business-like hair, and a dark, pinstripe suit. There was a briefcase on his legs. I wondered who he could be, and why he was typing our description. He wasn't with The Agency, or Kathy Lee would not have warned us.

Mom looked worried, too. She knew we would have to wait. Everybody's mind had the same question; who knew we were going on this trip, and why did they care?

The answers finally came when we switched planes. While we were in the airport Zip called with a message.

"Alex Bacon. Vice President of Porcel-Art. Suspected of ties to hard-line communists, listed as company to avoid. E-mail tracked to Peru. Be on guard. Look for your friends at Lima airport."

"I know him!" Mom said. "At least, I know about him! He was named on the plate we were to deliver when Rose and Susan were kidnapped!"

"But what's he doing here?" Richard asked.

"I think I know," Dad said. "I think they have ties to terrorist organizations, like Shining Path in Peru. They also have links to Columbian drug lords. When I announced our retirement in New York, we did not allow pictures. We've always tried to keep our identities secret. But they do know who we are. I'm betting they don't know what we look like in Peru, but someone knows we're coming. Our cover is a family vacation, but someone is worried we'll find out what's going on. That wire is being held up for a reason. Someone does not want The Agency computers updated."

"Why did The Agency take the contract with the Peruvians in the first place?" Richard asked. "They could have gotten the wire from anyone."

"Two reasons," Dad continued, "First the budget. They offered it to The Agency at half the price of other suppliers. Second, their offer raised a lot of flags and The Agency was very interested in their reasons."

"So, why didn't they go to a back-up when the Peruvians didn't deliver on time?"

"Well, they had paid cash for the wire. Half up front and half on delivery. It would be a large sum to write off and pay again to someone else. When Huntsville called and said the wire was late, and they would not be able to deliver the computers on time, The Agency waited as long as they could before looking for options. No one was anxious to tell the president until they had all of the facts. He's been under a lot of pressure about coordinating intelligence. Most of the experienced agents are gone or scattered around the world fighting terrorism, so they contacted us. Someone in The Agency is leaking information to the terrorists or they are simply watching us."

Mom was nodding the whole time. Her company not only kept track of other companies' performance, but also kept tabs on industrial spying and illegal activities for The Agency.

"Okay, so what do we do now?" She asked.

"We stick to the plan. Let the answers come to us. We spend the first week posing as tourists and nosing around. If all goes well, we spend the second week on a real vacation, somewhere nobody knows. Keep the COM links on. The Agency will keep eyes on us and Susan and Steven will also."

"Dad, why are we talking here? Isn't it risky?" I asked

"Yes, but not as risky as the next plane or the hotel."

Richard nodded. Under his breath he said, "There go the red-tailed catfish."

"Don't give up so easy, Richard. This is our first private contract. We can't quit now," Mom was tough.

"Any time we get into trouble The Agency will pull us out. Just don't leave Rose alone, or be alone yourselves."

"That's going to be a little hard sometimes, Dear," Mom reminded him.

"Yeah, well, as little as possible, anyway."

I was excited and disappointed at the same time. Here we finally get to take a vacation, and we are on the job. My thoughts of getting out on my own were flying away. I had felt like a prisoner in my own house ever since I came home from Russia. I wanted to show my parents they did not have to watch me every second! And poor Richard hardly ever got any time off since I've been home!

But still, it was great knowing what was going on for a change! And we were going to a different country! This would be good for my newsletter - and my schoolwork!

"One thing is in our favor," Richard said. "They won't risk hurting us. Their plan obviously has something to do with timing. They won't risk The Agency's wrath, and spilling the beans. They sure don't want attention ahead of schedule."

"Right," Dad said. "If anything, they will throw us red herrings to keep us off track. Our 'friends' will meet us in Lima, and we'll finalize our plans. The worst thing we can do is to look too worried."

Dad looked over at me. Now, he did look worried! "Rose, if you want to cancel the mission, we will."

"Are we any safer at home? Will we ever be? We need to do this. Other people need to know someone is doing something about this so they can take trips with their families," I said bravely.

"Yes, but you should have a normal childhood. We should not expose you to all of this. You are so young," Mom was choked up.

"What's normal, Mom? Not knowing anything about the world, and getting kidnapped on the way home from school by some pervert? Like some 'normal' kids I know? I see the news, too. People don't give enough credit to their kids. I'm not six any more. I still enjoy my age. Was the world any safer when you were kids?

I was angry. Angry at the world. Angry at terrorists and anything else that kept people from enjoying life. I had done some reading about Peru and knew half the population lived in poverty or barely survived. I had read about shantytowns and poor farmers surrounding a wealthy city where people went to the theater and opera. I had read about the gold in the mountains and the poor fishermen.

And I was angry with my parents for not understanding I understood! Sheesh!

The rest of the trip, Mom talked about what we would do on our 'vacation'.

We would be landing in Lima, the capital city and going to our hotel. Mom had laid out our itinerary, and said, "We will not spend the whole time working."

The list of events included sightseeing, museums, the theater, the zoological gardens and Machu Picchu.

Along the way we would see the oldest university in the western hemisphere, The National University of San Marcos, established in 1551.

We also had to dress for dinner! I had to pack a lot heavier than I did on my last trip! Mother also wanted to see me in a dress! Sheesh! I wanted to spend the whole time in shorts! The climate was hot and dry. Lima did not get much rain.

"What about the mountains?" I asked. "Won't we be seeing them?"

"It will be hard not to see them," Richard said. "They run from north to south through three countries!"

"I read about the Andes. They have the second highest peak in the world! They are also steeper, and more rugged than the Rockies." I said, anxious to show off my knowledge.

"They are so high they disrupt communication," Dad added.

"Of course we'll see them. The Central Railroad offers a tour."

The more we talked about the trip, the more excited we got. Soon everyone in first class was leaning into us, listening! I thought we'd have to take them all with us!

Richard would have loved that!

Finally we were talked out, and settled in with our thoughts. Still excited, I picked up the printouts and started reading. I was already planning my newsletter!

Mom tapped me on the shoulder. I turned as she smiled at me and said, "And we're going to do some shopping!"

Chapter Four

Richard was back in his 'agent' mode the rest of the trip, and we couldn't wait to land at the Jorge Chavez airport in Lima.

Our 'friends' were there to greet us. Posing as a tourist agent and driver, a man and woman greeted us by the luggage carousel.

I was the tip-off. "Two men, a woman and a twelve-year-old girl." They had been told.

As we picked up our luggage the woman approached us.

"Your suitcase is open," she said as Mom picked hers up.

"But the bag is zipped," Mom replied.

The woman smiled, and waved to her companion. He was smiling too.

"Welcome to Peru! Peru Travel Service at your service! Allow me to take your bags. I am Rico."

"And I am Gloria, your travel guide. Please follow us to the car. I have your itinerary all prepared."

Rico stacked the luggage on a cart, and we all followed Gloria to the parking lot.

They brought us to a renovated taxi with a sign on the top that said Peru Travel Service. Rico loaded our bags into the trunk.

There was just enough room in the old yellow cab, and I had to sit up front with Rico and Gloria. At least I got the window seat!

Gloria was about Mom's age, and had long dark hair. She was Latin, and I thought of Gloria Estafon

Rico was about the same age as Richard. He wore a bright red printed shirt. He was smiling and friendly, but I could tell he was an agent underneath.

I liked them both

"We will drive you to your hotel, there you can pick up your rental car. There are maps in the glove compartment, and all the directions you need to various points of interest. Also you will find directions to the Government Center, and the names and offices of anyone involved with manufacturing. You can reach us through Zip should you need anything. We need to maintain our cover so please remember to communicate with us in terms of travel agents.

Rico wheeled the car through the streets, and I looked around at the low buildings. Most of them seemed to be from one to three stories. It was a lot different than Steven's cab, and the skyscrapers of New York City.

Still, Lima was big. About 390 square miles! Rico pointed out the Zoological Gardens and the National Library. Not quite the tour guide that Steven was, but he was still proud of his city.

We were quiet most of the ride, listening to our new friends.

"The Agency does not want us to clock a lot of time on this. We will be here if you need help. Our current assignment is to track members of Shining Path. If you find a connection, of course things will change," Rico said as we wheeled up to the Lima Hotel.

It was a bright sunny day, and we were one of several cabs loading and unloading in front of the busy hotel. Rico unloaded our bags, and set them on the sidewalk.

"Here are the keys to your car. We can be reached by Zip. Good luck, and have a nice vacation!" Gloria said.

They drove off, leaving us standing by the luggage.

"I'll go in and register," Dad said, "I'm sure they will have someone to help us with our bags."

Dad went inside, and we expected a uniformed bellhop to appear and help us with the luggage.

Instead, a young boy about my age came out, pulling a large cart with a bar across the top. He was about my height, and had brown hair hanging on his forehead like it had been cut with a bowl. Dark brown eyes smiled at us. His teeth were white against his tan skin.

"Welcome to the Hotel Lima. I am Paolo. I will take your bags!"

Mom and Richard looked at each other in surprise, then shrugged. Paolo loaded the luggage onto the cart, and hung up the wardrobe bags. He struggled a little to pull the cart up the slightly tilted sidewalk and into the door. Richard started to help him but changed his mind.

"Do you really work for the hotel?" He asked him.

"I work for tips. I am a businessman! Self employed," Paolo announced with pride.

"I see," Richard replied, "an entrepreneur!"

Dad turned as the noisy cart led the procession right up to the counter.

The desk clerk smiled at Paolo and winked as he handed the room keys to Dad.

"You are in 301 and 303. Paolo will show you the way," he said in an official-sounding voice.

Paolo beamed at the recognition. He worked all over Lima to help his father and grandmother.

He led us past the tropical plants, and the gold ashtrays to the elevators, pulling the heavy cart across the deep carpet.

He pushed the button, and waited patiently for the elevator to arrive, trying not to look winded.

When the 'ding' sounded, the doors opened, and he resumed his work. Silent on the way to the third floor, he looked away shyly whenever our eyes met.

The cart rumbled down the hallway over the thinner carpet, and we arrived at the end of the hall.

Dad opened the door, and Paolo followed us inside. "Ladies and gentlemen first."

Unloading the bags from the cart, Paolo sat them on the floor and waited.

Usually, my father was not a big tipper, and we were surprised when he handed Paolo a twenty-dollar bill!

We held our questions as Paolo took the money with an even larger smile than he already had.

"Thank you, sir! If there is anything you need during your stay, just send for me."

Paolo stuck the bill inside his white pants, and pushed the cart through the open door.

We listened as it rumbled down the hallway and closed the door, then turned our attention to Dad.

"Well, he's a hard-working kid. Besides, it's on the expense account," he defended the tip.

"I hope I'm on the expense account!" I said as Mom hugged him, and Richard smiled.

"Sorry, Rose. We're tapped out," he teased.

"Sure, Dad. You know, I left my money at home! I guess I won't be able to buy you a souvenir! Darn!"

Dad looked hurt. "I guess we're even, then. I hope Paolo knows where the McDonald's is!"

"Okay, you two! Let's get unpacked. Speaking of food, I am hungry. Where is the local McDonald's?" Mom said.

Room 301 and 303 were adjoining suites. Richard got one all to himself! I got an extra bed in the living room in ours. At least we had two bathrooms!

"Can we really eat at McDonald's?" I asked hopefully.

"No, I don't think so, Rose. It was a long trip, and I know we are all tired. We will dress for dinner, and eat in the hotel."

"You're not going to make me wear a dress, are you?"

"Of course, dear. You are a young lady, and you should dress like one."

"Oh, Mom! What's wrong with what I'm wearing?"

"Shorts and tank tops are fine for traveling, but this is a nice hotel. We will be seen as a family, and dress accordingly."

Richard edged away as I rolled my eyes. I hated it when Mom got started on my dressing like a young lady! True, I usually wore jeans, Reeboks, and a ball cap with my ponytail stuck out the back, but what was wrong with that? Dad didn't mind.

"It won't do any good, Rose," Mom said, sternly. "I know all your arguments, but I'm still the Mom."

"So there!" I finished. "Okay, but I get the shower first!"

I grabbed my bag and headed for the big bathroom. If I had to dress up, they could use the small one! This was going to take some time!

I felt small in the big room. There were two sinks! Lots of fancy tiles surrounded the huge mirror, and the shower had glass doors! I made sure to lock the door.

"They want grown up, I'll show them grown up!" I said to myself. "Sheesh!"

I really didn't mind the dress. I had picked it out. If I had to wear one, I wanted to choose it. I tried to find one as grown up as possible without angering Mom any more than I had on the way to the store. What does a twelve-year old wear to look grown up? After putting Mom and the sales lady through every dress on the rack, I finally settled on my first choice.

It was blue and had short sleeves with white ruffles with a square neck and pleated skirt worn over white tights. Mom smiled in relief. I had passed up some pretty wild outfits!

"Wait 'till they see me in makeup!"

While I was getting ready, Mom and Dad were struggling in the smaller bathroom.

I smiled at the commotion, but knew if I was to have any freedom on this trip I would have to please Mom. She was so afraid something else would happen to me since my unplanned trip to Russia. I had to show my parents and Richard I was okay and could be trusted!

I wanted to know more about Paolo, too. Here was someone my own age – and he was cute, too!

The rumbling in my stomach was embarrassing as I stood before the mirror, looking at the new me. Now I didn't care where we ate!

An older, prettier Rose looked back at me. The ponytail was gone, replaced by long strawberry blonde hair, slightly curled above the shoulders and on my forehead. The ponytail barrette went to the hair on my right side, above my ear.

Secretly it was a COM link, Dad had said no one would suspect it. Plus, I would never get separated from it as I had with the jacket in Russia.

I wanted to show him I was wearing it

I had gone easy on the makeup, not wanting to scare Dad and Richard. Just some blush, and a little mascara.

I slid on the black, shiny shoes and picked up the matching purse.

"Ta-Da!" I said as I finally opened the door, and stepped into the living room.

"Oh my..." was all Mom could say.

Dad was in shock. "Can this be my Ramblin' Rose?"

"Depends," I said, "Can this be my Dad?"

Richard opened the door from his room, and stopped suddenly.

"Who are you - and what have you done with Rose?" He teased.

I smiled as Dad linked arms with his two girls, and Richard followed behind to the dining room.

My plan was working perfectly!

Chapter Five

I felt pretty special as we walked into the hotel dining room. At first I thought we would be too formal. It was summer here and we were on vacation!

Dad and Richard had both worn suits with bright-colored ties. Mom was wearing a white summer dress. About half the people there were dressed up, and the other half wore Hawaiian shirts!

Still, I hadn't been dressed this fancy since I had worn Anna's dress in Russia. Mom was pleased, and both Richard and Dad treated me extra special.

In the dimly lit dining room, surrounded by adults, I almost felt like one! It was scary!

I looked around the other tables but did not see anyone else my age. I began to think I would spend this trip as a prisoner of grownups!

The menu didn't help, either. Seafood. Fancy dinners I could not pronounce. Sheesh!

"Rose, what would you like?" Mom asked.

"McDonalds!" I shot back, then softened up a little. "How about chicken?"

"You know we didn't come this far for McDonalds. Yes, they do have chicken. I'll order for you," Mom said.

"And a Coke!" I added. Something to look forward to.

"Okay. I know this probably seems boring to you, but it means a lot to your Dad and I."

"I'm sorry, Mom. Guess I've been acting like a kid again," I said.

"We wouldn't have you any other way," Dad said, smiling.

While we waited for the food we listened to music by a local band walking around the tables playing guitars and maracas.

It was fun, and one of them stopped by our table, and played for me. I blushed.

While we ate, we made plans for the week. Next week we would go to Machu Picchu. Mom wanted us to go as a family.

And Richard wanted to go fishing in the Amazon! We would drop him off at Cuzco, the ancient capitol of the Incas. There he would hook up with a fishing guide.

"But what about Rose?" He asked

"Rose will be with us, Richard. You deserve a vacation. Take the fishing trip. We can stay in touch with you through the COM link. Rose will be wearing hers all of the time," Dad told him.

"Yes, Richard. Have a good time; we'll meet up in a few days. After tomorrow we will start our 'research'." Mom said in code.

I was getting excited again. Machu Picchu! Ancient cities! The Amazon! I had done some research of my own. This was a fascinating part of the world! It was already interesting to think there was snow back in Minnesota, but it was summer here. Being in the southern hemisphere was like being upside down. This was going to be fun!

"And tomorrow, Rose, you and I are going shopping! In the Plaza."

Dad rolled his eyes, "Maybe I should not have tipped that young man so well, after all."

I smiled thinking of Paolo. She hoped she would get to see him again.

Later that night, Mom sat on the edge of my bed. I knew she wanted to talk.

"I just finished saying goodnight to Sam," I said. "I always say goodnight to him at home, and I said goodnight to him every night while I was in Russia, too. I miss him."

Mom winced, remembering how Sam laid on my bed, and moped while I was gone

"Yes, I miss him, too," he said. "At least he has Aunt Susan and Uncle Steven to keep him company."

I decided to change the subject. "I can't wait to see Machu Picchu!"

"There's a special reason I wanted us to go there, you know." Mom said, glad I switched topics.

"What?" I asked

"That's where your Grandma and Grandpa met."

"Tell me about it, please."

"I will, tomorrow. Now it's time to sleep. We'll need our energy."

"Great. How do you expect me to sleep now? I'm too excited as it is!"

"Well, we don't have to get up that early. Gloria and Rico are going to be our guides. They'll be here at nine."

"This ought to be real interesting! You sure they won't drive off on us?"

"No, they won't. Now go to sleep, breakfast is at seven-thirty."

"Sheesh! Some vacation! Can't even sleep late!" I grumbled.

Mom just smiled, and shook her head as she walked away.

"Good night, Rose."

"Good night, Mom."

The last light switched off, and I laid in the moonlit darkness thinking of the coming day. I was anxious to hear the story of how my Grandparents met. Knowing Grandpa I shouldn't have been surprised it would have been in a place like Machu Picchu!

As I drifted off, I remembered his story about the wire forests. Soon I would find out how much of it was real.

I could almost see him standing there, smiling as he read my thoughts.

"Good night, Grandpa," I said softly.

"Good night, Rose," he whispered back.

Chapter Six

"Rose, time to get up," Dad's voice brought me out of the wire forests I'd been dreaming about.

"What time is it?" I mumbled, eyes still shut.

"Six-thirty. Breakfast in the dining room at seven-thirty. Thought you'd like to have some time together before I leave."

"Where are you going?" I asked, sitting up half-awake.

"I'm taking Richard to the airport. He's flying to Cuzco for his fishing trip. Then, while you and Mom are touring the Plaza, I'll be doing some investigating."

"Can't I go with you, Dad? I am an experienced agent, you know."

"I know you are, Rose. That's why I need you and Mom to tour the Plaza. Get a feel for the town and watch for our friend from the plane. If we split up, it will be harder to watch us."

"Oh, I know, like decoys," I said, fully awake now.

"Now you've got it! I'll be posing as a businessman, and talking to government officials. Our cover is a family on business vacation. You are an important part of the team."

I knew Dad was right. I didn't like being a decoy; I wanted to do something more important, but I knew it was a very important part of the operation. We can't all be captains.

"Besides, your Mom is looking forward to spending time with you, too."

And maybe I'll get to see Paolo, I thought.

At seven-thirty we were all seated in the dining room. Mom and I were casually dressed, as was Richard.

"What's on your mind, Richard?" I asked, noticing his face as he stared at the menu. He was always on duty.

"Nothing, as usual," he kidded.

"Well, you're a poor liar," I kidded back. "It's never, isn't it?"

"Ouch!" He said. "Actually, I was wondering how you're going to get along without me. Who's going to keep the boys away?"

"Maybe that's exactly why you should go fishing." I said, drawing a sharp look from Dad. He seemed to age right before my eyes!

Mom smiled. "Men!" She said, "Sheesh!"

"Actually," Dad piped up, "They will be watching for four of us. It will help our cover if we split up even more. Besides, we have our guides, Rico and Gloria. They will keep an eye out for us too. And, they know whom to watch for. Keep your COM links open, and we'll be fine."

"Yeah, you men go do your macho stuff. Us girls can take care of ourselves! We're just going shopping in the Plaza," Mom said as she closed her menu.

"Yeah, we'll be fine!" I agreed, trying to put Richard at ease. I wanted him to enjoy his fishing trip.

"Okay, so you don't need me," he sniffed. "Who needs to be needed anyway?"

"Of course we need you!" Dad said with compassion. "You're paying for breakfast!"

We all laughed, and dug into our food - but inside we knew we all needed each other.

At nine a.m., Gloria and Rico's car pulled up outside of the hotel.

"That's our cue. Phase One underway," Dad said, getting up from the table.

We left the restaurant and split up, Dad and Richard in the rental car while Mom and I climbed into the converted cab of the Peru Travel Service.

"So far, so good," I winked at Mom in the back seat. None of us had seen the man at the table by the window, parting the curtains to watch us as we drove away.

Our city tour of Lima began with our trip to the Plaza. Actually it was known as the Plaza de Armas, which, Gloria informed us, has been declared a World Heritage site by UNESCO. Running along two sides were arcades with shops, Portal de Escribanos and Portal de Botoneros. In the center of the Plaza was a bronze fountain dating back to 1560. Also in the plaza was the Cathedral.

"Note the splendidly carved stalls and the silver covered altars. Also, the fine woodwork surrounding them," Gloria said, like a true tour guide.

"The mosaic-covered walls bear the coats of arms of Lima and Pizarro," Rico spoke up. It was important for us to act like tourists. It wasn't hard to do, especially surrounded by the beauty of the Cathedral. I took notes, and put them in the light nylon backpack I had worn today.

Other tour groups were beginning to arrive, and we moved on to the Archbishop's Palace. This was famous for its Sicilian tile work and paneled ceiling. I was most interested in the catacombs under the church and monastery.

"That was quite a tour!" Mom said, putting away her camera. "Got some great shots!"

"Maybe I can use them for my newsletter," I said, putting away my notebook.

"Sure can," Mom said.

"Can we leave you to do some shopping in the Plaza? We have another group this morning. Rico says the Plaza looks today," Gloria said in code.

"Of, course. Rose and I can handle the shopping ourselves," Mom laughed.

We headed for the shops.

"Charge!" We said in unison as we watched Rico and Gloria drive away.

Chapter Seven

It was easy to get carried away as we walked up one side of the Plaza, and down the other; stopping at every shop catching our eye. We agreed not to buy not too much - because it would be hard to carry everything. My backpack grew heavier and heavier as the "not too much" piled up. Soon I was sweating in the afternoon sun, and we sat down at some sidewalk tables for a light lunch.

We bought some handmade shawls and silver trinkets as souvenirs for Dad and Richard. Some things, like a new braided rug for the house and a mat for Sam, Mom arranged to be shipped

She took charge of the handmade fishing knife for Richard, and I took charge of the carved onyx horse for Dad.

We wore some of the jewelry we had bought for ourselves.

"Mom, tell me about Grandma and Grandpa," I asked, sipping the Coke I had ordered.

"Well, they met at Machu Picchu. Your grandfather was here on business; your grandmother was a university student. She was studying archaeology and geography. They fell in love with the rain forest, and each other. That's why your Grandmother's portrait shows her holding an orchid. More than ninety species grow here."

"What kind of business was Grandpa on?"

"Well, Peru is one of the largest producers and exporters of copper in the world. They also export several other ores as well as anchovies and fish food and handmade crafts. Grandpa was here to negotiate shipping rights, and he also kept his eyes open for The Agency."

I felt a sudden chill, as if someone was watching us.

"Let's go, Mom," I said.

"What's wrong, Rose? Are you okay?"

"I'm okay, but I think someone is listening to us."

I looked around the other tables, but saw no one suspicious. Mom looked worried now.

Disoriented, we clumsily stood up, and gathered our possessions. As we turned to leave an elderly man stood in front of us.

"Excuse me, ladies." He said. " I could not help but overhear. Did you say her Grandparents met at Machu Picchu?"

"I don't mean to be rude, sir, but we were not talking to you," Mom replied.

"Forgive me, it is none of my business. But I knew your father. You remind me of him."

"My father is dead. Please excuse us."

But the man would not let us pass.

"Why have you come to Peru?" He asked.

"Again, sir, that is none of your business. Now, must I call the police?"

"No, of course not. I must be mistaken. Forgive my intrusion on your day."

My heart was racing as we left.

"Who was he Mom? Why are we walking so fast?"

"Lots of people knew my father. Some were friends, and some were not. He didn't call him by name. Dad said all of his friends called him by name."

We were walking faster now. And someone was following. As our footsteps picked up speed, so did his. The old man must have motioned to someone to follow us.

Mom and I looked over our shoulders. There was a man chasing us! He was getting closer, and started to reach for Mom's shoulder...

There was a crash behind us, and people were yelling. We turned to see the man struggling with a vendor, and Paolo getting to his feet. He had tripped the man who went crashing into a vegetable cart.

"Follow me!" He said, racing across the street to another shop.

We ran behind him into the little store featuring handmade shawls and lace needlework.

"Grandma, hide us!" Paolo said, parting the curtains and stopping in the small room behind the counter.

The old woman did not question him as we followed.

Mom took out her cell phone as the woman reached for a wooden bat under her counter. She looked like she knew how to use it, too!

"Zip, Code One," Mom said.

Paolo stared at the phone and us. "Who is Zip?" He asked.

"A friend," I said.

"Like me, eh?" Paolo smiled.

"Yes, like you, Paolo" I said.

Within minutes the Peru Travel Service appeared, and so did Dad.

Code One meant "agent in trouble". Any available agents would home in on the signal, and come to their aid.

"Dad! Are we glad to see you!"

Paolo introduced his grandmother, Rosa. "Just like my name!" I said, introducing myself.

The three of us told the story as Rosa listened and smiled. She stood with the bat, ready for action.

Rico and Gloria had gone to check the area.

"They are gone," he said when they returned.

"Who were they? Who was the old man?" Mom asked.

"The old man is a member of the Shining Path. His name is Luis Alejandro. He knew your father had ties to The Agency. Your father was responsible for his arrest many years ago. We don't know who the other man was, he ran away too quickly. But you are not hurt?"

"No, we are not hurt. Thanks to Paolo and his grandmother," Mom said.

"We are grateful, Senora," Dad said

"My grandson is quick thinking. Do you think we will be safe from these men?" She asked.

"We don't believe they know why we are here. Luis must have recognized me from knowing my father. But since he is still active, we will have to be careful," Mom said.

"We don't think they saw Paolo or where you ran," Gloria said. "They were too busy trying to not make a scene on the street."

"Why are you here?" Rosa asked.

"We're on vacation!" We all said at once.

"Excitement in travel is our slogan!" Rico said.

"Well, it is a pleasure to meet you all. Rose, you must come for lunch at our house while you are here. Paolo has so few friends, and I would like to get to know you better. We have the same names, you know!" Rosa smiled.

Paolo blushed. "But Grandma, they are on vacation and we are poor."

Rosa bristled. "We are not rich in money, true, but your father is a proud fisherman, and works hard to take care of us. Are your friends too good for honest folks?"

"No, of course not, Rosa. Let us check with our friends, and if it is safe for all of us, Rose is welcome to visit. We would not want to endanger your family."

"No one has asked me if I want to go," I said.

"Well, do you?" Paolo asked hopefully.

"Only if it's okay with my folks," I said, casting puppy eyes at Mom and Dad.

"We can drive her, and cruise the area." Rico said.

"I don't know..." Dad said.

"You'll have to face it sometime, Dad. You can't keep me in a cage forever."

Mom stayed silent. She knew what it was like to be a young girl. She felt for our situation and wished again we were 'normal'.

"Well, you'll have to decide soon. There is not enough room in here for all of us, and I have a business to run."

Rosa parted the curtain and motioned us out of the little room. Mom and I stopped and looked at some of Rosa's work. Dad walked out with Rico and Gloria. I watched as they stood on the street by the car, talking.

Finally Dad came back in. He looked at Paolo, then Rosa, then Mom and me.

"What time would you like Rose to be there?"

Chapter Eight

I was shocked! After what had just happened I thought my parents would never let me out of their sight!

In a way, I was right. I didn't know then Dad had talked to Rico and Gloria about things other than transportation. Mom didn't either, and kept throwing questioning looks at Dad while they talked to Rosa.

Paolo just looked at me and shrugged. I shrugged back.

"Come on, Rose. Time to go 'till tomorrow at noon. Thank you for your help," Dad said to Paolo and Rosa as we left the shop. He waved at Gloria and Rico, who waved back and drove away.

Back on the Plaza we followed Dad to one of the sidewalk tables and sat down.

"Okay Dad, what's going on?" I demanded.

"Yes, 'Dad' what's going on?" Mom echoed.

"Well, Rose, honey, you need some time off on this vacation. We need to make sure you'll be okay. Rico and Gloria know Paolo's family, and assure us they are safe. They will also provide transportation and keep an eye on the area in case you have unexpected company. We can't keep you in a cage forever. Besides, we need to know if we are being watched."

"Oh, I get it, I'm the bait."

"Dear - you can't be serious!" Mom said

"Rose will not be in danger - - just chaperoned. We all know why we are here. What we don't know is whether they know why we are here. Our cover is being on a family vacation. We have to mix business with pleasure. Rose, you yourself told us we have to go through with this mission; remember?"

"Yes, Dad, I - remember. It's okay, Mom. If we are going to be in a family business as spies, we'll have to get used to it. We all live in a world of cameras anyway."

Mom sighed. "Yes, we do. I lived with security and bodyguards as long as I was growing up, guess you will, too."

"At least it's not the paparazzi." I said.

"Rose, you know I would never put you in harm's way," Dad said, eyes tearing up.

"I know, Dad. I want to visit Paolo and his family. It will be good for my education, and the newsletter - and Paolo is a friend. I like to have friends. The only question I have is do I have to wear the COM link?"

"'Fraid so, kiddo," Dad said with a smile. I knew he was worried about me being with a boy.

"Great, no privacy," I grumbled.

"Don't worry, Rose. Dad will be tuned out. I'll be listening on the COM. Susan and Steven only get tracking anyway."

I could handle Mom listening. Dad was another matter!

"While we are outside, dear, what did you find out today?" Mom said to Dad.

"The Minister of Commerce promised to arrange a meeting between me and Peru Wire. There are two companies here battling for our business, and only one is contracted to work with the Peruvian government. Both companies make everything from fine electrical wire to chain link fencing. One goes after government jobs, supplying fencing to the army, the other works the private sector, going after world markets. The companies are feuding over the right to secure contracts with the U.S. Our company does not supply the military here. The U.S. feels it would be a conflict of interest should tension develop between the two countries. I told them I was a businessman here with my family on vacation, and looking for a supplier for my company back home."

"Sheesh! And you call me a rambler!" I said.

"So far, that's all information I already have. We need details. Can we get copies of the contract from The Agency?" Mom asked.

"No, they are classified, and we no longer have clearance to those documents. What we need to know is why the company is dragging its feet. Why are they stalling? Its not lack of raw material. Peru is the world's second largest producer of copper. Most wire is made from copper or aluminum. Both are mined in the Andes. I suspect they are trying to delay the new computers The Agency has ordered. They don't want them upgrading, at least not yet."

"Makes sense," Mom nodded. "But why?"

"Timing is everything. Could be the stock market. Could be world events or trade talks. Could be they just want to use their contract with the U.S. to line up other countries? Maybe their 'war' with the other wire company is slowing them down."

"I'll use my laptop, and do some digging tonight," Mom said.

"Good. I'll send a report to The Agency and update Susan and Steven," Dad said.

"What can I do, Dad?"

"You can show me what you bought today!" He asked.

"What makes you think we bought anything today?" I teased.

"The large bulge in your backpack, for one."

"Well, we might have picked up a few things, but I couldn't find anything for you," I fibbed.

Mom looked at me with a questioning expression on her face. Dad hung his head in mock shame and I looked at Mom and went, "Shhh!"

We told him all about our sightseeing, and showed him everything but the horse; I was saving that for later.

"Hey, what about dinner?" Dad said.

"Yes, Dear, what about dinner? I'm on vacation!" Mom teased.

"Just so happens we have a restaurant back home," He said, referring to the hotel.

"Is that the best you can do? Where is your imagination?" Mom countered.

Dad looked across the street for inspiration. He found it!

"How about McDonalds?"

Mom groaned, and Dad looked at me for support.

"You're not putting me in the middle on this one, Dad," I said

"What's wrong with where we are? We are outside a café," he said.

"Yes, we are. But where are the waiters?" Mom asked.

"Let's go in and find out." Dad said, standing up.

We followed him inside. Walking up to the counter, he asked about service.

"Our waiter was injured this afternoon in a fall. You are welcome to eat inside."

"No thanks!" Dad said, knowing what had happened earlier.

From the McDonald's he called Rico and Gloria. They would track the waiter and report back.

I smiled as I bit into the Big Mac.

That night after writing my newsletter notes, I said my prayers and good night to the three S's-Susan, Steven, and Sam.

I switched off the light, and thought about lunch with Rosa and Paolo tomorrow. I thought about Grandma and Grandpa, and the rain-forest. I knew there were lots of butterflies there.

I didn't know why, but some of them must have gotten into my stomach!

Chapter Nine

This time I was the one who woke everybody up for breakfast! I was excited about going to Paolo's for lunch!

"Come on, sleepy heads! Breakfast is at seven!" I said as I shook Mom and Dad awake at six in the morning.

"Sheesh! Some vacation!" Dad grumbled as he dug further into his pillow.

"We're coming, we're coming!" Mom repeated as she sat up against the headboard.

"What a turn around! Some secret agents you are!" I teased.

"Okay, Rose, you scoot, and we'll get up," Dad said.

"Okay, but if you are not ready by seven, I'm leaving without you!" It was so much fun to be on the waking up crew for a change.

I went back into the living room, smiling. Sure, it was only a few hours, but I had something to do. I wasn't just a tag along. I knew I'd be watched and listened to, but that did not matter. I wasn't interested in doing anything wrong with Paolo anyway.

While I was waiting for my parents I made preparations for the day. I unloaded my backpack, and took one of Mom's canvas bags. It would be easier to deal with. I packed my digital camera and notebook. I was a reporter, after all. I decide to wear shorts, sandals and a t-shirt, since Paolo and his family lived near the coast. And a light nylon windbreaker seemed like a good idea. Maybe we could go out in his Dad's fishing boat! At the last minute I decided to bring my CD player also.

By the time Mom and Dad came out of their room, I was ready to go!

"Well, too bad we couldn't get you going like this on school days!" Mom said.

"I wonder what Rose could be so excited about?" Dad said to Mom, as if I wasn't there.

"Hmm, I wonder…" Mom replied. "Couldn't be a boy, could it?"

"Naw. Must be the job. I think we have a first-class employee on our hands." Dad said, winking at Mom.

I blushed, partly out of embarrassment, and partly out of anger. How dare they tease me about boys!

"Okay, you two! You paid me back. Can't a person just be hungry?" I said, defensively.

"Of course! She's just hungry, dear," Mom said.

"Come to think of it, so am I," Dad said back.

"Let's go eat while we're still friends!" I smiled through my teeth.

"Okay, Rose. I'm sorry we teased you. We are hungry. Let's go see what's for breakfast."

And with that, Dad opened the door, and we headed for the hotel dining room.

The restaurant looked different in the daytime. There was a large buffet set up, and the great thing about it was I got to pick whatever I wanted. When we had all loaded our plates, we sat down at one of the window tables.

"By the way, Dad," I said, digging into my scrambled eggs, "did Richard get to the airport on time for his fishing trip?"

"Uhh, yep, got him there okay. He's probably on the Amazon right now."

Something about Dad's answer did not sound right. I decided that Dad must have a good reason for not telling us everything. Maybe it wasn't safe to talk in the dining room, although there were not many people here so early. The buffet ran until eleven. I decided to ask him later.

"Mom, when do we get to go to Machu Picchu?" I asked.

"As soon as we find what we are looking for. In the meantime, there are a couple of museums we could check out."

"You said you were going to tell me about how Grandma and Grandpa met." I reminded her.

"Yes, I know, but after yesterday's events we have to push up the program. We can reschedule."

"Okay, but before the trip is over," I said

"We've got some calls to make after breakfast, then we'll get ready for this afternoon," Mom said, business-like.

"Rico and Gloria will pick us up at eleven," Dad said.

"Why so early? Paolo does not live that far way," I asked.

"They are going to drop Mom, and I off before they take you there," Dad said quietly.

"I'm already packed. What can I do while we are waiting?" I sure did not want to twiddle my thumbs all morning.

"Well, you could start on your next issue of the newsletter," Mom suggested.

"Good idea. I could write about the Plaza, and the places we saw yesterday!" I already knew there were things I could not write about!

So after breakfast I took out my laptop, and went to the website. Having been the editor of my school paper was good training for writing a newsletter. In fact, many of the things I learned at school would probably come in handy. Like the first time we ate in the dining room. I knew which fork to use!

Before I knew it, it was ten o'clock and time to get ready.

"Okay, Rose. Let's check your COM link," Dad said, tapping the barrette in my ponytail.

Mom had her earphone in place. "Got it," she nodded.

"Now, remember Rose, we are not spying on you and Paolo. We're just watching over you in case we run into uninvited guests. Susan and Steven will be tracking your signal through Zip and so will we.

"I know, Dad. I've had some experience in the field, you know." I appreciated what they were doing. They could have held my hand the whole trip, and not let me do anything - and who would have blamed them?

I gave them both a hug and picked up my bag, double-checking the contents like a good agent would.

There was a knock at the door. Mom looked through the peephole.

Our escorts had arrived! And so had the butterflies! I was nervous and excited at the same time. This was going to be some day!

Chapter Ten

The butterflies got worse on the way to Paolo's house. Rico and Gloria made small talk as we rode along in the converted cab. I sat alone in the back seat, slipping from side to side on the hard fake leather upholstery. I hardly heard a word they said.

Mom and Dad had waited a few minutes before leaving the hotel room. They were following in the rental car, but taking a different route. I knew Mom was listening in. She was probably tiring of Rico's chatter. I had tuned everything out.

I was trying not to think about the fact back home Aunt Susan and Uncle Steven were following my 'blip' on Zip, and my parents were chaperoning my first 'date'. If that weren't enough, Rico and Gloria would be watching from a distance.

Sheesh! I felt like the president's daughter! Oh, and let's not forget the possibility several bad guys were probably watching too!

This was too intense! I had to do something to get a little privacy! So, as the car pulled up to the little house on the coast, I finalized my plan.

"Thanks for the ride," I said as I climbed out of the cab, canvas bag slung over my shoulder.

"See you at three," Rico said as they drove away.

By now, Mom and Dad were in position, parked on a scenic overlook, binoculars in hand. Rico and Gloria were headed to another lookout spot. For further security neither location was mentioned. This would also keep me from giving the whole thing away by staring or glaring at my spies!

Knowing Mom was listening, I let Rosa come out and greet me as I walked to the door. As soon as lunch was over I would switch the COM link to tracking only.

"I am so happy you could come, Rose!" Rosa said as crossed the little yard in front of the little house.

"Thank you for inviting me, Rosa. It's so nice to get away from my parents for a little while. I love them, but sometimes they worry about me too much! It seems like they watch my every move!" I knew Mom was wincing at that one!

"Now, Rose, I was young once like you - and I was a parent too. Some day you will thank them for watching over you. But today, I am young like you." She winked at me, and turned away from the door.

"What do you think of my flowers?" She asked.

"They are beautiful, Rosa!" I said, looking at the bright red roses growing in front of the house on either side of the door. They looked even redder against the sea shell pink stucco.

"My husband, rest his soul, and I planted these when we built this little house. This was a shantytown you know. We started with a few boards and bricks, and built one room. My husband was a fisherman, and I set up a shop for my needlework, and crafts in the plaza. As time went on we had a son and added another room. As we grew, the house did too. The town grew also, and stretches along the coast."

I looked up and down the street of similar houses. I saw the pride of hard-working people, and realized what a different life I had. Yet, my parents worked hard, as did their parents before them. I was lucky to live in the United States.

"Well, lunch is ready, and I know Paolo is waiting to see you," Rosa said, opening the door.

I stepped into the living room of the house. The walls were plastered, and painted bright white. Brightly colored mats hung here and there, hand-made by Rosa. There were also photographs and hand-carved figures of wood done by Paolo's father. It was warm and inviting.

There was a small table in the kitchen at the back of the house. The table was set with hand made placemats and colorful dishes. I could smell the tortillas and chili.

"Where is Paolo?" I asked.

"He was here a moment ago. I asked him to set the table," Rosa said.

The back door opened, and Paolo walked in holding a rose.

"For our guest," he said, handing it to me.

"Thank you," I said, blushing as I took the flower.

"Let me put it in some water," Rosa said. "Sit down and eat, children."

"Paolo, did you pick one of your grandmothers' roses for me?" I asked, concerned about him being in trouble.

"No, I have some of my own, in back of the house," he smiled.

"Paolo has many talents," Rosa said as she returned with the rose, and set it on the table, "like his father and grandfather."

Tradition was strong in this family. I realized we were more alike than different.

As we ate, my nervousness faded. I forgot about myself and let the reporter in me take over. I learned about Paolo's family and Rosa's business.

"Where is your mother, Paolo?" I asked.

"She died when I was born. My father says I look like her but I think I look like him."

I looked at Paolo's dark hair and eyes. I hadn't seen his mother or father yet.

"Her picture is in the living room, next to Paolo's grandfather," Rosa said. "He died on the fishing boat. His heart gave out pulling in a net of fish. Biggest catch they ever had, his brother said."

"I'm sorry. I guess I'm lucky to have both my parents."

"Rosa is like my mother. She raised me. I am lucky to have my grandmother!" Paolo said. "Do you like your Grandparents, Rose?"

"They are all gone. But my Grandpa and Grandma on my mother's side met right here in Peru! At Machu Picchu! My mother is going to take me there, and tell me the story!"

"After lunch I will show you the pictures. Father should be home soon, and he has promised to take us for a boat ride!" Paolo was excited.

The food was great, and soon we were in the living room of the little house. There on a shelf was a little shrine with photographs of Paolo's mother and grandfather.

"She was beautiful!" I said, looking at her dark black hair and dark brown eyes. "What was her name?"

"Luisa. And my father's name was Juan."

I turned at the sound of the new voice. Paolo's father had come home.

"And you are...?" He asked.

"Father, this is Rose, the girl I told you about," Paolo introduced me.

"A pleasure to meet you, Rose. I am Pablo, Paolo's father," he bowed.

"It is nice to meet you, sir," I replied, impressed with the charm of their manners.

Rosa beamed with pride at the family. "Come, Pablo, have some lunch," she said.

"Father, did you remember the boat ride?" Paolo asked.

"Yes, Paolo. You and Rose visit while I eat, and we will take a ride after," Pablo smiled.

I liked his dark, rugged face, and sad, smiling eyes. His hands were weathered, and hard working. I looked at his carvings of driftwood.

There were a seagull, a fishing boat; a rose, and an unfinished bust of a woman.

"I started carving after Luisa died. I have never been able to finish her likeness," Pablo said as he walked to the table.

Paolo tugged at me. "Let's wait outside on the beach."

I grabbed the canvas bag, and followed him out the back door.

Paolo showed me his rose bushes. "They are beautiful, Paolo. Is there anything you can't do?"

"Not according to Grandmother. She says I can do anything if I try hard enough."

We went for a walk along the beach. I pointed to a funny looking bird.

"What is that?" I asked.

"That's a Booby. The sailors named them that. They live off tropical islands, and along the coast. Father says they are important for their guano."

"What's guano?" I asked.

Paolo laughed. "Uh, it is used for fertilizer. It is important to the farmers. Father says the guano is drying up because of over fishing the anchovies. Peru is one of the largest exporters of anchovies in the world. They are also used to make fish food, of which we are again the largest producer."

"Yes, I read a lot about your country before we came. Is it true there are more than six million people in Lima?" I asked.

"I don't know, I never counted them!" Paolo said, laughing again.

We both laughed and sat down on some rocks. I took out my sun hat and CD player.

"Would you like to hear some music?" I asked.

Paolo nodded and took the CD player and headphones. Ignoring the CD, he tuned in the radio.

"We have many radio stations," he said, and tuned in the local teen station.

"If we are going in the boat, I better put on my sun hat," I said, using it as an excuse to switch the COM link in my barrette from voice to tracking only.

Now my parents would have to rely on their binoculars to watch us! At least we could talk in private.

But before we could do any talking, Pablo walked up and waved us to his boat!

Chapter Eleven

Pablo's boat wasn't very big, but it was big enough for a small crew. It was an old boat, but well cared for.

"This boat feeds many families." Paolo said. "It is not like the big commercial boats that work on the coast. My father and his three brothers are independent fishermen who sell their catch to the fisheries. They fish for tuna and anchovies. Sometimes I fish with them. Every man splits the take and my father counts as two. It is his boat."

Pablo smiled from the pilot house as Paolo showed me around the boat. I took notes for my newsletter. I was glad I had listened to my English teacher, Miss Langtree. She taught me the things every reporter must include in their story, the five "W's", Who, What, Where, When, and Why. It also gave me an outline for telling the story.

"What are you doing, Rose?" Paolo asked as I jotted down notes.

"Taking notes for my newsletter. I am a reporter," I said.

"You are a reporter? For who?" He asked.

"For myself right now. Last year I was the editor of my school paper. Now I am home-schooled, and write a newsletter on the Internet. Someday I will win the Pulitzer Prize!"

"Wow," Paolo said. "You will be famous!"

"Maybe. Well, yes I would," I said.

"Look, Rose, there are the factories. If you are writing about Peru you must talk about them. Father says they are our future. We compete with the whole world, he says. Only China beats us in tuna catching."

Pablo had slowed the boat, and I listened to the motor chug quietly as the boat eased along the shore. We stayed far enough out to avoid the other boats and ships busy with their work. Paolo pointed out the fisheries, the handicrafts, and other industries Peru was known for.

"And there are the wire factories. The wire is made from copper and aluminum from the mines in the Andes."

Paolo was proud of his knowledge

"You know a lot about your country," I said, impressed.

"Father says I am the future of Peru. He does not want me to become a poor, drunken fisherman,"

"Someday you will be famous too!" I said.

Paolo smiled, and stood a little taller.

My mind turned to my parents. I wished I hadn't turned off the COM link. I knew they would be watching, though.

"Paolo, can you show me the wire factories?"

"I just did," he said with a quizzical look.

"No, I mean take me there."

"Sure, but why?"

"Well, it's a long story, but let's just say I want to write about them."

"Okay. I could see you at the hotel tomorrow. I will be working there in the morning. At lunchtime maybe your parents would let me take you."

"We can't tell them about it," I said. "But maybe they will let you take me to McDonald's. Then we could go to the factories."

Paolo agreed, and we made our plans. I knew my parents would not let me go alone, and I knew if they were there, they would never find out anything. I didn't tell Paolo I wasn't just a reporter; I was a spy, also.

Pablo took us out to the fishing grounds. I took the camera out of my bag, and took pictures of Paolo and his father. I took pictures of the other boats and the scenery. I had been careful not to take pictures around the factories. You never knew who was watching!

Pablo took us back to the house and at exactly three o'clock Rico and Gloria drove up.

I said goodbye to Rosa and Pablo, and walked to the car with Paolo.

"Thank you for the nice tour, Paolo. See you soon," I said as I climbed into the tour car, winking at Paolo

He nodded at the wink, knowing as kids do, that something was supposed to be a secret. He didn't know why, but went along with it.

"See you soon," he repeated, shutting the door of the converted cab.

I knew I was in for some questions!

I braced my self for the five "W's"!

Chapter Twelve

"Well, young lady how was your day?" Rico asked as I slid across the slick back seat.

I did not like Rico's tone. Why was it all adults called you "young lady, or young man" when there were upset with you?

"Well, 'Dad', it was very nice," I replied tartly. Only my parents had the right to call me 'young lady'.

"Your voice link was off, Rose. We were worried about you," Gloria said defensively.

"You weren't supposed to be hearing me," I said.

"No, we weren't. Your mother told us she had lost voice. You didn't do that on purpose, did you?"

"Why, no," I said, "It must have accidentally switched off when I put my sunhat on."

Gloria looked at me, and kind of smiled. It was hard to fool another woman! Especially an agent!

"Well, everything turned out fine. We did not see any threats." Gloria said more to Rico than me.

Rico relaxed, and I launched into a description of the boat ride, conveniently leaving out the wire factories. I bored them with facts about fishing they already knew.

By the time they dropped me at the hotel, they were convinced I was just another twelve-year-old kid, and they were glad the babysitting was over.

Mom and Dad were another matter. They arrived at the same time. Dad dropped Mom at the door and went to park the car. I didn't give Mom a chance to ask anything. I ran up to her with my digital camera to show her the pictures.

"Hi, Mom! Look at these neat pictures! I got to ride in the fishing boat! Look at this one!"

I was so happy and bubbly Mom forgot her questions. She did not want to spoil the good time I had.

By the time we got to the room, and Dad walked in, we were both laughing about boys.

Dad did not have a chance. He walked into the room ready to fire questions, but stopped in his tracks when we both looked at him and started to laugh.

"Hey, what's so funny?" He said.

At that we laughed again. Soon he was laughing too.

"Boys!" Mom said, looking at me.

"Yep!" I said, smiling lovingly at Dad, who melted under it.

He started to say something, but stopped and shook his head. He would never figure it out.

"Well, Rose, how was your day?" He finally asked.

"It was great, Dad. Can't wait to show you the pictures!"

There was no way Dad was going to spoil his daughter's joy. After all, here we were safe and sound, laughing and having fun. Everything was fine.

I showed him the pictures on the digital camera, and talked about the newsletter.

"I must admit, Rose, we were a little worried when we lost your voice link. We watched your boat ride through the binoculars. At least your tracking was on," he said.

Rats! I thought I had gotten his mind off that!

"Must have been my sunhat, Dad."

"That's what we figured, too," he said, winking at Mom.

Sheesh! Could a girl ever get any privacy in this world? At least they weren't mad at me.

"You know, Dad, Rosa said she remembered what it was like to be a parent and a kid." I said, thoughtfully.

"We do, too," he smiled.

"She said I should be glad I have parents who care about me,"

"We do, Rose. We care about you having a good time, too. Remember, we are on the same side. So many kids think parents are their enemy. We know you wouldn't get into any bad things."

I felt bad about my secret plan to visit the wire factories, but knew Mom and Dad would never agree with it. I wanted to help them on my own. I decided to not to tell them.

"Hey, where are we going to eat tonight?" I asked, switching tracks.

"Well, we had a busy day. How about right here in our room?" Dad said.

"Okay by me. I can download my pictures onto the website and work on my newsletter."

"Yeah, and we have to coordinate with Susan and Steven," Mom spoke up.

"Can we put them on Zip?" I asked. "I want to see Sam! I miss him."

"Sure can," Mom said.

The best thing a girl can do after a date is spend lots of time with her parents! That way they don't worry about losing their little girl!

We ate in our room, and called home.

"Susan, Steven! Good to see you!" Dad said to the hologram on Zip.

It was like having them in our room. I knew we were appearing the same way there. Sam barked at our images, and I reached to pet him. He whined when he didn't feel my hand, and cocked his head from side to side. Finally he lay down, and whimpered a little.

"What have you found out?" Dad asked.

"So far, someone in the Agency is a mole. We are checking records now to see who is tipping off the Peruvians about your presence there. We are sure he or she is part of the plan to delay the shipment of the wire. Your theory about delaying the updated computers to The Agency seems correct. Someone is planning something big, and does not want us to find out before it happens," Steven reported.

"Have you identified the waiter yet?" Mom asked.

"Yes. Pedro Alveraz, known student of the Old Fox of Shining Path. Your father tipped the authorities to his activities in the Seventies who led to the arrest of most of the Shining Path members. They know his shipping contacts were only part of his reason for being in Peru. They see your visit there as more than a vacation, and getting information will be very hard for you. They will do nothing to damage relations with the United States again - especially if they are involved in the coming event. They will only stall you, and throw out false information."

"How can we get around it?" Mom asked.

Susan spoke now. "Keep tracking communications through your business computers. Look for any links you can establish or coded messages. Maybe they have been careless here and there. They will not allow you access to their computers physically. You will have to work through Zip, Rico, and Gloria."

"I have a meeting with the wire company tomorrow " Dad said. " At least I will get to look around. I am posing as a businessman, but they know better."

This was news to me! I hoped Dad would not be at the factory the same time I was.

"Keep your COM link on, and your button cam," Steven said. "What time is your tour?"

"Eight a.m. I should be out of there by ten."

Whew! I was planning on being there with Paolo about twelve-thirty.

"Any news on the man on the plane?" Dad asked.

"We've been tracking his movements," Steven replied. "His presence seems to indicate a joint effort in the plan between the hard-line Communists, and the terrorists. Whatever they are planning must be pretty big. So far we have the Al Quida terrorists, Shining Path, and The Communists working together. I wouldn't be surprised to run into the Colombian drug lords too."

"Somebody's computer must have information in it!" Mom said. "I'll hook up tonight with my company computers. There must be flags somewhere."

"With all The Agency's resources, why haven't we heard anything?" Susan said.

"Word of mouth. They must be setting it all up with a code of silence," Dad said.

"We'll keep working from this end," Steven said. "Right now we're going to have some breakfast."

"We just finished supper," Mom said

"Good night, Rose!" Susan said as they signed off. Samson The Great barked as I faded out,

"Good night," I said, choking back a tear at Sam's bark.

The rest of the evening was spent working on laptops. I edited my newsletter and Mom searched her company computers for information. Dad read up on wire production and mining.

Finally it was time to get ready for bed. I stood on the balcony looking out at the lights of Lima at night. Everything looked so peaceful. I watched the cars below, and listened to the traffic. I wondered how many people knew something terrible was being planned.

Maybe they just didn't want to think about it.

Chapter Thirteen

But I did think about it. All night long. The excitement I had planning my espionage with Paolo faded with the realization of world events. All my brave talk seemed to click off with the light. I felt like a twelve-year-old child.

Eventually I did drop off to sleep, just before dawn. The light shining through the curtains brought some of my courage back. Stumbling to the bathroom, I gave myself a good talking to.

"Get a hold on it, now," Grandpa used to tell me when I'd fall off my bike. "Get right back up and tame that horse!"

How was I ever going to be a world-class reporter if I couldn't go after a story? I could never look myself in the eye again if I backed out now. I decided to get back on the bike.

I put on jeans, a t-shirt, and my Reeboks. I threw my hair into a quick ponytail, and put on my Yankee's ball cap. I packed my canvas bag with a note pad, and my digital camera as I had done the day before. I made sure my barrette was in place, and switched to tracking only.

There was rain forecast for Lima today so a windbreaker would be wise, too.

Finally suited up, my courage restored, I stepped into the living room of the suite and said, "What's for breakfast?"

Mom and Dad were both up and sitting on the couch. They had been talking quietly so as not to wake me. They were surprised to see me.

"Well, good morning, Rose. My, you are up and at 'em today." Mom said, setting down her coffee cup.

"Going to the ball game?" Dad asked.

"No, the T.V. said rain today, that's all," I replied matter-of-factly.

"Well, we both have to work today," Dad said. "Let's catch the breakfast buffet and we'll talk about our plans."

"How late were you going to let me sleep?" I asked

"Just until you woke up," Mom said. "I'll be here all day, and I thought you might hang out with me while I work."

"That sounds exciting, " I said flatly.

I was trying to find some way to have lunch with Paolo so we could get away long enough to check out the wire factory.

"Well, let's eat. I'm hungry," I said, turning toward the door.

Mom and Dad looked at each other and shrugged. They figured I was just cranky, and not excited about sitting there all day, especially when we were supposed to go to Machu Picchu today.

Ah! There was my leverage! I would pretend to be so disappointed about our change in plans Mom would have to let me go with Paolo! I smiled as we trudged down the hall to the elevators.

Nobody talked in the elevator. I think it's a law or something. I used the silence to maximum advantage. I wanted my parents to feel guilty about having to work.

By the time we got to the dining room, I knew I had them!

"My, you sure are hungry, Rose!" Mom said as we sat down.

"People eat more when they travel, I heard," I replied, setting down a heaping plate of scrambled eggs and fruit. "Isn't that right, Dad?" It was still good strategy to play one parent against the other.

"So I've heard," he said, straddling his chair as he set down his plate.

"What time are you leaving, Dad?" I asked.

"Right after breakfast, sweetheart. I have to be at the wire factory at ten."

I put on a sad face, but did not want to over-do it. I did not want him to cancel his tour on my account.

"Look," Mom said, "isn't that Paolo?"

There was Paolo, dressed in his hotel whites, at the buffet. He was loading a big plate also.

Looking up, he noticed us and waved

Dad waved him over. "Come and sit with us, Paolo," he said.

"Dad, don't do that!" I scolded.

But it was too late. Paolo came to our table, and sat next to me.

"I get a free breakfast when I work at the hotel," he informed us.

"Well, we wanted to thank you for showing Rose your father's boat yesterday. "She had such a good time," Mom piped up.

"Yes, thank your grandmother for us, also," Dad said.

I wondered why Paolo was not dressed like me, and then realized how smart that was! This way no one would suspect we were planning anything. I figured he would work until noon, and then change into his street clothes.

"Well, you kids are sure eating well this morning," Mom said again. Paolo and I had laid out our plans yesterday on the boat. We would both dress in jeans and windbreakers, and eat a big breakfast. I would find some way to get Mom to let me eat lunch at McDonald's and instead we would run down to the wire factory and look around. We wanted to disguise ourselves as a couple of American kids just looking around. We could gather information to help the investigation and at the same time I could show my parents I could help too. After all, I was twelve years old!

"Well, I have to get to work," Dad said, pushing his chair back. "You kids have a nice day."

"You, too, Dad," I said, kissing him as he bent down, embarrassing Paolo a great deal!

"Yes, Dear, you be careful out there!" Mom said as he kissed her too.

"I must get to work, also," Paolo said as he stood up, holding his empty plate.

"I hope you don't expect a kiss!" I teased.

Blushing, he looked at Dad. "Yech! Why would I want that?

Now my face was red!

Dad laughed and walked away. Mom was holding back a laugh also.

"Serve's you right for teasing Paolo like that," she said.

I kept my smile to myself.

My plan was working perfectly!

Chapter Fourteen

I started on Mom as soon as we left the breakfast table. I knew guilt would be my only weapon in getting her to let me go with Paolo.

"Aw, Mom, do you have to work today? I thought we could go to Machu Picchu or something."

"Now Rose, you know how important this is. Why don't you work on your newsletter? Besides, it's supposed to rain anyway."

I could hear the guilt in Mom's voice. Perfect!

Turning the key to our suite, Mom opened the door and let out a sigh. She wasn't excited about working either. I only hoped she wouldn't change her mind. I had to be careful not to lay it on too thick.

It was nine-thirty. Both of us had been slaving away at our laptops for a whole half an hour! I let out a "Ho-Hum" followed by a soft sigh just loud enough for Mom to hear it. Her ears cocked in my direction just like Sam's did. She did not turn her head.

We kept working in heavy silence.

Paolo got off duty at noon. He changed into his jeans and sneakers, and stepped into the elevator, ready for part two of our plan.

By now, Dad should be finished with his tour of the wire factory. We had to hurry so we would not cross paths.

Paolo knocked lightly at our door.

"Well, Paolo. How nice to see you! Please come in," Mom said. "Are you finished working today?"

"Well, sort of," he replied. "I have to go into the plaza to pick up some supplies for the hotel. I could use some help, could Rose come along?"

"Oh, I don't know, Paolo. Rose should stay here until her father returns."

"Oh, can I, Mom? We have been working for hours! I'm so bored! Please," I pleaded.

"But it may not be safe, Dear," Mom defended her position.

"I'll wear my COM," I said, anxious to reassure her.

"She will be safe with me," Paolo said, standing tall and throwing his shoulders back.

It was so cute Mom was thrown off her guard.

"Well..." s-he said.

I knew she was starting to crack.

"It's only for an hour or so," Paolo said.

"Really, Mom. We'll be okay,"

"Oh, I hope your father doesn't find out,"

"Gee, thanks Mom!" I jumped ahead.

"Wait a minute, I didn't say it would be okay."

"But you were going to, weren't you?" I said, with big innocent eyes no parent can resist.

"If your Dad finds out..." Mom threatened.

"I'll get my windbreaker!" I said, grabbing the bag I had already prepared.

"Let's go! Thanks Mom, you're the greatest!" I shouted as we rushed out the door.

"Be back in an hour..." She shouted down the hall as we vanished into the elevator.

The silent whoosh of the closing doors signaled our escape. I looked at Paolo and smiled.

"Nice work, partner!" I said, shaking his hand.

"Nice work, Partner," he repeated.

"Let's get out of here before Dad comes back. I hope you know the way, Paolo.

"Of course I do! This is my town," He said, smiling.

By the time we heard the "ding" of the first floor elevator we had synchronized our watches and finalized our plan.

The spies at the wire factory would be no matches for us!

Chapter Fifteen

Paolo turned right as the doors opened. We were going out the back. On the way he picked up his windbreaker. No one paid attention as we went out the back door of the hotel. They were used to Paolo coming and going.

The sky was dark and cloudy, and there was a light rain falling. This was unusual for Lima, and most people welcomed the rain. The air smelled fresher, and the streets were wet and shiny.

Paolo knew all of the back streets, and soon we were not far from the coast highway. It was too far to walk to the factories, but Paolo said we were going to meet his uncle.

His uncle was a truck driver. He owned a van, and picked up shipments at the airport. He delivered them to the factories along the coast.

"Paolo, you are one minute late!"

"Sorry, Enrico. Rose, this is my uncle, Enrico."

"Nice to meet you, Enrico," I said, climbing into the van behind Paolo.

Enrico ground the gears and the van lurched forward. I grabbed the handle of the side door, and hung on as the van picked up speed. We lurched through every gear until at last we were rolling along the coast highway.

"So, you are a reporter, eh?" Enrico said. "They start young in your country, eh?"

"Some day I will win the Pulitzer Prize!" I said, smiling under my Yankee's hat.

"Paolo tells me you only need a little time to take some pictures. Will you take one of me? Maybe you will write about my delivery service, yes?"

"I'll take one when we jump out." I said.

"Well, here we are. I will be back in half an hour. I have deliveries to make. You must be here, or find your own ride."

"We will, Uncle," Paolo assured him.

"Smile!" I said as I snapped the camera

"What kind of camera is that? It does not look like other cameras. Do you have enough film?" Enrico asked.

"It's digital. It doesn't need film," I explained.

Enrico smiled as I took the picture, seemingly unconcerned about our "mission".

"Half an hour!" He reminded us as he drove away.

Paolo and I stood in the rain looking at the chain link fence of the Peru Wire Company.

"Don't get too close, rose," he cautioned.

I started snapping pictures of the giant wooden spools of wire and cable behind the fence.

It was just like I remembered from Grandpa's story! There were spools of different colored wire! Each of the giant spools sat in a big open area, and there was a forklift moving them around, probably to make room for more.

I wished we could have gone on the tour with Dad to see how the wire was made. I had read about how wire was made on Zip.

The copper or aluminum was made into rods, and forced through diamond cutters that shaved them down to the thickness desired. The blades had to be made of something very hard so as not to wear out.

I had also read about the growing wire business in Peru and how the two wire companies were at war with each other for business. Curiously, wire imports to the U.S. from Peru had doubled six months before the last election.

"Rose! You are getting too close!" Paolo whispered as I continued snapping pictures.

"I need to get the lens through the fence," I explained. "Keep watch for me."

Paolo was getting nervous. He did not like the cameras so close to the building, where they could be seen.

"Rose..." he started to say.

"Shhh!" I said as I heard voices from the wire yard.

We both stood silent, listening

"I tell you, I don't trust that American businessman!"

"Of course we know he is a spy. He is here to investigate the delay in the shipment of wire to the US."

The voices were coming from between two spools of wire. I motioned Paolo to be quiet, and moved a few steps to the right. Now I had a better view. The men were dressed in business suits, and one of them looked familiar!

It was the old man from the Plaza! The Shining Path member my grandfather had put away years before!

Paolo recognized him also, and tugged at my sleeve. I squatted down low as the two men continued talking.

"This plan has taken years to put together. All by word of mouth! The few things the Americans can find on their computers will not be enough to stop it unless they succeed in their plan to upgrade their computers, and link them all into one network. Our part of the plan is just to stall the wire. We must not draw undue attention to ourselves. We will not interfere with the American or his family. As president of this wire factory, I am taking all the risks, delaying our delivery."

Now I recognized the other man! Alex Bacon, the man on the plane!

"I say we stop the Americans now!" The Old Fox said. "They can find out too much! We can make them vanish. This is the largest combined terrorist effort ever conceived! All of the anti-U.S. forces are involved! We cannot risk the plan."

"Our orders are just to delay and confuse. We will stick to the plan! By time the Americans get their wire, all three bridges will be destroyed, and their economy will be in ruins!"

Paolo was crouched low, and backing up. There was a growing look of terror on his face. This was a bigger story than he wanted to know! My heart was pounding as I snapped a picture of the two men.

"Which three bridges?" I whispered.

"The Brooklyn Bridge, The Golden Gate and the..." the Old Fox said almost as if he had heard me, but before he could finish his sentence I fell backwards into Paolo's lap. He fell backwards into the street, and the horn of a passing car caused the men to look right at us

We scrambled to get to our feet, slipping on the wet pavement. The camera went sliding along the curb as we grabbed each other's windbreakers, and tried to stand up.

By the time we did it was too late! Standing behind us the two men clasped each of our necks with their big hands.

The Old Fox took the Yankee's cap from my head and spun me around.

"The girl from the Plaza! The American's daughter! And my old nemesis' granddaughter."

I wished I had turned on the COM link! I hoped he wouldn't see it! They searched our jackets and my bag.

"What are you doing here, children?" One of them asked.

"What did you hear?" The other asked.

"Nothing. She is a tourist. I was giving her a tour." Paolo said, bravely.

"I just wanted to see a factory." I said.

"What should we do with them?" The president asked.

"I know what I would like to do with them!" The Old Fox replied.

Both of us were scared now!

"We will make them disappear!"

"You mean kill them?"

"We could, but it would bring too much attention. I know there is a wire on the girl. She must be spying for her father. Ah, think I know…"

He was looking at my hair! He had found the COM link! If only I had set it to voice we would be rescued soon! But it was set on tracking only!

"Come with us, children," he said, as he removed the barrette from my hair, and replaced my cap.

Paolo struggled, and I kicked but it did no good! They dragged us through the gate into the wire yard. Just before we got to the garage door the Old Fox stopped

"Hold them!" He said, taking the COM link and slowly inching his way towards a booby bird perched on one of the spools.

"Oh no!" I whispered as I saw what he was about to do.

Many of the Booby's were tame, and he reached into his pocket as if to take out some food.

The bird fell for the deception, and with one quick move the Old Fox grabbed it, and fastened the COM link to its leg. Then he threw the bird into the air, yelling and terrorizing it so it would not return.

Our hope of rescue was headed for parts unknown.

"So, you want to see a factory, eh? Well, now you will have a personal tour!"

As we were dragged inside, I looked at Paolo. I knew he was thinking the same thing. They didn't know about Enrico, and the camera lying in the street.

At least we had some hope of rescue!

198

Chapter Sixteen

"Smile, children, or else!" The Old Fox said as we walked through the garage door, hands still clutching our necks. We smiled at the fork-lift driver, and he smiled back. The workers rolling big wooden spools of wire from here to there all smiled as we walked by, apparently delighted to see two smiling young children in their dreary world.

No one seemed to think anything unusual was happening. They smiled for their boss, too, who seemed to be steering us away from the factory and toward the offices. We stopped at his office.

Still clutching Paolo's neck, the man from the plane opened a door with a different name on it.

Alexis Bogdonovich, President and C.E.O. of The Peru Wire Company! Aha! Things were beginning to make sense now!

"What are we going to do with them?" The Old Fox asked.

"Patience, Bernard! I have an idea!"

"Bernard?" I asked. "Your name is Bernard? No wonder you call yourself The Old Fox!" My anger popped up in sarcasm.

"Quiet, feisty one, or I'll solve the problem right here! I do not call myself The Old Fox. It is a sign of respect from the members of The Shining Path."

"Oh, I get it, they would laugh at Bernard!" I just couldn't keep quiet.

"We will take the children on a real tour, then we will show them where the copper comes from - or used to come from -" Alexis said.

I wondered if he knew Vladimir, and realized his other identity was the president of Porcel-Art, the supplier of cheap mass produced phony Russian porcelain Vladimir sold to discount stores across the USA to raise money for the Communist hard-liners. I remembered Dad saying how the terrorists needed financing, and camouflage to operate.

"Yes, that is a good idea" Bernard said, nodding. "No one would suspect anything."

Paolo was quiet through the whole conversation. I knew he was scared, and so was I, but he was looking for a way to escape.

The door opened, and again the big hands were placed on our necks as we were steered out of the office and back into the factory.

We were led past big steaming cauldrons where the copper was separated from the ore, then past the cooling bins, and finally the molds where the hot liquid copper and aluminum were made into rods.

Then we were hustled by the cutters where the rods were forced through diamond jigs where they were reduced to various sizes of wire. We watched the process with little explanation from our tour guides.

Along the way some workers smiled at us, and others looked annoyed. Alexis stopped a man and said something to him. He smiled and nodded, then left. We wondered what his assignment was until we were led to the roof of the building, and a waiting helicopter.

The chopper was plain white with only call letters on it. It was executive class, though and we instinctively ducked as we were pushed on board.

As soon as we were thrown into our seats the pilot lifted off.

The rain had stopped and the clouds had blown away. Lima was once again the sunny, historic city we had known.

Even though I was used to flying, my heart was pounding. By now, Mom must have figured out we had not gone out for supplies. Dad would be back, and very angry. No, probably scared - worried something had happened to us.

I wished I had never thought of my brilliant plan! I clutched my canvas bag and looked at Paolo. It looked like he had never flown before. I thought about the camera and Paolo's uncle, Enrico, and hoped he would find it. With the COM link gone the way of the booby, it might be our only hope of being found.

I wanted to talk to Paolo about it, but stayed quiet.

As we headed toward the mountains, Bernard spoke up. "We could drop them, you know."

"No. Our part of the plan is only to delay and confuse. We cannot risk killing them. We will leave them in the old mining shack at the top of the mountain. No one has been there during the winter. If they escape, they will have to survive the mountain, and by the time they could return, if they return, it will be too late. We cannot risk our contact, and if they are found dead, they could link them to the factory and set off an investigation that could shut down the mission.

"You are just afraid of losing your position and money!" The Old Fox replied. "I have a score to settle with this one," he said, pointing at me.

"Your score was with her grandfather," Alexis said.

I looked out the window at the mountain peaks. They were high, rocky, and covered with snow. The thaw had just begun, and we could feel the cold air. At least we were wearing some kind of jackets!

I hoped they would be enough.

Chapter Seventeen

The nylon windbreakers weren't enough. I could feel the chill already. Paolo was toughing it out, but I could see he was cold, too

"Where are we?" I demanded to know

"We are finishing our tour. Here is where the wire comes from. This is a copper mine approximately fifteen hundred feet high. This mine is now played out, and ceased production last fall. Here is the mining shack. This completes our tour. You will now follow us inside the shack for a closer look at the miner's life." Alexis said in a tour guides' voice.

"That's okay," Paolo said, "I am not that curious."

"Oh, but I think you are!" The Old Fox tightened his grip on Paolo's neck and pushed him inside.

"You, too, Rosie," he said, reaching for my neck also.

"Don't call me Rosie! It makes me angry. You wouldn't like it when I get angry!"

"Angry is good. It will give you a chance to survive," he said.

"We will survive! We'll get down and tell what we know and then you'll be in big trouble! When my Dad and Uncle Richard get through with you…"

"If you do survive the mountain it will be too late, and we'll be gone. The world will change, and your father will be powerless to stop it. Remember, we could kill you - but we won't. We are giving you a chance."

"My grandfather stopped you once, and I will stop you again!"

"Enough threats, child. Hold still while I tie your hands or it will hurt more."

Before long, Paolo and I were tied up and sitting across from each other on the floor of the old shack. We listened to the helicopter take off, powerless to stop it. Soon we faced the reality of being alone, tied up in an old shack 1,500 feet high in the Andes Mountains.

On top of that, the bad guys were getting away! Three bridges in the USA were about to be destroyed. Thousands of people would die! The whole world economy would suffer! Our parents were worried sick about us! If we could get down from the mountain, they would probably kill us themselves!

I wanted to cry, but I was facing Paolo. I didn't want him to see me. I wanted to be alone but was glad I wasn't. I remembered being kidnapped in Russia. I got through it okay with the help of some new friends. I would get through this okay, too.

Paolo was trying to be brave. The same thoughts must have been running through his head also. He couldn't cry in front of a girl.

"Rose, slide over to me. Let me untie your hands!" He said.

I used my feet to inch across the rough floor of the shack. I was glad I wore jeans! Reaching Paolo, I turned around and let him untie me. Even though his hands were tied also, he was able to use his fingers, and worked at the ropes until at last they fell away.

"Now I'll untie you!" I said and went to work on his ropes.

Soon we were both free, and standing in the old shack. We looked around for anything that could help us.

"Have you ever been in the mountains, Paolo?" I asked.

"Not this high. Just the foothills. Have you?"

"Once, at camp in Arizona. But I never really did any climbing. It was a riding camp. My Uncle Richard did teach me some survival things, though."

"Well, let's see what we can find to help us. It's a long way down," Paolo said

I looked around the old shack. There was a coil of rope, an old pickax, and a box of crackers with one unopened sleeve. I hoped they would be edible. My stomach was growling already.

We opened the crackers right away. They were dry, but okay. Water. There was no water! What I would have given for a Coke!

"What will we do for water?" I asked.

"Well, there is a stove and one old pan. We could melt some snow," Paolo said, excited.

"Good idea!" I said, grabbing the old pan.

There were a few unburned logs stacked alongside the stove, and Paolo threw some in and looked for a match.

We were lucky to find some on the ledge of the old dirty window and while Paolo worked on the fire, I went outside to get the snow.

The wind was blowing, and the afternoon was beginning to fade. I knew it would get colder.

I stopped to look around. The view was amazing! There were mountains in all directions! At this altitude all I could really see were snow covered peaks and clouds.

As I walked around the shack with the pan I looked down on green plateaus and ledges. Far down to the east I could see the Amazon River and the treetops of the jungle.

I wondered if Richard was enjoying his fishing. By now, he would have been called back to look for us.

As the smoke wound from the little chimney in the shack, I realized how small I really was.

"Needles in a hay stack," I said to myself as I carried my thimbleful of snow to the little shack.

"Needles in a haystack." I repeated.

Chapter Eighteen

"Needles in a haystack," Richard said when he got the news. "Two kids lost in Lima, needles in a haystack!"

I did not know Richard had not left Lima. He wasn't on a fishing trip. He had gone deep undercover into the nightlife of Lima to find information. He was hanging out at the kind of clubs that kids aren't supposed to know about.

Waking up at five p.m. in a sleazy hotel room, he read the message on the cell phone. It said ZIP.

"The suitcase is open," he said into the phone.

"But the bag is zipped. Richard! Rose is missing!" Came my father's frantic voice.

"What? How can that be?" Richard asked, suddenly awake.

"She went with, Paolo to pick up supplies for the hotel this afternoon just before I returned from the wire factory. She never returned, and Paolo is missing too!"

"What about her COM?" Richard asked.

"She must have set it on tracking only. We are getting a signal, but can't get a fix. It seems to be moving all over Lima. First by car, and then by boat. Doesn't make sense!" Dad was trying hard to control his feelings.

"What do you mean?" Richard asked.

"Well, first the signal is on land, then it seems to be over the water. We have the Lima police, Rico and Gloria tracking the signal, but they haven't got a sighting yet."

"Where was the last permanent fix?"

"Outside the wire factory. Rose must have gone there on her own with Paolo's help. I think she is trying to help us with the case. The police are there now."

"Where are you?" Richard asked.

"I'm here with her mother. She blames herself for letting Rose go. One of us needs to stay here in case they return or we get a call."

"Do you want me to come in?" Richard asked.

"No. Stay undercover and see what you can find out. You might be the one who can get a lead. Susan and Steven have been alerted and all The Agency computers are looking for any communications."

"Okay. I was just getting ready for the night shift. I have a date with a former Shining Path girlfriend. I'm seeing her tonight at the Pizzaro Club."

"Good. Let's hope someone drinks too much and talks too much! We'll send word by Zip as soon as we hear anything."

"Okay. I'll set my phone on Vibe, and call you if I get any leads. They better pray they haven't harmed her!" Richard said.

"We'll both pray they haven't!" Dad said, signing off.

Richard went into the shower.

"Needles in a haystack. You always find them the hard way!"

The trouble was, they were looking in the wrong haystack!

Chapter Nineteen

We were tired, cold, hungry, and scared. Even though we wanted to start climbing down the mountain, we decided to wait. It would be too hard to see in the dark. Too dangerous, and too cold.

We would have to wait until morning. Sitting on the floor of the old shack, we made our plans. First, we divided up the food. One stack of crackers was not going to get us far!

"I wish we had some peanut butter or jelly," I said, hearing my stomach rumble.

"I wish we had anything," Paolo said.

"You need peanut butter to keep the jelly from running through the holes in the crackers," I went on.

"Well we don't have any jelly so what is the difference?" Paolo asked.

"The difference is it gives me something to think about besides being stuck on top of this mountain!" I snapped back.

Paolo winced. "I'm sorry, Rose. I should have never showed you the wire factory. Now everyone will be worried about us."

"I don't know what got in to me! I guess I just wanted to show my parents I could do something on my own!"

"We'll be okay, Rose. I am a survivor and from what you have told me, you are too! Were not just kids."

"We have to figure out a way to sleep," I reminded him, a little embarrassed.

"And other things, like the bathroom," He blushed.

"That's easy, we just take turns," I said.

"As for sleeping, there is an old rug by the stove. We could shake it out, and you could sleep on it. I will sleep sitting up against the wall," Paolo said.

"Well, the first part is okay but it will get cold even with a fire. In survival training they told us the best thing to do in the cold was to sleep together to save body heat," Now I was blushing

"Okay. Let's do our chores before it gets too dark. Then we can sleep, and get up at first light. We have a lot of hiking to do tomorrow," Paolo took charge.

I looked at the old, braided rug. I sure did not want to put my face on it. I decided I could empty my canvas bag and sleep on that.

I stood up and stretched. Grabbing the old rug from the floor I was surprised at how heavy it was. It was not very big, and must have been full of dirt and mud. Years of miners tracking it up. Sheesh!

Paolo helped me drag it outside. We hung it on a rock and beat it with sticks. Clouds of dirt and dust flew in the wind. Finally, it was lighter, and we shook it out. We decided to hang it on a rock for a while to freshen it up.

Paolo went around to the other side of the shack to freshen himself up. I stood looking down the mountain trying to find a path. That's when I saw the smoke!

"Paolo! Come here! Quick!" I yelled

"What is it, Rose?" He asked, running around to my side of the shack.

"Smoke! A chimney! Someone lives on this mountain!" I was so excited I was still yelling.

"That's great! That is wonderful!" Paolo was yelling, too.

"Lets plan a route!" I said.

The smoke was coming from below us and to the west. We had to guess but it looked like it was about a quarter of the way down. It looked like we could reach them in a few hours.

"But not tonight," Paolo said.

We went back inside, and laid out our gear. The rope was about twenty feet long, we guessed. The pick ax, matches, crackers, and my canvas bag. Inside my bag were the CD player, headphones, a notebook, a pen, and a water bottle with a cap! The bottle was empty from the day before, but we could fill it up with melted snow. The tin pan could stay behind.

We could make it!

We were too excited to sleep, and too nervous. We stalled as long as we could. We brought in the rug, and took off our shoes. We didn't have a blanket, and would have to find a way to keep our feet warm.

"Why are we taking off our shoes?" Paolo asked.

"Because our feet will sweat, and be colder in the morning. We have to hike in them," I said.

"But how will we keep them warm tonight?" He asked.

"Well, before we go to sleep we can put them on loosely without tying them. That should be enough to keep them from sweating and still keep warm."

"Okay, that sounds like a good idea," he said.

We each took a cracker to sleep on and a sip of water. There was only one log left, and we put it in the stove. It would have to do.

We talked into the night, and finally gave up. We would have to find a way to sleep. The fire was not warm enough, and the wind howled through the cracks in the old boards. We wouldn't freeze but it would be close.

I wished I had Sam with me. The big old Newfie snuck up on my bed many times, and I used to pretend not to notice. I woke up with my arms around him many mornings.

"Paolo, you lay down and face the wall. I'll lay with my back to you."

"Okay," he said, nervously.

"It's a matter of survival," I said, matter-of-factly.

"Yes, you are right. Goodnight," he replied.

As the moon came up through the dirty window, and the glow of the fire flickered on the wall through the door of the stove, I smiled and shook my head.

"Too intense!" I thought as my back rubbed up against his. I put my head on the canvas bag, glad that mother had suggested I bring it on the trip.

"Good for souvenirs and shopping," she had said.

I felt bad for Paolo sleeping on the old, dirty rug. He did not move or say a word.

Soon, I found it more comfortable to turn the other way, and I threw my arm around him, cuddling up as if he were Sam. I felt him stiffen and relax - and just before I fell asleep, I thought I could feel him smile.

Chapter Twenty

The sunlight woke me up. Paolo was gone, and the fire was out. I stood up and stretched. My stomach woke up too, and I listened to it growl. I looked around for the crackers.

There were not many left. I did not want to think about that. I reached for the door, wondering where Paolo was.

My eyes had to adjust to the light as I swung open the door and stepped out. It was cold. I stopped to lace up my shoes. There was something ghostly about this place. I listened to the wind that never seemed to stop, and could almost feel the spirits of ancient civilizations.

The altitude must have been working on my mind. Even in the sunlight this was a scary place.

I stood up and walked around, looking for Paolo. I could have called out for him, but something stopped me from breaking the silence.

I moved away from the shack towards the mountain. If this was a mine, the entrance would not be far away. And if it was a mine, they must have some way of getting the ore down the mountain!

Tracks! There must be tracks! I was excited now, and began to walk faster. Close to the face of the mountain I almost stumbled over them! There were tracks here! We could follow them!

Staring at the ground I followed the tracks to the east. Around the bend on the other side of the peak was the opening of the mine and the end of the trail. And that's where I found Paolo.

I walked up behind him and tapped him on the shoulder. He jumped a foot, and almost fell off the mountain!

"Geez! Did you have to scare me like that?" He said angrily.

"Well, good morning to you, too! I'm sorry. I did not mean to scare you!"

"I'm sorry I snapped at you. Look, Rose! Here is the mine!"

"I can see that. The tracks are what I was thinking about!" I said.

"Yes. Me too. We can follow them down. But there are places too steep for walking. See how the tracks are notched? This is so the cars won't slide down the steep places."

"If there are places too steep for walking, how do we get down?" I asked.

"Well, the mine was here before there were trains. The ancient people mined here also. They used trails and mules. The old trails are here too. We could follow the tracks until they get too steep, and then follow the trails."

"Sounds okay with me," I said.

"And we don't have to climb all the way down! Only to the farm house we saw last night!"

"Great! Let's go!" I said, anxious to leave this place.

"Don't you want to see the mine?" He asked.

I looked at the entrance of the mine. It was just a hole in the rocks. No sign, no boards across the opening. Just an old cave. I knew caves were dangerous. There could be poison gas inside.

"Naw. Caves are dangerous. I'll wait for a tour. We have to get back home!"

"Yes, but maybe there is something inside we could use." Paolo was edging closer to the dark opening.

"Paolo, what are you doing?" I said, pulling him back.

"I don't know, but I have to look," he said, twisting out of my grasp.

He ran ahead to the mouth of the cave. I wondered why they called it a mouth. I could almost see it swallowing up Paolo!

"Rose, come here!" He called as he disappeared inside.

"Paolo! Come back!" I yelled, running for the mouth as it sucked him in!

"It's okay, Rose! Look what I've found!" Came his disembodied voice

I stopped at the dark opening. The sun was just high enough to light the entrance. My eyes adjusted to the dim light as I peered inside.

"Paolo? Are you there? What is it?" I asked.

Paolo's big, toothy smile greeted me as he stepped back into the light.

"We have a ride!" He said, waving his arm towards the old ore car parked inside.

"A ride?"

"Yes! It's an old ore car, and it has a brake. We can ride it down the mountain!"

"No way! It's too dangerous! The mountain is too steep. We are not chunks of ore!"

"We don't have to ride it all the way, only to the farm below. It has a brake, and we can stop it if we have to."

"Even if we could - and I'm not saying I would - how do we know we can stop it?"

"Well, they said the mine was closed for the winter. They must have been using this car not too long ago. The brake must be okay. We'll just have to take our chances."

I didn't like the idea of spending hours or days hiking down the mountain without food, and very little water, but I sure didn't want to take a roller coaster ride in an old mining car, either!

Paolo examined the brake, pulling it back and forth.

"We can do it, Rose."

There's a time for thinking, and a time for doing. Sometimes you can think too much!

"Okay, let's do it!" I said. "Now, before I change my mind!"

Paolo released the brake.

"Help me push it outside!" He said.

We pushed the old car out into the light. It was heavy and we slipped more than once, falling onto the ground behind the old rusty bucket.

Finally, it sat in the sun, held by the brake. We walked back to the shack, collecting our few, meager supplies.

"How do we get it rolling when we are inside?" I asked.

"There is a long pole inside the cave. I saw it standing against the wall. I'll get it!" Paolo said, running back inside.

I climbed into the old bucket. We would have to sit on the ends facing each other.

Paolo came out with the pole.

"Once we get started, I'll throw the pole away. Then I can work the brake."

Paolo climbed in.

Sheesh! I would have to ride backwards down the mountain! Not only that, I would have to look at Paolo all the way! I did not want him to know how scared I was!

"Here we go!" He said, standing up, and facing backwards as he used the pole to push off.

He strained and strained - and very slowly the car started to move.

I stared at the sky and the mountain peaks. I saw an eagle in the clouds. I did anything I could to keep from thinking!

The car picked up speed, and Paolo threw away the pole. He sat on the edge; hand ready on the brake.

Soon we were rolling faster. The old shack we had stayed in passed in and out of my view. The butterflies were dancing in my stomach, and I vowed if I lived through this I would never ride a roller coaster again!

Chapter Twenty-One

"Susan, any news?" Mom talked to her laptop on Zip as the sun came up in Lima.

"Not since last night. All the Agency computers register the same tracking signal. It's almost like the perpetrators keep moving the kids around. On another note, though, we feel we are closing in on the mole. Seems a certain employee has ties to the Peru Mining Company, and pushed the proposal for the Peru Wire Company contract to the Director. We're checking the officials at Peru Mining for possible terrorist connections. The company is partly U.S.-owned and runs the copper mines in Cerro de Pasco supplying Peru Wire."

"That's where my research led, too," Mom said.

"We must be getting close to the answer, or they wouldn't have grabbed the kids," Susan said.

"We've been in touch with Richard, too," Mom went on, "Seems like our run-in with the Old Fox and the Shining Path wasn't just a coincidence. Oh, why did I let her go with Paolo?"

"I know the feeling," Susan remembered her decision to take me to New York that led to our kidnapping. "Has there been any contact or demands?"

"No, but we think the kids are probably safe. The tracking signal gives us hope. Apparently the kidnappers haven't found it yet. Besides, we think they will probably contact us today with instructions. Oh, why did we come here?" Mom was trying hard to be professional, but ran into being a professional mom.

"Don't do that to yourself," Susan said. "There's always going to be that danger whether you are home or not. The only way to avoid it would be to change our whole family history, and then the danger is still there! That's the kind of world we live in. That's why we are in this business, remember?"

"Yes, I know but I keep going around in circles. If only…"

"Keep your chin up, and we'll find them," Susan said.

In the background, Samson barked as if to give Mom hope.

Dad was on his cell phone talking to Richard, "What news?"

"Seems the Old Fox has a protégé who was one of the four Shining Path members arrested in 1998 for urban terrorism in Lima. Last night he came to the Pizzaro club looking for his old flame. He had too much to drink, and went nuts when he saw me with her. He tried to slug it out with me, and landed right in the booth! Then he tried to impress her by talking about the "glory" days in '98. Once his tongue started wagging he went on to say the Old Fox was back in business again. Something big went down yesterday - but he wouldn't say what."

"Sounds like we're onto something!" Dad said. "The timing is too coincidental. We must have gotten too close at the wire factory. Maybe the kids followed me, or maybe they were taken there."

"Right, that's where the last stationary signal came from. All the evidence points to the wire company, and a plot to stall The Agency from upgrading their computers. But why?"

"To keep us from finding out what's coming. The next big terrorist attack! Where is the protégé now?"

"Sleeping it off in a cheap hotel. I'm going to follow him today as a new recruit."

"Good. When we find the kids, we'll find the answers," Dad said.

A knock at the door interrupted the conversation. One of the Peruvian policemen swung open the door to escort Paolo's father into the room. He was holding a camera, my camera!

"Hold on, Richard, I think we got a break…"

"Hold on Susan, someone just came in…" Mom said.

Everything stopped as Pablo stood in the middle of the room holding the digital camera.

But nothing stopped where we were!

215

Chapter Twenty-Two

Where we were was picking up speed as we rounded the bend to the other side of the mountain. The ore car went faster and faster as the tracks wound down the far side of the peak. No wonder we hadn't seen them last night!

We hung on to the edges of the cart, trying to keep our balance. Paolo's face was contorted, and his mouth was wide open. All we could do was stare at each other; everything else was a blur

The combination of being cold, hungry, fifteen thousand feet up, and rapidly descending in a roller coaster car was almost too much! I was sure we would barf on each other as the car bumped along - almost leaving the tracks!

Paolo's hand was frozen on the brake handle, and seemed unable to move! I couldn't see where we were going, and we had no idea how far the tracks went. Maybe all the way!

But they didn't. About a third of the way down the car hit a bumper, and we spilled out onto the ground, landing on top of each other, rolling into a pit.

A deep pit!

"Paolo? Are you okay?" I asked, afraid to move.

"I think so," he said, "But I'm laying on the axe."

I had landed on top of him. Now that I knew he was okay, I rolled off, and helped him to his feet.

"What a ride! Where are we?" I asked.

"I don't know. Some kind of pit. Must be where they dump the ore to be picked up by the train."

"Can we climb out?" I asked, trying to climb, but slipping back in on the loose rocks. The pit was about fifteen feet deep. I looked up at the rectangular patch of sky.

"It's too steep!" Paolo said as he gave up trying to climb the steep sides.

"How will we get out?" I asked, leaning back against the side of the pit to rest.

"Do you still have the rope?" He asked hopefully.

"Yes! The bag fell in with us," I said, grabbing it, and pulling out the rope from the mining shack. "But what good will that do? There is no one to pull us out!"

"We'll pull ourselves out!"

"How?" I asked.

"Like this!" He said, tying one end of the rope to the axe and standing back against the far wall.

I was catching on!

"All we have to do is throw the axe until it catches something! Then we can use it like an anchor, and pull ourselves up!"

I found a safe place to stand as Paolo swung the axe and let go. It fell straight back down, and almost killed us!

He tried again. The axe was heavy, and he was not quite strong enough.

"It's no use. It's too heavy and there is not enough room to swing it!" He said.

"Don't give up so easy! Let me try!" I said.

"If I can't do it what makes you think you can? You're a girl!"

"Big news, Mr. Smarty-pants - girls are strong, too!" I said angrily.

Getting beat by a girl must have given him the extra adrenaline he needed. With an anguished look on his face he let out a roar of frustration, and flung the axe again.

This time it sailed out of the pit, and landed with a metallic 'clunk'. It had caught the wheel of the cart!

We both let out a laugh. "I'll go first!" He said.

Testing the rope to see if it would hold, he dug his feet into the side of the pit. It held, and soon he was scaling the wall.

He scrambled over the top, one leg at a time, and rolled out of sight.

"Come on, Rose! Your turn!" He said, looking down at me from the top.

I was glad I had learned to climb ropes in school!

Soon, we were both standing on the edge. We were a little scuffed up, but still in one piece.

"I think I know where we are!" Paolo said.

"Where?" I asked.

"Tarma! Or somewhere close to it."

"Where is Tarma?" I asked, trying to remember my research.

"It is one of the three passes across the Andes. There is a pass the Central Railroad takes from Lima to Tarma. It is about forty-eight meters high. About fourteen thousand feet. I watched the helicopter as we climbed the mountain. We must be near Cerro de Pasco. There is a mining company there, just north of La Oroya."

"Yes! I remember now! Most copper is mined in Northwest Peru! La Oroya is where the ore is smelted, but it is more central Peru," I said.

"But the train is not here. The pass is just opening up. We are still a long way up the mountain," Paolo sounded discouraged.

"The farm! We have to find the farm!" I said.

Gathering our supplies, we looked at the sun, and found our bearings. If we hiked south and west, we should be able to find it.

But hiking on the steep, narrow trails would be harder than it sounded!

Chapter Twenty-Three

It was a little warmer now. Five hundred feet can make a difference! Since our kidnapping we had spent the last twenty-four hours in our windbreakers. Now we were hiking, and it helped to warm us up.

The rumbling in our stomachs kept us going. We had eaten the last of the crackers, and the remaining crumbs after our fall into the pit. A little snow was all we had, and we had packed the plastic water bottle with it.

Paolo still carried the axe he had fallen on. Now and then he would put his hand to his side. It was bruised badly. We had to stop and rest a lot. The altitude and being hungry had a lot to do with that.

We followed the tracks until they became too steep. The pit we had fallen into was on a spur, beyond the regular route of the Central Railroad. We had found the tracks for a small work train designed to pick up the ore from the pit, and take it to the smelter.

Unfortunately, the winter season wasn't over for the miners yet, and no trains ran up here. Nothing would happen until the pass was fully open. There were no phones, so we kept walking, using the trail the ancient miners used. It was designed more for mules and llamas than people, and overgrown with bushes.

More than once, Paolo had to use the axe to cut through the brush. The long handle did not help. Sometimes he used it as a crutch. My ankle was sore from the fall, and I thought of using it as a crutch too.

"Rose, you are limping! What is wrong?"

"I think I twisted my ankle back there in the pit."

"Let's stop and rest," Paolo said, looking for a rock or something to sit on.

The mountain was terraced, and we stopped at the next opening in the brush. We sat on the trail, and hung our feet over the side, looking at the mountains around us. At this altitude we could see the vegetation covering so many of the mountains here.

"They look green," I said.

"Yes. We are on a terrace. I think we are nearing the farm."

I remembered reading how the farmers grew their crops on the terraces. The pictures I had seen of Machu Picchu were like that

"Paolo, how far is Machu Picchu?" I asked.

"A long way. It is to the east and south on the other side of Peru."

"Have you ever been there?" I asked.

"No. Some day I will see it, though. I know it is not going away. Were you not going to see it while you are here?"

"We were supposed to go today. It keeps changing. Mom and Dad have to keep working. We will see it before we go home. If I ever want to see a mountain again! Why haven't you seen it? You live here."

Paolo smiled. "My father has to work. Can you walk?" He asked, getting to his feet.

"Yes, I think so," I said, standing and testing my left ankle. It was sore. And throbbing - but not as bad as before. Probably a minor sprain.

"It must be about noon. The sun is almost directly above us.""Let's get to work!" I said, picking up the canvas bag, draping it around my neck, and under my right arm.

Paolo picked up the axe, and we started back on the trail. Cutting through the brush, slipping on loose rocks, we headed south and west toward the "farm".

I noticed in the clear stretches how Paolo kept leaning on the axe handle and bending to his left. I knew he was in pain.

"Paolo how is your side?"

"It is sore. It will be okay."

"Doesn't look okay. Maybe we should stop," I said.

"We will never get home if we do," he replied.

I watched the sun move lower in the sky. It stayed ahead of us, and the glare made it hard to see. We limped along, not knowing how far we had come, or thinking of how hungry we were.

As the sun moved lower, so did we. Our jackets were tied around our waists now, and we walked like zombies, one painful step at a time

"Paolo, we have to stop."

"Yes. We must stop," he said, zombie-like.

There was a rock with a large flat top ahead of us. We headed for it, slumping down on it as if it were a bed.

"Let me see your side," I insisted.

He said nothing, but sat still while I lifted his shirt. He cringed as the t-shirt slid over his ribs.

"Oh, Paolo!" I said, seeing the large, purple bruise covering most of his right side. He was having trouble breathing, too.

"I think this is more than a bruise. You might have broken a rib," I said, carefully lowering his shirt.

Paolo was sweating and looked feverish. I put my hand to his forehead. It was clammy.

"How is your ankle?" He asked.

"Sore, but I'll live."

"Me too."

There were only a few hours of daylight left now. I knew we had to find help soon.

"Paolo, stay here and rest. I'm going to look around."

He did not argue. I stood up and hobbled to the side of the trail.

Looking up beyond the brush, I could see the top of the mountain. We had come quite a ways but still were quite high. The canopy of trees and brush kept me from seeing much else and just as I was turning back to the trail; I saw a wisp of smoke.

"The farm!" I yelled, smelling the cooking coming from below. I knew it was not too far now!

Heart beating in anticipation, I ran back to Paolo ignoring the pain in my ankle.

The butterflies in my stomach came to a sudden stop as I approached the rock. Paolo had slid off of it and was slumped over on the ground.

"Paolo! Are you okay? Paolo! I found the farm! Paolo..."

This couldn't be happening! Not now! Not after all that!

"Paolo...come back! Come back..." I shook him again and again. Finally I sat on the ground next to him and cried.

Chapter Twenty-Four

I must have fallen asleep. I remembered crying, afraid Paolo was gone. But he must be okay, I thought, his hand was on my shoulder trying to wake me up. My eyes were still closed, waiting for his voice.

The gentle shaking continued and I still did not hear him say anything. I opened my eyes, unsure of what I would see. Had the Old Fox found us? Was Paolo all right? I couldn't handle the curiosity. I opened my eyes, awake, and wary.

It wasn't Paolo shaking me, and it wasn't a hand either! It was a nose. A nose belonging to a young Alpaca. I sat very still, and thought back on my research. I remembered that Alpacas were mostly found in the high plateaus of the mountains. As far as I knew they were friendly and would probably not hurt us - though they did spit like llamas and camels. This one was brown, and his wool would be highly prized when he matured.

The nudging stopped when I opened my eyes and the Alpaca stood back as if waiting for me to do something. I smiled. He just stood there, expectantly. I shook Paolo.

"Paolo, are you okay? Wake up," I whispered.

"Rose? What happened?" He asked, lifting his head from my shoulder, and wiping the sleep from his eyes.

"Shhh! Don't scare him away."

"Scare who away?"

"The Alpaca!"

"Oh, OH!" He said, suddenly awake, and staring at our new friend.

"You must have had a fever; you passed out while I was scouting the trail. When I came back I found you on the ground. I thought you were dead." I said, relief in my voice.

"I did not mean to scare you. The thin air must have gotten to me. I was so tired," he explained.

"I'm just glad you are okay!" I said, still whispering

"What is he waiting for?" Paolo asked.

"I don't know. He almost acts like a pet, or an animal that is used to people." It was too hard to keep whispering so I let my voice get a little louder.

"Rose! What if that is not a farm? I think it may be a ranch. Maybe they raise Alpacas for their wool."

"That would make sense. Anyway, farm or ranch - it makes no difference. There are people there, and they can help us!"

"Maybe the Alpaca can lead us there. We must be close!" Paolo was excited now, and struggled to his feet holding his side.

I stood up, too, expecting the Alpaca to run, but he didn't.

We picked up our supplies, and turned toward the ranch. The smell of cooking was still in the air, and though the sun was getting low - we still had daylight.

The Alpaca followed as we started walking, then ran ahead and took the lead on the trail.

We smiled, and followed him.

"I guess he is used to getting fed. Maybe he will lead us right to his pen," Paolo said.

And that is exactly what he did! We were happy not to be alone anymore, and the animal knew the trail. Soon the ranch was in sight.

The trail broadened. Soon it looked more like a road, and we were walking faster now. In the distance we could see a house, and two large fenced areas, one on either side of the road.

The light was fading now; and we could just make out shapes in the pens. Llamas, and Alpacas! There was a glow of firelight coming through the window of the house, and the sound of a barking dog.

It was a small dog, a border collie, most likely. The Alpaca was immediately herded in the direction of his corral

The dog was followed by another small figure. A girl. She was yelling something at the dog in Spanish, and stopped suddenly when she saw us.

I guess we would have been a surprise! Up here where few visitors ever come, especially two young children limping and carrying an axe!

We stopped. Paolo said something to the girl. Since I didn't know much Spanish, I relied on Paolo to translate.

"Her name is Maria," he said, as he introduced us. "I told her who we are and that we needed help."

"Si!" She said, motioning us to follow her as the dog ran behind us, nipping at our heels as if it was herding us!

"Peso!" She scolded the dog. "No, no!"

Peso kept herding us anyway, and we laughed as we followed Maria up to the door of her house.

Chapter Twenty-Five

I would not have recognized Richard if I had seen him that night. He had let his beard grow since we had arrived, and was wearing an eye patch. A wig with a ponytail completed the look. The silvery gray shirt tucked into his black dress pants helped make him look like a successful drug dealer.

He was deep undercover and the news of our kidnapping gave him an anger that fit the character he was playing.

As Paolo and I were limping up to the ranch on the mountain, Richard was riding through Lima with his new "friend".

"Where is this place, Marcos?"

"You in a hurry?" Marcos said as he stepped harder on the gas pedal, almost running down the pedestrians in front of the bars.

"Hey, watch out!" Richard snapped. "We don't need the police bothering us."

"You talk like an old lady. Maybe my driving makes you nervous?"

"It's not your driving, it's you who make me nervous," Richard said, relieved Marcos had slowed the car down. He could see people shaking their fists in the rearview mirror.

"Okay, okay. I was just having some fun. You will see where we are going when we get there." Marcos turned the corner and headed towards the coast.

He did not see the small black car pulling out a block behind him with the lights off.

"So, you think they will like me?" Richard asked, trying to keep Marcos' attention.

"We are always looking for a few good men," Marcos laughed. "If I like you, they will like you!"

Richard knew Marcos had fallen out of favor with the leaders of The Path. He was the kind of man who wanted to act tough, and impress his peers. They used him accordingly. He was also the kind of man who drank, and talked too much. They used him for that, too. Whenever they wanted to plant some 'red herrings' they gave him false information and wound him up. Then they set him loose after plying him with alcohol

Marcos knew what they were doing, but told himself he was useful. He traded his pride for the association and the booze

Rico and Gloria knew about Marcos, and had suggested Richard contact him. They took Richard to the bar, and set up his room at the cheap hotel. Now they were following at a safe distance and listening to the conversation on Richard's COM link

"A few good men. Like the U.S. Marines. That's funny." Richard said without laughing

"You don't laugh, yet you say that's funny. Maybe you are funny," Marcos said as the car rolled along the dark highway

"If I say it's funny, it's funny. Maybe you would like it if I laughed at you?" Richard's voice was threatening

"Why would you laugh at me? Am I drunk? No, not tonight. People laugh at me when I am drunk. They say, 'Get Marcos, I need a laugh.' Then they send me out on a fools' errand. Are you playing me for a fool, friend?"

"If I was, would I tell you? No, if you doubted me we would not be riding in your car. I am beginning to doubt you, though. Do you really know The Fox?"

"You see," Marcos, said, "You don't believe me. If I say I know The Fox, then I do."

"Okay, I believe you. Your joke was funny too," Richard laughed and broke the tension.

Rico and Gloria relaxed as they followed behind.

They finally came to a stop at the docks. Marcos parked the car and set the alarm. Richard followed him to a fishing boat.

Once on the boat they went below decks, and into the captain's cabin. Were three men were seated at a small table who did not introduce themselves.

"Marcos! Good to see you again! And this is your new friend?" One of them said, as he stood up to shake hands.

The other two nodded and smiled, but did not stand up.

"This is my friend, Crocker," He motioned to Richard and used his alias.

"And you are...?" Richard stuck out his hand.

"The man with no name," came the answer. "The rules here are no names."

Richard, 'Crocker', dropped his hand. "But you know mine," he said.

"We know Marcos called you Crocker. We have yet to know you. Until we do, we do not shake hands, or use our names. You don't just walk into this organization on the strength of a nights' drinking."

The boat had pulled away from the dock, and was headed out to sea. Richard had expected something entirely different, a camp in the hills, or maybe a meeting in town.

When they arrived at the dock, he saw the possibility that maybe this is what happened to Paolo and me. The tracking signal on the booby bird had been over water at times.

"You are a smart man," Richard said. "I would not like to work with stupid ones."

"No, we are not stupid, Mr. Crocker. Right now your picture is running through our computer. If you are not who you say you are, we will know."

"And if I am?" Richard said.

"Sit down, Crocker. We will play cards. Do you like to gamble? Of course you do. You would not be here if you didn't."

"Cards?" Richard asked.

"You can tell a lot about a man by the way he plays cards. You pick the game."

"What are the choices?" Richard said, looking at the faces in the cabin.

"It could be poker or it could be go fish," the man smiled.

"I don't play cards with people who don't give their names," Richard said, as he stared at the faces in the room.

"A smart move, but you didn't get the joke."

"Oh, I got it, I just didn't think it was funny."

"He doesn't laugh at funny things," Marcos broke in.

"I don't trust a man without a sense of humor," the leader said, searching Richard's face.

"And I don't trust a man who laughs at another man's fate," Richard replied.

The men at the table turned their heads from one to the other as they watched the verbal poker game between their leader and Richard. Marcos was beginning to sweat. If they found out that Crocker was not who he said he was, both of them would die.

Dying was not the worst of it, though. First they would be tortured to find out who had sent them.

Richard knew that, too. He waited for the knock at the door. But he had an ace up his sleeve!

After all, you don't just walk into an organization like The Path.

Chapter Twenty-Six

Richard was not the only one waiting for a knock on the door. Back at home Susan and Steven waited for their contact at The Agency.

"Why are we meeting at a restaurant?" Susan asked as they parked the car at the giant Mall of America.

"We can't trust the computer," Steven said as they locked the car, walking toward the skyway, and into the Mall.

The mall was always busy, and Steven seemed unconcerned about being overheard.

"I suppose you are right. Any one at The Agency could monitor our communications. I just hope our informant has some information for us," Susan's frustrations were showing through.

Paolo and I had been missing for thirty-six hours, and both Aunt Susan and Uncle Steven were weary of Zip.

"I just wish we were here under different circumstances," Steven said as they found the restaurant on the map, and checked his watch.

"Me too," Susan sighed. "This was supposed to be a routine investigation! I can't believe Rose is a hostage again!"

"Well, now we're pretty certain the delay in delivering the wire is part of a terrorist plot. Maybe tonight we'll find out what they are up to," Steven held the door for Susan, and they followed the host to a table.

They ordered drinks and waited for the contact to appear. Steven liked getting to a rendezvous early. It gave him the chance to scout the area and an advantage over his contact. He also liked watching the entrance.

A determined looking man approached the door and checked his watch. He held it up to his ear, and tapped the face of it twice. That was the signal.

Steven smiled and waved the man over.

Well, "Fred", good to see you! Thought you got held up at the airport. Any trouble with your luggage?"

"Steven and Susan! Good to see you, too. Yes, my suitcase was open." Fred said as he sat across from Steven and Susan.

"But, fortunately, the bag was zipped?" Susan said, giving the countersign.

"Yes, all my I.D. was in there. I was able to retrieve it, though. I'll tell you all about it while we eat."

Over dinner, Fred told them they had identified the "mole", and watched him while they traced his activities. The noise of conversation, and clinking silverware made it difficult for anyone who might be listening in.

"Seems Mr. X, is well connected. As you know, Peru Mining is partly owned by the U.S. Having worked as assistant to the president of the company, he was recommended for a similar job with the director of The Agency. He was hired almost two years ago, and his performance has been flawless. Once he gained the director's trust, it was a simple matter to slide the contract proposal from Peru Wire onto his desk. When the director asked him for his opinion on it, he said he thought it would be good for relations between the two countries. Not to mention the price, which was much lower than other suppliers - and would help The Agency's budget. It all sounded good, and made sense - so the director approved it."

"Seems so easy," Steven said as "Fred" took a drink.

"Yes. That's how they work. Right under our noses! Anyway, the director was under a lot of pressure from the White House. The president was taking a lot of flack for the information breakdown and The Agency pointed to the fifteen-year-old computer system. They needed to tell the public they would be updated in spite of budget constraints." Fred stopped to eat a few bites.

"Well, this latest incident will not help relations with Peru," Susan said.

"On the contrary, Peru is denying any involvement and is cooperating in the search and the investigation. They have vowed to find the people responsible, and are pointing to The Path. They believe there is an international conspiracy by the terrorists for an even bigger catastrophe than 9/11," Fred finally finished his dinner.

"What about the kids?" Steven said. "Do you think they are hostages?"

Fred pushed his plate away, and motioned to the waiter for another drink. He avoided looking at Susan.

"No. We don't believe the children are hostages. Rose's camera was found by Paolo's uncle. On it were pictures of the president of Peru Wire and The Old Fox, a member of the Shining Path. We believe they might have seen and heard too much."

Susan dropped her fork. Steven's face went white.

"We think they are still alive, though. As you know, Rose's tracking signal is still coming in. We think we've finally got a fix on it."

"Do you think they are hurt?" Susan's voice was barely a whisper.

"No. If they were they wouldn't keep moving them. Right now there is a Seal team in motion. We'll find them, and bring in their captors."

"We have to go in!" Steven said. "We can't just sit here…"

"No, we need you and Susan here. There are lots of people looking for those kids, including their parents, and the Peruvian police. We need you to take the information on Mr. X, and the officials of Peru Mining and Peru Wire to find out what the plan is."

"Why don't you just arrest them?" Susan asked

"No, they would just clam up. Obviously the whole plan depends on secrecy. It's better if we just watch them, and track their communications. I have a feeling it will all lead to the same place."

"Why are they keeping the kids alive if they know too much?" Steven said.

"Could be timing. Obviously the event is still a ways off and they don't want to antagonize the anti-terrorist squads too much. The kids are a problem to them, but they can't risk anything happening to them. If they turn up dead, it could hurt their plan. I think they are buying time by moving them around."

"Makes sense. I hope you are right. I hope the Seal team finds them!" Susan was holding back her tears.

Back at the house, Sam was lying on my bed. He was crying, too.

Chapter Twenty-Seven

None of the fishing boats detected the submarine as it glided silently underneath them off the coast of Peru. Hovering near the bottom, it waited for the five Seal team members to return.

Pulled along by personal underwater craft, the team was nearing the shore. Each was wearing a special tracking receiver set to my COM link.

The operation was set for dusk, since this was the hardest time to see. The Seal team, wearing black scuba suits arrived at the shore just as the sun was disappearing from sight.

It was also dinnertime, and most people were either eating or relaxing after a meal, and paying little attention to anything. So no one noticed as they slid their underwater craft onto the remote stretch of beach.

There wasn't anyone around this stretch of beach anyway.

Using hand signals, they converged on a sand mound where the COM link signal had finally come to rest.

Where were the guards? Where were the kids? The signal was still coming in.

They looked around for a building or vehicle. There was nothing but mounds of sand, and a few sprigs of weed.

Looking at each other, guns drawn, they decided to storm the sand hill.

And that's when they woke the booby bird!

The startled bird flew up into the darkness, only to be shot at by five laser rifles.

The night vision goggles revealed the bird somehow managed to avoid being hit. But before it flew off, the goggles revealed the COM link attached to its leg.

"Cease fire!" The squad leader yelled.

"It's a bird! A booby!" One of them said.

"We're the booby's!" Another one added.

After searching the beach the squad leader radioed in

"It appears the perpetrators have thrown a red herring at us, sir. They attached the tracking device to a booby bird! No wonder the signal kept moving around so much!"

"You mean the children are not there?" Came the reply.

"There is nothing here, sir, except five very embarrassed Seals."

"Then we don't know if the children are alive or not."

"No, sir."

"Secure the area and return to base."

The squad leader looked at his team. Each one was thinking the same thing. First, were the children still alive? And second, if news of this raid ever got out, they would be the laughing stock of the entire Navy.

Back on the sub, the commander reluctantly picked up the phone.

There were a lot of anxious people waiting for news of the rescue, but the most anxious ones were the children's parents.

This was a call he hated to make.

Chapter Twenty-Eight

Mom and Dad had been pacing the floor of the suite. The news of the rescue attempt had given them hope we had been found. Neither had even wanted to think we might not be alive.

"Oh, why did I let her go?" Mom was still crying.

"That's about the one hundredth time you've said that. That won't help the kids." Dad reminded her.

"I know, but what else can we do?" Mom said, wiping her eyes.

"We can have faith in Rose. She's a tough little kid. Those terrorists don't know what they've got their hands on! And Paolo! There is a smart kid, too. Somehow I know we'll find them, and they will be all right!" Dad was convincing.

"I hope that Seal Team finds them!" Mom said.

"They will. The signal is still strong. It's the longest stationary transmission they've received. If the kids are there, they will find them! We should be getting the call any minute now."

As if on cue, the phone rang.

"Yes, Commander?" Dad said as he picked it up.

Mom watched as Dad's hopeful look disappeared.

"I see," he said. "Thank you for calling."

The phone dropped from his hand.

"What is it?" Mom was frantic.

"They didn't find them."

"Where was the signal coming from, then?"

"A bird. A booby bird," Dad was in shock

"A bird? How?" Mom was in shock. "It was attached to his leg. He's been flying around from here to there ever since the kids disappeared."

"Oh no! That means they could be…"

"Don't even think it!" Dad said. "They must be alive. Rose would never have told them about the barrette, so one of the kidnappers must have been familiar with The Agency. He put the barrette on a booby to throw us off, and buy time."

"Or, he took it after he…" Mom couldn't say it.

"No, if he knew who Rose was, then he would know about the investigation. So far their whole strategy has been to delay The Agency's upgrade of their computers. They have been stalling for time. Time to get their plan in motion without being detected. They didn't expect Rose to show up and take their pictures, but they must not have known about the camera. Paolo's uncle found it in the street outside the wire factory where he dropped them off. My guess is they will stick to their plan. They put the Com on the bird to throw us off and buy time. I don't think they would risk killing the kids and having their bodies show up somewhere."

"I have to think you are right." Mom said. "But what do we do now?"

"Two things, first we start all over with good, old-fashioned detective work. We put too much stock in the COM link, and they used it against us. We've wasted time. Second, we start searching for the men in the photos Rose took. Find them, and we may find the kids."

"Richard should be getting close to the Fox, by now," Mom said. "Susan and Steven are tracking the 'mole' at The Agency. It won't be long before we close the noose on these terrorists!"

"Right! Now to hunt down the kids!" Dad said.

"Where do we start? They could be anywhere! There must be a million people in Lima, and a million miles of ground in Peru!"

"We have to use all of our resources. Call Rico and Gloria, and the Captain of the Peruvian Police. I'll get on Zip, and call Susan and Steven. Oh, and one more thing, find out where Vladimir is."

"Vladimir?" Mom said.

"Yes. Our friend from Porcel-Art is also Russian and the new President of Peru Wire."

"Our past comes back to haunt us," Mom said, thinking of Vladimir and the porcelain mines in Russia.

"Then it's time to lay old ghosts to rest," Dad said, picking up the phone, and handing it to Mom.

Mom took the phone and called Rico and Gloria.

"Rico, pick up Paolo's family, and bring them here."

And so the largest, quietest, kid hunt in The Agency's history was launched.

Again.

Chapter Twenty-Nine

They had to keep our kidnapping quiet. They couldn't risk the terrorists changing their plans and they did not want to scare them into doing something drastic - like killing us.

They also knew the odds of finding us alive were better than finding us dead. So, Paolo's father and grandmother started spreading the word along with Paolo's uncle how the search for us had to be very quiet in hopes of keeping us alive. Everyone they knew was sworn to secrecy. No media were allowed and only word of mouth was to be used.

The Agency and my parents were working the same way, as were the police. This made it harder to get information. Even the Internet and e-mail were blocked. Descriptions and pictures were passed on one person at a time. Questioning suspects was tough.

Dad returned to the place where the camera was found and started piecing the trail together with good old-fashioned detective work. He knew we must be alive, and waited for Richard to contact him.

Richard was waiting, too. On board the boat with Marcos and the leader of this little pack, the Man With No Name. Locked in a verbal poker game, hoping the right card turned up.

Someone handed the leader a note. He smiled and looked up at "Crocker".

"Well, Crocker. It would seem you are who you say you are. Quite an impressive background. Drug smuggling, gun running, caught - but never convicted. We could use a man with your talents. And you play poker very well. You never broke a sweat. Now, that was either because you are who you say you are or you know something we don't. Either way you are a cool hand."

Marcos let out a sigh of relief. Now that his new friend was accepted, he had risen a tad higher with his peers.

Richard had stayed calm the whole time. The ace up his sleeve was The Agency and the Crocker identity. He knew what the terrorists would find when they checked his name.

"Crocker" was a code name taken from Betty Crocker - it meant something was in the oven. It had been set up for Richard for use when he was under cover. In this case the computer synthesized his current activities into an appropriate cover.

As soon as the name was typed into a computer, flags went up at The Agency, the source of inquiry was tracked and a whisper copter was dispatched to the location of the boat.

"Should we move in now, sir?" the pilot asked his commander.

"No, protocol is twenty-four hours. Give Crocker time to see what's cooking. We only break protocol if Crocker contacts us, or seems to be in imminent danger. We'll stay in the shadows, and keep him in sight."

Richard knew he had twenty-four hours to find us, and find out as much information as possible about the terrorist's plans. After that he would be picked up, and the crew arrested.

Now he had to be careful and ask the right questions.

All of this was taking place as Paolo and I followed Maria to the front door of the mountain farmhouse. The sun was setting into the red sky silhouetting in the mountains. Peso was running behind us, herding us, and nipping at my swollen ankle. Paolo held his bruised ribs, and both of our stomachs rumbled.

Safety and food was here. Everything else would have to wait.

Maria opened the door and the smell of cooking flooded over us as several shocked faces turned towards us and froze.

A man, an elderly lady, two other children, an older boy, and a younger girl were seated at the table in the kitchen.

Paolo interpreted as Maria introduced her family in Spanish. Her mother was standing over the pot of stew on the stove, dishing up the food for each one.

"Madre de Dios! Maria, what have you found?" Her father asked, standing up from his chair.

"Father, this is Rose and Paolo. They need help."

"What are they doing on the mountain? How did they get here? What has happened to them?"

"Set a place for them. We will eat and then ask our questions," her mother said.

Chapter Thirty

Maria's father cleared his throat, and there was immediate silence. I knew he was about to say something.

"You must forgive our manners, it is not often we have visitors here. I am Roberto Ricardo Garcia. This is my wife, Christina Maria, her mother Isabella Sanchez, my son Miguel, (he motioned for Miguel to stand) our daughters, Maria and Clarissa. Welcome to our home."

I could tell he was very proud of his family and home. Tradition was very important here, even in the presence of two strange children.

"I am Paolo Rodriguez, and this is my friend, Rose. It is a pleasure to meet you all

Paolo was not to be out done, even though I had started to speak first.

Roberto and Miguel sat back down, and after prayers we all started eating some kind of delicious stew, and homemade bread. I had an idea what kind of stew it was - but I was afraid to ask.

"It is llama," Maria's mother said.

I was relieved both of Maria's parents knew English.

"The llama is very important to people here. For more than two thousand years the natives have used them for work, food, warmth, and milk. It is with much respect we serve this stew," Roberto said.

"I've just never had it before. It is very good," I said, trying to get the image of the animal out of my head

"In Bolivia they raise beef. We only have beef when we go to the markets," Roberto added.

Paolo and I were so hungry anything would have been delicious!

While we ate, we learned how Maria's grandmother was half Spanish and half Quechua, one of the native peoples. She had inherited the skill of making the beautiful handcrafts decorating the dried brick walls of the ranch house. Some were blankets woven with the figures of llamas, while some had Aztec-like patterns and designs. She also made beautiful shawls and scarves of fine needlework

Christina too, made beautiful things from the wool of the llamas and alpacas. Maria was learning the crafts as well.

Each spring, when the pass opened they would bring their wares to the market in Lima. Paolo was surprised to learn some were sold in his grandmother's shop!

"The name, Rodriguez was familiar to me. How nice to meet the boy I have only heard about!" Christina smiled.

Maria also helped Miguel with the chores, feeding the animals and cleaning the pens, helping Peso herd them, and doing some shearing.

Miguel was fifteen and becoming a man. He worked closely with his father, and watched the transactions at the market where some of the llama were sold. They also rented both llamas and alpacas to occasional teams of geologists and people exploring the mines.

Clarissa was five and a handful for her mother, who worked from "from sun up to sun set" taking care of her home and family as well as the animals and crafts.

"She never sits still! She is so curious about everything!" Christina said.

I liked Clarissa instantly.

When the table was cleared and a fresh log put on the fire, Maria's father turned the conversation to our predicament.

"We must find a way for you to get home. But first we will attend to your injuries."

Isabella took me to her bedroom and inspected my ankle.

"Hmmn," was all she said.

"How bad is it?" I asked, not knowing if she could understand me or not.

She smiled and tried to reassure me, understanding my tone more than my words.

"Is okay," she said as she wrapped it with a red cloth soaked in something that must have been medicinal.

I felt a tingling on my skin as the wrap was applied, and I felt some relief from the throbbing pain I had been ignoring.

Christiana attended to Paolo, wrapping his side in a similar way. Pulling down his shirt, she said, we must get some rest.

"We will find places for you to sleep tonight, she said."

Back in the main part of the house, we talked to Roberto and Miguel.

"We have no phone. The closest one is in Cerro de Pasco. The pass is opening, and the miners are coming back. Some of them live there all year long. The train will be running soon, and will take us to Lima. Cerro de Pasco is about one day from here. We will be leaving tomorrow to bring our wares to the market. Your timing is good. You can go with us. From there you can take the train to Lima," Roberto smiled and Miguel nodded.

The whole family was excited about the trip. Miguel had a far -away look as he talked about Lima. I suspected there might be more than just the big world waiting for him. Probably a girlfriend.

Christina and Isabella joined us after putting Clarissa to bed. She hadn't wanted to go with the excitement of company here.

"Isabella and I will give up our train fare so you and Paolo can go home." Maria's mother said.

"No, that wouldn't be right!" I said, "You have waited all winter for this trip!"

"I have money at home. We can re-pay you." Paolo said humbly but with pride.

"The right thing to do is to get you home." Roberto said. "We do not have much, but will share what we have."

"I will stay," Miguel said, straightening his shoulders.

"I will stay, too!" Maria added.

We were overwhelmed by their generosity. I felt bad for being a burden on them.

"I know lots of people are looking for us. You will be repaid...wait! Where is my canvas bag?"

Maria looked around. The bag was hanging on the wooden pegs by the door of the house. She went to get it

She handed me the bag.

I reached inside and found the zippered pocket in the side of the bag. I unzipped it and reached in. My hand found the money tucked inside.

"Emergency money," Mom had said.

I counted the five twenty dollar bills, thanking my mother with every one. No one had to stay behind!

But there was something else we had to think about, the Old Fox and Alex Bacon, our kidnappers!

Chapter Thirty-One

"What's wrong, Rose?" Paolo asked, seeing the look on my face.

"I was just thinking, what if the Old Fox and Alex have someone watching for us? What's in Cerro de Pasco? Will we be safe?"

Paolo talked with Roberto in Spanish. Roberto nodded, "Si the mining company is there. People are coming back with the end of winter. I have friends there, and family, it is where I grew up. We board our animals there when we go to Lima. We can disguise you. If those men are they're watching, they will think you are part of our family. When we load our goods onto the train they will not notice you. There is a telephone at the train station. You can call your family and let them know you are safe."

"We will not let anything happen to you!" Miguel said.

"Thank you all so much," I smiled, relieved we would not be alone.

"We must get a good night's rest if we are leaving tomorrow," Christina said. "Rose, you can sleep with Maria, Paolo can bunk with Miguel. We must rotate our baths. Rose, you can have yours first."

While we were talking, Miguel put a large pot of water on the wood stove. Off the little kitchen was a 'bathroom' and though they did not have running water this was a place where you could bathe and shave. There was a mirror and a cabinet for razors and soaps. Hand-made towels hung on wooden racks, and the room was warm and cozy.

The tub was just large enough for one person, and it was covered in white enamel. It reminded me of movies I had seen of the old west. It took several trips to the mountain stream outside to fetch the water. Everyone joined in on a bucket brigade, and soon the tub was half full. Then the hot water was poured in, and with the soaps and perfumes ready, it was a nice hot bath.

Mine was short but sweet. Isabella made the soap from llama tallow and used flower petals to scent the water. I relaxed as much as possible, and my ankle felt much better after a soak. Isabella wrapped it again when I was dry.

The whole process was repeated three more times, the men interrupting their work for the bucket brigade. Miguel kept the pot full on the stove, throwing more wood into the fire when needed.

It was late night before the baths and preparations for the trip were made

"What about the guys? When do they get their baths?" I asked Christina, as we got ready for bed.

"They take their baths in the morning, in the stream," she said.

"Brrr! Isn't it cold?" I said with a shiver.

"Of course it is, but they will never admit it," she smiled and shook her head.

I wondered how I would talk with Maria as we climbed into the hand-made wooden bed. The woven blankets were soft, and though the bed was small, it felt much better than the floor of the old mining shack.

When we were all settled in, Peso jumped on the foot of the bed. The little dog curled up between our feet, and made me lonesome for Sam.

"You are sad?" Maria said. She could see my face in the candlelight. She spoke some English.

"I miss my dog."

Maria nodded as she blew out the candle. She put a comforting arm around me, and we fell asleep in the moonlight listening to the sounds of the mountain

The night went fast. I had not realized how tired I was, and the pain in my ankle must have given me dreams. It was all a blur, but I was surprised how rested I felt as the sun came up.

Morning came early and I woke to Maria prodding me to get up. We had to wait in line to brush our hair and teeth.

I was not even awake yet, and already the house was full of noise! Breakfast was cooking on the stove, and there was an excitement in the air. This was a big day.

Outside, the noise of the llamas and alpacas and a barking Peso mixed with the sounds of laughter.

"So, Paolo! In the city you take warm baths, eh?" Roberto smiled as he emerged from the cold mountain stream. It was a cool morning at 14,000 feet. Miguel smiled at the 'city boy', then jumped into the stream to submerge himself in the shallow water.

Paolo jumped right in after him. "I never had a hot bath. We are not wealthy," he said, splashing water at Miguel.

It was cold, but like Christina had said, not one of them would show it.

Of course, we could only hear them splashing. The bathing spot was secluded from sight.

Most of the work had been done the night before. Blankets were folded and piled. The pickup truck was stacked on one end with months of work. The girls and women had made woven mats, decorated blankets, wall hangings, scarves and fine needlework. The men had things to sell also.

Roberto had coils of rope braided from the long coarse hair from the llama. Miguel had made leather wallets and purses from tanned leather.

"Wow! This is intense! How did you make so many things over the winter?" I asked as we stepped outside to load the last few things.

"Most of what you see was made long ago. We are always making new things, and some things take much time. Not all you see was made this winter," Christina smiled.

"Of course, how silly I am," I said, blushing.

I remembered Dimitri's family in Gzhel. Once again I was reminded of the importance of art.

"My father carves driftwood. He is very good," Paolo announced.

"I would like to see it someday," Roberto said.

The front seat was reserved for the grownups to ride in. The rest of us had to find places in back; at times Miguel would ride on the running board, talking to his father as he drove.

When everyone was ready, Roberto called Peso.

"Peso, you stay and watch the flock. Protect the house while we are gone."

Though he wanted to go along, he knew he had to stay. He sat; tail swishing the ground as Miguel climbed on to the old truck.

With a whine and a groan the pickup started off.

"Come on old girl, let's go," Roberto prodded the truck affectionately.

Chapter Thirty-Two

I watched my feet swing back and forth as we moved along the dirt road. Maria had lent me a pair of sandals and a red dress her mother had made for her. I wore it over my jeans. A matching jacket and a brown hat to hide my hair completed the outfit. My Reeboks were safely hidden in my canvas bag, and tucked under piles of blankets with Paolo's.

Paolo was also wearing a hat, and though his complexion was darker than mine, he still needed a disguise.

For my complexion, which was pale and freckled, Isabella had mixed up a special make-up. From a distance I could pass for one of the family. If it worked once, it was all we needed.

I sat next to Isabella on the tailgate. Maria and Clarissa rode farther up in the bed, sitting on the load. We would take turns on the tailgate.

The morning sun behind us, we were headed west and slightly south. The road gradually got narrower as we moved away from the ranch to lesser-used paths. The old truck seemed to have no problem negotiating the trail.

Maria wanted to know about my life back home. She had heard many stories of life in the United States. Yes, I thought, we are all rich and happy. To her, we would be. Hot water, telephones, television, and all the things she did not have would seem like an impossible dream.

There were other things she wanted to know, girl things that Paolo would have to translate. I was careful not to embarrass him too much. Besides, there are just some things boys don't need to know. Girls need their secrets.

We stopped for lunch, and I was grateful for the hat that helped to block out the sun. We had been driving away from it all morning and now it was above us. We would be facing it the rest of the day.

Finding a clearing next to the road, Roberto stopped. Christina and Isabella laid a blanket on the ground, and set up a picnic lunch. The men joined us, and we sat quiet for a while enjoying the view of the mountains.

"I've never seen such beautiful scenery," I said, eating a slice of homemade bread.

"You have never been in the mountains before?" Miguel asked.

"Yes, I've been in the Rocky Mountains, but the scenery is different. They are not green like these mountains."

"I have never been in the mountains," Paolo said, "I have always seen them, but my father is a fisherman. We live on the coast."

"I would like to go on a boat someday," Miguel said. "But I will probably take over the ranch."

"It must be a lonely life, how did you come to live on the mountain?" I asked between bites.

"My grandfather married Isabella's mother. She was a Quechua, and he was Spanish. She left her village, and they built a house on the mountain. My mother was born there, and one day my grandfather died. On a trip to Lima, she met my father. They wanted to get married, and Isabella, with no husband to help her anymore, offered them the ranch. So, the rest of us were born there. I will probably continue the tradition. Some day we will have enough money to build and add modern conveniences to the ranch. I have big plans and the Internet and computers can help our ranch grow. Our first need is electricity." Miguel was excited about his dream.

"Cerro de Pasco is growing," Roberto said. "There are more year 'round residents and someday the town will expand. As it grows, the possibility for electric service grows also. Until then, we will have to use a generator. Fuel is expensive here, and we do not use it more than we have to."

"Yes, someday the world will catch up to us," Christina said.

Isabella rolled her eyes. She had liked the life she made, but like the day she left her village, she knew things would change. She was determined to keep tradition alive in her crafts.

Soon we all sat, nodding at the universal concept of family and home. I knew it was time to move on.

On our feet again, we picked up the blanket, and started up the engine

The sun was finally behind us. We rode and talked into the evening.

Two-thirds of the way there we looked for a campsite for the night. It was too dangerous to drive at night. Once we found a suitable place, we set up a makeshift tent and started a campfire. Paolo and I helped gather the wood, and soon the crackling of a lively fire sent sparks drifting even higher into the air.

Sparks that led to smoke. Smoke that was seen.

"Where there is smoke…" The Old Fox lowered his binoculars.

"You don't think that is the children?" Alex said.

They had come to Cerro de Pasco suspecting Paolo and I might make it down from the mountain.

"No one lives on that mountain," The Old Fox said, raising the binoculars again.

"Maybe it is just tourists, mountain climbers, or explorers." Alex said hopefully. He had never been eager to kidnap the children in the first place. He was a businessman, and had been okay with his part of the plan, just to delay the wire.

"Maybe, but can we take that chance?" the Fox asked. The Path had a lot to lose if the plot failed, and much to gain if it succeeded. He was not above eliminating children for the cause.

"We don't even know if they overheard us, or what they know." Alex reminded him.

"I know who the girl is, though. She and her family are here for only one reason. Like her grandfather, they are not what they seem. I will not let history repeat itself."

"Revenge! That is what you really want," Alex was angry.

"If this plan fails, the terrorists in the east will have their revenge, and it will be on us - possibly the whole world! If there is a chance those children overheard the plan, they must be silenced!"

"Soon it will not matter what they know! The hour is drawing near for the event! They may never survive the mountain anyway," Alex was still angry.

"Fool! Do you not see how close they are getting? They are on the way to Cerro de Pasco! There they will find a phone, and the train! Once they contact their parents it will be all over!" Now the Fox had lost his composure.

"We will stay here and watch. When they arrive, we will stop them," The Old Fox had cooled a little; he lowered the binoculars, and turned. They were standing on the roof of the Peru Mining Company.

As the last of the sun disappeared they walked to the door and descended into the building. Watching the smoke from the fire, I wished I could send signals like the American Indians did.

Paolo sat studying my face. He got up and walked over to me. Sitting down again he put his arm around me.

"Don't worry, Rose. We'll get home."

"At least we found some nice people to help us," I said.

"Yes, who knows what kind of people we might have found," Paolo agreed.

Home. Sitting on a mountain half way around the world, I was as far from home as a kid can get. I recognized the queasy feeling in my stomach I had first felt in far off Russia.

Would I ever get used to it?

Chapter Thirty-Three

Morning found us on top of the blankets huddled together, Paolo, myself, Maria and Clarissa. The adults slept in the tent.

The smell of eggs and coffee on the campfire stirred us from sleep. I was happy we had not slept on the ground. We straightened and refolded the blankets then lined up for breakfast.

In spite of our situation, it had been fun. I couldn't help thinking what my parents would say when we got back. I would even take being grounded again just to be home.

But we had something important to tell them! Something important enough to kidnap and strand us on a mountain for. We knew their plan! I wondered what was going on below. Of course our parents and The Agency would be searching for us, and trying to uncover the terrorist plot. How much had they learned?

And time was running out! I couldn't wait to get to a phone in Cerro de Pasco! Things were happening back at home.

"You've got to call him now!" Steven said to the hologram of the Director.

"I know, and you're right. We should have done it sooner. The delay in the wire has been an embarrassment, and a strain on The Agency's relations with the President. But you've got to understand, careers are on the line!" The holograph pleaded.

"Careers! Thousands of lives are at stake! And now two children who just might hold the key to the terrorist plot! A couple of twelve-year-old kids who managed to do what all your sophisticated equipment couldn't!" Susan was angry and Sam growled.

"Up until now we haven't had any hard evidence to share with him," the Director smiled.

"We have enough evidence to arrest the mole, Alex Bacon, and the whole Path if we want to! Bring them in - and make them talk!" Steven's voice was rising. The hologram image vibrated from the tension.

"We can't just arrest a whole country on the basis of two missing children, and a photograph. International relations are touchy. We need the details of the plan; time, dates, and targets!" The Director fought back.

"Our best chance of getting that kind of information is to find the kids! Still worried about your career? If the terrorists carry out a major strike, you won't have a career left to worry about! And if I find out we could have saved the kids, and stopped the terrorists you'll have more to worry about than just your career!" Steven was shouting now, and Sam was sitting up and barking.

Zip almost lost the image quivering under Steven's voice.

"We don't work for you anymore," Susan said, "if you don't call the President, we will. We'll get him to authorize the arrests."

"Okay, okay. The Agency will authorize the arrests, but not for twenty-four hours. We have to give "Crocker" the standard time before we move in," the Director sighed.

"You mean you need twenty-four hours to put a spin on things, don't you?" Susan said sarcastically.

"You know the procedure. The suitcase is closed," the Director disappeared.

Susan looked at Steven. "I'm sure glad we got out when we did. Rose's Dad was right to make a move into the private sector."

"Yeah, those budget cuts were a dangerous thing to do. Most of the senior agents are gone now, and the young lions are lost without their computers," Steven replied, stroking Sam's ears.

"Well, there are two lion cubs out there who didn't need computers to find out what's been going on. I know they will be safe until the event takes place. A couple of aces in the hole," Susan hoped she was right.

"All we can do now is wait for "Crocker", I hope he can find out where the kids are," Steven echoed the thoughts on everyone's minds.

Sam was pacing the Ready Room. All he could do was bark.

Richard was pacing, too. What was wrong? His "Crocker I.D. had been accepted, and he was told he could meet the Council of the Path. He had been hoping to see The Old Fox. Instead they had taken him to this little room, and told him to wait. That had been hours ago.

Finally, the door opened

"Marcos! What's going on?" Richard asked as his new 'friend' stood in the doorway.

"Come on, they want us on deck," he motioned with his hand for Crocker to follow.

"About time!" Crocker said.

He followed Marcos up the steps to the deck. There the 'leader' and his companions stood with smiles on their faces.

"Crocker! Marcos! So nice you could join us," he said, smiling.

"What is going on? I come offering my services, and you treat me like a prisoner! When do I get to meet the real boss?" Richard said angrily.

"Why is that so important? A job is a job..." the man with no name replied.

"I only deal with the top card," Crocker said. "I thought we were going to meet him."

"How do you know you haven't?"

"Because he would have told me he was, once he checked my identification," Richard did not want to tell him he would have recognized him.

"There are only two people in this organization who are stupid enough to brag about it, and Marcos is one of them, the other has made another unscheduled trip," The leader said.

"An unscheduled trip?" Crocker went fishing.

"Yes, his actions were never sanctioned by the Council, but we have to stand behind him to protect the cause. So he went to tie up a couple of loose ends."

Richard's heart was pounding. Was he talking about the kids? He had to control his anger and his excitement.

"Loose ends?" Crocker asked.

"Yes, like shoelaces, you can trip on them. Loose ends are dangerous."

Something changed in the air. Marcos started to sweat and Richard looked around. Twelve hours had gone by since they boarded the boat, and now the morning sun was glinting off the water. There was no land in sight.

Relaxing a little, Crocker smiled. Surely they would not do anything in broad daylight.

"Yes, I understand. In my business I cannot afford loose ends either."

"Then you will understand this!"

Without warning, the men rushed Crocker and Marcos, knocking them against the side of the boat, and dumping them overboard!

Bobbing in the water, they began dodging bullets.

"Dive!" Richard said, grabbing Marcos and pulling him under.

The bullets followed them down.

Chapter Thirty-Four

Marcos was not a swimmer. Richard had to work hard to pull him under the surface, and keep him there. In the process his 'Crocker' wig came off, and floated back up to the top.

The bullets kept coming, following the air bubbles from the struggling men. Finally, Marcos settled down and held his breath. Richard did not know how long he could hold his own. He only hoped it would be long enough for the shooting to stop.

He didn't dare look up for fear of rising to the surface again. He listened for the sounds of bullets in the water, twisting and pulling Marcos with him as they came.

Suddenly, the shooting stopped.

"Look! There he is!" One of the men on the boat saw Crocker's wig.

The shooting started again, and the wig was riddled with holes. Finally, it sank under the water, out of sight of the shooters.

"Let's go. They are dead and drowned," The man on the boat said.

Richard heard the boat churning away, and soon the water was quiet.

Lungs about to burst, he let out some air, and started upward with the near-unconscious Marcos in tow.

Breaking the surface, they both gasped for air. Richard looked around, and saw the shredded wig, thankful for the disguise.

The boat was nowhere to be seen, and he knew they had narrowly escaped death. But now they were stranded in the middle of nowhere, floating in the water with no land in sight.

Richard reached up to the cross around his neck. Worn under his silk shirt it had helped complete the look of the drug dealer he had been playing. He prayed and pressed the back of the cross between his thumb and forefinger.

Would the tracking signal still work?

Still hidden underwater near the coast, the Seal Team sub had been monitoring communications with The Agency.

"Sir, we have a signal. It's Crocker's pick up call," the sonar man informed the captain.

"Co-ordinates?" the captain responded. "Let's not keep the good Crocker waiting."

When the co-ordinates came in the sub came alive.

"Right full rudder. Full speed ahead. Seal Team prepare for rescue."

"Pray for me, too," Marcos gasped, dog paddling to stay afloat.

"Don't worry. Help is on the way," Richard said, letting go of the cross to fan the water.

"Who are you and what happened to your hair?" Marcos asked.

"You'll find out soon enough," Richard replied. "Save your energy."

"Sir, a message from the sub," the aide said as he rushed into the director's office.

With mixed emotions the Director read the message.

"The oven is open. Crocker is served," was all it said.

"Get me the President."

"Yes, sir," the aide walked to the phone.

"Sir, I have the Commander-In-Chief on the line."

"Good afternoon, Mr. President. I need to brief you on current events..."

"Sir. A message from your wife," the Peruvian police officer said as he left his car after talking on the radio. He walked over to Dad, who was interviewing local residents in the streets surrounding the wire factory.

Was it good news or bad? Was it about the kids? So many possibilities rushed through his mind as he walked with the officer back to the car.

Susan and Steven paced the Ready Room. Still upset with the director, they wondered if he would call the president now that Richard had come back in. They were grateful he was alive and well.

"It's a good thing you didn't let Sam bark while we were on hologram," Steven said.

"Yeah, his bark is like thunder. Usually only Rose can keep him from barking. She showed me how to do it once," Susan replied.

"Kind of like keeping a sneeze from happening, eh?" Steven said.

"Yeah, kind of like that."

"Never works for me. Eventually the sneeze has to happen." Steven said, sniffling as if he had one coming.

"Oh no! Not that!" Susan said in alarm.

"Ah, ah, ah, CHOO!" Steven's feigned sneeze had become a real one.

The force of the sneeze penetrated the Ready Room and reached Samson's ears. A noise like thunder ripped through the neighborhood, vibrating the bunker door of Richard's Ready Room.

The barking continued until Susan made it outside in an attempt to quiet the furry giant.

"Eventually it has to happen," she said, putting a careful hand over Samson's nose.

"Eventually, it has to happen," the Old Fox said to Alex as they approached the telephone pole outside the Peru Mining Company.

"Once a plan is set in motion nothing can stop it. The Path has too much at stake to just back out," he continued.

"We have done our part. The hard line communists have put me in these offices to co-operate with the anti-U.S. interests. We have a large stake in this event also. But I do not agree with killing the children. Every plan must have a back-up plan, and killing the children would be bad for public relations after the event," Alex remained firm.

"You are in my country now. I will give the orders," the Fox was equally firm.

"I will go as far as delaying the children, kidnap them again if we must. As long as the event takes place all parties will be satisfied."

"Then help me cut this wire. We must not allow them to call home."

"E.T. phone home." The famous line from an old movie played in my head as we approached the town of Cerro de Pasco.

"I saw that movie!" Paolo said as the truck bounced along, garbling his words.

"We have to get to a phone!" I said, kneeling on the pile of blankets to look ahead over the roof of the truck.

"First one we see!" Christina shouted as we pulled into the outskirts of the town.

"There! Stop there!" I yelled, jumped out of the truck and ran to a phone booth alongside the street.

The truck squealed to a stop, and everyone jumped out, surrounding the booth.

"I hope it works," I said as I picked up the receiver.

"A dial tone! Hello, operator..." I started to say then stopped in mid-sentence.

The look on my face must have told everyone what happened.

"It's dead. Just went dead." I was in shock. "Someone must know we're here!"

Paolo shook his head. "No. We are so close!"

No one spoke. Little Clarissa, who had been so quiet sleeping most of the trip, put a hand to her face.

"Ah, ah, ah..." she stopped. There was a sneeze coming on.

I reached out and put a finger to her nose. It reminded me of how I would get Sam to keep from barking.

"A sneeze is like a bark," I said, "once it gets started, it is hard to stop."

Clarissa looked up at me, and smiled. Sneeze averted!

I smiled back and took my finger from her nose, grateful for the distraction that kept us from panicking about the current events.

The smile quickly faded from her face.

"Ah, ah, ah, CHOO!"

Chapter Thirty-Five

"I know they are here," the Old Fox said as he put the wire cutters in the trunk of the rental car.

"How do you know?" Alex asked.

"I can feel it."

"What do we do next?"

"First we stop them from communicating their information, then we must stop them from getting home. The event is only two days away. If we can keep them from talking all will be well. The terrorists will get what they want; the Path will get what they want. Your friends will also. Everyone who knows the plan is sworn to secrecy; except those two children."

"How do we find them?" Alex asked. "And how did they manage to escape and get this far?"

"They must have had help. There must be someone on the mountain we did not know about. Someone from Cerro de Pasco, maybe. A miner or farmer. If the children have told them, they must be silenced also."

"How do we do that?"

"Really, Alexis! How did you get to be an executive? We kill them, of course. Eliminate the competition."

"I don't like it. Too much killing."

"And just what do you think will happen when the plan is executed? It is much too late to think about your qualms. A few lives are nothing added to the thousands you signed on for," the Fox was disgusted with Alex's lack of courage.

"But the plan seemed so remote, so far away."

"So, killing is okay when you can't see your victims? Like a far off war?"

"Yes, like a war. For a cause," Alex was sweating now that he was closer to the events they had talked about. It was no longer an abstract idea.

"Enough! It falls to you and I to deal with this situation. There is only one way out, and that is to die. Do you wish to die?"

"No. I do not wish to die," Alex hung his head. He knew he would do whatever had to be done. That is how he got to his position, after all.

"What do we do next?" He asked the Fox as he turned the key, and started the car.

"We must find them. I believe they will take the train to Lima. We must get to the station and find out when the next one is due. We must be there when they get there." The Fox said as he put the car into Drive.

"They know we are here," I repeated as we all climbed back into the truck.

"How do you know that?" Paolo asked.

"The phone going dead was no accident. They must have been watching, and seen our campfires. They must have been worried we would escape the shack, and find a way off the mountain in time to warn The Agency. Remember, the Old Fox wanted to kill us, but Alex, or Alexis would not let him. They must have had second thoughts."

"The wire company gets the copper from Peru Mining," Maria's father said, "This man, Alexis, must be connected with them also."

"Yes, I think so. Time is running out. There are only two days left until the terrorists carry out their plan. We must get word to The Agency!"

"How?" Paolo asked. "They have cut the phone lines. What will they do next?"

"They will try to find us and keep us from getting off the mountain. We must get to the train!"

"Si!" Roberto said, climbing into the driver's seat and starting the old truck.

"Hold on to your seats!" He yelled as the truck lurched forward.

The gears growled, and the old pickup jumped with every shift. Soon we raced down the streets of Cerro de Pasco, the transmission giving off a high-pitched whine. It was the fastest this old truck had gone in a long time.

"Ahh, Ahh, CHOO!" Clarissa sneezed again, and fell off her pile of blankets into Maria's lap.

"This is like a race," Maria said as the truck bumped along,

"I just hope we can win it!" I replied, grabbing the rolled edge of the metal box.

Clarissa sneezed again.

"It must be the dust from the road," Miguel said.

"The tires are kicking up a lot of it!" I said.

"Yes," Miguel replied, "this old truck is nothing to sneeze at!"

Chapter Thirty-Six

"Time is running out," Dad said. "Whatever the terrorists have planned will happen soon - I can feel it."

"That means we have to find the kids soon," Mom said. They were talking on Zip to Steven, Susan and Richard on a three-way conference call.

"We may have a break," Susan said, "Seems Alex Bacon was recently named CEO of Peru Mining also. No coincidence, I'm sure. His ties to the hard-line communists suggest the terrorist event may be a joint project with other enemies of the U.S."

"Lately he has been seen in the company of the Fox. Seems the Path has an interest in wire, too." Richard said from his window on the laptop. "I found out the old guy had to make an unscheduled trip."

"Yes," Dad said, "the staff at the wire factory said Alex was at a high-level meeting, and couldn't be reached. My guess is the mining company in Cerro de Pasco."

"Could be where they are holding the kids," Mom said hopefully.

"Should we send in the troops?" Steven asked.

"No. We don't want to endanger the kids. Our best chance of rescuing them is to not tip our hand. Besides, we still don't know what the target is. If we rush to get the kids, we may jump-start the event," Dad was trying to stay cool and professional.

"We could send Rico and Gloria. Their tour car is a good cover and would probably go unnoticed," Mom suggested.

"No, they can't take the car. The only way to get there is by train or fly in." Richard pointed out.

"Lets put them on the train. They would not be conspicuous and a plane or chopper may alert the bad guys." Dad said.

"One good thing," Richard spoke, "the leader on the boat said the Fox was acting alone. Chances are it is just him and Alexis we have to deal with."

"Good. That gives the kids a better chance. Keep searching for clues to the terrorist plan, we'll contact Rico and Gloria and send them in." Dad's voice showed excitement.

"Just got some Intel from The Agency; seems the phones are down in Cero de Pasco." Susan broke in.

"Looks like we are on the right track!" Mom said.

The train was at the station when we arrived. We parked the pickup truck and loaded the goods onto a cart for the freight car. I felt clumsy in my disguise and worried about my hat falling off. I was sure we were being watched!

Paolo was used to this kind of work as he had often helped his grandmother unload blankets and handcrafts for her shop. He looked like one of the family.

No one seemed to be paying any attention to us as we loaded the car but still I could not shake the feeling that the Fox and Alex were there. I tried to look around without being conspicuous.

There were several families, businessmen and tourists, relatives who had come to visit. Not much different than people who wait for a bus in my country or people at an airport.

This was the first major run of the season with the pass opening up. Maria's family made this trip every spring and fall.

Still, I didn't see anyone who looked suspicious. The conductor talked about the phones being down and no way to communicate except the radio on the train.

If only I could get a message out! Of course, that is exactly what the Fox wanted to avoid. If I tried I would blow our cover! I decided to get on the train and try to get us to Lima. I had given Roberto the money to buy tickets for Paolo and I. I thanked my mother silently again for putting the money in my canvas bag.

Maria's family kept an eye out for us too. I relaxed a little and finally put my bundle into the car.

And that's when my shoe fell out!

"There! That family loading the freight car! That shoe looks familiar. The girl, Rose was wearing those shoes in the Plaza! She must be wearing a disguise!"

The Fox and Alex were parked around the corner from the station, using binoculars when no one was looking.

"What do we do?" Alex asked, lowering the binoculars and handing them back to the Fox.

"We could get on the train and try to grab them all! But that would mean we would have to hijack the train, and give ourselves away. The kids are obviously under the protection of the family they are with. We could follow them to Lima and try to stop them there, but the risk is too great. We have to make sure they do not talk to anyone."

"But what about the radio on the train? Or in the station? One message is all it would take, and we would have The Agency here in little time, or in Lima waiting for us!"

"Yes, you are correct, Alex. Let them think they have safely boarded the train. They will not try to radio anyone soon. They will think they have avoided us, and wait until they get to Lima. We will make sure they never arrive!"

Alexis was shocked. "What do you mean, never arrive?"

"There is some dynamite in the trunk of the car. We will get ahead of the train and plant it on the tracks!"

"But what about all the innocent people on the train? Women and children!"

"Casualties of war. It is regrettable - but do I need to remind you again of our part in the plan? Millions will die, and economic chaos will break out in the U.S.! What is one train?"

"No! I won't be part of this!" Alex was firm.

"Then I will simply kill you now and do it anyway," the Old Fox was cold and Alex knew he meant what he had said.

"Okay. Then let us do it quickly!"

We found our seats as the train pulled out of the station. Thankfully, nothing suspicious had happened. It almost seemed too easy, and I remembered what Susan had once said in New York; "If something seems too easy, watch out!"

"Rose, you must tell us all you know," Roberto said. "If something happens at least more people will know, and someone will be able to get a message out."

"He is right, Rose," Paolo said.

I had avoided saying too much to Maria's family. I had not wanted to put them in danger. But after all that had happened, it seemed like right thing to do.

I gave them as much background as I could, and finished with the plan we had overheard at the wire factory just before we were kidnapped.

"We must get to Lima, and alert your parents! We must stop these madmen!" Roberto said.

"My God! The Brooklyn Bridge and The Golden Gate? But you said there were three targets," Christina said.

"The third target is symbolic. They plan on bombing three casinos in Las Vegas. All of this is set to happen at the same exact time the day after tomorrow. It has all been planned by word of mouth for the last few years, ever since the 9/11 attacks on the Twin Towers. Each cell or member of the plan had a specific job to do and delaying the wire needed for The Agency's new computers was an important part of the plan. It would help delay the coordination of information to tip off the authorities to the plan. My family was sent to Peru to investigate the hold-up in the delivery of the wire The Agency had contracted for." Whew! I lived up to my nickname on that one!

"But if the U.S. is on alert, how will they avoid detection?" Miguel asked.

"Well, there is a battle going on at the airports for a better system of profiling travelers. Some people want to adopt the European system, and some people complain about privacy. The terrorists use this to their advantage. They know the holes in the system. As far as the actual bombings, unsuspecting people will carry them out.

People driving to work do not know their car is carrying a bomb. Tourists in Vegas do not know their luggage has been tampered with. Once someone tried to blow up the Brooklyn Bridge. He was profiled and identified. Al Quida had trained him. He was stopped. Now they figure no one would make a second attempt on the bridge.

I did not care who was listening now, and most of the passengers were. The looks on some of their faces were skeptical, though. Just a child's imagination

Everyone was silent for a few minutes, digesting all that information. The train rolled along steadily, and we looked out the windows, wishing this were just another routine train ride into the city.

I watched the scenery flash by as the train picked up speed. We were traveling down the mountain now, and in a few hours we would be safe in Lima.

But hours were precious now. I wondered if there was a way to get to the radio in the engine car?

Just as I thought of it, I saw the black car on the road alongside the train. It seemed to be racing us.

The two men in the car looked familiar!

Chapter Thirty-Seven

"That car!" I said. "It looks like the Old Fox and Alex! I think they are trying to beat us to the crossing!"

"But why?" Paolo said, climbing over Maria to see out the window.

"They're trying to stop the train!" I think I said it a little too loud. The passengers were all crowding over to the left side of the train. Panic was growing! The conductor headed for the engine to tell the engineer.

Up front, the engineer hadn't seen the car yet. Everything was humming along normally, just another routine trip to Lima. This job could get boring, he thought.

He checked his watch, proud of his record for being on time. Well, here was something to accomplish, anyway.

The black car sped ahead, finally catching up with the speed of the train, and then passing it! Alex was behind the wheel.

"Well, Alex! I see you have come to your senses!" the Fox smiled.

"Yes, we must beat that train!"

"We will! When we reach the crossing, stop the car in front of the track. I'll jump out and plant the dynamite!"

Alex just nodded and kept his foot on the pedal. The pedal was on the floor!

"Rose! We must stop the train!" Roberto said, reaching for the emergency cord.

"No!" Miguel stopped his father. "Not at this speed! We may all be killed by the sudden stop."

"He is right. That black car cannot stop this train anyway. The men in the car will be killed," one of the passengers shouted. "But we will be okay."

The time for action had passed. There was nothing we could do now but brace ourselves for the impact. I had seen the news story on television about how long it takes for a train to stop. And I had seen what a train could do to a car!

I hoped the conductor would reach the engineer in time, but in my heart I knew we could not do much. I was more worried about what the men in the car might do! I did not believe they would kill themselves by putting the car in front of the speeding locomotive!

"What is it, Rose?" Paolo asked, noting the change in my expression.

"I don't think they are going to try to stop the train," I said.

"Then why are they racing it? What do you think they are going to do?"

"Well, mining companies use explosives, right?" I said, not wanting to come right out and say what I was thinking.

"Yes, so?" Paolo was catching on. His voice was shaking a little.

"I think they are going to blow it up!" I whispered, finger to my lips.

The Engineer looked up from his watch. The track ahead looked clear. They would be approaching the crossing soon. Almost time to blow the whistle! Blowing the whistle was his favorite part of the job. Usually no one was around to blow it at. Sometimes kids would be at the crossing, playing a dangerous game of daredevil, but no one had been hit yet. Once in a while a car would try to beat the train across the tracks, but that had not happened for a long time. This will probably be just another whistle blower, he thought.

Being in the third car back, the conductor had to open the door, and walk to the other car. He walked through that car, trying to calm the passengers as he hurried up front. One more car to go! He hoped he would reach the engine in time!

The black car was passing the engine now, approaching the crossing ahead of the train.

"Faster, Alex!" the Fox shouted. "I must have time to plant the dynamite!"

"My foot is on the floor!" Alex shouted back.

The car finally passed the engine and the Fox unbuckled his seat belt and unlocked the door. It looked like they would have just enough time!

The engineer reached for the whistle cord. He blew the approach signal. Out side at the crossing, the familiar 'Ding-ding-ding' sounded as the striped arm lowered and the red stoplights flashed.

Two more blasts of the horn and they would sail across the intersection.

Just then, a black car came to a screeching halt in front of the arm at the crossing. A man jumped out of the car, and ran to the trunk - opening the lid just as the conductor burst into the engine compartment.

Suddenly, nothing was routine

Alex sat at the wheel, the car's motor running. Just seconds now! Only a few seconds were left to determine the fate of so many people! Outside, the Fox had grabbed the dynamite, he was lighting the fuse and running to the tracks.

The engineer blasted the horn! Knowing he could not stop, he pushed the engine faster. Maybe they could plow right through it!

Inside the cars there was panic. We were helpless. There was nothing we could do but pray! I looked at the frozen faces of Maria and her family. Somehow, I felt responsible for all of this. Why hadn't I listened to my parents?

"We'll be okay, Rose. We all will! I have prayed to Saint Rose of Lima!" Paolo said.

I remembered reading about Saint Rose in the church I had toured with Mom. She was a Roman Catholic nun who lived from 1586-1617. She was born in Lima and became a nun in 1606. She became famous for the austerity she practiced, and was the first native-born saint of the Americas. I felt a connection with her name.

"It will take a miracle to get out us of this!" I said, hoping for one.

The Fox was holding the dynamite. Ignoring the screaming whistle, he turned around, facing the engine and looking at the engineer for a second.

Alex had the motor running. He put the car in gear just as the Fox was turning toward him. He stepped on the gas!

Instead of going in reverse, the car lurched forward; blasting through the wooden arm, and hitting the startled Fox, pushing him - and the dynamite across the tracks just before the train flew by!

There was an explosion as the dynamite blew up in the Old Fox's hand. The car went up in flames as the gas tank exploded, and we could see it out the train windows as we rolled safely by.

Alex had made his decision.

Chapter Thirty-Eight

"Sheesh! That was too intense!" I said, sitting back down. The passengers all breathed sighs of relief, then sat quietly in shock of what had just happened.

Christina was the first one to break the silence. "I made a lunch. We should eat."

It seemed strange to eat at a time like this, but it also seemed like the thing to do. I thought about it while she passed out the homemade fajitas.

"Mom, why do we eat at a wake? And what is a wake?" I had asked at my Grandparent's funeral.

"We eat to bring normalcy back into our lives. Life goes on even after someone we love dies. We must go on," she said sadly.

"But why do we have a party?" I asked.

"It's not really a party. When someone faces death, people gather around, and surround the family with life. We need support and comfort. Food is something that brings people together. It gives them emotional strength as well as physical strength. We go through a lot of stress, and we need energy. Besides, we need to celebrate life - and let each other know our loved ones are not really gone, just somewhere else."

Well, I wondered who would miss the Old Fox and Alex! But we were still alive after a close call! That was reason to celebrate! The food never tasted so good! Normalcy.

Besides all that, Peru was a country used to chaos. There had been wars and struggles throughout its history. The people on the train were quick to return to normalcy.

But I suspected they would talk about this trip for a long time!

Back in Cerro de Pasco, Rico and Gloria stood outside of Peru Mining. They had gotten off the train as it arrived, and started their search for us, believing we were being held hostage.

Renting a car at the station, they had not seen us loading the train. Our disguise had fooled them! They also did not see the Fox and Alex, who were parked around the corner, watching between the buildings with their binoculars as we boarded the train.

The trail of evidence had led them to the mining company.

"There's no one here. Where could they be?" Rico said.

"It's a big mountain, they could be anywhere," Gloria replied, looking through her binoculars.

"They must be here somewhere! The phones don't just go down for no reason," Rico was frustrated.

"If the phones went down, maybe the kids were trying to call home. That would mean the Fox and Alex probably cut the phone lines so they could not call! That would mean the kids escaped!" Gloria knew she was on the right track now!

"You're right! Maybe the kids are trying to get home! If they couldn't call, maybe they are trying to get back to Lima!"

"But that would mean they might be on the train we just got off, and we did not see them," Gloria was thinking back to the train station, replaying the scene in her mind.

"Maybe we did not see them because they were in disguise, or were planning to stow away."

"That makes sense. They might not have any money, or could not risk telling anyone. Maybe the Fox and Alex were on their tail."

"And they would not have seen us if they were not expecting us to be there!" Rico knew they were getting closer.

Their deductive reasoning was interrupted by a call on Gloria's cell phone.

She picked up the call on Zip.

"An explosion? Where?"

"We think the train is okay. We are hoping the kids are on it," Dad said.

"We were just figuring that out, here too," Gloria said.

"We think they are trying to get home, and someone is trying to stop them. They must know something about the terrorist plan."

"If the train is okay, what caused the explosion?" Rico asked.

268

"A car. We don't have much information yet. Satellite photos picked up the explosion and the wreckage of a car. We are sending Richard in a chopper to investigate.

"Have you talked to the engineer yet?" Gloria asked.

"No, the radio on the train is out. We are hoping that means the kids are still alive, and someone has cut the radio so they cannot call," Dad's voice was cracking with emotion.

"Then, it would mean someone is still on the train! If the car were trying to stop the train, whoever was on it would not have been able to cut the radio. We have to catch that train!"

"Gloria, look over here!" Rico called out.

He had spotted the cut in the phone line outside of the Peru Mining Company.

"Let's go! We have a train to catch!" She said, running to the rented car.

The train rolled along while we ate. Other people in the car had taken out their lunches too. The conductor was offering refreshments and the engineer was busy trying to get the radio to work. The steady clack of the wheels became a comforting sound in the background, lulling the passengers into a sense of security.

My thoughts were on Lima, and seeing Mom and Dad again. Paolo also was thinking of home.

Maria watched us eat; anxious to talk when we were finished. Her eyes kept going to Paolo when he wasn't looking, and I could see she had a crush on him. I smiled, thinking of Dimitri, the boy I had met in Russia who had a crush on me. I liked Paolo too, and was surprised when I noticed Maria's looks how I wasn't jealous.

Dimitri would have been pleased!

Maria's family was also aware of Maria's attention, but did not seem too concerned. "Just children, nothing to worry about," their eyes said.

Grandma smiled.

There were three cars on this train. We were in the lead car, there was a second car of passengers, and there was a third car with the freight and luggage. It was just a commuter train on a routine trip to Lima.

No one in the second car paid much attention to the man in the back when he stood up and walked to the front of the car.

Wearing jeans and a striped peasant shirt under a woven poncho and a round hat, he looked like many of the natives in Peru. His weathered face had a kind smile showing a few missing teeth. He smiled at people, and they smiled back.

When he reached the door of the car and stepped out, no one thought anything of it.

He stood on the metal platform, and watched the ties fly by underneath. The sound of the wheels seemed to cloak him from sight as he climbed to the back of the first car, and opened the door.

Stepping into our car, he quietly shut the door, the sleepy passengers taking the sound for the conductor.

He stood for a moment until he spotted his destination and walked slowly down the aisle, smiling at the few curious looks he received.

Seated across from Paolo and me, Roberto looked up, and saw the friendly stranger. He smiled, nodded, and the man smiled back.

Something sent a chill down my back. I could feel eyes on the back of my head. I wanted to turn and look back, but something in Roberto's manner told me not to.

The chopper landed at the crossing, and Richard climbed out, telling the pilot to wait and keep the motor running.

He examined the wreckage of the car and looked for traces of the occupants.

Climbing back in the helicopter, he told the pilot to take off as he picked up the radio's microphone.

"The kids were not in the car," he told my parents, relieved. "I think they are on the train. We are in pursuit of it now."

Rico held the pedal to the floor, flying along the road at full speed

"Do you think we can catch them?" Gloria asked.

"We sure are going to try!" Rico replied as he pushed down on the pedal even harder. Maria looked up, taking her eyes off Paolo for the first time since we had started eating. Little Clarissa looked up, too.

They were smiling at someone.

Chapter Thirty-Nine

The smiling man had been sent by The Path. They hadn't liked the Fox working alone, and had suspected him of kidnapping us. The plan was too important to them. They had their own reasons for being involved. So they watched without the Fox knowing it.

Rico and Gloria might have spotted the man at the train station, but he had seen them first. He had also seen us buy tickets and board the train. Our disguises did not fool him.

He had reasoned we would not be traveling alone, and knowing the Fox was looking for us, it was simple deduction we would come to the station.

Now he stood before us with the disarming smile of a simple peasant.

He reached under his poncho and drew a gun, ready to shoot us all

Rico and Gloria were gaining on the train. "I see it!" Gloria shouted as the car bumped along, kicking up dust on the dirt road.

"We can catch it!" Rico shouted back.

"What do we do then?"

"We stop it!"

"How?"

"I don't know yet!" He said. "But we'll think of something."

The helicopter was much faster than the car.

"There it is!" The pilot said.

Richard looked out the window as the copter banked towards the tracks. He could see the train now and something else.

"There's a car chasing it, too.

"What do we do when we catch it?" The pilot asked

"Fly in front of it and get the engineer's attention. Try to get him to stop!"

The pilot nodded and pushed the stick forward.

"Hi, mister," Clarissa said, her big brown eyes catching the smiling assassin.

It was just the hesitation Roberto had hoped for! He jumped out of his seat, arms outstretched and reaching for the gun!

The gun flew as Maria's father landed on top of the would-be killer. They rolled in the narrow aisle as people picked up their feet, surprised at the sudden commotion.

The smiling man rolled on top of Roberto. He drew a knife and was ready to thrust it, when a sharp crack from Grandma's cane crashed into his head!

The knife fell from his hand, and Roberto pushed him off, rolling out from underneath him.

"Miguel, get me some rope! Let's tie him up."

"Who has any rope?" Miguel asked the passengers. "Anything, before he wakes up!"

"I have something!" One of the passengers stood up, holding up his bag. He dug through it, and pulled out a pair of long leather laces for his work boots.

Stepping over the lady next to him, he gave them to Miguel, who helped his father wrap them around the smiling man's wrists and feet.

"That should hold him. If he wakes up, hit him with your cane again!"

"Rose! Look out the window!" Paolo shouted. "There is another car!"

"Sheesh! How many killers are after us?" I said

But there was something familiar about the people in the car. "It's Gloria and Rico!"

Gloria looked out the car window. Keeping pace with the train, she could see the passengers now. She looked up, and saw me waving and smiling.

"The kids are okay!" She shouted to Rico

The helicopter finally caught up, and the pilot ignored the speeding car. He flew ahead of the train to give himself room to turn around. Now he flew towards the train as if playing 'chicken'

The startled engineer shook his head. "What is going on? First the radio, and now this!

He watched as the helicopter repeated the maneuver, this time seeing the men signaling him to stop the train

"They want me to stop the train? They must be terrorists! Or robbers! We are close to Lima now and I will not be late!"

He didn't stop even when the conductor burst into the engine with the news of the smiling man.

The train rolled into the station in Lima with a helicopter escort, and the black rental car of Rico and Gloria's in pursuit

The engineer was met with guns as Dad and Mom and several police descended on the train. He shrugged and looked at his watch.

"Right on time!" He said, smiling.

"Mom! Dad!" I yelled as we herded off the train. Police and security surrounded us. All the passengers were detained and questioned as the press was held back behind hastily constructed barricades.

"Rose!" They both said together. I could hear the mixed emotions in their voices, relief, and anger.

Paolo's father and grandmother were there as well and Rico, Gloria, and Richard were making their way through the crowd.

As much as I was happy to see them, I felt an urgency to tell them what I knew.

I hoped it wasn't too late!

Chapter Forty

Monday morning. Every T.V. and radio station in the free world was interrupted with the news of the latest terrorist attack.

"Las Vegas, Nevada. At six a.m. this morning a bomb hidden in an ambulance destroyed several casinos and killed hundreds. Hundreds more were injured. Details are sketchy but those numbers could run into the thousands. The ambulance and its occupants were completely destroyed by the bomb, which experts are saying was nuclear. The danger of radiation may render the city uninhabitable for years! We have cancelled all programming to bring you the story as it unfolds."

It was six-thirty, a.m.

While the world listened in shock the president was preparing to face the nation. Picking up the phone, he called the Director of The Agency.

"I want every security person available in Vegas, now! And I want you here with me! You are going to explain at the press conference how this could have happened!"

At six forty-five, he president was interrupted by another news bulletin even as his chief of staff rushed into the Oval Office.

"The Golden Gate Bridge has just collapsed!" The newscaster, already in shock from the Vegas disaster was now reporting a second attack!

"No, I can't believe it! The Brooklyn Bridge is gone!" He continued. "Thousands of motorists trapped in their cars have died! The morning traffic jam on both coasts has turned deadly!"

Live cameras from helicopters covered the scenes of horror. Cars on fire plummeted into the water as the bridges collapsed. Trucks were thrown into the air, only to land on other cars and roadways, killing more people, and blocking roads in New York, spreading a chain reaction of explosions and crashes that would paralyze the country!

People were paralyzed - frozen in disbelief in front of televisions and radios in every home and workplace. It was as if the whole world had stopped!

The press conference at the White House was a disaster, as both the president and the Director of The Agency had no answers for the questions.

"How could this have happened?" One reporter demanded to know.
"Why didn't we see this coming?"
"Are we at war?" Another asked.
"What happened to our security?"
On and on the questions went.

"Apparently the attack on Las Vegas was both symbolic, and a decoy. While we focused all of our attention on the disaster there, the terrorists were able to send nuclear car bombs to the bridges. Clearly, their plan is to cripple our economy," the president said.

"We had a special team on the job," the director said. "They were close to discovering the secret terrorist plan, and when they finally did it was too late."

The director had already made a deal with the president. When it was time for heads to roll on this one, it wouldn't be theirs!

The day wore on into a week as the images were repeated time and time again. Experts appeared from everywhere, explaining their theories, and speculating on how such a massive plan could have been kept so quiet for so long.

The death toll continued to rise as well as the casualties. The numbers were staggering!

The economy of the U.S. was near breakdown and the ripple effect was spreading to the European Community and the Third World.

Thousands of businesses were closed - some forever - as their staffs had perished in the tragedies.

It was the longest, darkest, day in history.

Unless you were a terrorist!

"I'm sorry we were too late! We tried, we really did!" I said through hot tears that felt like lava flowing down my face.

The world sat stunned, waiting for the next terrible announcement.

I would have been glad to see a commercial!

That's what would have happened if Mom and Dad hadn't listened! Fortunately, they did!

At six o'clock on Monday morning, Tony Shiffer left the roadside motel on the way to Vegas. He was almost there! He had managed to save five hundred dollars over the last year from the various temp jobs he had held all year in Sioux City, Iowa.

Now he was on his way to Vegas in his old, rusted Buick Skylark. Forty-five and a failure, he would take one more roll of the dice and strike it rich! And if he lost... he didn't want to think about that. There just wasn't anything else to live for.

While he slept, a car rolled quietly into the parking lot. One man dressed in black, wearing a stocking hat walked over to Tony's car. He bent down, and took a package from his pocket.

Silent and quick, he reached under the rusted door panel and found the car's frame. There was a metallic 'click' as the magnetized bomb bonded with the metal. The man stood up and jumped into the waiting car, which drove quietly away. None of the occupants of the motel were awakened.

Tony was hungry and resisted the urge to stop at the truck stop diner. He could eat in Vegas! His plan was to arrive at six-thirty.

And he would have, if he had better tires! Somewhere between the motel and Vegas, on an open stretch of road there was an explosion! Tony fought to keep the car on the road as the right front tire went flat from the blowout. He managed to pull the car over to the side.

"Darn! No spare!" He said, looking at the empty trunk. He had already known that, but decided to look for one anyway. Who knows?

Slamming the trunk, he started walking away from the car. Back to the gas station he had seen on the way.

After about fifteen minutes the rest of the tires blew!

"Funny, didn't sound like tires," he thought as the blast knocked him to the ground.

Picking himself up, he looked back in the direction of his car. The small speck he had seen a few minutes ago was gone.

"I got a bad feeling about this," he said to himself as a black Suburban pulled up alongside him.

The dark-tinted window on the passenger side rolled down. There was a man with a high-power rifle.

"Get in!" He said.

Tony didn't argue.

"Sorry about your car. I didn't even get the shot off when the tire blew by itself! Boy, you must have had crappy tires on that thing! You must have an angel too!"

While Tony sat, bewildered, in the back seat, the man opened a laptop computer.

"Steven, the suitcase is closed," he said, and closed the laptop again.

Tony wondered what he had gotten into!

Back at the Ready Room, Steven and Susan high-fived each other! One down, two to go!

"I'm glad you thought of that plan!" Susan said.

"A stroke of luck. After we got the information from Rose, I tried to imagine how they would get a bomb into Vegas. It seemed like the only way. Terrorists are famous for car bombs, anyway. The long-range security would have profiled an operative, and so it seemed logical to choose a random innocent driver and plant a bomb on the car. There weren't too many driving to Vegas so we decided to shoot out a tire here and there."

"Why his car?" Susan asked.

"I don't know. Guess I just don't like old rusted Buicks.

"What about the other two targets?"

"My guess is they will use the same scenario."

"Good thing we closed the bridges at four a.m."

"Yeah, there will be a lot of angry commuters today!"

"Angry, but alive!" Susan said, turning back to Zip.

The split screen showed the two bridges. The liaison from The Agency was on the Brooklyn side. Another agent was on the Golden Gate side

"The suitcases are packed and ready," they said, reporting in.

"Good. Get ready to meet your travelers!" Susan said.

Chapter Forty-One

But the suitcase wasn't closed! While Tony sat being questioned in the Suburban, emergency vehicles rushed to the scene of the explosion!

Police and security agents combed the area for clues as motorists began stopping for the barricades. Soon, the area was full of people. Reporters rushed to the scene and crowds of spectators had gathered.

One man in a radiation suit held a ground sweeper looking for radiation. It was standard procedure, and so far he had not found any radiation from the bomb in Tony's car.

Satisfied, he shrugged, and made his way back to the perimeter.

It was when he passed the ambulance where Tony was now undergoing examination when the Geiger went off.

"Got something here!" The man said through the radio in his headgear.

"Residual?" The question came back.

"No. Too strong! It's live! I think we have another bomb!"

"Where? What's the source?"

"Seems to be coming from the ambulance!"

"Medical equipment?" The voice asked.

"No. Too strong!" The man in the suit said as he swept the vehicle.

"Get them out!" The voice said.

In seconds, agents descended on the ambulance, herding the crew and Tony into the Suburban.

The police used bullhorns to evacuate the area as the Suburban pulled out, taking the ambulance crew and Tony away for questioning.

Back at the Ready Room, Susan, and Steven were interrupted by a call on Zip.

"The suitcase is still open! I repeat the suitcase is still open!"

"What's happening out there?" Steven asked.

"Apparently, the bomb in Tony's car was a decoy. It was a real bomb, set to go off on signal, but only as an excuse to send in the real bomb, which was hidden in an ambulance. The second bomb is nuclear!"

"My God!" Susan said. "What's the status of the ambulance?"

"The Bomb Squad has already located the bomb, and is diffusing it now. It's small, but deadly."

"Does the crew know anything about it?"

"At this point, neither the ambulance crew or the driver of the car, seem to know anything about it. We think the bombs were planted without their knowledge. Judging by the one found on the ambulance, both bombs were small packages magnetically attached to the frames of the vehicles," the agent reported.

"Makes sense," Steven said. "Good way to get past our security, unknowing carriers no one would suspect!"

"First bomb goes off, send in the ambulance!" Susan said, shivering from the thought.

"My guess is they will use the same plan for all three targets! They have learned from 9/11!" Steven speculated.

"Right! With the heightened security since 9/11, they would not risk open communications. That's why the 'chatter' has been so low. Word of mouth passed in code, delaying the wire for more sophisticated computers for The Agency, and using carrier pigeons instead of operatives to deliver the packages! Ingenious! Thank God it didn't work!" Susan sighed.

"Good thing the bridges are closed!" The Vegas agent said.

It was precisely then that two more explosions were reported, one in New York, and one in San Francisco.

The T.V. monitors in the Ready Room showed scenes from both coasts now as reporters followed the new explosions. "Details are sketchy…"

Zips monitor divided into three views covering all three locations. Amazingly, no one was killed in the explosions. Both cars were parked and the streets were littered with debris. Chain reaction fires and explosions from nearby cars and houses continued to rock the neighborhoods.

Apparently, both owners were in their houses when the bombs went off, delaying their morning commute to work with the news that the bridges they normally used were closed.

Steven was talking to both sites at once. "That's right, check all the emergency vehicles! All of them!"

Back in Vegas, the bomb squad had disabled the second bomb.

"Steven, Susan, we have some info on the bomb," the Vegas agent broke in.

"What have you got?" Steven said.

"If it wasn't nuclear we would never have found it. The package contained a low-frequency receiver. It was set to go off on signal; a radio signal," he said, holding up his hands, showing a 9-volt battery, and a small red wire.

The same kind of wire my Grandfather had used in his ham radio!

"There's some writing on the wire," he continued.

"What does it say?" Susan asked.

"It says 'Peru Wire Company'."

"Bingo!" Susan said, high-fiving Steven's hand.

Chapter Forty-Two

The fire vehicles were delayed a few minutes as each one was inspected for the hidden bombs. The delay was costly, but necessary.

Eventually, the bomb in Brooklyn was found on the lead fire truck of the closest station. It would have been the first on the scene had the car blown up on the bridge. The nuclear charge was designed to make sure the bridge was destroyed.

A similar scenario was discovered in San Francisco.

Mom and Dad were following the events on T.V. and Zip.

"Apparently, the terrorists were planning on crippling the economy rather than destroying it." Dad was saying.

"Yes, we've thought for a long time they are more interested in 'hit and run' than in a World War, or totally destroying the U.S.A." Mom added.

"Yeah, truth is, they need us. Much of their funding comes from unsuspecting citizens."

"Not to mention other groups who have a bone to pick with us, or a financial interest in causing chaos."

"Like the Path, the drug lords, and the old hard line Communists," Dad concluded.

We turned our attention back to the T.V.

"Many people are rushing to churches across the USA and the world today. The president is assuring people we are not at war, and as bad as the attacks were today, they could have been much, much worse. As it is, our agents in the field have been able to short out the second part of the terrorist's plan, which at this point looks like three targets-"

The T.V. suddenly blanked out, causing our heart rates to jump suddenly. When it came back on, the network had gone to commercial.

"Looks like a news blackout." Dad said.

"Yeah, it is an election year!" Mom nodded.

"Eventually the whole story will come out. For now the news people have plenty to talk about and cover," Dad said.

"When all the facts are in, they'll put a spin on it," Mom said.

"But that's how it works in the Good Ol' USA!" I said.

Mom and Dad looked at me and smiled.

The next few days were filled with 'official' activity. Mom and Dad took me everywhere as they were interviewed by The Agency and filed their reports.

Paolo went with us along with his father and grandmother. Maria and her family were brought along as well. Rico, Gloria, and Richard were our bodyguards, and a special team was sent to assist them.

We were driven in four separate vehicles for extra security. Every trip was a covert operation!

Paolo and I told our story over and over again! It was fun for a while but soon we got tired of it all.

"Mom, when do we get to go to Machu Picchu?" I asked as we rode in the black limo to the Government Building in Lima.

The leather seats were slippery under the dark blue dress I had been forced to wear. Paolo and his father were in suits and ties and Maria, wearing a white ruffled dress, smiled every time she caught Paolo looking at her.

We were on our way to an unofficial, official, dinner to honor us all for our part in the foiling the terrorist plot.

This would be a night to remember, and a night we could never talk about! Sheesh!

"Soon, Rose. We'll be staying an extra week, and I promise we'll have our vacation. We'll get to Machu Picchu.

"What about Richard? Will he get to go fishing?"

"Yes, though I don't think he's anxious to get in the water.

Up front, Richard turned around and smiled as the car turned into the drive in front of the Government Center.

I thought about Sam. Right now I needed somebody to hug.

Chapter Forty-Three

We felt like celebrities on Entertainment Tonight as we stepped out of the limo, and were surrounded by special agents in suits all wearing little coiled wires in one ear.

We were escorted to the dining room in small, separate groups for our safety. The room was full of important-looking people dressed in tuxedos and gowns. The tables were all set with fancy china and glass-ware on white tablecloths.

There was a round of applause as we walked in, and were escorted to the tables set on the stage. A microphone and podium were set up between the two long tables we were seated at. Above the podium was a large video screen.

I blushed at the applause as it grew to a standing ovation. Paolo bent his head sheepishly as the three sets of parents beamed with pride.

"Ladies and gentlemen, may I present our guests of honor..." The speaker began.

The Vice President of Peru!

I don't remember what we ate, or much about the night. I know I was nervous as I stood at the microphone accepting a plaque from the Government of Peru, and an honorary agent status from The Agency

When all the talking was done, the lights were dimmed and the video screen came to life.

It was the President of the United States! Using a video link with Zip and the cameras in the room, we were able to talk to him.

"Rose, Paolo, and your families, I want you to know you have our gratitude for what you have done to stop the latest terrorist plan. Your families have banded together in this fight, and we have won this round. Because I cannot be there in person we set up this video link and I now present you all with a Congressional Medal of Honor. Unfortunately, for security reasons we cannot make this public. Nor will anyone hear the full story. This is being done for your safety and I ask that everyone in the room agree to the secrecy in all our best interests. Please raise your right hands now to signify your agreement."

Everyone did and the president continued. "We want you to know this investigation has just begun. We will not stop until we know all the details of the plan, and have captured those involved."

There was a round of applause for the president as he signed off, and the lights came up to full.

The local Agency director talked to us as we ate our deserts, telling us the battle for a safe world never stops and how even two young children can make a difference.

There were a lot of introductions, and hand shaking at the end. Finally, we were led back to the cars, and taken to new rooms in the hotel.

Paolo and Maria's families stayed at the hotel also.

Plainclothes men were stationed throughout the hotel and I wondered how long we would be watched

Alone in our new suite at last, I snuggled on the couch between Mom and Dad.

"Sheesh! That was intense! What's going to happen tomorrow?" I asked.

"Tomorrow, Mom and I have some work to do with The Agency. We will file our reports, and look at participating in the on-going investigation," Dad said, as he removed his bowtie.

"Do you think you'll get more jobs as private contractors?" I asked.

"Well, thanks to you and your shenanigans…" Mom had a serious look on her face, and I began to worry.

"Oh, oh," I said, waiting for the lecture I knew was bound to come, "here it comes!"

"As I was saying," Mom said in a stern voice, "thanks to you and your shenanigans, we have a five-year contract!"

"That is, after our vacation next week!" Dad said, smiling

"Just remember one thing, Miss Rose…" Mom continued, "just because you are an honorary agent doesn't mean you can go running off with boys anytime you feel like it!" Mom got the lecture in after all!

That night, I slept in the in my own private room. I said goodnight to Grandpa and Grandma as I always did and thought about Samson The Great.

He'd love this bed!

Chapter Forty-Four

Eventually, they did find out how the terrorists planted the bombs. It was a simple matter of scheduled maintenance, and records kept online.

Using the skills of experienced hackers it was not too hard to get into the computers of the fire companies, the hospital, and view the maintenance schedules of the vehicles involved.

Knowing when and where the oil changes were done, the terrorists planted a man at the scene. Using fake I.D.s, three Americans sympathetic to the 'cause' were given part-time jobs well ahead of the planned event. Gaining the trust of their employers was easy, and when the vehicles showed up for oil changes they were given something extra.

A small 'package' containing a nuclear device was attached to the inside of the frames where no one would ever see or suspect it. Each contained a small receiver. The receivers were tuned to different frequencies of local ham radios. A small 9-volt battery powered the receiver. At the specified time, a signal would be sent over the hacked into frequency of the ham radio in the area.

Ka-Boom! Down went the bridges and Las Vegas, too!

Of course, by that time the 'employees' of the oil change garages had moved on, leaving no forwarding addresses or trail. People even forgot what they looked like! But everyone remembered what good guys they were!

The genius of the plan was there would be no operatives in the area when the blasts occurred. No one would be coming or going at the airports, there would be no suspicious movements of those being watched. It would be complete surprise!

The delay in the wire for The Agency's new computers was for two reasons. First, so the subtle probing into ham radio records the fire stations and hospital would not be detected, and procuring of plutonium needed for the bombs would not be traced.

The two-year plan was set up by word of mouth, and passed in code from one cell to another, each being given a part of the plan - but not the whole thing. The bits of code passed in restaurant conversations were to small to be noticed, and under penalty of death each person was sworn to secrecy.

To make up for the funds that would be lost in the disruption of the U.S. economy, interested parties were contacted and invited to partici- pate for a fee.

Hard-line communists, drug lords, and of course, The Path. Each had a vested interest in striking a blow to the United States.

It all would have worked if Paolo and I hadn't been in the right place at the right time! And, if Alex and the Fox had not talked about it when they did! The one mistake in the plan was letting them know what the targets were! Of course, it was necessary to secure their co-opera- tion.

Richard told all of this to Mom and Dad, winking at me when he mentioned Paolo and me.

That brings me back to the rest of the story!

Paolo's little house was full of activity as we all gathered for a farewell lunch. The two grandmothers and Christina were busy in the little kitchen, and Paolo's father took Roberto and Miguel for a ride on his fishing boat. Mom, Dad and Richard were busy setting up the tables and chairs in the back yard as Rico and Gloria served as waiters, run- ning food and beverages to the tables until it was time for everyone to sit down and eat.

Paolo and Maria and myself sat on the dock, talking about what would happen next.

"We'll miss you, Rose," Paolo said, his brown eyes tearing up.

"Yes - I will miss you, too, " Maria echoed.

"Sheesh! This is supposed to be a celebration! You have got me all choked up! You know I'm going to miss you too!" I said, holding back hot tears.

I sat quiet for a few minutes, watching the fishing boat make its turn and head back for the dock.

"I have something for each of you," I said, reaching into the canvas bag I'd had through everything that had happened.

I pulled out the gifts Mom and I had bought on the plaza; two portable CD players, one red and one blue, and a selection of music to go with each one.

"Which color would you like?" I asked them.

"Rose," Paolo said, taking the blue one, "I have something for you, after we eat."

"Me too," Maria echoed again, taking the red player.

"Okay, but no more crying. We will see each other again! And we can stay in touch. I'm still writing my newsletter on the Internet. You can still send me mail. We will still be friends. Promise?"

So we did as the boat drifted up to the dock. Miguel jumped out to tie it up, beaming from his first ride on the water.

From the house, Paolo's grandmother waved us in.

"Let's eat!"

It was decided Maria and her family be watched for their safety, and escorted back to Cerro de Pasco. They sold their goods to Paolo's grandmother, who lovingly displayed them in her shop. I proudly carried the hand-embroidered canvas bag made by Maria's grandmother, the beautiful Aztec design on the outside. Inside was the gift from Paolo, a hand-carved piece of driftwood in the shape of a rose.

"My father carved it for me after I grew the rose bushes," Paolo explained as he handed it to me, "I wanted you to have it."

So much for my "No More Crying" rule! I smiled as the tears rolled down my cheeks again! I was still crying as we all said goodbye.

Paolo and Maria were seen holding hands as they walked to the train that would take Maria's family home.

Paolo's father returned to his fishing boat, and Paolo returned to working at the hotel.

Rico and Gloria would keep an eye on him and his family.

As for me, I knew I was in a battle for independence!

"What should we do with you, Rose?" Dad said as we rode in the car on our way to Machu Picchu.

"Whatever do you mean, Father?" I said, formally.

"Well, you are now a target of the terrorists as well as the hard-line communists! We may have to send you to a convent!"

"You wouldn't!"

"Well, it is a thought..." Mom said.

"But, but..." I said, pretending I believed them.

"Actually, both the terrorists and the hard-liners are laying low. Obviously they are working on their next plan, and feel a vengeance strike against any of us would call attention to them. We believe they feel it is safer to just watch us like we watch them. But, it's still a factor we have to consider. Sheesh!" Dad said, sounding like me now!

Richard had been sitting quietly next to me in the back seat through the whole conversation. I looked at him for help.

"Now, you know they won't let me stay in a convent with Rose! I propose we release her under my supervision when you two are gone. I'll keep an eye on her. And don't forget the tutor! She'll be watching too!"

"And don't forget Sam!" I said, hopefully. "And the fact both my parents are agents! And my aunt and uncle, too!"

"Well, you have some valid arguments there, young lady. Why don't we make our decision after we see Machu Picchu?" Dad said as he pulled the car into the train station. The train would take us on the six-hour journey to Machu Picchu, where we would stay at the Tourist Hotel overnight. Rico and Gloria had made all of the arrangements, charging The Agency for their services as the Peru Travel Service.

"Okay, sounds like a deal under one condition; Mom has to keep her promise to tell me about how Grandma and Grandpa met in Machu Picchu and show me the "wire forest" Grandpa told me about."

"Okay, you've got a deal," Mom, said as we opened the trunk to take out our bags.

"It's a good thing Susan and Steven agreed to stay on at the house with Sam, even though their house is finished," Dad said, grabbing his bags.

"They have to stay and help with the investigation anyway," Mom said.

"Well, we finally get our vacation!" I said.

"And I finally get my fishing trip!" Richard smiled.

"See you in a week! Hope you catch the giant red catfish!" Dad waved as Richard walked away.

"I will! It's guaranteed in the fee! Oh, by the way, Rose, your suitcase is open!"

"What?" I said, ready for action.

"Made you look!" He laughed, disappearing through the doors of the station.

We all laughed as we followed him in.

Epilogue

Mom and I stood on the lookout at Machu Picchu. Below us was the road leading back into the forest, winding through the Andes Mountains.

"Your grandfather met your grandmother on a guided tour right here at Machu Picchu. It was the first time either of them had been here. This lookout is where he told her the story that landed him their first date. The very next day they went into the jungle where he promised he would prove to her his story was true."

"What story did he tell her?" I asked.

"Well, he told her about the wire forests! She was a college student and an archaeologist - and didn't believe a word he said, so of course she had to give him the opportunity to prove it! The next morning they had breakfast together and followed the tour into the rainforest. There they stood, under the canopy looking at the rainbow of colors from all the orchids that grow there. Grandma smiled as he picked one for her, and gave it to her with a wink and a kiss. And that is why she is holding one in her portrait."

There I was standing high on the lookout above the canopy, picturing my Grandparents young and in love and imagining the story he had told to win Grandma's heart.

There were tears in my eyes again! Grandpa, you sly old fox! He had won my heart the very same way!

"Come on, young lady, we have to get back. Early day tomorrow," Mom announced.

"Why? Where are we going tomorrow?" I asked.

"Your Grandpa wasn't kidding when he told that story." She said with a hint of intrigue.

Dad had stayed behind examining the ruins. He waved as we approached.

The next morning, after breakfast, we followed the tour. Under the canopy of the trees I saw the orchids and the Wire Forests of Peru.

The End

Kool-whip
Incorporated

Ramblin' Rose

Prologue

The big grandfather clock in the dining room of my Grandparents' house tick-tocked in the silence. Everyone had stopped talking

We had just finished Thanksgiving dinner. Grandma, Mother, and Aunt Susan had gone to the kitchen to get dessert. Dad and Grandpa sat back in their chairs, full from the turkey and potatoes. They fell into silence, anticipating pumpkin pie and wondering if they had left enough room for it

I did! It was one of the things my six-year-old stomach could always make room for! To me, the turkey and potatoes were just something you had to wade through to get to dessert

Being the rambler I am, it was hard to sit quiet and wait for the pie. I listened to the big old clock as it grew louder and louder in the big house by the sea.

Grandpa took out his shiny gold pocket watch with the picture of the sailing ship on it. It was a gift from Mom. He admired the picture, rubbing his thumb over the surface, tracing the lines of the sails

My Grandparents owned a shipping business, and Grandpa was a sailor at heart. He always said Grandma was the only woman who could keep him on dry land

I looked up at Grandma's portrait. She was a beautiful dark-haired lady. The portrait showed her standing on the 'Widow's Watch' holding an orchid and looking out to sea as if waiting for Grandpa's ship to appear. The wind blew her dress against her and wisps of her hair seemed to brush across her face.

I wanted to be like Grandma some day

Grandpa watched me as I stared at the portrait. He opened the watch and checked the time, then clicked it shut, snapping me out of my trance just as the pie came bustling in with Mom, Aunt Susan and Grandma

"Ah!" He said, "Now a piece of 'hard to resist-ance!'"

"Amen!" Dad said

"Well, I guess the dessert prayer has been said!" I reported as I reached for the fork and the big, plastic bowl of Kool-Whip in the center of the table.

Everyone laughed and dug into the pie.

Soon we were in the living room, Grandpa in his rocker and I on his lap. Mom, Grandma, and Aunt Susan were busy cleaning up in the kitchen.

"Grandpa," I asked, as I ran my little thumb over the shiny watch, "where does Kool-Whip come from?"

I knew story-time was coming, Grandpa loved to tell stories of his travels.

"Why, Kool-Whip comes from the Arctic, up around the North Pole," he said, smiling and winking at Dad.

The women returned from the kitchen just as Grandpa was about to launch into the rest of his story.

"Oh, he's at it again! Telling tales! He's been doing that since I met him! Matter of fact, that's how he got his first date with me!" Grandma said, sitting in her chair, and picking up her embroidery.

"Don't look so innocent, Mother," Mom spoke up, "He used to tell us those stories, too, and you went right along with him! You even helped him! Some of the best ones were yours!"

Aunt Susan nodded in agreement with her sister. They were Grandma and Grandpa's only children.

"Well, how do you know they weren't true? Remember, there is always some truth in every story!" Grandma defended herself, smiling.

I ignored them all. I was getting sleepy after eating so much pie, and I wanted to hear the rest of the story. Grandpa was so good at telling them, they did sound real.

"AHEM!" Grandpa said, giving the signal for silence. Someone had asked him to tell a story.

"Like I was saying, Kool-Whip comes from the arctic. They blast out big chunks of the glaciers, and float them down the coast to California, where they melt it down and dehydrate it into a powder. Then they mix it with a little bit of water, and whip it into a creamy state, where they pack it in the plastic containers like the one we just dipped into. But you see, it's a secret. They don't want you to know how things are really made."

Grandma smiled and shook her head as she embroidered, not daring to look at him and laugh out loud. Mom and Aunt Susan smiled and wondered where their father came up with these crazy ideas.

My Dad was a 'Secret Agent' for the government and saw a lot of the 'bad side' of life. He looked at Grandpa with wonder. He loved listening to his stories as much as the rest of us. In defense of my grandfather, I suppressed a laugh. Even at six I knew what was real, and what was not... or, so I thought.

I gave him a hug just before I fell asleep on his lap.

There I was with Grandpa, in my dream, on a ship in the frozen waters. We stood by the rail, and watched as a large chunk of arctic ice broke off and fell into the water. We smiled at each other, and high-fived as the ship towed the mighty chunk of ice through the frozen maze

Grandpa took out his pocket watch, "Right on time!" He said. He took my hand, and led me to his cabin

"You need some rest, Rose. Lie on my bunk awhile. I'll wake you when we get to California."

I was tired, and sat on the bunk yawning, listening to the steady tick-tock of the Captain's clock as the rolling sea gently rocked me to sleep.

Chapter One

"Rose?" Dad's voice came over the intercom as I put the finishing touches on the latest issue of the Internet Newsletter.

"Hi, Dad. What's up?" I replied as I hit the 'Enter' key and put the last picture of Machu Picchu in place.

"Come on down to the kitchen, we're having a family conference."

"Okay. Be down in a minute," I said, switching the computer off.

I looked at Sam, who had been sitting patiently next to me while I worked. "I hope they haven't been reading my e-mails to Dimitri again!"

Sam cocked his head, and whined at my worried tone.

"Come on, Sam. Let's see what kind of trouble we're in now."

The big black Newfie, known as Samson The Great at the dog shows, followed me out of the upstairs bedroom. I know he was thinking he hadn't done anything wrong!

The two weeks since we had been home from Peru had been quiet. I caught up on my schoolwork, and worked on the newsletter.

I also caught up on a lot of e-mail! There were lots of messages from readers to answer. People seemed to like my stories, and the newsletter was growing. I was drawing a lot of traffic and letters. I wrote a lot of responses to fans.

I also kept in touch with my new friends, especially Dimitri.

Life had gotten a little more normal since our return from Peru. My parents had settled into their new role of private contractors to The Agency, and I felt a little less like a prisoner in my own house.

Richard still accompanied me almost everywhere, and I was still monitored on the 'Net. The cameras in our house became invisible and I had grown accustomed to being watched.

As we rounded the corner into the kitchen, I wondered again what this was about. I hadn't broken anything, or gotten into any trouble I knew of, but there were Richard, Mom, and Dad sitting at the table.

I sat down in the one open chair, Sam at my side.

"What's up?" I asked.

"Well, Rose, we've been talking..." Mom started out.

"I knew it!" I said, defensively. "You are going to send me to a convent!"

"What?" Dad Said, "A convent? Relax, Rose."

Mom started to laugh. "Yes, Rose, relax! We've been talking and feel life has settled down enough to do some things away from the house. The Westminster Dog Show is coming up, and I have entered Sam. The Agency has asked your father to supervise the security.

"Wow! The Westminster Dog Show! Can I go, too?" I said

Mom and Dad both winced.

"Well, honey," Dad, said, "We thought you might like some time away for yourself. Your cousin Abigail has asked if you would come and visit for a week."

I sat with mixed emotions. Dad never called me 'honey' unless they were going to try to convince me to do something I wouldn't like. Still, a trip by myself sounded pretty good. Maybe I could finally regain my parents' trust. But Sam was my best friend! How could I not be there for the biggest event in his life? Why didn't they want me there?

"What's the catch?" I asked, warily.

"The catch is your Aunt Rebecca has offered to paint your portrait. Your Mom and I would like her to do this while you are still the age you are. It is the only week she can do it."

Oh, great! My dreams of independence were melting before my eyes. What fun could I have sitting for a portrait? And my cousin Abigail was two years younger than me! I didn't want to end up baby-sitting a ten-year old!

"What about Richard? Will he be going too?" I asked.

"The Agency has called me in for a refresher course. I'll take you to the airport, and see - you get on the plane safely. Then I'll report to school."

"So, why can't I go to the dog show?" I asked.

"Well, there are some security issues - and The Agency thinks you might be at risk at Westminster. They feel it's better if we are not all in the same place at once. Sam has a shot at winning this one, and your

Mom wants me there. We know it's a tough deal, but maybe you can volunteer for Sam's sake."

"Sheesh! Guilt trip, major! I suppose I have to wear a dress, too!" I pouted.

"We don't want you to feel your being punished, Rose. I really would love to have Rebecca paint your portrait. She is very talented and hard to get. Matt has promised to look after you, and has guaranteed you'd have a good time. Abigail is so lonesome!"

Matt was Dad's brother. He was a captain in the Coast Guard. He was very nice, and I did not get to see them often because they lived in Alaska. Abby was always sending me e-mail and wishing I could come and visit. She liked to take pictures, and had just gotten a digital camera. She was a pretty good photographer for a ten-year old. She envied my adventures and my newsletter.

"After all, every star reporter needs a photographer!" She had said in one of her letters.

I sighed. If I had to get some independence this way then I would leverage it!

"Okay, but I have a few conditions of my own," I said matter-of-factly.

"Conditions?" Dad said cautiously.

"Yes. First, I get a raise in my allowance. Second, I don't wear the dress-if you want to capture me now then do it as I usually am. Third, I want unsupervised time while I'm gone, and when I get back home."

Sam whined at that one. His tail thumped the floor.

"Hmmn." Mom said. "Why the raise in your allowance?"

"I'm saving for something special."

"What?" Dad said.

"I can't tell you," I replied.

"If you can't tell us, how can we trust you?"

"If I have to tell you, you don't trust me."

"Okay, we'll negotiate that later. As to the dress, that's non-negotiable. Years from now you'll be glad you didn't do it in jeans," Mom said.

"On your third demand, I'm sure we can give you some more privacy, but only as afforded to any twelve-year-old girl. We know you are not average, but the world doesn't."

Two out of three wasn't bad. I decided to go for the raise and reluctantly wear the dress.

"Do I get the raise?" I asked.

"Yes," Dad nodded, "but we'll talk about the amount later. A lot has to do with what it's for."

"Okay, so when are we leaving?" I asked.

Richard looked at me, and shook his head.

"Smooth operator," he whispered.

"Friday morning. We'll all be back here two weeks from Monday." Dad replied matter- of- factly.

"Two weeks? I thought you just said Rebecca only has a week?" I said, surprised.

"Well, Matt said he would take you and Abby to Sea World the second week.

"Sheesh! Why didn't you say that in the first place?" I asked.

"Well, we wanted to give you the chance to hit us for the raise. We know you're saving for a trip to see Dimitri," Dad smiled.

"And here I thought you didn't trust me."

"Oh, Rose, honey, we trust you. You have to learn to trust us," Mom said as she stood up from the table, arms outstretched.

Tears on my cheeks I ran to give my parents a hug.

Sheesh! Two weeks away? I was sure going to miss them!

Saying goodbye to Sam was the hardest part! Seems like I was always leaving these days. Tears ran down his big furry neck as I hugged him.

"This time we both get to travel, Sam. Just not together," I told him as he whined a little.

Sam was no stranger to travel. Entering dog shows was my mother's hobby, and Sam always had to leave a week ahead with his trainer. This time he would be leaving two weeks early.

"You can do it, Sam! I know you can! Best of Show!" I said, standing up and drying my tears. I always told him 'Best of Show' when he left.

The Agency had sent a special car to take us to the airport. As we pulled out in the black limo, I looked at the house through the darkened windows of the car. It seemed strange that no one would be here at all.

Richard set Zip to guard the house, and turn the lights on and off according to our usual routine. The mail was re-routed and no one would know we were gone. The phone calls were automatically forwarded by Zip, and could not be traced to our present whereabouts.

"Good luck in school, Richard!" I said as we split up at the airport. He used to drive me to school, now I felt like I was escorting him to the bus stop!

This time my COM link was my cell phone. Tied into Zip, it contained a tracker and quick connects to Mom, Dad, Richard, and Aunt Susan - and a distress call button to Zip. It was also a picture phone!

"Now, I expect regular calls so I can see how Sam is doing at the show!" I told my parents as I hugged them goodbye.

"Don't worry," Mom said, "We'll stay in touch!"

"Be careful out there, Rose," Dad said as I hugged him.

"Don't worry, Dad. It's just a visit. How much trouble can I get in with my cousin? Besides, I'll be sitting for a portrait!"

"That's exactly what worries me," Dad teased.

I was anxious to show my parents they could trust me. After all, I was a world traveler!

"Now, if you can't reach us, call your Aunt Susan. She and Steven are moving into their new house in Connecticut," Mom reminded me.

"Sheesh! Let's go already! Sam and Annie will be out there before we even get on our planes!" I said.

Annie was Sam's trainer and handler. Mom was way too busy with her company to do it all.

So, we were finally ready to leave. Dad got a green light on his phone. As far as anyone could tell we were not being watched.

Chapter Two

The plainclothes agents watched as we said goodbye, and boarded three separate planes. I had mixed feelings seeing my parents and Richard walk away.

This was the first time I would be traveling alone. I felt like a grownup, but the butterflies in my stomach were telling me I was just a child who wanted to be with my mom and dad.

A handler was transporting Sam. She had been checked by The Agency and had handled him many times in previous shows.

Reluctantly I checked my bag, and showed my Agency I.D. Bypassing security I clutched my canvas bag, and walked to the plane.

I brightened up when I saw the friendly smile of the stewardess.

"Hello, Rose. Nice to see you again!"

It was the same stewardess I had seen on my other trips!

"Hello, yourself. Are you assigned to me or is this just a coincidence?" I asked.

"Call me Erica. And yes and no," she replied, putting a finger to her lips.

I felt a little better seeing a familiar face.

"But, I thought your name was Kathy..."

"Please take your seat, miss," she said, her eyes telling me not to say her real name.

I felt silly for not realizing she was using an alias, but she hadn't used the passwords.

Well, of course she wouldn't. She was supposed to be a stewardess.

I blushed and found my seat. Putting on my headphones, I listened to a CD and looked at the in-flight magazine. It was all about Alaska.

This was my first trip to Alaska, and I was surprised at how much I didn't know about it.

Like the four climate zones, maritime, continental, transitional, and Arctic. Kodiak, the Aleutians, southeastern, and south central Alaska have climates primarily influenced by the sea. Rainfall is quite frequent, but temperatures do not vary much. Western Alaska has a transitional climate, with lower temperatures, and less rainfall. High winds and blowing snow are more frequent. Arctic Alaska has very little snowfall, cool summers, and frequent high winds. The interior of Alaska has a continental climate with great temperature variations but only moderate rain and snow.

I was going to Anchorage where Matt, Rebecca, and Abigail lived. There is usually little snow all winter. It can get as cold as 20 below zero, though. That was something I was used to in Minnesota.

I was curious about the 'midnight sun', too. In Barrow, on the Arctic coast, the sun is not seen from late November until late January. Also in Barrow, there is continuous daylight from early May to early August.

Anchorage is a seaport, and Uncle Matt was a captain on a Coast Guard cutter, patrolling the waters. The Coast Guard has many responsibilities besides rescue. They watch for smugglers and enforce maritime laws. They have served in every major war the U.S. has been involved in.

Anchorage is the largest city in the state, covering 1697.6 square miles, with a population of about 251,000.

The article was full of other facts and figures but the one that really got my attention was Portage Glacier. Huge chunks of ice can be seen falling off the glacier's face into the lake below - just like the dream I remembered having on my grandfather's lap so long ago.

Another interesting place was Earthquake Park, where visitors could see depictions of the 1964 earthquake that destroyed much of the city.

I was also interested to read about Eklunta Village, which has exhibits of the culture and traditions of Native Americans and Russians who have lived in Alaska for more than 350 years!

Reading about it made me think of Vladimir and my unscheduled trip to Russia. I realized how close I was to where this whole business had started! I wondered what he was doing now.

Of course, Siberia was far from Gzhel, but in my mind it was close enough!

I wondered if I would get to see any of these places on this trip. How much could a person see while sitting for a portrait?

Matt and Abigail were going to pick me up at the airport. Rebecca was very busy in her studio. She was a very good artist, and very much in demand for her portraits.

She also liked to paint animals and landscapes, often working from photographs. Abby had become interested in photography watching her mother work, and took many good photos of the ships and wildlife in the area. Some of them were so good Rebecca used them for her paintings. Abby usually used her mother's cameras.

I had brought a gift for Abby, a digital camera of her own and I was anxious to give it to her. It was safely tucked away in my suitcase.

All that reading had made me sleepy, so I put away the magazine and the headphones then settled back in my seat.

Soon I was dreaming of Grandpa, the gold pocket watch, and his stories of where Kool-Whip really comes from.

"It's a secret," he said, "buried in the Arctic Ice. You see they don't want you to know what they are really up to!"

"Oh Grandpa! You're just kidding me!" I said, looking at Grandma for confirmation.

But she just smiled and said, "Remember, Rose, there is some truth in every story."

I didn't wake up until the wheels touched down at the airport in Seattle.

Chapter Three

We had a layover in Seattle. It would be an hour before the connecting flight to Anchorage. I sat in the plastic chairs under the watchful eyes of the Airport Security.

They had been alerted to the fact I was flying alone. Dad had seen to it I'd be watched. I wondered if I would ever be able to travel on my own.

I couldn't blame him though, after all, I was only twelve, and as much as I would like to think I was grown up, I knew I wasn't.

The snacks weren't bad in first class, but I was bored - and when I spotted the candy machine I decided to get a candy bar. I took off the headphones, and put away the CD player I had been listening to. I dug through my bag in search of my coin purse. It was loaded with quarters, and some rolled-up dollar bills.

The hidden pocket in the bag held all of my vacation money, and I carried my own ATM card for emergencies. But the coin purse was for occasions like this, and I took out two of the dollar bills, unrolling them so the machine would accept them.

"Sheesh!" I said, "a buck and a half for a candy bar!" But really, it was no more than at the local store or the magazine stand across the way.

I'd slung the bag over my shoulder instead of around my neck like I normally would. I needed both hands to feed the dollars into the machine.

That's when I felt a slight tug on the bag, and turned just in time to see a hand emerge with my CD player.

"Hey! What do you think you are doing?" I yelled at the teen-age boy who was obviously trying to steal it.

I grabbed at it, snagging the headphones, and forced him to stop.

The thin, blonde boy looked shaggy and tough. He wore dirty jeans and boots, and looked out of place in the waiting area.

He was trying to unplug the headphones!

"Stop or I'll scream!" I said.

He wasn't sure what to do. It was supposed to be a quick, easy lift and run. Now, he couldn't let go without dropping the player, and attracting the attention of the guards.

He looked around, nervously. He already had their attention, and one of them was walking toward us!

"I'm sorry, I bumped into you by accident, and it fell out of your bag," he lied as he walked back towards me, hand out to return the player.

"Is this young man bothering you, miss?" The burly security guard asked.

The young man's eyes pleaded with me. I could see he was desperate. But there was something else there. In spite of my background, and all of my 'training' I shook my head.

"No. Everything's fine. We were just arguing about which CD to listen to."

"Is he traveling with you?"

"No, we're just waiting together."

"Where are you headed, son?" The guard asked.

"San Diego. I'm going back to my Mother's. I was in Seattle visiting my Dad."

"Well, your flight is over there, I suggest you leave the young lady alone."

"Yes, sir," the boy replied as the officer walked away.

"Thank you!" the boy said to me when we were alone.

"I should have turned you in! What are you doing stealing from a kid anyway?"

"I needed the money. I could get ten dollars for that. That would buy me food for two days."

"You steal for food?"

"Only when I have to. I ran away from home to see my father. He's sending me back. My mother has custody. He had just enough money to send me back. My mother is on welfare, and the child support he's forced to pay."

"But why do you have to steal? Don't you get money for food?"

"My mother buys booze with it. She blames my father for everything. If you had turned me in they would have found out I have a juvenile record. I got in trouble a few times when they were breaking up."

It was hard for me to understand, my parents had always gotten along, and I never felt unwanted. This was a side of life I had never seen before.

"Look, if you need money…"

"I don't need your money!" He said.

"Well, you sure wanted my CD player!"

"Look, I owe you. If you're ever in San Diego, and you need help just ask for Shane. What's your name, anyway?"

"Rose."

"Well, Rose, I'm sorry I bothered you. Go back to your candy bar before someone grabs it."

I looked down at the tray in the machine. The candy bar sat waiting. I suddenly felt guilty about eating it, and thought about offering it to Shane, but when I looked up, he was gone.

I looked all over the waiting areas, but couldn't find him. Finally, I sat back down, clutching the candy bar - but no longer wanting it. I decided to put it in my bag before it melted in my hands.

I sat, staring at nothing, thinking about how lucky I was to have the life I had. The next time I looked up it was to see a woman standing in front of me.

"Erica! What are you doing here?" I asked.

"I'll be flying to Anchorage with you," she said.

"You will? Is this just a coincidence?" I asked, suspiciously.

"Well, I've never missed one of your flights yet!" She smiled.

"Sheesh! What does a girl have to do to get some privacy?" I asked half kidding.

"Put your headphones on, and listen to your CD player," she answered.

And that's what I did until we boarded the plane.

Chapter Four

Eventually, I ate the candy bar, looking around as if Shane were on the plane.

"Silly! He's on the way to San Diego. And he doesn't fly first class!"

There was something I liked about Shane. He must have been thirteen going on fourteen. He looked rough, and acted tough - but I knew he wasn't really bad.

I thought about Dimitri. I still had a crush on him. He was working hard in school, and trying to make a better life for himself. His parents were not rich, but at least they were together.

Then, there was Paolo. Though I never really had a crush on him I liked him as a friend. He worked hard, earning money wherever he could.

It must be harder for Shane. He was too young for a real job, but there must be something he could do. There were kids in my neighborhood that delivered papers or did yard work for money.

But I did not know where Shane lived. Maybe in his neighborhood there were no yards.

I hoped he would stay out of trouble!

It wasn't long before we reached Anchorage, and I turned my thoughts to Abigail and Uncle Matt.

This was the first time in four years I would meet them in person, and I would have been nervous about it except for my adventures in Russia and Peru. I was used to meeting people now.

Abigail had just turned ten, and Uncle Matt had promised her a trip to Sea World for her birthday. My visit was a special occasion so I would get to go, too!

They were waiting for me when I left the security area. I recognized them from their pictures, and they recognized me.

"Rose! Rose! Over here!" Abby said. She was so excited she couldn't stand still.

Uncle Matt smiled as I approached them

"Hello, Rose. Welcome to Anchorage!"

He looked a lot like my Dad, only younger.

I hugged them both, and we headed to the baggage area.

"I've got so much to show you!" Abby said.

"How was your trip?" Uncle Matt asked.

I always wondered why people ask you that. If you had a terrible trip - would they really want to hear about it?

"It was fine, Uncle Matt."

"We've been reading your newsletter on the Internet. You've got quite a promising future, young lady," Uncle Matt said.

"Thanks. I'll probably write about Alaska now, too. I have to keep writing anyway for my home school credits," I said as we watched the bags slide onto the kiosk.

"I wish I didn't have to go to school!" Abby said, looking at her father.

"It's not as great as you think, Abby. I miss my school friends, and now I have to force myself to do my schoolwork. It was easier in school because you had to do it."

She cocked her head to one side, pulling at her brown pigtails. Her pouty look changed as she thought about what I had said.

Uncle Matt appreciated my comments. I felt like a much older big sister giving advice to the younger one.

"Well," Abby said. "I am ten years old now, Double digits! Someday I will be a great photographer - and maybe I can work with you on your adventures!"

I smiled at Abby and said, "Yes, maybe we can work together. We'll share the Pulitzer Prize!"

She smiled back, happy again as we carried my luggage to Uncle Matt's car.

"Rebecca is excited too," Uncle Matt said as we drove out of the parking ramp and into the bright sunshine.

"Where is Aunt Rebecca?" I asked.

"She had to finish a portrait for a client. She is waiting at the house."

"I think Mom is more excited about doing your portrait than anyone she has ever done!" Abby said. "Even me."

I blushed. They were treating me like a celebrity.

"I don't know why she would be excited about painting me," I said, looking out the window of the big back seat of the SUV. Abby had tried to get me to sit up front, but I told her it was her seat.

Uncle Matt looked in the mirror as he drove; he smiled at me and shook his head.

"Well, we've got some great things planned for you two," he said, turning the car onto a side street off the main highway.

"We've been talking to your parents and my job is to see to it you want to come back and visit us more often."

The car started climbing a long hill. We were close to their house. They lived in town, and the white-sided house was much bigger than it looked from the outside.

About halfway up the block it was a four-level home with an attached building Rebecca used as a studio.

Sitting high on the hill, in back, the house dropped to the ground - and there was a small but comfortable back yard.

It all looked very picturesque, and for the first time in all my recent travels I was looking forward to a nice relaxing visit.

But what did I know?

Chapter Five

Uncle Matt tooted the horn as he parked the car in the driveway alongside the studio. It was a signal to Rebecca we had arrived.

Inside the studio, Rebecca wiped the paint from her hands, and smiled. "Perfect timing!" She thought. She had just put the finishing touches on a portrait of a very important client.

Admiral Foods, the giant of the food world was launching a huge advertising campaign. All the big executives were in Anchorage for the kick-off, and they had commissioned Rebecca to paint a picture of a very important person.

Checking the portrait one more time, she finally felt satisfied, and opened the side door of the studio. She walked into the driveway as we unloaded the luggage.

"Welcome, Ramblin' Rose! It's so good to see you! My, you have grown up haven't you?"

More hugs followed as I was swept into the house via the back door.

"We hardly ever use the front door," Rebecca explained. "It's more for salesmen and newspaper boys."

We walked into the family room on the lower level through the sliding glass doors.

The fireplace was glowing with crackling logs, and the whole house seemed warm and friendly.

Soon we climbed the carpeted stairs into the kitchen.

"Abby will show you your room," Aunt Rebecca said as Uncle Matt followed us down the hallway with the monster suitcase I had brought.

Abby had carried the smaller bag, and I was left with my trusty canvas bag and backpack.

A few more carpeted steps brought us to the upstairs bedrooms; Abby's and mine were directly across the hall from each other.

Uncle Matt set the bag down, and said, "Well, I'll leave you two to get settled. Come on down as soon as you can."

Back in the kitchen, Rebecca was on the phone. "Yes, Mr. Mirilav, the portrait is finished. You'll stop by tomorrow? That would be fine. Yes, it will be ready to pick up in time for this weekends events. Thank you, sir, we'll see you tomorrow."

"Another satisfied client?" Matt asked, opening the refrigerator.

"Yes. A nice commission! Especially with the upcoming trip to Sea World."

"I don't know what we'd do without your studio," Matt said, closing the refrigerator door. "This commission will establish you for life."

"Oh, we'd do okay. What were you searching for in the fridge?" Rebecca asked, knowing he had not even looked at anything.

"An unconscious habit, I guess," he said, realizing he had done this many times.

"Well, you know we can't talk about the portrait until the unveiling. At least, not publicly."

"Yeah, I know. Though it's hard not to talk about it, especially with my brother, the agent."

"Well, you are a captain in the Coast Guard! Your brother can't get all the top secret stuff!"

"I almost blew it when we called to invite Rose. They offered us money for her portrait and Sea World, I wouldn't have taken it anyway, but we sure don't need it now."

Rebecca nodded. "Admiral Foods has paid us well. Who would have thought I would paint a portrait of the Russian president?"

"You are a part of history now, dear. You have painted some important people before, but this product kick-off is a major milestone in U.S.-Russia relations. The first simultaneous launch of a new food product in both countries! The two governments are using the event to strengthen relations, and set a precedent for democracy, and free enterprise. Just think we'll get to meet the president!"

"Who would have thought we'd meet the Russian President before our own? I'll never forget the way Mr. Mirilav managed to sneak the Russian president from his hotel to our house for a sitting!" Rebecca smiled as she remembered the Russian Secret Service men.

"With a little help from the Coast Guard, I might add," Matt reminded her.

His crew had been chosen to provide the transportation from the hotel to the house. Working in plain clothes alongside the Russian Secret Service was exciting duty!

If the media had found out, it could have endangered the president's life, and ruined the diplomatic relations between both countries, not to mention all the plans Admiral Foods had made.

Rebecca had done some preliminary work on the portrait from photographs as she usually did, but had insisted on a live sitting. She always insisted on one before taking any commission to paint a portrait. Photos were fine for a start, but she needed the person to pose live in order to bring out qualities of a person often hidden by the camera. That artistry was one reason her works were in such demand.

"I told them I didn't want to risk my career, and the future of international relations on a few photographs - and they agreed. Boy, this will be a story to tell our grandchildren!" Rebecca said.

"Whoa! Slow down. Abby is only ten! Besides, they will probably read all about it in the history books!" Matt smiled.

"Or, on the Internet. A certain niece of ours does write a newsletter, you know."

"Are you going to tell her about it?" Matt asked, opening the refrigerator again and staring at nothing.

"Tell who about what?" Abby said as I followed her into the kitchen. I had gotten settled into the guest room, and we had come downstairs in search of food.

"Oh, you two will find out soon enough!" Matt said, closing the refrigerator door again, still empty-handed

"I get the feeling everyone is hungry," Rebecca said.

"Matt, why don't you run down to Kentucky Fried Chicken and get us supper?"

"Yeah," Abby smiled, "we'll celebrate rose coming to visit!"

"Okay," Uncle Matt said, "but only if you girls set the table."

"Yes sir, Captain Matt! I mean, "Aye, Aye, Captain!" Aunt Rebecca teased as Uncle Matt frowned at her

Abby and I both joined in and saluted Uncle Matt who, giving us a stern look, did not return it.

"Shoulders back! Eyes front! Sharpen up that salute, sailors!"

Pretending to be serious, all three of us snapped to attention and saluted again.

"Much better!" He said, returning the salute. "Now, prepare this galley for chow! I'll be back shortly!"

"Aye, aye, Captain!" We replied as Uncle Matt turned and marched out the door.

When he was gone we descended on Aunt Rebecca.

"Tell who about what?" Abby repeated.

"Top secret!" Aunt Rebecca replied as she turned to the cupboard, and handed down the dishes

Guest or not, I was put to work and soon we had the table set. We hurried so we could have more time to work on Aunt Rebecca before Uncle Matt returned with the food.

By the time the car pulled back into the driveway we had heard the whole story, and been sworn to secrecy, something I was already used to!

"Wow," I said as Uncle Matt was coming up the outside steps, "this is too intense!"

I couldn't wait to tell Mom and Dad!

Aunt Rebecca had called them when I arrived, and told them I had made it safely. I didn't talk to them because it was late in their time zone. We agreed I would call them tomorrow.

I could hardly sleep that first night thinking of everything that was happening! Sam was in the dog show, I was in Alaska, Aunt Rebecca's portrait, and the huge event that was to take place next week at Sea World!

Not to mention I was going to pose for my own portrait! In a dress, no less!

The camera for Abby would have to wait. Her birthday was not being celebrated until Sunday, and it was only Friday night.

All of Abby's friends were coming over for a birthday party next Friday. I would have to keep her present a secret until then.

For now, I had all I could do to try and sleep.

Chapter Six

That's the thing about secrets; they never stay that way!

Saturday morning at Westminster, Sam was rehearsing with his handler while Mom watched.

"Way to go Sam!" Mom shouted encouragement from the sidelines as the big Newfie pranced around the show floor.

Dad was busy with the security team hired by Westminster, checking COM links and monitors. He was pretty satisfied with the setup. Next would come the daily meetings and drills to ensure every member of the team knew their job and what to do in the event of a "situation".

The pulse of the cell phone interrupted him in his breast pocket.

"Time out, guys. Take ten," he said into his Com and reached for the phone.

The green light told him the call was on Zip, and the I.D. brought up Richard's name.

"Hey, what's up?" Dad said, avoiding using Richard's name.

"Something I thought you should know. How is Sam doing?"

"Look's good so far. I think he has a good chance."

"Glad to hear that!" Richard said.

"What were you going to tell me?" Dad asked.

"I'll be cutting out a few days early. Already had this class. I think someone goofed. Thought I'd look up Susan and Steven, and take in a show."

Dad frowned. It wasn't like Richard to talk in riddles, especially on Zip. The connection must not be safe. That meant no signs or countersigns should be used.

"Well, say 'Hi' for us! Give us a call when you get there," Dad knew he would probably have to wait and talk to Richard in person about 'something you should know'.

"Yeah, I'll call when I get there. Just wanted to let you know where I would be. Good luck with the show!

"Thanks. Talk to you soon," Dad said, shutting off the phone.

He was good at not letting anything show on his face even though his mind was running through all the possible scenarios.

"Hmm... Richard is at Arlington for refresher classes, but doesn't feel safe talking around the other agents, or on Zip. He's already had the training... someone wanted him out of the way... Susan and Steven are the only ones he can trust... and there is something I should know... correction; something we should know. Is it about the dog show, or Rose? The Agency? Not quite enough information..."

Mom's loud applause for Sam and his handler, Annie, interrupted his thoughts.

Sam basked in the approval, and Annie beamed.

Annie was about forty, and had been handling dogs for twenty years. She had worked with Sam many times, and Mom considered her the best.

Dad looked up at the applause, and saw Mom wave him over.

"He sure looks good out there," Dad said, sitting down next to Mom

"I think he's got a good shot at winning!" Mom said.

"Speaking of winning, we just got a call from Richard," Dad said.

"What did he want?" Mom asked.

"To wish us good luck and tell us something we should know."

"Something we should know?" Mom frowned.

"Yeah, but he couldn't talk just now," Dad replied.

"Okay, I guess we'll have to guess. Was it about Sam? Rose? The show?"

"Don't know right now. Best thing is to be on our guard, and stay sharp. He said he's cutting class, and probably will look up Susan and Steven. They'll probably take in a show."

"Well, I guess we'll have to wait to find out what they saw," Mom had caught on.

She knew she couldn't trust Zip now, or her cell phone. She was good at hiding her worry, too.

They both knew the 'show' they would take in was this one; the dog show, and the three of them would be coming. They would be there to watch each other's back. It was clear they could not trust anyone in The Agency during this situation and they would have to talk in person.

They also knew I was safe by Richard's deliberate act of not mentioning me. However, the situation might involve me somehow.

All of this was standard procedure in case the climate turned 'cold' as Dad called it.

Mom resisted the urge to call me right away. She did not want to tip off anyone who might be watching them.

"Break's over. Back to work!" Dad said, switching on his COM.

Mom nodded. "Okay, Annie, let's hit it again!"

They decided to call me later.

Chapter Seven

Sunday morning in church I couldn't keep my mind off Mom, Dad, and Sam. Mom hadn't said much about anything when she called, except how Sam was doing. I was happy to hear he had a chance of winning, but there was something in Mom's voice telling me she was worried about other things. I asked Dad if everything was okay, and he said things were fine. I instinctively knew something was troubling him. I decided to stay alert.

"Rose, snap out of it!" Abby was shaking my shoulder as the other people in the pew scowled at my lack of attention. I hadn't heard a word of the service.

"Huh? Oh, sorry, Abby. My mind was wandering," I said.

"Yeah, it looked like it got up and left the building!" She retorted.

"Okay, I'm back," I said, a little irritated.

Uncle Matt and Aunt Rebecca pretended not to notice, and I was glad when the service ended.

"Well, Rose, I thought you might like to see my studio today," Aunt Rebecca said as we rode in the car on the way back to their house.

"That would be great!" I said, even though I was not excited about sitting for a portrait. I wanted to see where the "very special" subject who would make history had sat. Maybe even the picture itself! I wished Aunt Rebecca had let me tell Mom and Dad about it!

When the car pulled into the drive outside the studio I couldn't wait to go in. I jumped out of the car, and headed for the door.

"Not so fast, young lady!" Aunt Rebecca said as she reached out and put a hand on my shoulder.

"But I wanted to see..." I started to say.

"I know, but Mr. Mirilav will be here at 1 p.m. to pick it up, and I have promised him no one would see it before the ceremony at Sea

World next week. Why don't you girls go upstairs until he leaves, then we'll have our tour."

"Okay, Mom. C'mon Rose, I'll show you my photo album," Abby said, taking my hand.

I shrugged and said, "Okay," but the reporter in me was making a plan 'B'.

At precisely two minutes to 1 p.m., a black official looking car pulled up in front of the house. A man in a black suit got out and said something to the driver

I was watching out the front window as he made his way around the side of the house to the studio door.

Again, I drew Abby's irritation as she tried in vain to keep my attention on the photo album.

"There you go again, Rose! I'm trying to show you my pictures, and all you can do is look out the window!"

"I'm sorry, Abby. I just can't stop thinking about the man in the black car. You know I'm kind of a secret agent and something about him looks suspicious. These pictures are really good! You really are great with a camera!"

"Thanks, Rose!" Abby said, beaming from the praise. "I took all of these by myself, and Mother says I can use her tripod and camera to take your pictures today."

"Take my pictures? I thought I would be sitting for a portrait." I said.

"Mother always arranges the poses, and takes pictures first. She says there is no need to sit for the whole thing. She works from the pictures until she gets ready for the face, then she insists on the person doing a live sitting so she can capture that unique 'something' the person has the camera can't see or feel. She says that's why her paintings of people look so lifelike."

"Wow! That makes sense. And I don't have to sit every day?"

"No, today she will set up the picture and background, then take some preliminary pictures. Or, I will. This will be the first time she has let me take the set-up shots!"

"Wow. It sounds a lot more fun now!" I said, relieved we didn't have to sit for hours every day. Now we could go places and see things!

I watched the front window with one eye as I browsed Abby's album. There were pictures of wildlife and landscapes of Alaska as well as pictures of ships, boats, and Coast Guard cutters. Abby had pictures of her parents, and friends as well. She really was talented for a kid her age. I couldn't wait to give her the new camera.

"I took all of these with my 35mm camera. Mother and Dad said I should learn the basics on one before I try a digital. My first cameras were instamatics. I got my first one when I was eight, and my parents told me how good the pictures were. They said I was a natural," Abby beamed again.

"Well, they were right! Say, Abby, do you have your camera ready?" I asked

"Yeah, it's right in my room. I'll show it to you!"

I looked out the window again. The driver of the car was getting out and opening the back door for the man dressed in black.

"Hurry Abby!" I said as she came back into the room.

"What's up? Why the hurry?" Abby asked as she came to the window alongside me.

Outside, the man in black handed the covered portrait to the driver, who carefully placed it in the back seat of the car.

He must have sensed us watching him because he turned around and looked up into the window. While he stared into the sun on the window glass, I noticed him pull on the pinky finger of his right hand. He seemed to do it unconsciously, and chills ran down my back.

"Take his picture, quick!" I said.

Abby set up the shot, not sure if it would turn out, and snapped the shutter.

I looked at the man again. I didn't recognize him. He seemed familiar, maybe because he was Russian. Mirilav, the name was not familiar either. Still, something tugged at me. I felt I knew him from somewhere.

"What was that all about?" Abby asked.

"I think I know that man. I'm not sure but I think I do. I want to send the picture to my parents, and check him out."

"Well, I think you've been playing spy too much. There are lots of Russian people in Alaska. They have lived here for three hundred years. Besides, that's Mr. Mirilav. He is in charge of the big publicity campaign for Admiral Foods. He's the one who hired Mom to paint that portrait. He is the one who is taking us all to Sea World next week for the big event."

Just then, Aunt Rebecca called up the stairs.

"Come on down girls. Let's have some lunch and get started."

On the way down the steps I wished I had given Abby the new digital camera.

"How soon can you get that developed?" I asked.

Chapter Eight

"As soon as we finish taking your portrait shots," Abby said as we rounded the corner into the kitchen, and headed for Aunt Rebecca's studio. "But why is it so important?"

"I'll tell you later," I answered.

Aunt Rebecca's studio was painted white, and was full of windows. There were plants in front of each one, and a stage-like area against the wall facing the house.

The 'stage' was set with a white satin drape hanging down in folds here and there and a high-back red velvet chair with brass studs on the front of the arms. It looked old fashioned.

"Classic is what I call it," Aunt Rebecca said, noticing my expression. "Your mother wanted a classic look to the portrait. It's a bit Victorian but I think it will work very well with the dress she sent with you."

I rolled my eyes. In my head I wanted the portrait to be somewhere between a world-roving journalist in jungle khakis and my Grandmother's pose as a young lady, looking out to sea, hair blowing in the wind as she held the orchid my grandfather had given her. Sitting in a chair with my hands folded was not what I had in mind.

I looked around at some of the portraits on the walls. Some were classic, some were modern; each one seemed to fit the subject.

"Oh, come on, Rose, it's not that bad. Why don't you put on the dress and we'll take a few shots to see what it will look like?"

Sheesh! The dress was white too! And I was to wear white pantyhose and dress shoes! How about a prom dress, maybe blue at least?

I looked at Abby for help, but she just shrugged. She stood behind the camera and tripod set up in front of the stage.

"Now, follow my thinking, Rose," Aunt Rebecca said, hand on my shoulder. The red chair will bring out your strawberry blonde hair and complexion, and you will be holding a rose. A rose for a Rose!"

"You mean a blooming Rose, don't you? Sheesh! People will think I lived a hundred years ago!" I pouted.

"Tell you what," Aunt Rebecca said, a hurt look in her eyes, "Your mother requested this. Why don't we take some sample shots we can show her, and then maybe we can alter the setting to fit you better."

That sounded like a reasonable plan, and I reluctantly agreed. Modeling was definitely not in my future!

Once I had the dress on, there was the question of my hair. My customary ponytail would just not do! But this was just a rehearsal so Aunt Rebecca brushed it, and placed barrettes on the sides to keep it in place for the photos.

"We'll have your hair done for the actual shooting. I work from photos first to frame up the painting, and put the details in later."

I nodded as she led me to the chair, and arranged the dress. I felt like Queen Elizabeth sitting on her throne! To top it all Aunt Rebecca handed me an artificial rose to hold, and it reminded me of a scepter! All that was missing was a crown of jewels - and loyal subjects!

"Okay Rose, now follow my suggestions as Abby shoots the pictures. Remember now, this is her first professional session, so help her out as much as you can."

The first shot was pretty unspectacular; me sitting stiffly upright holding the artificial flower - and trying to smile. I pondered different expressions. Should my expression fit the setting? Abby took several shots of my changing face. Smiling, grimacing, scowling, sticking my tongue out.

Aunt Rebecca just let us go. Soon we were having fun being silly and I started to relax.

"There we go, Rose! That's it! Now lean forward in the chair and think of something funny."

Click!

"Now, sit back in the chair and think of something far away."

Click!

"Now stand next to the chair with your hand on the back of it."

Click!

"Now, sit on the floor in front of the chair and lean back on the seat."

Click!

"Now stand behind the chair, now sit sideways and let your legs dangle across the other arm. Now let your left shoe fall off."

The camera clicked faster and faster, the poses changing and changing until I forgot all about the camera, the studio and everything except being me. Suddenly, the stodgy Victorian setting seemed full of life, and I realized the contrast was not my red hair against the white - but my spirit against the setting!

How much like the real world!

Soon I felt as much at home on the stage as I did in life and the boring photo session became an adventure.

"That was great, Rose! We'll develop the proofs and see which one you like the best! You know, you are a natural-born model!"

I blushed from the praise, surprised at myself.

Abby waited patiently behind the camera for her mother's appraisal of her work.

"Abby, you did great! There's no doubt in my mind you are a natural born photographer! Come on, let's go to the darkroom and see what we've got!"

The afternoon had somehow faded away, and soon I was back in jeans with my hair in a ponytail.

I couldn't wait to see how the pictures turned out! I almost forgot about the picture of Mr. Mirilav in Abby's camera.

It was the only cloud in a perfectly fun day.

What was it about him that seemed so familiar?

Chapter Nine

The man known as Mr. Mirilav settled into the soft, black leather of the limo. So far, things were proceeding according to plan. He wanted to smile in satisfaction, but his years of experience told him all was not well yet.

On the surface, things looked good, but the main event was still more than a week away, and many things could still go wrong

The portrait was finished, and was indeed a masterpiece! He allowed himself the satisfaction in keeping it a secret. Not only that - but the fact he could arrange such a secret sitting while the whole world was watching was amazing!

But the best was yet to come! This event would ensure his come-back, and his status in the new government...

The driver looked in the mirror at his silent passenger. He could see the deep thoughts etched on his forehead. A strange mixture seemed to alternate between joy and worry. Better to be a driver, he thought.

Mirilav checked his watch. By now the ship had arrived at the coor-dinates, and was waiting for its intended cargo. Only, this cargo would not go into the bays...

As the driver turned into the hotel's parking ramp he picked up the car phone and placed a call.

"This is Mirilav. Status report?"

"On schedule. Package will be picked up tomorrow. Everything 'cool'."

Mirilav smiled.

On board the Admiral, the flagship of Admiral Foods, the captain hung up the phone and smiled.

He was going to be famous! The largest launch of a new food product in the world! The largest publicity stunt in history, and a historic meeting of two presidents! After all these years of un-rewarded service - he was about to become a celebrity!

But why this particular chunk of ice? It seemed any iceberg would do. He had asked only once, and Mirilav had told him something about the engineer's calculations

No matter. It was just a piece of ice.

He turned his attention to the first officer who was patiently waiting news of the call.

"Everything is on schedule. Proceed as planned."

"Aye, captain.

Back in his room with the portrait, Mirilav paced back and forth unable to relax.

What was bothering him so? He thought back to the studio. To picking up the portrait, to loading into the car, to looking up at the windows of the house...

Somebody watching? But who? Why did it feel so familiar? It wasn't the paparazzi; it wasn't an agent... who would recognize him anyway? He had totally changed his appearance!

He had lost nearly fifty pounds, had his nose changed, shaved his goatee and mustache, put hair on his formerly balding head, and looked twenty years younger!

He had also assumed a new identity, and a completely new background. No one on Earth could possibly recognize him!

Yet, he had felt familiar eyes on him...

"Just nerves," he told himself. "Just nerves.

Back at Abby's house we watched the pictures come to life in the red glow of the darkroom.

I was more interested in Abby's shot of Mr. Mirilav from the window than the poses Aunt Rebecca had put me through. I couldn't shake the feeling I had seen Mr. Mirilav somewhere before.

"What is it, Rose?" Aunt Rebecca asked. "You seem more interested in Mr. Mirilav than the photo shoot for the portrait.

"Yes, Rose. What is it? Don't you like my pictures?" Abby asked.

"Of course I do! It will be hard to choose one! It's just that I can't get over the feeling I know that man from somewhere. He doesn't look like anyone I remember, but still there is something familiar about him. He is Russian?" I asked

"Yes," Aunt Rebecca answered. "He is Russian. He is in charge of the entire campaign for Admiral Foods' launch of its new dessert product. But there are many Russians in Alaska. The Russian community here is more than three hundred years old! I know you went to

Russia. You wrote all about it in your newsletter. Maybe he just looks like someone you saw while you were there."

"I thought about that already. I don't think so. I have a pretty good memory, and I don't remember anyone who looked like him. No, this is something more than that. Something familiar on a deeper level. Something in his mannerism..." I was thinking out loud now.

"Wow, this is like being with Sherlock Holmes!" Abby said.

"Well, whatever it is, I'm sure you two detectives will figure it out. In the meantime we have to pick a pose, and get started on your portrait. We must have it done before Abby's birthday party next Friday night. You know she is having a sleepover with a few of her friends, and we are leaving on Sunday for Sea World. I'll have to work fast."

I watched Aunt Rebecca take the pictures from the rinse as Abby hung them up to dry. Mr. Mirilav floated back and forth in the wash as the portrait photos were taken out one by one.

"You know, even if the portrait isn't finished by then, you can always send it to us," I said, my eyes still on the floating picture.

"Yes, I know," Aunt Rebecca answered. But we must have time for your final sitting!"

Finally, she took the photo of Mr. Mirilav from the tray. My eyes followed it to the hanging line.

It wasn't his face. Standing half turned and looking up it was his hands that I noticed.

His left hand was wrapped around the little finger of his right hand. He seemed to be tugging on it as if pulling it back into place.

That was it!

I had only seen one person in my life who did that!

But it couldn't be him!

Or could it?

Chapter Ten

"Who's this, Abby?" Aunt Rebecca asked as she hung up the picture of Mr. Mirilav. "It looks like Mr. Mirilav! What's it doing in here?"

Abby thought quickly. "I was showing Rose my camera and I took his picture when he was leaving."

"Well, I hope he didn't see you. This whole project is supposed to be a secret. Admiral Foods does not want the press to know."

Now my mind was spinning! Secret? Mirilav... Vladimir? I couldn't get over the feeling I knew the man in the photo.

"Rose? Are you okay?" Aunt Rebecca asked as I stared into nothing.

"Huh? Oh, I'm fine. I just remembered something. Come on Abby, let's look at the rest of your pictures."

With a puzzled look on her face, Abby led me out of the darkroom, and I followed her upstairs.

Rebecca looked at the pictures of the photo shoot hanging on the line. She shrugged and scratched her head. What was going on?

"Who's Vladimir?" Abby asked as we sat on the bed in the guest room.

"He's the man who kidnapped me and took me to Russia," I answered.

"Kidnapped you? I never heard about that! I thought you took a trip there!"

"I couldn't tell anyone but my parents and The Agency. It's classified."

"I read all about Russia in your newsletter but nothing about that!"

"I'm only allowed to write about certain things. My parents are both agents, were, and still are I guess. Now they work in the 'Private Sector'. You have to promise not to repeat any of this to anyone, not even your closest friends."

"Okay. But why are you telling me?"

"Because, if I'm right and that is Vladimir, he's up to no good - and your family is involved. Did anyone know I was coming?"

"No. Mom and Dad called your parents when they planned the trip, after they got the job from Mr. Mirilav," Abby said thoughtfully.

"What was the job?" I asked her, warily.

"Well, they said they wanted a portrait painted of someone very special and were looking for a local artist. Because they wanted to keep the whole thing out of the papers they had Dad and some of his crew pick the President up and bring him here for the final sitting. They said if anyone found out before the unveiling at Sea World we would lose the contract and not be able to go. Mom is going to be on the platform with all the big shots and both presidents!"

"Both presidents? Wow! I wonder why my parents didn't know about it?" I said.

"No one is supposed to know. Mr. Mirilav is in charge of the whole publicity thing. People are always watching and the safety of the presidents is at stake."

"What's the big new food product?" I asked with a queasy felling in my stomach.

"Kool-Whip," Abby replied.

"Kool-Whip? There's nothing new about that!" I said like the expert I was.

"A new kind of Kool-Whip. It comes in different flavors, and is 'low-carb'. They say it will replace frostings.

Kool-Whip? I remembered my grandfather's story about Kool-Whip being made from the Arctic ice. Sheesh! Who would have ever thought it?

"Rose, there you go again, spacing out."

"Oh, sorry, Abby," I said, shaking off the memories.

"Anyway, Rose, if that is Vladimir, what's he doing here and why don't you recognize him?"

"Well, he would have had to lose about fifty pounds, and grow hair on his head - or he could be wearing a wig. His nose is different, too. But all those things are possible. I thought he had been sent to Siberia."

"Siberia isn't that far from here," Abby reminded me. "Are you going to tell Mom and Dad?"

"No, not until I'm sure. The big question is what is he doing here?"

"Maybe you're wrong, and he just reminds you of him," Abby said, hopefully.

"I've never seen anyone else do that with his fingers."

"Well, someone else could have the same problem. Or habit."

"Yes, but there is just too much coincidence here. My instincts tell me we should check this out. Unless he's here to kidnap the president or something worse…" I didn't want to think about what else he might do.

"Or worse?" Abby seemed scared now.

"What else is going on around here?" I asked.

"Well, we could look on the Internet," Abby suggested.

"I wish I could talk to Zip," I said.

"Who is Zip?"

"A special friend."

"Why can't you?" Abby asked.

"Because we'd have the whole Agency listening in, and we don't have any evidence yet. We'll have to use the regular Internet."

"Okay. Come into my room. We can use my computer."

I thought about the first time I met Zip. Aunt Susan walked in on me - and off we went; kidnapped to Russia!

I wondered what would happen this time without him. It never crossed my mind that the Agency would be watching Abby's computer, too.

Chapter Eleven

While Abby and I were looking up current events, Mom, Dad, and Sam were getting ready for the big show.

"Sam is really doing great!" Mom told Dad as they sat for dinner at a restaurant.

"That's great!" Dad said, as he cut into his steak.

"How is security going?" Mom asked between bites of her salad.

"Piece of cake. I wonder why The Agency insisted on us being here. This is a routine assignment," Dad grumbled.

"Oh, come on now, aren't you the one who's always saying there is no routine assignment?" Mom reminded him.

"My words come back to haunt me!" Dad mumbled, trying to hide in another piece of steak. "But it's true," he said, looking up at Mom, "there are plenty of junior agents who could have handled this. There must be something bigger going on somewhere."

"So, you don't think Sam and I are important enough for your protection!" Mom was getting angry.

"Of course you are! That's not what I meant!" Dad defended himself with one foot in his mouth.

"It seemed like a perfectly logical assignment to me, what with Sam in the biggest competition of his life! And need I remind you of how much money is at stake with the prizes and the sponsors? Why, the television audience is immense! It costs almost as much to advertise on this show as the Super Bowl!" Mom was rolling now! She knew as much about security and world events as Dad.

"It just doesn't seem like a terrorist target to me," Dad said, finishing his steak.

"It seems like a perfect target to me, a blow against the decadence of the West and capitalism! Think of all the wealthy people here!" Mom was adamant.

"All true," Dad replied. "But after that call from Richard, I know something is up. It almost seems like someone wanted us out of the way…"

"Out of the way of what?"

"Something bigger," Dad said.

"What could be bigger right now? You saw the hot sheet on Zip. We bid the jobs like the rest of the private sector. Or did you forget we are not in The Agency any more?"

"Richard said we couldn't trust talking on Zip. How do we know it was a real hot sheet? My instincts tell me something else is going on behind the scenes." Dad drank the rest of his coffee and looked at Mom.

"I miss Rose," Mom said. "She should be here with Sam."

"I know. But we agreed to give her some space, and The Agency did not want her here for fear she would become the target. After foiling the plot in Peru she is still on the list. I wish Richard was with her."

"Don't you trust Matt and Rebecca? He is your brother, and a Captain in the Coast Guard. The only other people she would be safe with would be Susan and Steven," Mom waved the waiter over.

"Of course I trust my brother. And she will get her portrait painted. They wouldn't even let us pay Rose's expenses," Dad watched the waiter approach.

"And it's not every day she gets an invitation to Sea World! And it's a chance to see Abby. I worry about her not being around kids enough."

The waiter stood by the table. "Ahem," he said, impatiently.

"I'll have some of that delicious-looking cheesecake," Mom said.

"Another cup of coffee for me," Dad said.

The waiter nodded, and walked away.

"Dad looked at Mom. " I wonder what the kids are doing right now."

"Probably just kid stuff. Nothing Earth shattering I'm sure." Mom smiled as the cheesecake arrived.

"Yeah, kid's stuff," Dad said, sipping at the hot coffee. " What in the world could happen in Alaska?

"Abby, what was that?" I said as I felt a slight.

"Just an earth tremor. We get earthquakes from time to time, but we haven't had a big one since before I was born. Could be the glaciers breaking up, too. Or blasting. Lately they've begun drilling for oil."

"Sheesh! There seems to be a lot going on around here!" I said as the computer booted up.

"Yeah, always is. It's not a boring place to live. There are lots of science experiments going on all the time in the Arctic."

"Science? Research?" I asked.

"Yes, Dad says that ever since they detected the meteorite from Mars buried in the ice they have to stop people all the time. University students, 'gold diggers', and private research teams are all always trying to get at it. Then there's the global warming going on."

Abby was well informed about the world around her. Especially for a ten year old!

"Oh, you know, we get current events in school, and the Scholastic newsletter," she explained, seeing my surprised look.

"Besides," she continued, "I read your newsletter all of the time! You are always telling your readers to be curious about the world around them - just like my grandfather told us to be! You are not the only one with curiosity you know!"

Abby sounded a little annoyed at me. I did have a tendency to ramble as if I was the only one who ever thought about anything. My head hung down a little as the search engine came up.

"Mars has been in the news a lot lately," I said, "lets look up that rock you were telling me about."

"Okay," Abby replied, "but I don't see what possible connection there could be to this 'Vladimir' you are so worried about."

I didn't either.

Chapter Twelve

While we were reading up on Mars, Richard was driving up to Susan and Steven's new house.

Inside, Steven heard the 'Car Approaching' signal and watched as a smaller window appeared on the television screen as he and Susan sat watching a movie in the living room.

Using the remote, he zoomed in on the image of the car approaching the tall iron gates of the driveway.

"It's Richard," he said, pushing another button opening the gate.

"Just like his e-mail said," Susan replied, removing Steven's arm from around her shoulders as she stood up and stretched.

"Time to give the 'tour', I'll open the door," Steven switched off the P.I.P. and the movie, then went to the door.

Richard admired the brick drive sidewalk as he climbed the three brick steps onto the columned porch of the new house built to look like an older Victorian mansion.

The door opened before he could use the brass knocker.

"Richard! Good to see you! Come on in!" Steven shook his hand.

Stepping into the foyer he was greeted with a hug from Susan.

"Playing hooky? I thought you were supposed to be in school this week!" She said.

"Yeah, I skipped out. I've already had this class. Someone goofed. Nice place!"

"We'll give you the tour but first lets go out into the kitchen. I've got refreshments."

Seated around the table with coffee and rolls they made small talk about current events.

"And that brings me to why I'm here," Richard said as he put his coffee cup down.

"We thought you had more than one reason for coming," Steven said.

"From your e-mail, we guessed it wasn't safe to talk on Zip. What's up?" Susan asked.

"Something big is happening, and someone doesn't want us to know about it. They have us scattered, and are monitoring our communications. I'm guessing The Agency is behind it - or rather someone in The Agency."

"What makes you think that?" Steven asked.

"Loose lips. A couple of 'the boys' were bragging in class about the Big One that got away. Seems an old friend of ours left some critical information off the "Hot List' we bid jobs from. Seems he wanted his team to get the assignment, said it should be handled 'in house'."

"You mean Kyle Davis?" Susan asked.

"Yeah. He was always jealous of us even before we left The Agency. 'The Chosen Ones' he called us. Always getting the best assignments etc."

"Okay, I can believe that," Steven said, "but what was it he left out?"

"Well, no one would say that much, but I've got friends in the Secret Service. Seems the president will be in Sea World next week for a special kick-off event between two companies in the U.S. and Russia. The Russian president will also be there. Details are being kept top secret, but it has something to do with Admiral Foods, and a new food product."

"Well, that would be an Agency job anyway, and the Secret Service," Susan noted.

"Yes, but backup and perimeter security was biddable. We could have handled that job," Richard bit into a roll, and picked up the coffee again.

"Okay," Steven repeated, "we got aced out. We still wound up with the dog show - and it was a logical choice with Sam in it."

"So true," Richard replied. "So true no one would notice. No harm done. What concerns me is Rose will be at Sea World next week!"

"Rose at Sea World?" Susan said.

"Yes. She is visiting Abigail in Anchorage, and they are going to Sea World next week to celebrate Abby's birthday.

"Her mother did tell us about the trip," Steven said. "Just co-incidence?"

"I hope so, but you know as well as I do there is very little co-incidence in this world."

Susan looked at Richard. "What else do you know?"

"My Secret Service contact tells me the publicity campaign starts in Anchorage, and our family was involved. Seems the man in charge of the affair used Matt for an escort for a V.I.P."

"Why would they use the Coast Guard if they wanted things quiet?" Steven asked.

"They were in plain clothes. The Guard was happy to have a role. It's top secret until the event is over but it will bring attention to the role the Guard plays in national security. But here's the kicker. Seems that Rebecca will be on stage with the two Presidents."

"What? Where did Matt's team take the V.I.P?" Susan said, already suspecting the answer.

"To Rebecca's studio. She painted the man's portrait."

"I think you're right, there is no co-incidence here, but what about the dog show?" Steven asked.

"This is the first time they've used an Agency contract for security. They usually rely on locals. With all the terrorist activity, they decided to go with us. If Rose wasn't in the middle of this, I wouldn't think anything of it - but then there was the call for me to go to Arlington for updated training. Training I've already had. Could have been a clerical error…"

"Except that we are scattered to the wind," Susan finished.

"Have you told Rose's parents yet?" Steven asked.

"No. Can't trust communications. I suggest we all go there, and talk to them in person. We'll be there to cheer on Sam."

"And watch their backs!" Susan said.

"Let's make a plan in the morning. Come on, we'll show you the house," Steven stood up from the table.

"By the way, why is the publicity campaign starting in Anchorage?"

"Three reasons: One, there is a large Russian population there; two, Rebecca is a well-known portrait artist; and three, that's where the ice is."

"Ice?" Susan asked.

"Yeah, seems they are going to blast off a chunk of glacier and tow it to Sea World."

"Tow ice to Sea World?" Steven was mystified. "No wonder they wanted the Coast Guard's co-operation! What kind of product are they launching, anyway?"

"Kool-Whip," Richard said.

"Kool-Whip? That's been around forever!" Susan laughed.

"Well, there is something special about this stuff."

"How does Rose figure in to all this?" Steven asked as they pushed in the chairs.

"The man in charge of the event is Russian," Richard answered.

The hair on Susan's neck stood up as she remembered being kidnapped.

"Vladimir!" She said.

Chapter Thirteen

"What has Mars got to do with anything?" Abby asked as we continued our search on her computer.

"I'm not sure," I said, "but something about it rings a bell. Look, The Agency and the Secret Service will be protecting the two presidents. They are probably setting up for terrorists now. All the attention will be on the stage, and your mother's portrait."

"Okay, but I still don't see…"

"Well, The Agency knows Vladimir. That's why they had to change his appearance. When I was being held prisoner, I noticed he had a habit of pulling on his little finger - as if putting it back in place. Mr. Mirilav has that same habit."

"Okay, but why not use someone else?"

"Good question. My guess is they want his experience. He worked in the U.S. for fifteen years. He was also working for the hardliners, the old communists, and not for the government. Because of that, he was sent to Siberia. But what if it was a set-up, and he was really sent there by someone in the government to get him ready for this assignment! And my folks were sent to the dog show…"

I was thinking out loud. My Dad was the most experienced man in The Agency when he retired, and we went into business for ourselves. Mom has always wanted him to go to the dog shows with her, and everything seemed logical. But why didn't they know about Sea World? Or did they? If they knew I was going there why, wouldn't they want the assignment? Of course, The Agency would want to handle security for an event like this - but I'd heard Dad talk enough to know they use private security also. Maybe someone did not tell them about this! But why?

"I'm getting tired. Can't we do something else?" Abby asked.

"Sure, Abby. Maybe we can figure it out tomorrow."

"Abby, will you come down, and help in the kitchen?" Her mother's voice drifted up the stairs.

"Okay, Mom!" Abby said, pushing back the chair. "I'm going to help Mom." She said as she stood up. " You can keep searching if you want."

"Okay. There is something else I want to check," I replied.

Alone with the computer, I remembered some things Aunt Susan had said. "Trust your instincts." And, " When everything looks like it's all falling into place get ready!" And, "Things aren't always what they seem."

I searched for Admiral Foods, and found their company newsletter.

"SEA WORLD KICK-OFF SET FOR NEXT WEEK!"

Michael Mirilav, Special Project Director for Admiral Foods confirmed the kick-off of 'Kool-Whip Incorporated', the name given to Admiral Foods launch of it's new dessert product which will be simultaneously marketed in two countries, the United States and Russia.

"This will be an historic occasion," he was quoted as saying. "The announcement will be released to the press tomorrow. Two presidents will be in attendance along with leaders of industry and commerce. There will be a special ceremony coinciding with the arrival of Admiral Food's flagship arriving from Anchorage Alaska towing a huge iceberg. This is the largest advertising campaign in history and will be followed by several TV and radio spots. Of course, attendance at Sea World will be free to the public after the arrival of the VIPs and invited guests. The event will be televised and followed by radio."

There was more, but I had read enough.

A giant iceberg? Why not? It was Kool-Whip after all! I was impressed.

But what would Mars have to do with it?

I went to the NASA site. There was an article on Mars, and the plan to send Martian rocks and soil samples to Earth. The article said they would arrive sometime in the next decade!

Another article caught my attention. "Moon rocks disappear." Seems when we landed on the moon, several moon rocks were brought home to study, and all of them were eventually stolen either by fortune hunters, collectors, or jealous governments! Now they were afraid the same thing would happen to the Martian rocks...

Jealous governments? The article talked about information sharing. In the days of the space race both the U.S. and Russia wanted to be first. The Russian and Japanese governments were unhappy about the U.S. not wanting to share technology. They did not like being second to us in economics or technology.

And we had a Martian rock here all the time? Buried in the ice. Too hard to get at... Global warming, the Larsen B ice shelf disappearing, so much research in Arctic waters

What if the Russians found a way to get the Martian rock out of the ice right under our noses?

I had butterflies in my stomach! Somehow I knew I was right! But who would believe me

It made sense. Everyone would be focused on the events on the surface! The show, the presidents, the economic, cultural value of the product, and all the festivities while all the time a team could be working under the ice, digging out the Martian rock

If Mr. Mirilav were really Vladimir, he would not want my parents involved. He could have arranged for them to be at the dog show! But the director of The Agency did not want me there at the same time

The timing of my visit here and the portrait seemed too convenient. Did Vladimir know I was coming, or would I be a surprise?

If he knew I was coming, why was I here?

I switched off the computer. This wasn't fun anymore!

Chapter Fourteen

"What's the matter, Rose?" Aunt Rebecca said at the supper table. "You don't seem to be having fun."

I wanted to tell her and Uncle Matt all about my theory, but I didn't really have any proof! Besides, I didn't want to spoil things for Aunt Rebecca. This event and her portrait of a man I believed was the Russian president was too important to her.

I sure didn't want to spoil Abby's birthday celebration, either! I had to call my parents. But was it safe to talk? Was Vlad listening in? If it was Vladimir!

I decided to wait until after supper to call them. I would be careful about what I said.

"Oh, nothing. Just homesick a little I guess. I wonder how Sam is doing?" I said, picking up the forkful of mashed potatoes I had been drawing tracks in.

"Yes, that is so exciting! Having Sam in the Westminster! I think he has a shot at the title!" Aunt Rebecca was excited, and trying to cheer me up, too.

"This will be a year we'll all remember!" Uncle Matt said. "So many big things happening all around us! Especially Abby turning ten! Double digits, eh?" He said, smiling at his daughter, who was looking a little forgotten at the table.

Abby smiled at her Dad. All were redeemed!

I suddenly was homesick. Now I really needed to call my parents.

"Say, I know what will cheer you up!" Uncle Matt said, brightly. "How would you like a ride on a Coast Guard cutter? I could arrange it tomorrow on the Night Watch. I'll set it up through the Coast Guard Auxiliary, and you two can go on patrol with me!"

Abby beamed! "Wow, Dad! Can you really do that?"

"Anything for my birthday girl!"

"That would be intense!" I said.

"You kids are lucky! He hasn't invited me out on the cutter since we were dating!" Aunt Rebecca pretended to be mad.

"Would you like to come too, Dear?"

"I would but I have too much work to do. You guys go ahead without me."

The night air was cold but we were suited up in quilted jackets and life vests. Abby had brought her camera. We stood on the deck watching the lights of Anchorage, and the boats, and ships in the harbor.

Uncle Matt piloted the boat, looking down on us from time to time to make sure we were okay.

Abby took several pictures of the harbor lights, and some of the boats going by.

I listened to the steady churn of the cutter's motor and the sound of the water as we made our way to open water.

We were on patrol along the coast.

"Let me take your picture, Rose," Abby said, moving away from the railing.

"Okay, but only if I get to take one of you!" I said, assuming a pose.

"Deal," she replied.

"How's this?" I said, standing sideways, and looking out to sea.

"Looks okay, but why not look at me and smile?" Abby said.

"I don't want to look like a tourist," I said, holding the pose.

"Oh. Well, I guess..." Abby stopped in mid-sentence.

"Well, I can't stand this way forever. Are you going to take the picture?"

"Sure." Click went the camera

Click, click it went again and again.

"Abby, what are you doing?"

"Taking a picture of the ship behind you."

"What ship?" I said, turning to look in the other direction.

That's when I saw the Admiral Foods flagship. I knew it must be because it was towing a large iceberg behind it!

Abby took several pictures of the ship as it glided by.

I looked up at Uncle Matt. He was talking to someone on his headset.

For a moment I thought we were going to stop the big ship, and check their papers. The cutter motored steadily towards the flagship.

But instead of intercepting the ship, we turned and circled the iceberg behind it, inspecting the chains and towing gear.

Finally, we drew up alongside, and escorted the ship several miles along the coast.

With a wave and a blast of the cutter's horn we pulled away and turned back towards the harbor.

I couldn't help but wonder about that huge chunk of ice. Was it the one with the Martian rock?

"Are you going to tell my parents about your theory?" Abby asked.

"I don't know. I'm not so sure anymore. It sounds kind of wild even to me!"

"What about your parents? Are you going to tell them?"

"I'd like to have a little more proof, first. If I could see Mr. Mirilav close up..."

"Well, that won't be until next week at Sea World," Abby pointed out.

"If I could prove that Mr. Mirilav was really Vladimir then maybe someone would believe me."

"Well, I don't know how you can do that. Hey, are you going to take my picture now?"

"Oh yeah," I said, taking the camera from Abby.

She assumed the same pose I had, standing sideways to the rail, looking out to sea, only this time she was looking at the coastline.

"Smile!" I said.

"Smile?" She asked.

"Yes. I want you to look like a tourist."

I grinned and took the picture.

Chapter Fifteen

"Who would have thought that brat would be here!" Michael Mirilav, a.k.a. Vladimir said to the empty hotel room as he paced back and forth.

"I thought I paid Kyle enough to keep that family away from here! I even let him talk me into using her uncle and the Coast Guard! 'It would look good,' he said, 'It will help the cover-up. Think about it-it will throw off the Secret Service and the Coast Guard will like the chance to highlight their role in national security. And it will spite Rose's father! He's been a thorn in my side, and a roadblock in my career! I'm going to like setting him up!' Well, the money we paid him will soothe Kyle's conscience when it's all over."

Vladimir walked to the mirror. He leaned in close and smiled at himself. He couldn't help gloat over his transformation.

"I look ten years younger! And they thought I was finished! Banished to Siberia! Ah, to have friends in high places! Our poor Russian capitalist president has no idea who really is running the country! As for the Secret Service, they don't worry me! They will be so busy watching the two presidents they will have no idea what is going on below the surface! When the Party brings the Martian Rock home we will be a decade ahead of the U.S.! They will have to wait for the samples from Mars! We will steal it right out from under their noses - and get paid to do it! This will be better than the Moon Rocks!"

He smiled at himself again. "And the very best part is Rose's family will help us do it! Rose can be my ace in the hole! If anything should go wrong, she will be my insurance!"

Turning away from the mirror, he reached for the phone.

On the other side of the country Kyle answered the cell phone in his pocket as he drove along the freeway on the way to trials for the

Westminster Dog Show. It was not The Agency phone he had been issued.

"Yes?" He answered the ring after seeing the caller I.D.

"What is 'she' doing here?" Vladimir asked calmly, but with an angry edge to his voice. "I thought you had them all at the show."

"I didn't have a choice! The Director wouldn't go along with it. He arranged the visit with her parents."

"What about the rest of your plan?" Vladimir asked.

"The diversion is all set up. It will co-ordinate perfectly with the presentation. It will be sweet revenge!"

"There will be no revenge unless the plan goes smoothly! Be sure your plan works or you will be joining me in the cooler."

"Don't worry. I will keep my part rolling. Just don't drop the ball on your end!"

Kyle hung up the phone and smiled. He had an ace in the hole also! If anything did go wrong, he would simply pretend he was working undercover to stop Vladimir.

Either way, he would come out looking like the hero, and Rose's family would be left holding the bag!

He was smiling to himself as he put away the phone. Sure, there would be a record of the call. He was counting on it!

What he didn't count on was Richard. Every plan has a flaw, and Richard was it! Kyle did not know how Richard had already attended the terrorism class he had been diverted to.

Of course we found out about all of this much later

Right now we were returning home from the ride on the cutter.

Abby had fallen asleep on my shoulder as Uncle Matt drove us home. We were all riding in the front seat of the car. I had the window seat and Abby sat in the middle next to her Dad.

I envied her for a moment, and wished I could fall asleep on my father's shoulder.

"Uncle Matt?" I said, breaking the silence.

"Yes, Rose?"

"If I tell you something, you won't laugh will you?"

"Of course not! Why would I?

"Well, it may sound kind of strange. It's about the presentation at Sea World.

"What about it?" He asked as he drove into the sunrise.

"I think something is going to happen there," I said, cautiously.

"Something like what?"

"Something no one will see."

I explained my theory. Uncle Matt listened, but shook his head.

"I can understand why you might think something will happen. Of course, you know The Agency is going to be there as well as the Secret Service. They will be protecting the presidents and the VIPs, as well as the crowd. But a Martian rock? You have a good imagination, Rose."

Uncle Matt did not know my background. Everything that happened to me since I first met Vladimir was classified. He only knew my parents worked for The Agency and his brother was an agent. I couldn't tell him how I knew about Vladimir, and why my crazy theory made sense.

The car pulled into the drive, and I thought about what I'd said. It did sound crazy! I didn't know why I thought anything had to do with the Martian rock at all. It was just a feeling.

But it wouldn't go away!

Chapter Sixteen

The newspapers broke the story the next day. 'ADMIRAL FOODS TO LAUNCH NEW PRODUCT AT SEA WORLD!

US and Russian presidents to sign new agreement at Sea World next week.'

The story was on all the news shows on television, too.

The paperboy had delivered the Anchorage paper and Aunt Rebecca picked it up and laid it on the table that morning.

The paper carried a front-page story of the largest publicity campaign in history being kicked off right here! It talked about being chosen as the site because of its large Russian community and the seaport where the Admiral Foods flagship would depart after being rigged for the most unusual cargo in the world! An iceberg!

Alaska was proud of its heritage, and the natural place for a campaign like this. Donald Price, the CEO of Admiral Foods was pictured in the story along with Michael Mirilav, the man in charge of the campaign. A sidebar to the story covered the dismissal of the Aaron Young, vice president of advertising. Apparently, Mr. Young was upset about the decision to bring an outsider in to handle the campaign.

Mr. Price defended the move, citing Mr. Mirilav's Russian descent and expertise. When asked about the security issues, Mr. Price said Mr. Mirilav had the highest recommendation by The Agency in charge of National Security.

Apparently, Mr. Young had retreated to an undisclosed location to spend time with his family, and could not be reached for comment.

The article did not say much about the new product except how it was rumored to be a new line of Kool-Whip. The details were being kept secret until the official launch at Sea World. A short history of Kool-

Whip followed, and the reporter speculated Admiral Foods was trying to maximize its' investment in the product and advertising campaign.

Other related articles talked about the new trade agreement and the international relations involved. The opinion page wrote pro and con commentaries on private industry directing foreign policy.

Several consumer groups had scheduled protests, and another sidebar worried about terrorist activity at Sea World. There was concern for the safety of the two presidents, as well as the crowds that would gather.

Finally, on the Arts and Entertainment page a story about Aunt Rebecca and her portraits appeared in response to the rumor she and her family would be attending in the VIP section. There was speculation about the reason for the invitation, and when a reporter talked to the artist, she only replied, "no comment'

There were also pictures of the flagship being escorted by the Coast Guard, and an explanation of the special towing rig constructed for the iceberg.

"Sheesh!" I said, finally lowering the paper as Aunt Rebecca set down a plate of eggs and bacon.

"Sheesh, what?" She asked. "You've been reading that paper for half an hour now! What could be so interesting to a young girl except a big sale or rock star?"

"As if you didn't know about the big story." I replied, handing her the paper as Uncle Matt and Abby sat down at the breakfast table.

Aunt Rebecca just smiled, and poured the orange juice.

Precisely at eight a.m. the phone started to ring. And it wasn't going to stop all day.

"Let the machine get it." Uncle Matt said.

Two minutes later the doorbell rang. The phone in Aunt Rebecca's studio rang also, and there was a knock at the back door, too!

"Better eat fast kids! I think we're going to have to make a get-away!" Uncle Matt said, ignoring the doorbell and the knocks.

"Shouldn't we answer the door, Daddy?" Abby asked.

"If we do, we'll never get to eat breakfast!" He explained. "There is probably an army of reporters outside. We'll be answering questions all day!"

"Is that why you took me out of school this week?" Abby asked.

"Smart kid," Matt said to Rebecca as the ringing finally stopped.

"Yes, honey, we knew this would probably happen, and so we arranged for you to have this week and next week off school for a family

vacation. Your school principal is sworn to secrecy. Mr. Mirilav and The
Agency both talked to her."

"Cool!" Abby said to her Dad. "But what about the sleepover? Won't
the reporters bother us then, too?"

"No. Mr. Mirilav has arranged for security for us. We will be staying
on the base. Your friends' parents are being asked to sign a secrecy
statement. Right now, a detail of M.P.'s from the base are on the way
over. They will escort us to the base today, and tomorrow we will have
your party."

"Why didn't you tell us before, Dad?" Abby said. "I thought we'd be
in my own room."

"I'm sorry, Abby. The Agency contacted me last night after you had
gone to bed. They talked to the editors of the papers and knew the story
would be coming out today. It's big news all around the country! They
hadn't thought about our part in all this before. If we hadn't signed the
agreement to keep it secret we wouldn't have to worry about it. We
would just have to put up with reporters all week!"

"If Mom hadn't gotten the contract to paint the Russian President
would we still go to Sea World for my birthday?"

"Of course we would, Sweetheart. We know how much you love
wildlife."

We had all eaten without realizing it, and as if on cue the ringing
and knocking started all over again!

This all seemed familiar to me after the trip to Peru, but it was new
to Abby. I sat quiet for a change and listened. Outside a crowd had gathered, and news vans and reporters were busy telling the story.

Aunt Rebecca turned on the local news on television, and we all
watched the 'attack' of the reporters. We didn't dare peek out the windows!

Two hours later at the Westminster Kennel Club Mom and Dad had
just gotten off the phone with the Director of The Agency.

The video screen at the arena was turned on, broadcasting the news
of 'Today's Top Story'.

"Look, Hon! There's Rebecca's studio!" Mom said, petting Sam as he
sat next to her folding chair.

"I see it," Dad said, a little angry.

They watched as the reporter talked about Rebecca's reputation as
an artist, and showed several portraits she had painted of celebrities,
and even the Governor of Alaska!

Since the artist could not be reached for comment the reporters speculated she had painted a portrait of one of the dignitaries who would be attending Sea World next week. Perhaps one of the presidents! Maybe the Russian president himself or the CEO of Admiral Foods, Donald Price

They showed her picture, and then moved to a story of her husband Matt, a captain in the Coast Guard, and the role they played in escorting the ship out of the harbor.

The Coast Guard commander talked about this opportunity to point out the role that the Guard played in national security and counter-terrorism.

The story moved on to the international issues of the product launch by Admiral foods and several experts were interviewed about security issues involving the two residents meeting in such a public place.

It was great publicity for Sea World and Admiral Foods, a chance to highlight the president's program for international relations, and the role of corporate America.

The stock market was up also, led by a jump in Admiral Food's stock with the announcement of the launch of its new product.

Everyone was impressed with the tight security that had kept the project under wraps for so long.

Everyone but my parents!

Chapter Seventeen

"I can't believe you left us out of the loop on this!" Dad was yelling at the Director of The Agency on his cell phone.

"Now, calm down. I was acting on the advice of the Agent-in-Charge of the Sea World operation. He had it on good authority the Westminster Dog Show was a target for a terrorist hit. With your dog in the competition, it seemed like a natural contract for you."

"And Rose is in Anchorage! How does that work? You told us she would be safer there! Now we find out on television about the Admiral Foods campaign and Rebecca's involvement..."

Dad looked up from the phone at the small group of people entering the arena below.

"I'll call you back," he told the director as he clicked off the phone. Richard looked up at him in the stands and gave him the 'cut' sign when he saw him on the phone.

Dad knew the line was not secure. He stood up and made his way to the arena to greet Richard, Susan, and Steven.

Mom and Sam got there first! Sam was busy licking Richard's hand, and being petted by Susan at the same time. His tail thumped happily!

"Well, this is an unexpected treat!" Mom said as Dad joined the group. "What brings you guys here so early?"

"Well, we were in the neighborhood..." Richard said, smiling as he shook Dad's hand.

"Glad you could drop in." He said. "It's good to see you all. But really, why are you here?"

"Like I said, we were in the neighborhood. I noticed the bag was unzipped, and thought I should see if anything was missing," Richard repeated.

Mom and Dad both knew Richard had information for them, but did not feel like talking here. It wasn't safe.

While Steven took his turn petting Sam, the rest made dinner arrangements. They would find a safe place to talk.

"Why here?" Abby was saying. I sure didn't plan a sleepover at the Coast Guard base!"

"Now, Abby, you know our house is surrounded by reporters. You don't want that either do you?" Uncle Matt tried to calm her down.

Abby wasn't spoiled, but she was upset. I would be too! This whole thing had gotten out of hand!

"And what about Rose's portrait?" Abby turned to her mother. "When is that going to get done? And our sight-seeing?"

"I'll have to finish Rose's portrait after Sea World. We'll still have the weekend before she goes home. Is that okay with you, Rose?"

"Sure, Aunt Rebecca. To tell you the truth I didn't want a portrait. It was Mom's idea. But after the photo shoot the other day, I realized how much fun it might be. And I sure won't mind being painted by a famous artist like you!"

Aunt Rebecca blushed at the compliment.

"What about your other clients?" Uncle Matt asked.

"I don't have any scheduled. I didn't take anything but Rose's portrait over Abby's birthday, and the Sea World trip. It would be impossible to work in the studio now anyway."

"Dad, what about the sleepover?" Abby asked, impatiently.

"Think about it, Abby. How many kids get to have a sleep over on a Coast Guard base? You'll have one the kids will never forget!" Uncle Matt was still trying.

"But won't there be reporters out here, too?" She asked.

"Yes, there probably will be. They are looking for a story and they will probably find one." He nodded.

"Well," Rebecca said, "If they are going to find one anyway, why don't we just give them one?"

"What do you mean, dear?" Matt asked nervously.

"I mean, why don't we go home tonight? If they are out there tomorrow we'll give them a story. We know what we can say, and what we can't. Why not use it to advertise the event at Sea World? Once we talk to them, they will go away."

"Yeah, Dad! Once we talk to them, they will go away!" Abby was smiling again.

"You know, you might be right! Maybe we should go home." Uncle Matt was coming around!

"What do you think, Rose?" Abby asked, pleading with her eyes at me.

"Makes sense to me," I said.

"The ship has already left port. The big news guns will be following her to Sea World. We can talk to the local press and cite security reasons for leaving out certain details," Uncle Matt was on board now.

"Now, that is something I'm familiar with!" I said, leaving out an explanation.

"Of course! Your Dad..." Aunt Rebecca stopped.

"Right. There are things I can't put in my newsletter, too."

"Okay. I'm familiar with classified information also," Uncle Matt said.

"So, when do we get to go home?" Abby asked.

"Tonight, young lady, after supper. By then the local reporters should be gone."

So we all agreed on what to eat, and got ready for Abby's birthday party the next day. I still couldn't wait to give her the digital camera.

And I couldn't wait to get to Sea World. Not just for the big events but also to see what Mr. Mirilav was really up to.

Later that night, back in Abby's house, I dreamt about Grandpa and the dream I remembered from that Thanksgiving so long ago.

There we were, on the deck of the big ship in the Arctic, watching the iceberg as it followed behind us, secured by ropes and chains like some giant whale we had captured.

"So this is where Kool-Whip comes from!" I said as Grandpa smiled and led me to his cabin.

I fell asleep to the gentle rocking of the ship, dreaming of pumpkin pie.

Chapter Eighteen

The muffled sounds drifting up from the kitchen woke me up early. There was still an hour to go before the alarm would ring

It was still dark, and I lay still - listening to someone making coffee, and talking quietly. I recognized the sounds of parents who did not want to wake up the kids

I knew Abby was still sleeping, and thought this might be my chance to talk to Uncle Matt and Aunt Rebecca before the busy day started

I could smell the coffee as I tiptoed barefoot down the carpeted steps. My stomach rumbled, and craved eggs and toast.

Uncle Matt and Aunt Rebecca looked up from the table as I rounded the corner. The conversation stopped, and I saw the look of surprise when they spotted me. They thought it would be Abby

"Well, mornin' Rose. What gets you up so early?" Aunt Rebecca asked

"I smelled the coffee," I said as my stomach rumbled again

"Didn't know you drank coffee." Uncle Matt said

"Good Gracious! Sounds like you're hungry, too!" Aunt Rebecca laughed hearing the rumblings.

Uncle Matt pulled a chair out from the table. I sat down while Aunt Rebecca put bread in the toaster, and took out the eggs.

This was a rare time, and I was happy to have some time alone with them. I smiled back at Aunt Rebecca as she poured a glass of orange juice for me, and asked if I wanted coffee instead

I felt like an adult and a veteran traveler. This gave me the confidence to bring up my theory

"I really don't drink coffee, but I like the smell of it. Sometimes, at home, when my parents are up early, and I need to talk to them about something important, I get up early and sit with them like this in the kitchen. Then we can talk before the busy day starts.

The eggs crackled and spit in the pan as the toast popped up. Soon we were all eating, and I knew Abby would be up soon. Then the birthday would officially start, and my chances of talking would be gone.

"Is there something you wanted to talk to us about, Rose?" Uncle Matt asked.

"Yes, Uncle Matt. It's about Mr. Mirilav."

"What about him?" Uncle Matt replied, a worried tone in his voice.

"He's not who you think he is." I said.

"Who is he then?"

"The man who kidnapped me and Aunt Susan and took us to Russia!"

"What?" There was shock in both of their voices.

I briefly told them the story, and answered their questions. I didn't care about security anymore. They were family, and I needed them to listen.

"And I think he's up to something! The coincidence of me being here now and going to Sea World…"

"If that's true, what do you think we should do?" Uncle Matt asked.

"I don't know. On the surface everything looks okay. Just a coincidence about Abby's birthday and Sea World coming at the same time as the dog show… my family split up and for some reason afraid to talk on the phone. I'm just thinking out loud now, but I know The Agency will have plenty of security at the unveiling. Vladimir looks different - but I know it's him. He was supposed to be in prison, so he must be working for someone in the Russian government. Maybe there is an assassination planned, but there will be too many cameras and security there. National and world news, too! That's why I think there is something else going on."

"Wow! You sure have been around! You sound like your Dad. But what else would he be up to - and why would The Agency say he was okay? Could he be a double agent? Is he working for us now? Maybe he has a new life, and is what he says he is and maybe he is not Vladimir after all," Uncle Matt was not convinced.

"If he is Vladimir - and he's not here to shoot anyone, then what would he be up to?" Aunt Rebecca was thinking it over.

"Well, that's where it gets a little wilder!" I said, laying out my theory about the Mars Rock, and the steps leading me to it.

Uncle Matt stood up and smiled as he pushed his chair in.

"Rose, I know you've been around, and your story sounds okay - but I'm not convinced about your theory," he said.

"It's possible," Aunt Rebecca said, "I've heard all the stories about the research in the Arctic, the global warming, and the disappearance of the Larsen Ice Shelf…"

"Look, I know how important this is to you both, and I sure would not want to spoil things for you or Abby. Maybe my theory is wrong but I know that man is Vladimir. All I'm asking is that you check it out. Put somebody on your crew to watch him. If I am right and he is Vladimir, remember he is a kidnapper and a Russian spy. He kidnapped a twelve-year-old girl for heaven's sake!"

"Now that makes me mad! Okay Rose, I'll put someone on to watch him. I sure wish I could talk to your parents…" Uncle Matt trailed off.

"They would never have sent me if they knew he was here! Someone in The Agency must be working with him. I know it's not safe to talk to my parents right now, and we don't want to tip him off. If The Agency is involved we can't trust them either. If we find out he is up to something, we'll have to stop him ourselves."

The alarm went off in my room, and I could hear Abby's feet hit the floor. Breakfast Number One was over.

Upstairs we could hear the sound of Abby's voice in the bathroom.

"Happy Birthday to me…Happy Birthday to me…"

The day was off and running!

Chapter Nineteen

There was a lot to do for Abby's birthday! Aunt Rebecca asked me to blow up balloons and help her hang up decorations. I turned blue in the face a few times on the balloons!

All of Abby's friends from school would be coming at five that afternoon for the party. There would be ten girls from Abby's class at school and two boys. The boys were coming a little reluctantly after being teased by the other guys in Abby's class. But they were friends. Only half of the kids would be coming for the sleepover, and the boys were not staying!

Sheesh! Good thing!

Abby talked a mile a minute at the breakfast table, and didn't even seem to mind we had already eaten. She was content to wait for her presents until the party.

The reporters had given up on us, or so it seemed. Uncle Matt had been right about that. They were following the story of the big ship and the iceberg being towed to Sea World. They would probably be back after the big events.

Aunt Rebecca had ordered a cake from the local bakery and buckets of chicken for the party. We would pick that up later.

I waited for the phone call from my parents

My parents were busy also. The dog show was set to be on TV the same day as the big events at Sea World. Dad was busy supervising his small staff of security agents, and Mom was watching Sam and his handler rehearse in the ring. The actual dog show would take place this weekend, and be televised on Monday.

It was a well-orchestrated show, complete with politics and bribes to judges. There was a lot of money in pets - especially dogs. The dog food companies had lobbied hard in the background for a big dog winner this year. Big dogs eat more.

Politics or not, Sam was in Dog Heaven. He loved the attention, and the sense of purpose he got from competition. Newfies were working dogs, and never happier than when they felt they were of service. They also loved kids, were natural guardians and lifesavers. "Good protection for a young girl", Mother was always saying.

When we were at home, Sam was always at my side - - under my feet or on my bed. I used to fall asleep on him in front of the TV.

When I wasn't home, he moped and whined. At least at the dog show he could keep his mind occupied!

Dad's mind was occupied with security. He took his job seriously, and even though this job was not as big as some of the ones in his government career, it was just as important. But the staff he was working with at Westminster was experienced and knowledgeable. He was impressed with their crowd control, surveillance, and was satisfied with the general security.

What they needed was his experience in other fields. Agency work and international assignments as well as counter-intelligence and terrorist training.

Still, Dad felt that any of his former Agency team members could have handled this assignment. His mind was on Sea World and the familiar high-stakes security he was used to.

"Sheesh!" He had said at dinner with Richard and Susan and Steven. "What a rock/hard place scenario!"

"It's obvious that someone in The Agency wants us out of the way," Richard said. "They split us up and send us to opposite corners under perfectly natural-seeming circumstances. Meanwhile, someone at The Agency, Kyle, probably, gets the big, juicy assignment you'd have had if you were still on the inside. I'll bet he's the one who put the bug in the director's ear about Westminster."

"You might be right, Richard," Steven nodded, "I did some nosing around, and found there's hard evidence about a terrorist attack on the dog show. Doesn't mean it's not a real threat, but all eyes are on Sea World."

"And Rose is out there!" Mom said. "At the director's suggestion - I might add!"

"But at least she's with Matt and Rebecca. Your brother is getting a lot of overdue recognition for the Coast Guard. It's about time someone pointed out their role in Homeland Security."

"Amen!" Dad said, nodding. "I feel better with Rose being there, as far as that goes."

"But talk about high profile!" Mom said. "Rebecca was just mentioned on the news, and there is speculation she had a personal sitting with the Russian president to finish his portrait to be presented at the Admiral Foods launch next week! Rose is the youngest member of our team, and she's the one sitting on the powder keg! Is it possible someone wanted her out there?"

Dad stood up abruptly, his chair catching on the thick carpet and falling over, causing quite a stir among the guests at the posh little hotel restaurant.

"I can't take it anymore! We're leaving!" He said in an unusual loss of control.

"Whoa!" Richard said. "Remember what you always tell us? Keep your head. It's not that simple. If Rose is a pawn, we could put her in real danger by tipping our hand. Then there is the dog show. Real or not, something is going on - and your wife and Sam need you there."

"Do you have any better ideas?" Dad asked.

"I do!" Steven said.

So, here it was, Abby's birthday, and even though Uncle Steven's plan was in motion, Dad was anxious - and he was thinking about Sea World. He looked at his watch.

Waving to Mom, he pointed at his wrist. "Time to call Rose."

The phone rang just before the first of Abby's friends pulled up to the curb.

Chapter Twenty

I sprang for the phone. "Hello?" I said.

"Rose, honey, is that you?"

"Hi Mom! Yeah, it's me! How is Sam?"

"He's fine, dear. He's doing great. I think he has a chance of winning!"

"I know he does! Can I talk to him?" I asked, tears welling up in my eyes.

"Don't you want to talk to your Dad?" She asked.

"Duh! Of course I do! But maybe we should put Abby on first, her friends are arriving for the party."

I waved Abby over, away from the door, and one of her friends who had just handed her a present on the way in. Aunt Rebecca took charge of the arriving guests, and Uncle Matt came over to the phone with Abby.

"Happy birthday, Abby!" Mom said

I waited until the phone had been passed around on both ends, thinking of a way to talk about 'other' things over an open line.

Uncle Matt had taken the phone after Abby, and from the look on his face I figured he was talking to Dad.

"Oh, she's fine!" He said. "No trouble at all! We might just have to keep her longer," he said, smiling and winking at me. He was quiet for a while, listening and nodding as Dad talked.

When I finally got to talk to him, I still didn't know what to say.

"Guess what, Dad. I think I need a new suitcase! Mine is ripped open!"

"How did that happen?" He asked. "Did you catch it on something?"

"Yeah, a sharp point. I'm not sure where or when though. I've looked around and think I know how it happened.

"Well, a good suitcase is hard to find these days. You'll just have to wait until next week. We may be able to send you one. Perhaps your Uncle Matt could help you out?"

"Good idea! I think we could look around out here! I don't like shopping on-line, though. Too many hackers. Wish we could just Zip through it like the old days! Seems like a lot of trouble to go through for just an old suitcase. Especially one from overseas!"

"Well, Rose, honey, it is an old case. You shouldn't be so fussy. Mom has connections at some of the local businesses, and she can find some good leads for you. Right now you should get back to the party. We'll call tomorrow before the big trip!"

"Okay, Dad. Love you! Now can I talk to Sam?"

I choked back the homesick tears from the phone call, and wiped my eyes. At least Dad and I had understood each other. I hoped he was proud of the way I talked in code. Anyone listening from The Agency might have figured it out but anyone else would have thought I was just a fussy rich girl upset over an old suitcase.

It was a chance we had to take.

Car after car pulled up to the curb, and suddenly the house was full of girls! The two lonely boys seemed caught between us and Uncle Matt - probably wondering what in the world they were doing here!

If anyone were going to sneak into the house, this would have been the time to do it! The noise level rose steadily, and soon the birthday party was at full throttle!

It must have been a dangerous place for any male because Uncle Matt slipped out to get the chicken, taking the two boys with him!

I wondered how he could have left us alone!

What I didn't know then was Uncle Matt had arranged for some of his off-duty crew to watch the house during the party.

Some of the things I had told him, and the recent events with the Sea World connection had given him an uneasy feeling. Having a young daughter himself, he thought about the possibility of her being kidnapped, and talked to some of his friends

So we were safe for the party, which lasted until bedtime.

Abby opened her presents, and saved mine for last.

"Oh, Rose! I love it! A digital camera! We can use it at Sea World!"

I won't bore you with the rest of the details, but finally, two relieved boys left the party. They did not even consider staying around to spy on the girls for the sleepover!

Especially after Aunt Rebecca put Uncle Matt in charge of the cleanup crew!

"Nobody goes anywhere until every paper plate is in the bag, and the deck is cleared!" He announced.

One by one we filed up to the giant yard bag with our plates, cups, and plastic forks.

Aunt Rebecca smiled as Abby said, "Aye, Aye, Sir!" and led the way, giving him a salute as the trash went into the bag, setting a precedent copied by every girl in the place! Including me.

When the dining room - excuse me - Mess Hall, was clean, we marched to the steps and down to the family room - where the real party would start!

As I brought up the rear, I smiled at Aunt Rebecca, who hooked arms with her husband and said, "There are some advantages to being a military wife."

Finally free from the eyes of Captain Hook we hit the couches and pillows and sleeping bags ready to talk about- what else? Boys

Being the oldest one there - and an outsider at that, I listened more than I talked. That was unusual for me, being a rambler and all. But finally they had exhausted the local gossip - which everyone seemed to know anyway, and turned to me.

"What about you, Rose? I'll bet you have lots of boyfriends!" One of them asked.

"Yeah, I've read your newsletter on the Internet! You've been around the world! What are the boys like in Russia? Are they like the Russian boys who live here?"

"Boys are the same no matter where you go," I said, in a worldly way. I had their full attention now, and I knew once I started ramblin' it would be hard to stop

I looked at Abby, not wanting to take the attention from her, but she was as anxious to hear about my adventures as the rest of them! I had to be careful about what I told them.

"Tell us the things you couldn't write about!" They said.

"Yeah, tell us about the things you didn't tell your parents!"

Sheesh! As if there was anything to tell!

So I told them about Dimitri, Paolo, and even Shane - the boy I met at the airport on the way here who had tried to steal my CD player.

Soon, the popcorn was gone, the movie was over, and one by one the room full of pajamas was falling asleep.

The sound of silence drifted down the carpeted steps. Uncle Matt and Aunt Rebecca had gone to bed, and only the hum of the refrigerator was left, lulling me into sleep, too

Like I said before, if anyone was going to sneak into the house, a good time would have been at the party with all of the noise.

But they didn't. They waited until the middle of the night.

Chapter Twenty-One

It was two a.m., and something woke Aunt Rebecca from her sleep. She lay awake perfectly still in a shaft of moonlight sneaking around the edge of the shade and listened

She knew the sounds of the house. She filtered out Matt's snoring and the refrigerator. Her sharp ears even reached down to the family room, and scanned the sounds of all the sleeping kids

She heard the occasional popping of a nail as the house grew used to the cold, and even heard the brittle night wind coming down from the Arctic.

There wasn't anything unusual at all.

But something had awakened her.

She told herself she was being overly protective with all the kids in the house. Other people's children, yes, but still in her home - and just as precious.

With all the excitement in their lives right now, it was only natural her senses would be heightened!

But she trusted her instincts.

She pushed on Matt a few times trying to wake him, but he was deep in sleep, and she knew it was hopeless.

Some protector, she thought, and decided to investigate herself.

She got out of bed silently, the way you can only deep in the night and checked the alarm panel in the bedroom without turning on the light.

The indicator was steady, and she knew it was working. Still, something pulled at her like a gentle ghostly hand and she glided quietly down the carpeted steps to check on the doors and windows as she had so many times before when Matt had been away at night.

The front door was locked and silent, nothing to tell. The back door, too. That left the studio.

She held the bolt as she unlocked the inner door connecting the studio to the house, trying to make as little noise as possible

Her heart beat faster as she stepped into the studio, bare feet hitting the cold, tiled floor.

Still being cautious, Rebecca left the lights turned off. The eerie silhouettes of the canvasses stood motionless in the moonlight. Some of them were draped; some were not. All of them seemed to be just as she had left them.

She stood and stared at the outside door. It gave no signs of recent use, and Rebecca began to think there was nothing to worry about after all.

Then she thought of the darkroom.

Her heartbeat had been slowing down, but was on the rise again! There was an unmistakable feeling of someone having been in the room recently, and she approached the door slowly.

She stood outside the door afraid her slamming heart would give her away.

Finally, conquering the urge to turn and run, she boldly turned the knob and swung the door open

Nothing.

Switching on the light she surveyed the narrow closet-sized room.

Everything was in its' place. Abby's pictures of Rose clipped to the runner line just as they had left them.

Then she saw it!

One picture was missing!

It was the picture Abby had taken of Mr. Mirilav from the upstairs window. They had left it here, hadn't they?

If so, who would break in to take it - and why? And how did they get past the alarm system without setting it off?

It must be someone with advanced technology training and experience. An agent? Surely not a reporter!

Instead of being reassured by the lack of a prowler, Rebecca was more uneasy than ever. Not only had their house been violated, but also the alarm system had failed to warn them! She no longer felt safe in her own home.

Sure, when they first talked to Mirilav, they wondered about the wisdom of having him come to the studio for a sitting. It was a remarkably risky thing to do. Almost reckless!

But they had been caught up in the excitement of the situation, and impressed with Mr. Mirilav's influence to set such a thing up. Not only set it up - but also have the Russian president agree to it!

Monumental egos at work! And hers was no exception!

The press would have a field day with the story, and Rebecca wondered now if their house would be free from publicity ever again!

What were we thinking? She asked herself.

She thought about my story. The picture was the only thing placing Mirilav at their home. Though he was always quoted in connection to the Admiral Foods story, his picture was rarely seen. He kept a low profile, only appearing in person when necessary.

With me in the house, Mirilav might have a reason to worry about the picture he knew was taken. If he were indeed, Vladimir, he would have a reason to steal the picture that might link him to her.

The upcoming launch of Admiral Foods' new Kool-Whip, the world and economic factors that went with it were just too much to risk! The release of the picture could ruin the whole plan.

Rebecca was now convinced I was right, and it would change everything!

Chapter Twenty-Two

Like any good agent, Mr. Mirilav sat in his room going over the plan. Tomorrow he would leave for Sea World and the busy week ahead. It would be twice as busy for him!

On the one hand he had to play the top executive in the biggest advertising campaign in history, and on the other hand he was the top agent in the biggest technological rip-off in history!

This one operation could change the balance of power in the world!

"I sure hope this rock is worth the trouble!" He said to himself.

He recalled the conversation with the scientists in Siberia.

"The information is top secret, Vladimir!"

"Yes, I know, Pachenko! But we are both loyal to the old line. This time, however, we have the backing of the government! If I am to be in charge of this operation I need to know everything!"

"You only need to know what they tell you! You only need to know your part of the plan! Your part is to lead the publicity campaign for Admiral Foods. Your job is to keep The Agency at bay. Your job is to see that all eyes are focused on the surface events, and not the extraction of the rock from the iceberg."

Pachenko pushed the swivel chair away from his desk and stood up.

"This conversation is over," he said.

"It is not over. You have gone to a lot of trouble to get me to this 'prison', this secret research center. I have lost weight and re-shaped my body and my face! I have studied for months for this assignment. You have told me this operation will change the balance of power in the world, and restore the Old Party! 'The Soviet Union will rise again', you said. If this is true, if you trust me to pull this off, then why don't you trust me with all of the facts?"

Pachenko sighed. It was too late to find someone else. Mirilav must appear at Admiral Foods soon. The timing was politically perfect. The United States was actively involved in a private venture with Admiral Foods and its plan to launch its new Kool-Whip in Russia. Many careers now depended on a successful launch of the project.

More than that, here was a chance to get a jump on the U.S. For years they had led the space program while The Soviet Union struggled to finance its own program. The once glorious project was now space junk for museums and collectors.

When the United States brought home the moon rocks, they locked them up and refused to share their secrets until they had studied them first. The Star Wars program would see to it the Soviets would never have them.

So, we stole them. What choice did we have? The U.S. never admitted to it. How embarrassing that their precious rocks had disappeared! Now, the Martian rock at the bottom of the Arctic - so close to Siberia, and our hands - could be ours! The U.S. had said the Martian rocks would be arriving sometime this decade. One sample could prove our theory and provide a weapon making us invincible!

And here was a sample buried in the ice! Oh, how many people would never know why the Larsen B Ice Shelf really disappeared, or why so many experiments were really being done in the Arctic. Or why, the average temperature in Alaska was slowly rising!

But we do! And the United States - so mighty - was afraid. Afraid we would find a way to dig the rock from the ice and the minerals buried within! Minerals not found on Earth! One in particular, named Pachenko!

"Okay, Vladimir. Come to the laboratory. I will tell you a story."

Vladimir smiled as he followed Pachenko down the white-walled corridor to the labs. This was a part of the 'prison' the outside world would never see!

Passing the benches full of men in white coats, he followed the head scientist to a room beyond.

Soon, they were seated in a small lecture room, and Pachenko held a remote to run the slide show.

The lights dimmed, and Pachenko began his story as an image of Mars filled the room.

"Research has led us to believe the planet Mars was not always void of life. There was a race of people, and beings not unlike our own. They would have been dark-skinned to protect them from the closer proximity to the sun, and the ozone layer would have been thicker than Earth."

Click. Artists' conceptions filled the screen. Images of humanoid people, animals and mammals not unlike the ones on the Antarctic or the Eskimos.

"Something happened on Mars," Pachenko continued. "Not an asteroid. All planets are bombarded daily. We think it was a biological time bomb. A mineral found in such abundance it was of no more value than dirt."

Vladimir leaned forward in his seat. Here was something he knew about. Like the clay producing the world's fine porcelain.

"What is this mineral called?" He asked.

"Why, Pachenko! What else? Named for the man who discovered it!" The scientist answered.

"What does it contain that could destroy a world?" Vladimir continued his questioning

"Air, lots of air." Pachenko said, smiling.

"I don't understand," Vlad was confused.

"You see," he said, "the molecular structure of this mineral was full of space. It is lightweight, pliable, and appears when processed like a metal. When it is compressed the friction of the molecules increases, and it becomes as hard as it once was pliable. Compress it even more, and its power outgrows its physical realm! BOOM!"

"But, Mars did not explode." Vladimir stated, confused.

"Of course not! But still the metal permeated the planet. Like our trees taking the poisonous carbon dioxide out of the air and giving off life-giving oxygen, Pachenko sucks the oxygen from the air as it decays over time." Pachenko gave Vladimir a moment to absorb the information. Then he gave him some more. " Soon there is not enough oxygen in the atmosphere to feed the hungry rock."

Click. Vladimir watched the slide show as Mars began to deteriorate, choking on its own dust.

"The atmosphere, now short on oxygen, begins to suffocate, depriving the planet of rain. The surface becomes a desert as the vegetation begins to die. No longer able to clean the air or grow, the plants are soon gone. People are driven from the surface by the harsh conditions. They go below. Technology crumbles as the raw materials dry up. Soon, the surface is barren, worn down by constant wind and sand. The Pachenko leeches into the atmosphere, and eats away at the ozone layer. The planet becomes more susceptible to meteors as the atmosphere thins. The sun dries up the remaining water, leaving only the canals. Pieces of the planet ricochet from meteor strikes, flying out into space.

One lands in our Arctic zone millions of years ago, eventually being trapped in the Arctic ice."

Vladimir watched the computer simulation on the screen.

"And this is the rock we must sneak out from under the noses of the world?"

"Yes. Our tests show the element, or mineral, Pachenko is contained in the rock. This is what the United States does not want us to have. It has been too cold, and too deep, to extract - and it will be another hundred years before the Pachenko in the rock will eventually eat away its icy prison. If we could get it to warm water, extract it and duplicate its properties..."

Pachenko looked at the screen, his voice trailing off into his own twilight zone.

So, Vladimir shook his head, and was once again in his hotel room. All of his hard work, the preparation was about to pay off!

From bribing the jealous Kyle at The Agency, to splitting up the one family Vladimir feared, to orchestrating the publicity, and supervising the deception allowing them to tow the coveted iceberg to Sea World and the distraction that would remove the capitalist traitor from the Russian Presidency and embarrass the United States, no step had not been thought of!

Mirilav looked down at the small table by the bed. Pulling his little finger absentmindedly, back into place, he picked up the snapshot taken by the girl.

The one photographic link that would place him at the home of the artist, Rebecca! He thought about how easy it had been for the agent he had sent to retrieve it!

Chapter Twenty-Three

Kyle smiled as he rode in the black Suburban through the gates at Sea World.

"What a perfect plan!" He said to himself. "At last! The director listens to me instead of that middle-aged egotistical…ah, but no matter! When this was over - no one would hire that family again! I'll be the Number One Agent In Charge of Security! "

He patted himself on the back as the car full of agents approached the Main Office.

"And that meddling Rose! Well, here is a chance for Vladimir to get his revenge! I owe him that much for his help embarrassing her family! Of course, Vlad might get away with her as a hostage but I needed to win his help. Tit for Tat. Who cares about an old rock anyway? The chance to foil a hit on the Russian president will secure my future forever! Of course, no one will know it's staged, just like the one at the dog show! I'll save the day here, and Rose's precious dad will watch helplessly as "terrorists" attack the dog show! "Kidnapping" the judge is a stroke of genius on my part if I do have to say it myself!"

He smiled as he walked inside to the waiting army of agents.

"Now to put it all into motion!"

The average visitor to Sea World would not have noticed too much out of the ordinary as they walked through the gates, except for the large Admiral Foods flagship - which was really a cruise liner owned by Admiral Foods, used to host business meetings, and special events. Oh, and there was a large iceberg floating behind it.

It seemed like a natural air conditioner as the Pacific winds blew across the ice, bringing a chill to the air around the west side of the park.

It was a crowded place anyway, especially now with news of the big events taking place on Monday.

There was a lot of activity by the whale tank though, where a stage had been set up, with several men in black suits and earphones stood guard while workers put the last touches on the podium.

The stage was covered in red, white and blue - crowned with two flags, the Russian's and the Stars and Stripes. Floating above the whole thing was a big white banner that said, "Admiral Foods".

Saturday night, Abby and I camped out on the overnighter. She was excited about all the pictures she would take tomorrow with her new camera, and all the marine animals we would see.

"Rose!" Are you awake?"

"I am now! Abby, it's two o'clock in the morning! You have to get some sleep or you will be too tired tomorrow! I have to get some sleep!" I said, exasperated.

"How can you sleep with all this happening?"

"Training. Now leave me alone!" I snapped as I grabbed the blankets and rolled over in a huff!

At least I had gotten the top bunk!

It was finally quiet! Abby held her tongue, and eventually fell asleep. But now I couldn't!

I had noticed a lot of things today as we walked around the grounds. Men in suits were everywhere! My eyes had instinctively looked up and spotted watchers on the rooftops. There were small surveillance cameras, heads bobbing up now and then, squelches of radios drifting down from the outposts.

Even the trees were watching. Here and there a wire ran up a trunk. When one is tuned into an Agency member, they notice more than other people.

I saw signs of The Agency everywhere.

The T.V. cameras and reporters didn't seem to notice. The stage was surrounded by news vans, parked at a secure distance.

Reporters and cameramen were taping the stories in advance and commentaries were being rehearsed in the newsrooms around the world!

The only event that would match it was the Westminster Dog Show.

Now my mind went there, and I wished I were with Mom and Dad and Sam.

I fell asleep dreaming we were all in the same place, only I couldn't tell if it was here or there...

It was five a.m. Sunday morning, and both Mom and Dad were up getting ready for the day.

"You know what to do?" Dad asked as they drank coffee in their room.

"Of course. How about you?"

"Yeah, I think I've got it down. Richard's plan is a good one. I'm glad he will be here. I don't know if I can trust the crew."

"Well, we'll find out today! I hope Susan and Steven make it to Sea World okay."

"They will. Their disguises are perfect. I hope Stevens hair all grows back!"

"Yeah, he looks pretty funny bald," Mom laughed.

"And the rings in his ears..." Dad shook his head.

"I thought the phony biker tattoos were a good touch! And Susan as a biker chick! Pregnant as she is!"

"I just hope there's enough in our budget to cover the Harley!" Dad said.

"Don't worry. My company will use it in a promotion when this is all over."

"Let's hope no one will think it's unusual for a couple of bikers to be flying to the West Coast. Good thing our friendly stewardess will be there to get them on the plane."

"Yes," Mom said. "If she wasn't Richard's girlfriend I don't know if we could trust her either."

"When will they pick up the bike?" Dad asked.

"As soon as they leave the airport they will go right to the shop. The bike is already paid for. They'll go straight to Sea World and look for Matt and Rebecca."

"Richard was right, the only way to get a message to them is to talk to them in person. I'm sure Kyle is behind this plan to keep us split up, and out of the loop," Dad slammed his right fist into his open left palm.

"Me too. I just wonder what's going to happen here at the dog show," Mom put her cup down and stood up from the table

"Yeah, and what's going to happen at Sea World," Dad added.

"Any idea what Richard will be wearing?" Mom asked as they left the room, and walked down the carpeted hallway.

"No, he wouldn't say. Doesn't want us to give him away by looking for him. He'll be in the crowd somewhere."

"Well, let's get Sam," Mom said. "It's a big day for him too."

Chapter Twenty-Four

Sunday night was a big night! It was hard to sleep even back in our hotel room. I sat at the dining table in our hotel suite; chin resting in my hands, looking out at the lights on the water.

There was the Admiral Foods ship and at least a dozen smaller boats around it. One of them was the Coast Guard cutter usually piloted by Uncle Matt. His crew was on board, and Uncle Matt was technically on leave

The full moon danced on the water, and rippled the lights. It was a pretty sight. But underneath that pretty sight was a lot of activity

At Uncle Matt's order, the cutter initiated sonar scans of the area around the ship and the iceberg itself. Normally, sonar around the ship would have been enough for security but after reconsidering my 'theory', Uncle Matt had expanded the area to include the iceberg

So far, all was quiet

Abby had finally given up and gone to bed, tucked in by her parents and assured all the excitement of the coming day when her mother would be on stage with all the dignitaries to unveil her portrait of the Russian president

"I'll have my new camera ready!" She assured them.

"And you'll need all your rest, too," Aunt Rebecca told her as she tucked her in. "A good photographer needs to be alert!"

"Good night, Rose," they said to me as they left the room.

"Good night," I replied from the other bed.

"Good night, Rose, see you tomorrow!" Abby said as the light switched off, and the door closed.

"Good night, Abby. See you tomorrow!"

Soon the suite was quiet, almost too quiet. I couldn't sleep. I finally got out of bed in my pajamas and went into the dining room.

So I opened the blinds, and stared at the lights on the water, thinking about everything all at once and especially, Sam.

Rose? Is that you?" Aunt Rebecca said as she opened her door.

"Yes," I said quietly.

"What are you doing up so late."

"Couldn't sleep. I miss Sam. I wish I could be there tomorrow. It's a big day for him, and I have missed the whole thing," I sniffled.

"I know. It's a big day all around. I hope you know what it means to Abby to have you here. Me, too." Aunt Rebecca stood behind me, and put her hands on my shoulders. I missed my mother's touch.

"You know," I said, "I used to dream about going places, and doing exciting things; how much fun it would be! But now that I have, I realize it's not all fun and games. You think I'd be used to being homesick by now."

Aunt Rebecca pulled up a chair next to mine.

"You know, Rose, it's okay to be homesick. If you ever stop being homesick, then you have something to worry about."

We sat quiet, side by side for a while, looking out at the lights.

Soon, I was alone again.

"Grandpa, please send a message to Sam for me. Tell him I love him and I wish I was there."

I like to think that all the way back in his kennel at Madison Square Garden; Sam got the message, and smiled in his sleep.

"Rose! Time to get up!" Abby was shaking me awake.

"What time is it?" I asked groggily, wondering how I had gotten back into bed.

"Six o'clock! Time to rock!"

I groaned. Six o'clock was just too darned early!

We sat around the dining table having breakfast, and going over the plan for the day. It was Monday morning, and the Big Events were taking place at last!

"Okay, Rebecca, have you got your itinerary for the day?" Uncle Matt asked.

"Yes, it starts at eight this morning with interviews and photos with the local media. At nine we meet with the two presidents and their entourages and more reporters. Ten o'clock with the president of Admiral Foods, and at eleven we all hit the stage for the unveiling at noon."

"Which just so happens to meet head-on with the start of the Westminster Dog Show on the East Coast," Matt added.

"How about you? Have you got the plan down for your day?" She asked.

"Well, I'll be spending the morning with the girls, and checking in with the crew on the cutter. At eleven we will be in our front row seats just in front of the stage to watch the unveiling."

"And I'll be wearing my headphones, and watching the Dog Show on my cell phone!" I said.

"And I'll be taking pictures! Award-winning pictures with my new camera!" Abby said, smiling.

Soon there was a knock at the door. Matt answered, and after checking the I.D.s of the two men, let them into the room.

"Rebecca? My name is Kyle. I'm here to be your escort this morning. This is Agent Vance, he'll be escorting you also."

"Kyle?" I thought. The name sounded familiar. I remembered Dad talking about Kyle. He didn't seem to like him much. My 'spidey-sense' was tingling!

"Shall we get started?" Kyle asked, holding the door for Rebecca.

At least I knew he was with The Agency! I decided to say nothing, and just smile as they left.

"Come on, girls!" Uncle Matt said. "We have a big morning ahead! Abby, got your camera ready?"

"Sure do, Dad," she replied, jumping down from her chair, and racing for her bag.

"How 'bout you, Rose? Ready for the big day?"

"10-4 - I mean - Aye, aye, sir!" I saluted as I picked up my trusty canvas bag, reaching for the cell phone, and the headphones. I wanted to be ready when Sam made his big appearance!

"By the way, Uncle Matt," I said as we walked down the carpeted hall to the elevators, "I thought I fell asleep at the table last night."

"You did," he said. "I carried you back to bed. You were talking in your sleep."

"What was I saying?"

"You said, 'Good night, Sam'."

Chapter Twenty-Five

Mom and Dad watched Sam go through the paces with his handler.
"Bravo!" Mom said.

"He sure looks like a winner!" Dad said.

"Well, I was a little worried about him yesterday. He seemed depressed. Probably lonesome for Rose. But this morning he seems much better."

"He probably gets homesick once in a while," Dad said. "I know I do."

"Well, it will all be over tomorrow," Mom, sighed.

"Amen to that! This is the last time I listen to the director! From now on, we stay together. Us, Rose and the team!"

"If we get anymore Agency jobs."

"I thought about that too. There is plenty of money in the private sector. We can stay there. We don't need The Agency anymore."

"I just wonder what is supposed to happen today," Mom said.

"Whatever it is probably won't happen until tomorrow. If it is a 'terrorist' plot they'll want maximum viewers, and we are up against the events at Sea World. Today is the presentation of the portrait and the official handshake of the two countries, tomorrow will be specials about life in Russia and interviews with Rebecca and other people as well as a special on Sea World. They estimate the country's viewers will be split pretty evenly between the two events."

"Yes, I heard the Westminster Dog Show is the longest running sports presentation in the country second only to the Kentucky Derby."

"One way or another, all eyes will be on us and Rose," Dad said as they stood up from the padded chairs at ringside to welcome Sam back from his practice run.

Dad and Mom split up as the spectators began to pour in for the show. Dad went to the Security Office to watch the monitors, and talk to the team.

As the seats filled up, he looked for signs of suspicious people and Richard, who would be in disguise.

He felt better knowing Richard would be there to watch his back. He had reviewed the profiles of all the security team members, and could find nothing suspicious in any of them. But then again, money will make people do things they wouldn't normally do.

He decided to run a check of all their bank accounts.

While the check was running he watched the outside monitors.

A small group was protesting the commercialization of pets and shouting accusations of pay-offs. They were citing the public's abuse of the winning breeds, charging how people often pick a pet unsuited for them because they are suddenly stars.

Dad knew the Westminster echoed these same concerns, and reinforced the message with every show. He decided to watch the group in case they were a cover.

Generally, protests at the Westminster were rare and peaceful. He turned his attention to the announcers who were pre-recording information about the lighting of the Empire State Building.

"This year, again, the Empire State Building will honor the Westminster by being lit in the Purple and Gold colors of the Kennel Club on Monday night. Tuesday the tower will be lit in red in honor of Valentine's Day."

"Absolutely right, Dave," the other announcer said. "You know, the Empire State Building has a history of being lit in different colors to celebrate holidays and major events. The building is beautiful when it's lit and featured on postcards and calendars around the world. It is quite an honor for the Westminster Kennel Club to have the building lit in its colors."

"It certainly is, Joe, and it shows how much New Yorkers have embraced this event, indeed, the whole country. And what a great way to point out the value of these dogs, and their service to society."

Dad turned from the monitor to scan the crowd again. The report on the financials came back, but showed nothing unusual.

But then again, there was always cash

Cash may be king, but Susan and Steven were glad for electronic funds transfers when they strolled into the Harley-Davidson dealer to pick up their new bike.

The salesman who handed them the keys was just a little perplexed when he checked their I.D.s and saw their bike had been paid in full.

He was still scratching his head as they mounted the bike and drove away. Susan turned to smile back at him. The salesman himself could not have afforded that bike - and here were two - well - what the heck was he doing wrong, anyway?

Agents, agents, everywhere! Every place we went that morning I could spot them! They were at every concession stand, every pool or cage, on every roof and behind every tree! The security here was intense!

And under all this attention, Vladimir, a.k.a, Mr. Mirilav, was up to something!

I could feel agents watching me, too. Certain ones probably connected to The Agency. This was in addition to the ones watching Uncle Matt.

Happily, Abby seemed not to notice, and continued taking her 'award winning' photos.

Something still nagged at me about Agent Kyle. Of course! He had always been jealous of Dad. Always in his shadow, Dad had said. And here was the biggest security event in history! And my father not running it!

Still, on the surface it all made sense. Everything seemed logical. Who could question any of it?

But that 'spidey-sense' would not stop tingling!

Could Kyle have something to do with Mr. Mirilav?

Chapter Twenty-Six

"Earth to Rose! Come in Rose!" Abby was waving her hand in front of my face.

"What..." I started to say.

"Where have you been? You've been like that all morning. You've missed almost everything."

"I'm sorry, Abby. I guess there's just too much going on, and I keep trying to figure it out. Where's your Dad?"

"He got a call from the cutter. He said he was going to take it in the rest room. He'll be back in a minute. We are supposed to wait for him here."

I looked around. The rest rooms were about fifty feet away. We were standing in a clear spot, watching couples and families milling about. The Admiral was behind us and we were facing the park's entrance.

There was a lot of commotion around the gates. Groups of protesters had gathered and were chanting things like, 'Leave the animals alone!' 'No commercialization!' 'No corporate world!'

Security kept them out, but the news people made sure they got on camera. As I watched the gates, I noticed a couple entering the park. They looked like bikers.

Uncle Matt finally returned. He looked excited about something.

"Come on, girls, let's go find our seats."

"What's up, Uncle Matt?" I asked.

"Got a call from the cutter. Sonar detected activity around the iceberg. I sent a diver in to check it out."

My heart started to beat a little faster. Maybe I was right!

We hurried to the stage where people had already gathered. Front row seating was marked with name cards, and we quickly found ours.

On stage, Aunt Rebecca waved to us and smiled. She was seated with a small group of speakers on the right side of the stage, next to the podium. In front of her was the portrait, covered by a veil.

Most of the dignitaries were present and one by one the rest filed in. All in all there were about two-dozen people seated on the stage, and about two-dozen agents surrounding it. There were also about a dozen news services, and cameras set up.

There were large, flat monitors on either side of the stage and throughout the park. They all came on, and all activity stopped as the logo for Admiral Foods appeared everywhere.

A taped message gave an introduction to the day's events and the first commercial for the new Kool-Whip. A split screen showed two families, one in Russia and one in the United States. Two super cute kids, about ten or so, were busy in the kitchen. They were working on a recipe, talking to each other on a videophone call as they made their own desserts.

"My mom says this stuff is good for us!" The U.S. kid said, holding up the plastic container for the camera. It was labeled 'Chocolate'.

"My mother likes the different flavors, and says there are no trans-fats! And it's low carb!" The Russian kid replied as he took a big spoonful of the stuff, and spread it on the chocolate cake in front of him. It looked like strawberry.

The kid in the U.S. spread hers on the white cake and both continued until the cakes were covered.

"Makes a great frosting! Even kids can use it!" Both of them said as their mothers walked into the kitchens with a surprised look on their faces.

The two kids cut a piece of cake and placed it on a plate, handing each one to their 'mother'.

The kids smiled and said, "Mom, can I go to Sea World this weekend?"

Both mothers nodded as they rolled their eyes in appreciation of the divine taste of the New Kool-Whip.

The commercial ended with a voice and text saying: Admiral Foods - bringing the world together one bite at a time!

There was a spontaneous eruption of applause all through the park as well as on stage

The picture changed to a view of the Admiral and the floating Iceberg behind it replaced the message on the screen. The picture faded and reappeared showing the stage.

The two presidents had been escorted onto the stage under the cover of the commercial. Two motorcades of black limos had arrived at the back of the stage and dropped off their passengers, and were now streaming away.

"Pretty clever!" I thought.

The monitors cut to a local broadcast of the event, now live from Sea World. The commercial had been seen all over the world!

The cameras panned the park, and gave an introduction to Sea World as it scanned all the people - and eventually focused on the President of the United States.

"Ladies and Gentlemen of the World, today we begin a historic new venture. A joining of resources and common interests. A new world of common values - family and friends - this new venture by Admiral Foods represents our shrinking world. A shrinking of differences. By following the footsteps of other ventures, soft drinks and food vendors who have gone before them, they have brought for the first time products into the kitchens and hearts of two great countries in a way never done before. Our economies have long been intertwined, and this administration believes only good can come out these efforts. In the sprit of international cooperation I would now like to introduce the President of Russia and present him with this token of our new business spirit."

The Russian President rose to the applause of the people, moved to the podium, and began to speak. Saying much the same thing as had our president. He thanked everyone for the hospitality he had received while he was here, and nodded back to our president - who asked Rebecca to stand up as he introduced her, and listed some of her accomplishments.

Wow! This was too intense! My Aunt Rebecca and two presidents!

Rebecca blushed. Nervous and excited, she approached the portrait. A translator echoed her words as she unveiled the portrait.

The camera zoomed in on the painting. It was a perfect likeness of the man, with a warm smile - and a kind look not usually seen in the news. Almost Norman Rockwell-looking.

The President was pleased, and hugged Rebecca.

Cameras flashed everywhere! Abby was standing and snapping away through tears of pride!

Uncle Matt was wiping the tears of pride from his eyes as he stood and clapped.

The Russian President thanked the Coast Guard for its hospitality, and waved Uncle Matt to the stage!

And that's when all heck broke out!

Chapter Twenty-Seven

Dad was wrong about the 'terrorist' attack on the dog show. It would have come tomorrow for maximum exposure if it had been a real terrorist plot. But it wasn't!

It was part of the plan of a jealous agent to make my father and his family look bad to the director.

Sam had won all of his events in the preliminaries. Now the Working Group was on stage, competing for Best in Breed.

The spotlight was on Sam. The announcers began their commentary.

"The Newfoundland is one of the few breeds indigenous to the North American continent. His forebears may have been the big black bear dogs of Norway left by Leif Ericsson around 1000 A.D. or descendants of the Tibetan Mastiffs that crossed over from Asia. What we do know is early explorers found large Mastiff-like dogs on the isle of Newfoundland in the 17th century."

As the judge examined Samson The Great, the announcers continued their commentary.

"The Newfoundland is a massive, strong, docile, and gentle dog. His intelligence and disposition make him an excellent guardian for children. His double coat and webbed feet make him a good swimmer and lifesaver, too. Common bloodlines with Labradors make him an excellent hunting dog also. His devotion to duty often exceeds his instinct for self-preservation, and he has been known to give his life in battle."

Now the judge watched as the dogs ran the show ring.

"The Kennel Club standard for the general appearance of the Newfoundland is an animal who is: well balanced, impresses great strength and activity, noble, majestic, exceptionally gentle and docile nature."

Sam ran the show ring to the mounting cheers of the crowd.

"Here is Newfoundland, Samson The Great a.k.a., Sam."

The crowd erupted with a standing ovation.

Almost half the eyes in the country watched as Sam trotted. But at least two people in the arena were not looking at the show ring.

An older, white-haired man, himself big and gentle looking as the Newfie below, was busy using his trained eyes to scan the security surrounding the event.

Dad also was looking at other things. His eyes went from the monitors in the control room to all of the exits, and each of the security team members assigned to it.

He watched the audience for any suspicious activity, also and the judges tables.

Both the man with the white hair and Dad saw it immediately.

A change of guard!

At each end of the arena, a substitution had taken place. As the new guard stepped in and whispered something to the other, who turned with a shrug and left.

No changes were authorized!

The replacement guards had taken the headsets from the other guards and Dad immediately tried to call them. But each one had turned the headset off!

He tried to call the neighboring guards to ask them what was going on. They shrugged, indicating they didn't know.

Not wanting them to leave their posts, Dad alerted the floor crew around the ring. They watched, but saw nothing unusual.

The white-haired man in the stand had seen it also. He watched the two unmoving guards, perplexed, he expected them to make a move toward the ring, but they did not. Why? Were they there to let someone in?

The answer came as he saw the two relieved guards appear at ringside.

The show judge was in the process of calling out the winning dogs. Each time Sam was passed, tension mounted. Would he make the cut, or was he Best in Breed?

Finally the judge indicated, and Sam trotted out with his handler.

He was Best in Breed!

Just then the two guards donned black hoods, and grabbed the judge! The commercial break came as people began to scream!

Holding a gun to the judge's head, the two men dragged him toward the exit.

Dad was on his feet, running to the ring. He ordered the others to hold their positions, and for the outside guards to block the exits.

But they did not reply!

Every one was frozen with fear or by command. Except for one man.

The big man with the white hair vaulted over the people in his row, and raced down the aisle to the exit, coming up behind the two kidnappers to block their escape!

Now, Dad was running at them from the other end, and Sam knew he had to do something!

Escaping his handler he raced at the men, growling. Like a giant black bear, he showed his teeth - and lunged at the gun hand of one of the men, grabbing his wrist with his massive jaws!

The white-haired man threw his arm around the other man's throat from behind as Dad raced up to disarm him.

There were cheers from the crowd as other guards rushed up to handcuff the kidnappers, and lead them away.

Dad patted Sam and shook hands with the other man.

"Good to see you, Richard!"

By the time the commercial came back on, the phony terrorist kidnappers had been led away. All of it had happened off camera, and instead of my father being embarrassed, he was praised for saving the judge - and the show!

The announcers who recapped all the events for the television audience praised Sam.

"What a great example of the Newfoundland's characteristics! There's no doubt in my mind that this dog is headed for Best in Show!"

About the same time things were going bonkers at Sea World!

Chapter Twenty-Eight

The other half of the country was watching the events on the West Coast.

Uncle Matt was on his way to the stage to the commentary at the event featuring the President of the United States.

"Many people do not realize the role of the Coast Guard and it's importance to national security. While many are aware of their life-saving role and maritime duties, few realize the vital security role they play against terrorism and illegal operations. This man and his unit were responsible for the safety of the Russian president during his stay here. This event has given us the opportunity to give credit to an organization that often goes unnoticed. Today, we salute the United States Coast Guard!"

There was a tremendous standing ovation and applause as Uncle Matt neared the steps of the stage.

Just then, one of the Russian dignitaries seated near Rebecca jumped up and shouted in Russian.

"Traitor!" He yelled as he aimed a pistol at the shocked president! Everyone froze, expecting the gun to go off - but it didn't!

Before she even thought about it, Rebecca snapped the veil she had been holding like a towel in a locker room, knocking the gun from the man's hand as Matt raced up the stairs and grabbed him.

The audience again erupted in applause!

Abby snapped pictures like crazy!

Before the commotion died down, the sound of gunfire drifted across the water from the floating Admiral.

"Sheesh! Now what's going on?" I said as the commotion continued.

The television crews turned their cameras to the ship as helicopter crews swarmed in - Coast Guard helicopters!

From here it looked like they were arresting people!

"The Mars rock, I'll bet!" I said to myself.

"Excuse me, Miss. Is your name Rose?" It was a policeman.

"Yes," I said, nervously, looking at a petrified Abigail.

"Your uncle asked me to escort you and his daughter to the stage area. Please, follow me."

It all made sense. Uncle Matt and Aunt Rebecca were still on stage, talking to security people. They would be worried about us.

We followed the officer as he led us around the back of the stage.

Something was bothering me again. My senses were tingling as we approached and saw Mr. Mirilav smiling at us, pulling on his little finger as he stood beside the open door of his limousine.

"Come in, Rose! And Abigail! Your parents have asked me to take you to safety," he said.

"Run, Abby, Run!" I said.

We ran under the stage, and out the front.

"Split up!" I yelled. "He can't catch us both!"

Mirilav slammed the car door, swearing in Russian.

He started running and watched us split up in the crowd. I was right he couldn't catch us both!

He was chasing me

Bewildered agents all over the park watched the chase unsure what to do. They knew Mirilav as Head of the Admiral Foods campaign and were trained to trust him. I ran on as people stepped out of the way, not wanting to get involved!

"Help!" I yelled.

But no help came. I began to hope he would run out of energy before I did.

But Vlad was in much better shape than the last time I saw him. I knew if he caught me he would use me as a hostage. Now I understood why he wanted my family split up, and me out here!

I wondered about Abby!

When the shots rang out across the water, Kyle knew Mirilav's plan had backfired! Now he knew his own backup plan had to be put in place!

He watched the monitors follow Abby through the crowd, and saw his opportunity. He would rescue the girl, and deny any knowledge of Vladimir and his plans.

Leaving the Security building, he put himself on a collision course with the young girl.

Abby saw him and stopped in her tracks. She recognized him from the hotel room that morning.

"Abigail, come to me. I'll take you to your parents. Everything is okay now."

But she backed up. Something in his voice told her he was not to be trusted.

"Come on, Abby. I won't hurt you! I really want to take you to your parents."

"No. I don't trust you!" She yelled.

"Come on, kid! I told you I wouldn't hurt you! I'm one of the good guys!"

He was yelling - frustrated Abby would not trust him.

"If you won't come to me, then I'll just have to come and get you!"

He ran toward Abigail, who turning to get away found herself against the wall of a building.

"Ah, I've got you now!" Kyle said as he closed in.

"Not so fast, Kyle."

Abby looked up to see a tough-looking biker standing between her and the Agent in Charge.

"Who are you? Get out of my way!" Kyle ordered the man.

"If you want her, you'll have to go through me."

Kyle thought about it then reached into his suit jacket for his gun.

"I don't know who you are, mister, but this is none of your business. Now, get out of my way!"

The biker just smiled as Kyle drew his gun.

Whack! The butt of another gun crashed down on his head as Susan, the pregnant wife of the 'biker' knocked him out.

He crumpled to the ground.

"We're friends of Rose," She said to Abby.

Meanwhile, I had run myself into a corner.

Caught between two buildings, I had nowhere else to go! I watched Vlad come racing around the corner and smile at my predicament.

I thought I was finished.

Suddenly, a foot came out of nowhere, tripping Vladimir and sending him to the ground.

When he was down, the young teenaged boy pounced on him, sitting on his chest, and punching him in the jaw.

"No one messes with my friends!" He said as Vlad struggled to get up only to be hit again.

Finally he passed out.

"Hi, Rose!" The boy said as he stood up.

"Shane! What are you doing here?"

"Well, I got to thinking about what you said back at the airport. I went out and got a job. I work here at Sea World. I'm in maintenance now - but who knows. I kind of like it. Might even go to school and study marine life."

"Well, thank you for saving me. How are your parents?"

"You know, I gave them a second chance. They might even get back together."

Shane and I talked about a lot of things.

Eventually, someone came to pick up Mr. Mirilav.

Epilogue

A lot of news was generated that day. The stories from both coasts hit the wires, and would fill the papers for weeks as the events were sorted out

The Russian president denied any knowledge of Vladimir, as did the CEO of Admiral Foods. The product was launched anyway, and the New Kool-Whip was a smash success!

Shane was invited to a farewell celebration at the hotel where Susan and Steven introduced themselves to Matt and Rebecca. I told him to keep in touch, and he said he would be a faithful reader of the Newsletter.

Abby's pictures from Sea-World were featured in the news. Her shots of the events, including Kyle and Vladimir were used in world news reports! I told her she could be my official photographer anytime!

Dad was offered his job back in The Agency again. He was praised for saving the dog show, and exposing a rogue agent. His work tracking down Kyle's "kidnappers" proved to be the evidence needed to convict them.

He turned it down.

Aunt Rebecca was swamped with offers as an artist and teacher. Pictures of her work were featured around the world.

Uncle Matt was promoted, and placed in charge of Security. He resigned, citing an offer to join a family business.

The Martian rock was at the bottom of it all. The hardliner, Pachenko and his associates in the Russian cabinet had staged the attempt on the president's life as a distraction in order to bring the rock to warmer waters, and steal it from the United States. They did not want to be left behind in the technology race.

Just as they had freed the chunk of ice holding it, the underwater team was interrupted by a group of Coast Guard divers. The rock was saved, and the United States now had a jump on the Russians!

"In the spirit of Kool-Whip, we will share our findings with our Russian friends," the U.S. president said.

Sam won Best of Show, and is busy doing public service with his handler, visiting hospitals, and raising money for charities, including an organization to educate people on properly choosing and caring for pets. His picture is featured on billboards, calendars, and endorsements around the world.

Mom's company handles his advertising, and endorsements. So far he has turned down all offers from dog food companies - except the one from Admiral Foods.

"Would you sit still, please?" Aunt Rebecca interrupted my rambling thoughts.

"I'm sorry, Aunt Rebecca. My mind was wandering again."

"Well, I need to get this portrait done. You are leaving tomorrow - and I need you now."

"Aye, aye, sir!" I said, smoothing the front of my white dress, and leaning back across the arms of the old, velvet chair.

I let my hair drape down over the arm of the chair, and kicked off one polished shoe, looking up at the backdrop of the blue sky and clouds. Holding a rose to my chest I thought of my Grandmother's portrait as she held the orchid in the wind, looking out to sea and waiting for Grandpa.

I smiled as I searched the sky for him.

"Well, Grandpa. Looks like you were right again!" I thought. "Kool-Whip really does come from the Arctic!"

"That's it, the perfect look! Hold that pose!" Rebecca said, triumphantly.

I fell asleep in the chair, watching Grandma smile as Grandpa's ship came into view. Holding the orchid high she waved as the ship blew its horn.

THE END

AFTERWORD

I was happy to see Richard when he came to pick me up at the airport. But he wasn't alone. Kathy, (Erica?) was there with him.

She smiled as I hugged Richard.

"I'm off duty now. Would you mind if I rode home with you?" She asked.

Richard blushed.

"Is there something you want to tell, me, Richard?" I asked.

"Yes, Rose. Your suitcase is open!"

"I know, but the bag is zipped!"

We laughed all the way to the car.

It seemed like months since I was home, and my heart beat faster as we turned the corner onto the parkway. I felt so much older now.

Richard and Kathy dropped me off in front of the door, and pulled the car around back.

I climbed the brick steps, and opened the door.

There was no surprise party.

I stood there alone for a minute, a little sad.

As I stepped onto the polished floor, my spirits soared. There was the familiar sound of webbed feet and claws looking for traction as Sam came around the corner with a big bark, and lunged at me, tongue at the ready.

My tears fell on his massive head even as I fell underneath him.

"Get off me, you big lug!" I said.

Sam found his old tug toy and brought it to me.

"You know what happened last time!" I said.

He whined and tugged anyway.

The slippery end slid from my hands, and as I went crashing backwards, the big black Newfie did too! Right into Mom's china cabinet!

There was a sickening crash as Mom's prize plates fell to the bottom behind the glass doors. There goes the raise I had asked for! Now how would I get to see Dimitri?

This was all way too familiar! I sat on my butt, looking up at the new portrait on the stairway wall. On the decorator table sat all my mail, letters from Dimitri and postcards from Paolo.

I paraphrased a famous movie.

"Oh, Sam, there's no place like home!"

We hope you enjoyed reading about Rose's adventures, in this book. Your comments and thoughts concerning *Ramblin' Rose and The Internet Newsletter* or AMI are welcome.

www.aspirationsmediainc.com

If you are a writer or know of one who has a work they'd love to see in print — then send it our way. We're always looking for great manuscripts that meet our guidelines. Aspirations Media is looking forward to hearing from you and/or any others you may refer to us.

Aspirations Media, Inc.
www.aspirationsmediainc.com